THE GOOD DAUGHTER

Diana Layne

THE GOOD DAUGHTER
COPYRIGHT © 2012 by Diana Layne

ISBN: 0615588832
ISBN-13: 978-0615588834

Contact Information: dianalayne@yahoo.com
        Cover Art by Shanel Anderson
        Editor: Theresa Zumwalt

Black Gold Books
PO Box 1683
Corsicana, Texas 75151

DEDICATION:

To my six children: thanks for putting up with the craziness of a writer and all that entails (including, but not limited to, irregular mealtimes with a lot of frozen pizza).

And to Beverly, Barb and Karen, best friends a woman could have.

ACKNOWLEDGEMENTS

Thanks to these wonderful, supportive people who helped make this book possible.

To Terry Zumwalt: Editor extraordinaire
To Shanel Anderson: Brilliant cover artist
To Detective Sergeant Hank Bailey: I would have been lost without the research help! (mistakes are all my own)
To Debbie Weierman, FBI Office of Public Affairs (again, mistakes are my own)

And last, but most important: thanks to you, dear reader, for taking the chance on my book. I sincerely hope you enjoy it.

CHAPTER 1

Naples, Italy

Hurry! *Dai, andiamo!*

Marisa Peruzzo slammed on the Audi's horn, the blaring sound having little effect in the din and congestion. The tangled morning traffic crawled, and the cobblestone streets crammed with cars and lined with historic buildings, were too narrow for her to pass. Trapped.

No! Her brother had too much of a head start for her to be trapped.

"*Merda.*" She hit the redial button on her cell phone. She had called the number ten times in as many minutes.

"Come on, Paolo, answer," she muttered.

His voicemail clicked on again. She screamed, raised her arm to hurl the phone, and just managed to stop herself before she smashed it on the dashboard. It would be of no use if it were shattered. And maybe, just maybe, Paolo would get her earlier frantic message and call.

"Be safe, be safe, be safe." Her chants alternated

2

with curses at her father and brother.

What she'd overheard—the casual way her father had told her brother to 'deal with them' and her brother's sinister laugh in response had her dashing out the door the first moment she could escape.

What did Massimo have planned to 'deal with them'? Them being Paolo and his father Giuseppe. It couldn't be good.

Her brother, capable of many atrocities, took a special delight in torture, breaking legs, crushing hands. Once he'd castrated a man for making a pass at his girlfriend.

Marisa's stomach clambered up high to her throat.

Don't think about it. Concentrate on reaching Paolo. If only she hadn't been delayed by her father trying to initiate trivial early morning chitchat. At least he hadn't caught her eavesdropping, hadn't learned her secret, that she'd been the one feeding information to the *Guardia de Finanza,* Italy's anti-Mafia force, in an attempt to stop him and his dealings. He would have had his ever-present bodyguards take her hostage if that had happened.

Carlo Peruzzo had that kind of power. After what he had done to her mother, Marisa wouldn't put anything past him. When she learned the truth that his actions had robbed her of a sane, cognizant mother, it only made Marisa more determined to bring her father down. Her life had been hell with no one to protect her from her father's machinations.

No, that she was still free to come and go was proof she hadn't been the reason for his order, and she grasped hold of the slender tendril of hope that he said 'deal with them' and not 'kill them'.

Paolo Zambrotta, a policeman dedicated to ending organized crime in Italy, was her chance to get out of the family crime business, her chance to make a new life for herself. Her chance for love, something she had never planned until she met him. Recently, she had even allowed herself to entertain visions of holding her and Paolo's child in her arms.

She couldn't let that chance be ruined!

Carlo had tried one warning already. He had ordered the Zambrotta family restaurant burned. Only Paolo's father Giuseppe had witnessed the crime and was willing to testify. Paolo now held hope of getting at least some *La Cosa Nostra*, if not her father, locked away.

It had to be the upcoming trial. Carlo must be worried about a conviction. Giuseppe had been sequestered and untouchable. Perhaps poppa thought to send another message to the older man by going after Paolo this time.

"Oh, hurry!" Marisa punched the horn again.

As if in an answer to her prayers, the snarl untangled just enough so that—

At the unexpected opportunity, she stomped the accelerator, bullying her Audi V8 through a small opening in the traffic, somehow managing not to crash into another car.

Springing free of the congestion, she sent her thanks heavenwards and floored the gas pedal, working the gearshift like a pro to race up the steep hill to Giuseppe's house. Paolo was due to pick up his father from protective custody for the first court date—she glanced at her watch—oh, no! Her heart thudded. He would have to pick Giuseppe up in mere moments to arrive at court in time.

More than a block away, she grabbed her phone again. Hit redial. She swerved around the corner onto Giuseppe's street.

The phone was ringing.

But she was almost there. She could see the house, Paolo's familiar dusty white Fiat parked out front. She smiled. The day suddenly seemed brighter. Relief almost made her limp—

The explosion rocked her Audi. Flames shot fifty feet in the air, glass shattered. She slammed on the brakes, her car screeching as it slid to a stop. The impact threw her head into the deployed air bag. The phone flew out of her hand.

Then everything went silent.

Her head pounding, blood dripping from her nose and a cut on her forehead, her vision blurred, she dragged her gaze upward and stared in horror at the fire blazing before her.

Paolo's car engulfed in flames.

CHAPTER 2

Five Years Later, New York City

Dave Armstrong watched the condensation collect around the neck of the beer bottle, roll slowly downward, and soak through to the napkin underneath. Another untouched and fast-warming bottle of brew going to waste.

No help for it. He was on the clock. He'd only bought the drinks because he needed to keep this table. The one his informant Sandro had specified when he guaranteed someone high up in the Peruzzo crime family would make contact tonight at ten. In a bar so far from Little Italy, Dave was sure it'd been chosen so the contact wouldn't be recognized.

He removed the piece of gum he'd been chewing, rolled it in the old gum wrapper, and opened a new piece. The last piece. Damn gum lost its flavor so fast, though the first burst of spearmint gave false promise it would last. Sort of like every relationship he'd been in, he thought.

Man, he was totally bored if he was comparing gum to women.

And the TV shows always made his job at the FBI sound so exciting. Yeah, right.

The waitress stopped by his table, providing a brief diversion. "You wanna waste another beer, good-lookin'?" she asked with what he now thought of as her trademark overly bright smile and hopeful gaze.

During the course of the evening, she'd been by often enough—he knew her name was Bobbie Jo and she was another Southern transplant like him, determined to make it big in New York. Only he didn't want to make it big in New York. Just catch the bad guys.

"Yeah, fine," he told her, doing his part to keep the tip money flowing her way.

Hoppin' John's Beer Bar had certainly lived up to its name this evening. The bar was crowded and noisy, full of women in tight jeans and halter-tops, and men with big belt buckles longing to get laid. After more than two hours, his head pounded in rhythm with the Country & Western wannabe band's attempt at honky-tonk. Their rendition of *Blue Eyes Crying in the Rain* made him want to cry right along with them.

Dave tapped his fingers on the table and mentally reviewed the top guys the FBI hadn't pinched in this last bust who might be willing to flip. Or was it one who already had been arrested and was willing to deal? The biggest bust in history, but Carlo had managed to escape the net. Truth be told, many of the mobsters that they got were going to walk without more information. And for certain they couldn't nab Carlo without more information, but chances on getting that seemed slim.

Carlo had a particularly nasty reputation for offing people who crossed him. And Dave couldn't come up with anyone that brave.

Yet Sandro had promised the contact would have useful information and he would know him as soon as he saw him—

Her. Dave corrected himself and sat up straighter when she entered the bar. He would recognize *her*. Sandro had never specified male or female, Dave realized as his heart rate kicked up a few notches. His jaw would have dropped if he hadn't been the kind of guy trained not to show his emotions.

Hell, who wouldn't be shocked? *Carlo Peruzzo's daughter. The Mafia princess herself.*

Her gaze scanned the room until she saw him. Though her lips were pressed in a straight line, a sparkle flashed in her eyes as if she did know just how she shocked him.

She walked purposefully toward him, making her way through the crowded tables. Black designer jeans hugged nice curvy hips, and her full breasts were covered with a pink plaid, pearl-button western shirt. Interesting color choice. A leather belt wrapped around her waist, and his focus narrowed. Best he could tell the belt was pink, too. And there were some kind of pink jewels inlaid in the buckle.

He hid a smile. The only thing that would complete the color coordination was if she had on—he looked down, yep, pink cowboy boots. Pretty-in-pink cowgirl-Mafia princess. That certainly wasn't an image he expected to see.

With her head high, and her gaze fixed on him she seemed unaware—or unaffected—by the attention she garnered. And she certainly got a fair share of stares. He saw more than one man pause with a drink halfway to his mouth, head swiveling to keep track as she walked past.

Dave had never seen the high-and-mighty Mafia daughter in anything other than expensive business suits, with her hair pulled back and her makeup understated, but tonight she wore this chic knock-off cowgirl look well. With her dark wavy hair swinging free around her shoulders, her smooth olive skin glowing, and lips a luscious color of pink to match as well, she could raise the lust level in a saint.

Dave was no saint.

But he was a professional, and he would make certain not to let her looks affect him.

Marisa slid into the chair opposite his. "Hello, Agent Armstrong." Her husky voice matched her hot cowgirl look and went a long way toward shattering all of his previous ice princess illusions.

Bobbie Jo chose that moment to bring his fresh beer. Suddenly, Dave was parched, his mouth so dry he could barely swallow, much less speak. On the job or not, as soon as the bottle touched the table, he took a swig.

"Oh, ho, so the boy does drink. Just waiting on your lady friend here before you started partying." Bobbie Jo's wink made his neck muscles tighten.

She turned to Marisa. "Keep 'em waiting, honey, good policy." Bobbie Jo gave an approving nod. "Whatcha drinking?"

Marisa looked at Dave. "Whatever he has is fine."

The waitress moved off, and Marisa raised her eyebrows. "You haven't been drinking?"

"Not while I'm on the job. Just been sitting here *for hours* watching the beer grow warm."

"My, you must have excellent *come se dice* . . . how do you say?" She held up a hand in question. "Oh, yes. Willpower."

Her sarcasm irritated him, and he couldn't stop himself from lashing back. "You pull off the cowgirl wannabe look pretty well."

"What?" For a moment she seemed to wilt before his eyes. Then she straightened, held her head higher. "Is there something wrong with the way I look?"

Had he imagined the brief moment of weakness? He decided to probe deeper. "A true cowgirl would wear something more practical than designer jeans. And it's not necessary to color coordinate everything down to your boots."

Her voice was still strong when she asked, "Which boots? On my feet or my ears?" She pushed back her hair, and he saw a dangling pink jeweled miniature boot hanging from each ear.

He couldn't help but stare.

"I had them special made, do you like?"

What game was she playing? Was she trying to convince him she liked playing dress up? He had a feeling they could go back and forth like this all evening, when all he really wanted was his information so he could leave. No, Dave, you don't want to be sitting here across from a totally hot woman, not at all. Information.

"You're late," he said, the blunt statement designed to throw her off guard while allowing him to regain his composure.

"It takes a while to put together an outfit like this. And these boots were really hard to pull on."

"You almost backed out," Dave guessed, trying hard to get onto the subject.

Marisa only smiled and leaned close. Dave leaned forward as well, anxious to get to business.

"Since you're still on the job, Mr. FBI man," she

said in a low voice, "you're not going to drink any more of that are you?" She nodded toward his beer.

Dave fought off a frown, tempted to lie. "Actually, I—"

"I didn't think so." She picked up the bottle, held it against her lips with her left hand, while she used her thumb and first two fingers of her right hand to stroke the bottle. The action injected Dave with the immediate idea of her stroking something much more personal.

"After all, you're working, no?" she said, her lips, shiny and pink, hovering over the bottle rim.

"Help yourself," Dave nearly growled, hating that this woman, this Mafia princess, was playing him so well and making him work hard to stay in control.

She moved the bottle in a cheering motion, put it back to her lips, tilted her head, and slugged down half the contents. Dave tried to ignore how her moist lips closed over the rim where his own lips had been moments before and focus, instead, that her actions indicated she needed a boost to steady her nerves.

He knew he'd guessed correctly that she almost didn't show, even though she had pointedly not answered his question. The realization provided a small comfort.

"You like this place?" she asked, looking around at the New York City bar that was pretending to be country.

Dave shrugged, now resigned a long night was going to get longer. "It serves its purpose."

"Which is?"

"It's far away from Little Italy. That's what you wanted, isn't it?"

She finished the beer before she answered. "Certainly I didn't want to be seen by anyone I know, but I thought you'd like this place since you're from Texas.

Don't you Texans like country-and-western?"

"I've been gone from Texas a long time."

"Ah, but I've heard Texas is like Italy—you can leave it, but it never leaves you." A wistful look clouded her dark eyes and she seemed in another place before she turned her gaze back to him. "Once a Texan, always a Texan."

"And once an Italian, always an Italian," Dave echoed.

"*Si,*" she said softly. "You are correct."

Bobbie Jo brought Marisa's beer and picked up the empty bottle. "Need another?" she asked Dave.

"No, thanks." He'd spent enough money tonight on beer he couldn't drink. When the waitress left again, he asked Marisa, "You want to go back?"

"To Italy?" Marisa shrugged. "I haven't really thought of it. I'm getting used to the States."

Dave knew she'd been in the city three years, her father cleverly moving the family before the Italian authorities could solidify a case they'd been working on against him. At the time, Dave had just finished his first massive mob bust when Carlo moved in and dirtied the turf again with one of the bloodiest family takeovers the city had ever seen.

Ever since, Carlo had remained slippery as a well-oiled snake.

"If you don't want to go back, what's your game?" Dave asked, needing to understand why she was willing to turn witness.

She raised one perfectly plucked eyebrow.

Dave rested his elbows on the table, steepled his fingers. "What do you hope to gain by helping me?"

She stared at him, her cocoa brown eyes

unflinching. "I want justice."

"Justice for your father would be prison." Dave narrowed his eyes and leaned closer for emphasis. He wanted to be very clear they were talking the same language.

"Yes, at the very least," she agreed, her tone laced with venom.

The lady was full of surprises this evening.

While he would privately admit a criminal like Carlo, who made it a habit to destroy lives for his own gain would be better off dead, Dave wondered what Marisa had been through which led her to at least appear to share his opinion.

"It's my job to gather enough evidence to arrest your father," Dave continued. "Sandro said you're willing to help."

She nodded. "This is true."

"You and Sandro are old friends, right?"

"We've been friends since we were children, *si*." She drank from her own bottle this time. "I know what my father is doing to him."

"So you're here to help out an old friend?"

"That's one reason."

"An old *married* friend?" He didn't know why he threw out that comment except the pain of remembering who Sandro had married distracted Dave momentarily from the dark-haired and dangerous woman across from him.

There was also the fact Marisa and Sandro had once been engaged—something Dave learned on his own. Had Sandro dumped her to marry his wife? If so, why would Marisa help him? Or maybe Marisa dumped Sandro. Dave would love to know the story.

"I'm aware Sandro is married, Agent Armstrong," Marisa said at last, interrupting his speculations. "And I said helping him was one reason. I didn't say it was my only reason."

"Which is? Your main reason, that is."

Marisa took another drink and surveyed the bar again. "Can you dance like those people?"

Dave turned and followed her line of view to the small dance floor in front of the stage. "The two-step? Sure."

She set the bottle firmly on the table. "Dance with me, then."

Her request wasn't what he expected, but he resigned himself that she wasn't going to make this as easy as he'd hoped. All in a day's—or night's—work.

There could be worse things besides dancing with a beautiful woman. He stood and held out his hand. "Shall we?"

She slipped her small, manicured hand into his and let him lead her to the dance floor.

He turned, and she moved into his arms, closer than he would have liked, her head fitting neatly under his chin. He made himself ignore the erotic feel of her warm, firm body pressed against him, the soft smell of her musky perfume, as he taught her the steps.

"You think dancing will make me forget what I asked?"

"Shh, I'm counting so I don't lose my step." She stared at the ground. "I like your boots."

He led them to a more isolated corner and stopped dancing. "Marisa."

Forced to stand still, she looked at him. Her dark eyes studied him with a cool, casual gaze. He was

14

tempted to move closer, see if he could make the coolness melt away.

He held his place instead. "Why are you willing to help?"

"Why is it important?"

"Motivation. Everyone has a reason for what they do."

"My reasons are my own."

"I need to know you're trustworthy." He knew when she narrowed her eyes she understood his meaning.

"You think I'm trying to set you up?"

"It's been known to happen."

"What good would that do me? If you were *removed*, someone else would take your place, no?"

"Maybe this isn't about you. Maybe I'm causing your father too much trouble. Granted, I haven't been able to arrest him yet but I will—"

"You think this is about you? You think I care nothing for my friend Sandro at all?"

Her regal, indignant tone made him feel like he was getting a dressing down from his superiors.

"I don't know what to think," Dave snapped.

"Bah!" Her gaze flashed fire. "Sandro must be desperate to use you."

"Yes, I believe he is. Quite desperate. I can help." Dave didn't want to gloat, because Sandro, a transplanted Italian soccer star who had unwittingly found himself in Carlo's clutches, *was* in a desperate situation. Even though it wasn't so many years back when Dave would have gloated. Would have hoped quite fervently for the downfall of the man he once considered his rival.

"Maybe you can help him. Maybe you can't. But I don't think you can help me, Agent Armstrong." She released his hands, stepped back, and turned toward the door.

"Marisa, wait." How had he lost control of the situation so fast? "Don't go."

She paused, glanced over her shoulder. "Why?"

"I...um, I apologize. For . . . my naturally suspicious nature." He held out his hands, hiding nothing.

She pivoted to face him, gazed at him steadily, as if debating with herself. "This is a dangerous business," she finally said.

"Exactly." Dave kept his tone level, though inside the clamp released around his windpipe. "And of course being suspicious keeps me alive."

"What about me?" She moved closer to him.

He closed the space between them even more, took her hands in his again. "I'm not sure I understand."

"Will your suspicious nature keep me alive, Agent Armstrong?" She squeezed his fingers. "Can I trust you with my life?"

CHAPTER 3

It was well after two a.m. but Marisa went through her normal nighttime routine, even though she felt anything but normal. She tried to deny an overwhelming sense of déjà vu. Her body wasn't cooperating. Her hands shook as she swiped away make-up, her stomach rolled with nausea. Tossing the used cotton pad in the small garbage can, she braced her hands on the sink.

Today had been a long day, starting out with a visit to her mother. While Marisa no longer lived with her parents, she made a point to stop by and see momma a few times a week. She had some good days. Other times she was unresponsive. Today was one of those unresponsive times. Did her mother realize what that brute who called himself her husband had done to her? Did she ever remember what she'd been like before? Marisa couldn't tell.

She stared at herself in the mirror. And just what was *she* doing?

She was doing what she had to do. In order to live with herself, she had to bring her father down. Make him pay. What he'd done to her mattered little; what he was doing to Sandro was another thing. And what he'd done to her mother—and Paolo—was unforgivable.

Tonight she'd set things in motion which could not be reversed. By agreeing to help Dave, she hoped she found a way to accomplish her goals. What she had not intended was her reaction to Dave. Did she simply have a fatal attraction for men in law enforcement?

No, before Paolo, she'd never associated with cops, went out of her way to avoid them because that's the way it was in her family. Until Paolo approached her and opened her eyes and stole her heart. She was twenty-one then and while she'd been with men, had been used and abused, she had never experienced the joy of being in love.

And she would have never allowed herself a chance if Paolo hadn't gained her trust and then told her what really happened to her mother. It was a tale much different than the version she'd been told.

Not long after she'd been sent off to school, after the incident with her brother's teenage friend and the stiletto she learned to carry, her father told her momma had deliberately overdosed on sleeping pills. She'd been revived, but the damage had been done. On her best days, she appeared to be off in la-la land, the land of the happy where nothing bad ever happened. And on her worst days she fell into a near vegetable state, where she sat in a wheelchair all day and had an attendant to take care of her every need. The change in her mother from a vibrant, flamboyant woman to this stranger had been drastic for Marisa, at a time when she desperately needed her mother's protection.

But she never had reason to doubt what her father told her happened, and how he let her think she'd been the reason for momma's overdose. Marisa had kept quiet about the teenage boy she stabbed—like poppa told her—but always thought momma somehow found out and couldn't accept it. Her father never did anything to make Marisa think differently.

So the truth, when Paolo at last told her, had been hard to believe, and so much worse. Her mother never overdosed. The changes in momma were not Marisa's fault. It was hard to let go of her guilt, but Paolo had proof Marisa could not refute. Evidence that made real the fact that her father was a monster, not only for what he'd done to momma but for letting Marisa believe it had been her fault.

Paolo helped her accept the reality, and his kindness and goodness was unlike anything she'd experienced. And there had been no turning back.

Until poppa stole Paolo away as surely as he'd stolen her mother.

For Paolo, for momma, for herself and all those many nameless people her father had hurt so much, Marisa marched on in her quest for some way to right the many wrongs.

Especially when Carlo turned his greedy sight on Sandro and his uncle and their restaurant. History repeating? No, not this time. No more.

Which led her to Dave.

Marisa was skeptical whether Dave could help but she'd researched him well and aside from finding him fascinating, he did have a track record for bringing down mob guys. Maybe he would be successful and she wouldn't have to utilize "plan B" as they said here in America.

But going to Dave for help put her at risk for another—unanticipated—problem.

Dave had felt the same intense feelings as well. From the unconscious way he licked his lips and let his gaze flit across her body, Marisa knew he wasn't immune to her.

She wouldn't allow it to matter. She dressed to distract him, she reminded herself, so she could get a read on him. A slight miscalculation on her part; she had not counted on a reciprocal attraction.

Hadn't counted on the spark she'd thought long buried when he took her in his arms. She only asked Dave to dance to reduce the intimacy of sitting directly across from him at that small table. Who knew the two-step could be so sexy?

With a sigh, she turned on the faucet to wash the last of the make-up from her face. Dripping water, she reached for the towel when her cell phone rang. Patting her face dry, she glanced at the caller ID and stiffened.

Gigi. She wanted to ignore his call, but that would be stupid.

Marisa wasn't stupid. She pushed the button.

"*Ciao*, gorgeous."

He sounded chipper, must have been a good night. She tried to make herself sound tired and sleepy in contrast. "*Ciao*."

"Why don't you grab a cab to the *ristorante* and let's have a late dinner. I feel like celebrating."

Never mind that it was closer to breakfast time, and going to eat was the last thing she wanted to do with him. Next to last thing, rather. Worse would be if he wanted to take her to bed, and if she met him tonight, bed would be inevitable. One day, one day, she'd be past having to use her body as she'd been taught. But today was not that day. Nor tomorrow. But only a little longer. She clung to that thought.

"Have a good night?" she asked. He and his friends often got a private room at Sandro's restaurant for all night gambling.

"I'm on a hot streak and now I'd like to spend some time with my hot Italian woman."

This, on top of the day she'd already had. No. No. "*Amore mio*, I am already in bed," she lied.

"Bed. Just where I like you best."

He must've been drinking heavily, that's when he got all sexy—or what he thought passed as sexy. It would be laughable if it wasn't so distasteful.

"But come here first," he continued. "Let's eat and then we can go back to my place."

"Gigi. Did you hear?" Her temper flashed but she tamped it down. "I'm in bed. I've already taken off my make-up."

"Can't you just slap some back on?"

She heard the irritation rising in his voice and debated whether she had the energy to fight. Yes, she decided. She hardened her voice. "No, I can't 'slap some back on.' I was asleep, I'm tired. I'm going back—"

"Wait," he cut her off. "Why don't I have Georgio pack us a meal and you meet me at my apartment? You can go there without getting dolled up. Don't even bother getting dressed, just throw on your coat."

"Gigi, I—"

"Or..." he cut her off again and added slyly, "I could bring the food to your place."

No! She deliberately kept Luigi away from her apartment, wanting her own space. She had conceded by renting the apartment from him in a building he owned in the first place, a calculated move on her part to appease him, but she had never invited him over to stay the night. This was her private haven. He knew her rules and only presented the option to provoke her.

It worked. "*Va bene.* I'll meet you at your place in a half hour." As much as she didn't want to she resigned herself to spending the rest of the night with Luigi, knowing she had to keep up this charade for her plan to work.

At least by going to his place, she'd be able to add the new snooping software to his phone. No, Dave didn't know about it, but there was a lot he didn't need to know.

He didn't know all the things that'd been forced on her. The men she entertained because of her father...and her brother. And that Luigi was another one poppa had set her up with. Although this time she knew enough to turn the tables on them both. Without having to use her stiletto. She hoped.

Dave didn't know the things she'd seen. Whole fingernails lying on a table, acid poured on a widow's legs, a man's tongue cut out. Dirty old men's shriveled—
.

She cut that thought short. If Dave knew those things, he'd realize she was slowly losing her humanity. And that her biggest fear was that she wouldn't be able to stop herself from becoming an animal like everyone else in her family.

CHAPTER 4

FBI headquarters, New York City, two weeks later

"Damn, Tony must've made the coffee today."
Dave grimaced as he forced the sludge in his cup down
his throat.

"Hey, be grateful I got here early enough to make
it." Tony shoved more paper into the printer. Always
such a mother hen, Tony was.

Dave walked back toward his office through a row
of desks in the main room. "That's something to be
grateful for?"

Two other men chuckled, but Dave saw a third
man hadn't cracked a smile. Frankie sat at his desk,
headphones on his ears and a cup of coffee, probably
long forgotten, placed to one side. Beneath his hand lay a
notepad, the page nearly full of scribbled notes as he
translated last night's tapes.

"How's it going, Frankie?" Dave tapped the
frowning man on his shoulder.

"Hang on a minute, boss. This isn't looking good."

While waiting, Dave loosened his tie and
unbuttoned the top button on his shirt. As much as he'd

wanted to be an FBI agent, following in his father's footsteps, Dave had never gotten used to feeling choked.

"So, what do they say?" he asked, drumming his fingers on the edge of Frankie's desk. "Has our bug paid off already?"

Though Marisa had been cantankerous and elusive, she'd finally come through. She hadn't offered many specifics about Carlo's business ventures, claimed to know nothing about the alleged weapons smuggling to the drug cartels beyond the border, but she did tell him where her father held his private meetings. It was a place Dave and his team had been trying to find for several months since previous wiretaps had netted them a big fat zero.

This new tap had been up and running less than a week. The fact Carlo and his men spoke in Italian, as Marisa had warned Dave, proved no challenge. Frankie had grown up in a traditional Italian-speaking home.

Dave looked around the room at his men, working in sync like any well-tuned machine. It had taken him eleven months to put together the original Organized Crime Task Force, but they'd worked side-by-side five years now and could read each other's body language, perceiving unspoken codes in eye contact.

He'd snatched Steve, a fellow Texan, just out of the Academy. Standing over six feet tall, with strawberry blond hair and blue eyes, an east-Texas accent and cowboy boots, Steve stood out among the dark-haired Italians they stalked. But he was quick-witted, easy going and strong as a draft horse. He could easily bench 450 pounds and yet charm the most hardened mobster with no one the wiser. Dave was happy to have Steve in his corner.

And Frankie . . . steady, dependable Frankie. He and Tony, Italians both, had been childhood friends in Brooklyn. They both knew all the goombas and spoke the language like natives. Good guys, both of them.

And last, but not least, the newest members of the team, Roberto and Greggorio, aka Bobby and Gregg. They'd come on board right after the big organized crime bust three years ago when Dave had lost one member to retirement and another to a long-term injury. They were the youngest, least-experienced and therefore the weakest link. But they worked hard to earn their spot, and Dave trusted them.

Dave's attention turned back to Frankie when he pulled off his headphones and read his notes aloud. "'This is no good,' Carlo says. 'I want him. First thing in the morning.'

"Now Angelo's talking," Frankie went on to explain. "He says, 'You want him dead or alive?' And Carlo answers, 'Alive for now. There is much I want to tell him first.'"

Dave set his coffee cup down and peeked over Frankie's shoulder. "Do they ever say who they're talking about?" Dave asked, though he knew the chances were slim. Carlo's guys were always careful, even when they thought they were safe. "Damn, I'd love to catch him in a slip."

"Afraid not this time. There's no mention who they're talking about, but I have a feeling they're onto Sandro."

Frankie's softly-spoken words rang ominously in the suddenly quiet office.

A burning lump which had nothing to do with the coffee he'd ingested settled in Dave's stomach. "What the hell are you talking about?"

"Well, Carlo goes on to say nobody ever sets him up and lives to—"

"Shit!" Dave sorted through the information, couldn't deny the facts. "You're right. He *has* to be talking about Sandro." From all they knew, it couldn't be anyone else. How could Carlo have found out? They had been so careful when Sandro offered them his help after Carlo had found Sandro's family-owned restaurant in Little Italy an irresistible place to launder money.

"Damn, that bastard's slick. Gregg, call Sandro's house," Dave ordered.

Greggorio obligingly picked up the phone. "He's probably already left for practice." He punched in the numbers, waited a few moments. "No answer."

A new panic hit Dave. Sandro's wife. "Where's Nia? Why isn't she picking up the phone?" Dave had known Nia longer than he'd known Sandro. Since she was in diapers, to be exact. They'd grown up next door to each other in Dallas. Now, in a strange twist of fate, they both lived in New York with Nia married to someone else instead of him.

Life was indeed ironic.

"Doesn't she take the kid to the park most mornings?" Gregg asked.

The park. The knot in Dave's stomach eased enough so he could breathe again. "You're right, she does. Maybe she's there." Even though it was unlikely since a cold front was fast moving in. But he didn't want to think something had happened to Nia, there was some innocuous reason she wasn't answering the phone.

"Yeah, nothing to worry about, I'm sure," Gregg added. "Frankie said Carlo didn't want Sandro picked up at home anyway. Wasn't any mention of bothering Nia, was there?"

"Yeah, right. It only sounded like he's after Sandro. At least for now."

Dave scanned the room. Somebody had betrayed them. No other explanation. He stiffened with the realization, clenched his teeth so hard he could feel his neck muscles tighten, ready to snap.

Who? One of his men? It had happened before to other teams. Dave looked again at each man, judging, questioning, until at last he mentally gave himself a shake, drew in a breath. No, it couldn't be. He trusted these men with his life. And they each knew the life and death importance of keeping information tightly guarded.

But someone had talked. Who? Marisa? Why would she talk? Had someone known she liked to show up at midnight for meetings and figured out her code name?

For Marisa to betray them would make no sense. They might joke about her, but Dave knew the woman was not only highly intelligent, she had street smarts. And she had seemed sincere in wanting to rat on her father, wanting out of a life of crime. Though she had never admitted to her main motivation, Dave suspected she had her own score to settle.

Had he been wrong about her?

Had it really been a set-up from the beginning?

He wouldn't get any answers here. "I'm going to the soccer field to look for Sandro. Steve, you and Tony follow as back-up. Frankie, you learn anything else from that tape, you call me yesterday."

Dave hoped to God he wasn't too late.

CHAPTER 5

One moment. Your whole life could change in one moment.

At the defining moment, Sandro Crocetti thought he'd made the right decision. But it had been wrong. It had forced this latest, more drastic decision.

"Did she believe you?" Marisa asked as she steered the BMW sedan away from the house.

"*Si.*" He leaned against the cool glass window, sick inside at what he'd done. *Forgive me, Nia, amore mia.* "*Si*, she believed me." He shook his head. "*Porca miseria.*"

"You did what you had to do. It is for the best."

"This does not make it easier." He turned to Marisa, a picture of confidence in her black designer suit, not a long dark hair out of place, the scent of designer perfume softly surrounding her. She was a beautiful woman, but she seemed so much harder now than when he'd known her in Italy. "I hope this isn't another mistake."

"There was no other choice."

Sandro knew Marisa never second-guessed her decisions, and normally he wouldn't either. But the stakes had never been this high.

Marisa glanced at him. "Will she leave?"

"I don't know. I believe so. I hope so." Fear and doubt sucked at his soul, made him feel as if he were directionless in a deep, dark fog.

"If she doesn't leave, I don't think she will be in danger." Her words offered no more than a hollow hope.

"I hope you are right."

Marisa's grip tightened on the steering wheel. "My father doesn't make a habit of harming women or children."

She sounded as if she were trying to convince herself. "But he has," Sandro argued. "I know this. You know this. Carlo could easily decide they need to die."

The ring tones *Lost Without Your Love* played out loudly. Marisa checked the caller ID. "It's Agent Armstrong. Do you want me to answer?"

"Dave." Sandro spat out the name and followed with a long string of obscenities in Italian.

"I'll take that as a no." She shut off the phone and laid it down. "I think we can trust this Agent Armstrong. You sent me to him in the first place."

"Bah! A mistake! It is because of him and his stupid FBI that I have a contract now on my head. If not for you, I could be dead. What I'd like to do to his man who sold me out—"

She took a hand away from the steering wheel and patted his arm. Her display of kindness stopped his outburst.

"You are sure you want to continue?" she asked.

"As you said, there is no other choice." No other choice if he wanted to live. No other choice if he wanted to keep his family safe. For too many years Carlo had controlled Sandro's life. Giving in hadn't helped. Running hadn't helped. It was time to stand and fight.

If only he could have kissed Nia once more. If only he could have held his son.

His heart stung with a mixture of anger and emptiness.

He turned to stare out the window at the houses they passed as Marisa, a skillful driver, pressed the stolen black BMW as fast as she could, expertly navigating the crowded, early-morning streets. He knew the New York suburban commuter traffic was no challenge compared to her native *Napoli* where the roads were as wide as a sidewalk, and all Italian drivers imagined they were a Formula One race car driver.

She'd almost gotten them to the city.

After minutes of sullen silence, he drew a deep breath, stiffened his spine, and turned back to Marisa. "I will kill your father, you know."

"*Si.*" Her lips pinched together, her eyes narrowed. "It is for the best."

CHAPTER 6

Hugging herself against the chill in the air, feeling an even deeper chill seeping through her veins, Nia Crocetti watched the black BMW drive away. When she could no longer see it, she still stared, the image of her husband with another woman seared into her brain.

He'd left her. Sandro, the love of her life. With another woman. The picture replayed itself in her mind. A woman sitting behind the steering wheel, with dark hair and sunglasses, showing no more than her profile. But then Sandro had gotten into the car and the woman had leaned over to kiss him. . . .

Nia's stomach spun, threatening to make her sick; her chest squeezed and contracted so hard it hurt to breathe. She hadn't seen it coming. There had been no hint, no warning. She reached into her memory for signs she might have missed. Barely noticing the cold wind stinging her face, she staggered back inside, shut the door, and collapsed.

Her marriage was over. Just like that. Nia fought to retain control over her emotions, part of her refusing to believe what she'd seen. Her throat clogged with choked back tears, her eyes ached. She pressed the heel of her hands against her eyes, wiped an escaping tear. She wouldn't cry. She was a trained athlete. She knew how to control pain. But it was damned hard.

What about their son, what would she tell him? And the pregnancy test she'd taken earlier this morning . . . Sandro hadn't known. She hadn't been able to tell him before he left.

Her gaze darted about the room. Her home. Their home. She loved every inch.

Drawn as if by a magnet, she moved to their wedding picture. She and Sandro looked so happy, so in love. Her white dress contrasted with her tanned skin and dark hair. Having done many commercials and photo shoots for the national team's various soccer sponsors, she knew she was an attractive woman. But on her wedding day, she had felt truly beautiful, like a princess. And her husband was the gorgeous prince with his formal black tuxedo, olive skin dark from the sun, curly brown hair and beautiful hazel eyes. Nia lovingly traced the frame, the metal cool under her fingers.

She smashed it to the marble floor. The shattering glass echoed in the room, the scattered pieces resembling her broken heart.

Shaking, she sank to her knees. Hiding her face in her hands, needing to escape reality, if just for a moment, she remembered. How crazy in love she had been, what a wonderful life she and Sandro had planned together, what a wonderful life they *had*. But he'd found someone else, and had no more use for her. How had it happened?

"Momma?" The little voice came from the top of the stairs.

Wiping stray tears and unanswered questions aside, she squared her shoulders and forced herself to her feet. She had decisions to make. But they would have to wait.

"Momma?"

"Coming, *amore mio*. Momma's coming."

She walked up the staircase. Daniele, a little miniature of his father with soft curly hair, stood behind the gate. At two years old, he was still too small to manage all the steps. She opened the gate, picked him up, snuggled against his fuzzy pajamas. He was still warm from sleep.

"My sweet *bambino*."

The doorbell stopped her soft, mothering sounds. *Sandro!* was her first thought.

Stupid. He wouldn't ring the doorbell. But who would this early in the morning?

She went down the stairs, carrying Daniele. At the bottom, she stopped before a mirror, briefly fingering her hair straight and wiping away the last traces of tears, though her eyes were still red. No help for it.

A chilly blast of air hit her when she opened the door. A huge man in an expensive black suit stood on her porch.

"*Buon giorno, signora.* I am looking for Sandro." He had a heavy accent, but he seemed pleasant enough in spite of his intimidating size.

Still, he was a stranger. Her alert system kicked in. She hugged her son protectively against her chest. "He isn't here."

"He is not at the soccer field either."

"Who are you?" Whoever he was, he knew where Sandro was supposed to be.

"I am only an old *family* friend."

She couldn't miss the emphasis he placed on the

word family, and for some reason her heart skipped a beat. Studying him, she decided he looked familiar. Perhaps she'd seen him at the restaurant? "You've come at a bad time. He's gone."

"When do you expect him?"

At that moment her phone rang in the background. First the door, now the phone. She didn't want to talk to anyone. She adjusted her son on her hip. "Never."

"*Scusi?*"

She shook her head. Why had she said that to a complete stranger? Shock, possibly. "He's gone," she repeated, struggling to collect her thoughts, which were bouncing around more than a soccer ball in a group of five-year-olds.

"I don't know when he'll be back," she corrected herself.

"This is most tragic," he muttered, whispering Italian under his breath.

Her interest sharpened. "Can I help you?"

"No, no, *signora*. It is a. . .private concern."

She wanted to question him more, but her instincts suggested it would be wiser if she didn't. "I'm sorry I can't help. It's cold." She nodded toward her son. "You'll understand I don't feel like chatting." She closed the door and squeezed Daniele closer to her.

Never still for long, Daniele squirmed to get out of her arms. Reluctantly, she kissed him and set him down. He moved toward the ruined picture on the floor. She had forgotten.

"It's broken, Momma." He bent down.

She snatched him up before he clutched a shard of glass. "Yes, it's broken, *caro*. Momma dropped it." She pulled out a small box of toys and sat him down to play away from the broken picture. "Be good while I clean up the mess."

Mess, was right, she thought, sniffing, still fighting not to give in to a disastrous crying jag. Suddenly her life was one big mess.

It hit her as she swept up the last of the glass. She *had* seen that man before at the restaurant. He was in the company of known crime boss, Carlo Peruzzo. It was a repugnant thing, the mob frequenting their family-owned restaurant, but what could they do? The restaurant was in Little Italy, and mob guys were known to be Italian. They paid for their food with money like—

Wait! The woman with Sandro! Nia only saw her profile, but the woman did resemble Carlo's daughter . . . Marisa, was her name.

Was that why the big Italian came to her door? Because her husband was having an affair with Carlo's daughter? Would Carlo be trying to hunt Sandro down over something like that? Or was she getting hysterical?

Dumping the idea away the same as she dumped the broken glass in the garbage, Nia put the broom and dustpan back in the closet and sat down to play blocks with Daniele. She knew she should be making plans, perhaps call her mother and ask advice, but the thought of admitting to someone else what had happened made her nauseous.

As much as Nia didn't want to think about it, the images tangled in her brain, twisted her insides. The fairy tale marriage of the soccer princess and soccer prince...was over. There had never been a clue he'd been unhappy. Surely there would have been at least a hint?

Somehow, she couldn't process that Sandro had left, even after watching him go. Or that he left Daniele behind without a goodbye.

She paused. "Wait a minute!"

Daniele looked up from his toys. "Momma?"

She realized she'd spoken out loud. "Momma's talking to herself, sweetie. Play with your toys."

When Daniele picked up a toy car, Nia's thoughts turned back to her husband. Sandro *wouldn't* leave Daniele behind without a goodbye. She knew it with every fiber of her being.

The more she thought about it, the more convinced she became he wouldn't leave her either. Family was Sandro's number one priority, coming even before his soccer career. He would never let lust for another woman overtake his obligation to his family.

Even if he had fallen out of love with his wife.

Nia frowned. Sandro's actions were too out of character. No way would he change so drastically in such a short time. He only wanted her to think he was leaving her for another woman. Why? And was the woman really Marisa Peruzzo?

Then there was the large, rather intimidating man who came to her door. Strangers didn't just show up on her doorstep. Not many people outside of close friends and family even knew where they lived.

Her heart pounded anew. She was onto something. She trusted her instincts. Something was definitely wrong. Sandro was trying to keep her from finding out about...something. What?

Determined to find the truth, she left Daniele playing happily with his blocks and toy cars while she searched for the number of her childhood friend turned New York FBI agent, Dave Armstrong. Though she didn't live in the city, having a ready-made friend living in the same state had been a reason she hadn't objected moving to New York instead of her home state of Texas when they had returned from Italy.

Now her friend could be useful as well. She had memorized the plates of the BMW Sandro left in, and if Dave could tell her who owned it, perhaps she could begin to piece together the puzzle. If Sandro were in trouble, she would find a way to help.

When she picked up the phone, she remembered the earlier missed call and checked the caller ID, but didn't recognize the number. They left no message, either. With a mental shrug, she called Dave. But of course with the sort of day she was having already, he didn't answer, and she had to leave a voice mail.

"Damn," she murmured. Now what?

"Momma, watch!" Daniele crashed his small cars into a block tower he'd built, clapping his hands when the blocks scattered.

She squatted down beside him, love for the tiny boy swelling in her battered heart. "Awesome crash, sweetie."

He giggled with delight and began to restack the blocks.

Perhaps Brad would know what was going on, she thought as she handed Daniele a red triangle block to put on top of his new tower. Sandro and the team's goalkeeper were almost as close as brothers. If anyone knew anything, he would.

Brad would still be out on the soccer pitch practicing and wouldn't have his cell phone. She could track him down but she'd need someone to watch Daniele. Since he was recovering from a recent ear infection, she didn't want to drag him out in the ever-increasing cold winds. Not wanting to disturb Sandro's aunt and uncle this early if she didn't have to, Nia called the neighbor's daughter hoping she would get lucky and the college girl would have no classes this morning.

Luck. Nia snorted. It would be nice to have a little good luck. It had certainly started out as a bad day.

CHAPTER 7

Nia pulled her cream-colored Mercedes sedan to the end of the long driveway and stopped. A black Lincoln Navigator blocked the end of her driveway. She couldn't go anywhere until it moved.

To her surprise, the passenger door on the SUV opened, and the big Italian who had been at her door earlier looking for Sandro stepped out.

Confused as to why he was still at her home, blocking her driveway, Nia became all too conscious of the chill crawling up her spine as she pressed the button to roll down her car window. A bad feeling hovered in the air.

She took a deep calming breath before saying, "I told you Sandro isn't home, and I don't know where he is. Would you move out of the way? I'm in a hurry."

"*Scusate, Bella,* but you must come with us."

"What?" Was he kidding?

"Please. *Vieni qua.* Come." His words were polite, but his look was deadly serious.

Her heart rate spiked, but she forced confidence into her voice. "I'm not going anywhere with you."

"Really, I must insist." He reached for the door

handle.

She hit the automatic locks and hurried to roll up her window, but the large man was sticking his arm inside—

Car tires screeched around the corner. The Italian turned toward the sound. A dark blue sedan squealed to a halt. Nia recognized the car and started to breathe easier.

Dave opened the door, gun drawn. "Freeze! FBI. Nia, get out of here! Go!" he shouted at her.

The Italian banged his fist against her now closed window startling a scream out of her. When he reached under his suit jacket and she saw a big gun, every nerve ending ignited with danger signals.

Escape!

Adrenaline flared through her and she stomped the accelerator, jerking the steering wheel hard to the right. The luxury Mercedes 230 shot forward, smashing small green hedges and brightly-colored ornamental flowers under unforgiving tires. The seatbelt clamped tightly across her chest as she bounced off the curb.

Shots rang out behind her. She looked in her rearview mirror. The Italian had dashed back into the SUV, shooting at Dave who had ducked behind his car door. Oh, God, Dave would be killed.

Then a new fear. With a burst of power, the Lincoln Navigator sped after her. In her rearview mirror, she saw Dave hop in his car and follow, firing shots after them. The big Italian was shooting back at Dave, out the passenger door window.

The black SUV pressed steadily closer to her own car. Were they after her? Or running from Dave? She pressed the gas pedal harder, and at the last minute, made a sharp right turn onto a side street, her tires squealing.

The Navigator made the turn soon after. God. They *were* chasing her! Her hands started shaking so much, she squeezed the steering wheel to keep a grip.

Glancing between the road and her rearview mirror, her fear grew when Dave didn't make the turn. She heard the pops as the big Italian shot out the tires on Dave's car. It careened and bounced off a red Corvette parked on the side of the road, before spinning around in a crazy circle. Immediately, Dave jumped out and fired off a few futile shots.

"No! Dave!" she gasped before her breath stuck in her throat.

Now it was the Italians. And her. A streetlight in front of her changed to red.

"Not stopping, watch out!" she warned drivers who couldn't hear her, hoping no one would get hurt.

She kept the accelerator floored, her heart rate as high as the speed of the car. Squinting her eyes to slits so she wouldn't see any oncoming traffic and hesitate, she barreled through the intersection. She heard honking horns and screeching tires but no one hit her.

A glance in her rearview mirror. SUV still there. Although she thought she was pulling ahead. The heavy Navigator was no match for the Mercedes' performance engine.

Then she felt it. A thud. Heard it. Then another. A crash of glass. She didn't need to look in her mirror again to know her back window had shattered. They were shooting at *her* now!

Forcing back the panic rising from her chest, she kept her head low as she weaved through the growing traffic, trying to make her car a harder target. She hoped someone else wasn't hit by mistake, but couldn't let that thought worry her.

She jumped as a loud explosion sent the back end of her car wildly careening. They'd shot out a tire. She let off the gas, fought the steering wheel. She struggled to steady the almost out-of-control car. Stopping would be the wrong choice. A ruined tire rim was nothing compared to being caught by those madmen.

"Help me, help me, help me," she prayed, her brain not able to form a more substantial thought. "Help! Me!"

Sweat beaded on her forehead as she wrestled with the car. In spite of her efforts, the car lost speed. She yanked the wheel, forcing another sharp turn, whipping in front of an oncoming car. The black SUV turned behind her, passed the other car, and soon loomed on her tail, closer than before.

The tire rim scraping on the pavement sounded worse than a metal file grinding against an axe. She clenched her teeth against the sound and frantically searched for a safe place.

A silver Lexus sped into the next intersection and squealed to a stop, blocking her way.

She slammed on the brakes. The car bounced and jolted on the bad rim. At the last second, she wheeled her car hard to the left to avoid crashing into the Lexus.

Trapped! Her heart sank. She would have to make a run for it. She snapped her seatbelt free and jumped out to dash away. She was the fastest player on her soccer team. She prayed her speed wouldn't fail her. There was a shopping strip ahead. People. Phones. Help.

Wait. Her cell phone.

No time to go back. She sprinted.

They came at her from everywhere. Five men with

guns. One woman. Bad odds.

Two of the men cut her off and grabbed her arms. Gasping to catch her breath, she tried to twist away.

"Where you think you're going, bitch?" This one was a native New Yorker, his Italian descent still obvious despite the accent.

"Careful, he don't want her hurt." The big Italian again. He was huffing and puffing from the chase. "He only wants to question her."

Who wanted to question her? "I told you I don't know anything. Leave me alone."

Gathering the fear pounding through her body into energy, she thrust a sidekick to her right. Connected with a knee. One captor fell in agony. Her legs were powerful. She jerked an arm free, but immediately, it was trapped again.

They dragged her toward the black SUV. No one rushed forward to help her. No one was even in sight. The people had disappeared like cockroaches in sudden light. She couldn't blame them. Five men with guns were bad odds for anyone.

Frantic not to get in the car with them, she dug her heels into the concrete.

"No fight, please," the big Italian said, not unkindly. "Carlo just wants to talk to you."

Carlo. Carlo Peruzzo. She was right. The realization made the fight momentarily desert her. If the well-known crime boss wanted her husband, then Sandro had to be in trouble.

What sort of trouble could he be in that involved men with guns?

She tried bravado. "Who are you?" Nia demanded. "What does Carlo want with me?"

No one answered.

"Leave her car here," the big Italian directed. "He'll find out faster that way."

Who would find out? Sandro? Was this a ploy to make him show himself? Or was fear making her illogical?

She knew she should never go to the second location. It was better to make a stand here than disappear into a car where no one could track her. She screamed. A hand clamped across her mouth. She bit until she tasted blood, and her attacker screamed as loudly as she did. Then the backhand came. She saw stars, and they pushed her into the SUV.

The New Yorker, the one who called her a bitch, slid in beside her. The big Italian and his driver climbed into the front seat. The other two drove off in the Lexus she'd nearly crashed into, and her cream-colored Mercedes was left sitting in the middle of the street. Punctured with bullet holes. Deserted.

What happened to Dave? Would he be able to find her? Was he okay?

The New Yorker aimed his big black gun at her. "So's you don't get no ideas about jumping out," he said when he caught her eyeing the gun.

What ideas? Death by gunshot or death by throwing herself from the car? No choice there. She could tell from his tone, his body language, he'd love it if she tried something. She wasn't stupid.

She sat tight. A way to escape would present itself. And when it did, she would be ready.

CHAPTER 8

Dave slid out of the disabled car before it stopped rolling. He squeezed off his last three rounds at the speeding black Navigator. One hit the rear door, one hit the left taillight, and the last one went wide.

"Damn it!" He slammed his hand on the hood of his car. "Son of a bitch!" He barely restrained himself from kicking the bullet-punctured tire.

"Come on, Nia. Get away from them," he muttered, though he knew it was useless. Pain gripped his heart knowing she had no chance, and his back-up wouldn't arrive in time.

What had gone wrong?

Once discovering Carlo was after Sandro, Dave had taken Steve and Tony with him to the soccer field, but Sandro wasn't there. Had never shown up, in fact. When the soccer team administrator mentioned they were the second group of men looking for Sandro, Dave felt hope. At least Carlo's men didn't have Sandro, even though he'd disappeared.

Dave left Steve and Tony behind to further question the administrator because at that point it was obvious the star player had indeed disappeared. Dave himself had headed for Sandro's house to brainstorm with Nia where her husband might have gone.

But they were too late. Now the mob had her. And Sandro was missing.

There was still Nia and Sandro's small son. The child Dave wished he had been able to have with Nia.

The boy hadn't been in the car with his mother. Dave had to find him, get him to safety.

* * *

Promising to return soon, Marisa checked Sandro into a hotel amidst his protests. Leaving him to puzzle over a new throw-away phone, she ditched the stolen Beemer, made a quick dash to the computer software store, and still arrived at work by ten-thirty, only half an hour past her normal arrival time. Not so unusual it would be noticeable.

This morning the office was in an uproar as sleazy looking men pretending to have fashion sense crowded the reception area. Loud voices could be heard from more than one office.

Of course, Luigi wasn't here. After calling in the order to get Sandro, with a little unasked for help from her sleeping drops, Luigi was sleeping off his winning streak from last night. She didn't see Angie either, which was unusual. Perhaps he was one of the men trying to find Sandro. Poppa would trust Angie.

As a boss, it was hard to find men to trust. Luigi and Angie, two of the most loyal Peruzzo Mafioso, had come over with them from Italy. She'd known Angie since she was nine. He'd tried to protect her, keep the cruelest things out of sight. Of course, there had been some things even Angie couldn't protect her from.

Her father. Her brother Massimo, who, in his way, was worse than her father. Massimo, cruel, lazy, indolent—of course he wasn't at the offices yet. He rarely made an appearance before late afternoon. Massimo had always gone out of his way to torture her.

Even after she'd put a stop to his side business where she was the commodity, he and his friends still seemed to delight in exposing her to the most perverse cruelties. Always alert, she'd noticed Massimo had begun to collect some of poppa's soldiers for his own. Carmine, Joey and most especially the little sleaze Mikey. Weasels, rats, carnivores, willing to eat their own. It wouldn't be long before Luigi and Angie didn't have the strength to keep Massimo's men at bay. Then a bloody war would start and innocent people would get caught in the crossfire again. She'd seen the ambition and greed in Massimo's eyes. She'd even tried to warn her father and Luigi, but they'd just responded "boys will be boys".

Which was fine. They could go on living in their make-believe world. For now. But soon, she would bring it all to an end.

Ignoring the melee, she dropped off her purse and coat in her office, as per her normal routine, and went to the coffee bar in the snack room to make an espresso. She usually chose coffee, but today, she needed the extra caffeine after a night of little sleep. She heard yelling from her father's office, then a door slam. She entered the main area in time to see two of her father's soldiers rush out the front door.

Marisa smiled grimly. She was one step ahead. Barely. It was a dicey and dangerous game, one her father wasn't even aware she was playing, but one in which she'd defeat him before he knew he had been challenged. Subtlety was always best; she learned that lesson after the stiletto incident.

She detoured by the accountant Roberto Torino's office. Roberto wasn't a made member, was truly a CPA, and one of her father's most trusted people. He kept his head down, nose clean and did his job. For that, he was paid a lot of money.

"What's going on?" she asked with a nod of her head in the direction of her father's office.

"Not really sure, seems like someone Mr. Peruzzo is looking for has disappeared."

Roberto wasn't as naïve as he appeared; he simply managed to keep a low profile. She almost hated what they had planned for him as he worked so hard to stay good.

She gave a deliberate shrug and smiled to disarm him. "Business as usual, I suppose."

He barely cracked a smile at her joke.

She took a sip of her espresso and changed the subject. "I stopped by to let you know I'm updating software on the computers. Why don't you leave yours behind at lunch?"

This time, he actually cringed. Roberto did hate to be parted from his computer.

"Unless you have something else you could be working on and I'll just take care of it right now," she added, hoping he'd say no since she didn't have the software ready yet she wanted to put on his computer.

"No, lunch will be fine."

"Okay, I'll be back then. *Ciao.*"

Once in her office, she pulled out the new disk-imaging software. To access her father's money and move it into new accounts, she needed the account passwords. Luckily, as her father's IT person, she had the ability to get to those passwords.

She powered up her notebook and opened the software packaging and the flash drive to practice making a mirror image of her hard drive. The faster she could make a copy of Roberto's hard drive, the better.

It wasn't luck or an accident that she was the IT person. Marisa liked to build things, and she'd always had an interest in computers, had built her own desktop when she was thirteen; but it was at Paolo's suggestion that she made herself invaluable to her father.

Her heart ached with nostalgia. Paolo had been dead over five years now, but she still missed him. For him, she would see this through, no matter what.

Roberto didn't go to lunch until one; until then she busied herself with other computers, making imaginary updates on the other computers so he wouldn't get suspicious.

He found her before he left. "I'm going now."

"Great, I'll go to your computer next. I plan to wrap up early; I have some errands to run this afternoon."

If he thought her being gone from the office most of the day unusual, he didn't say. Roberto generally kept his nose in the books and didn't make trouble for anyone. Which is why she hoped to convince Sandro to let Dave help again. They needed help getting Roberto out of the way. If he noticed the money transfer in progress, he would stop it and ruin their plans.

She hoped Dave could help by having Roberto picked up and held in custody for a short time. If not, the options for her and Sandro to remove Roberto out of the picture were limited to murder, use poison to make him sick and send him to the hospital, or kidnapping. None of those options were appealing, or even practical.

Their best hope was Dave; he could have Roberto picked up and held without charges for at least three days. Would Dave agree? He seemed so honorable. How far would he bend rules to get to her father? She didn't think he'd bend them far enough if he knew her ultimate plans, but there was no need for him to know.

He just needed enough information to be useful. If, and she realized it was a big 'if', she could convince Sandro once again that Dave could still be of use to them.

For now, she needed to make herself useful and get that information from Roberto's computer. And then, they'd need to move as quickly as possible afterwards to be certain he didn't change the passwords as part of his routine security.

She grabbed the software CD and the flashdrive and headed for Roberto's office.

CHAPTER 9

The air in the downtown office of the Federal Bureau of Investigation reeked of bureaucracy. Electronic key card, security badges, checkpoint after checkpoint. Dave wound his way up one elevator, down two halls to his office.

The employees in this building had worked hard to get here, and they hadn't left their egos behind. They might wear similar ties and look alike, but behind each tailored wool suit was a strong personality waiting for a chance to shine.

Dave walked into his office after meeting with his Task Force when his phone rang. He fished it out of his jacket pocket. "Armstrong here."

"Are you in your office?"

An Italian accent. Sandro. Dave's mental sigh of relief was chased by a stomach lurch at the thought of telling Sandro about Nia. Dave lowered his voice. "Where are you?"

"Are you in your office?" Sandro repeated, more forcefully.

"Yes, I am. What difference does it make?"

"Go outside, someplace private. I will call again.

51

Five minutes."

"Why?"

"I will tell you later. Go outside." Sandro disconnected before Dave could ask more questions.

As he retraced his steps back out of his office and rode the elevator down to the ground floor, he puzzled over the strange request.

He found an isolated corner in a near alley by the time Sandro called back. "Where are you?" Dave demanded as soon as he punched the connect button.

"You are alone?"

"I'm no amateur," Dave snapped. All this mystery was wearing thin. "Of course I'm alone. What's going on? If Carlo has the ability to monitor phone calls, my being out here won't do any good."

"It is not your phone which is dangerous. Your office is bugged."

Dave went still. "What? No way!"

"You have checked for this?"

"We have top security. We do sweeps for bugs. Besides, nobody from the outside could get in to plant one." He was trying to remember when they last did a sweep when he realized that if no one could get in to plant a bug, then—

"Nobody from the outside did get in," Sandro said.

Yes, that was it. Someone from the inside would have had to do it. Dave's head started to pound. "Christ! Would you stop being so elusive? Are you saying one of my men— No, that's ridiculous." Yet for the second time that day Dave had reason to wonder about his team. "Where the hell are you?" he snapped.

"Definitely the bug was planted by someone with top security clearance. This we will discuss later. If you are being watched, it will be suspicious for you to stay on the phone."

Dave blew out a breath. "We need to meet." He didn't want to tell Sandro about Nia over the phone.

"*Si*. Soon."

"It's important we meet now." Dave emphasized the word 'now'.

"Carlo knows I was working with you, which means it is likely they're watching you. If you rush off now, after talking on the phone outside they will know you have been talking to me. It will be hard to lose them when they are so alerted."

"Okay." Dave conceded, beginning to pace. Ten feet left. Ten feet back again. "When and where?"

"You will be very careful no one follows you?"

"Look, damn it, I know how to do my job." He raised his fist in the air, briefly wishing Sandro's face was there before he realized his anger might draw unwanted attention. He dropped his hand.

"I trusted you before. I have a contract now on my head."

"Don't you think I know that?" Resisting an urge to squeeze an imaginary throat, Dave ran the fingers of his free hand through his close-cropped hair. "How did you find out?"

"Marisa."

"Is she the one who told you my office is bugged?"

"*Si*."

"She could be making the whole thing up. They could be using her to set you up right now."

"Has she not given you good information?"

"She could have given us the information to look like she was cooperating." Dave's palms began to sweat.

He coudln't afford to screw this up. One wrong move and he'd be pushing papers for the rest of his career. And that was the least of his problems. One wrong move and Nia could—

"She saved my life this morning. Which is more than you can say."

She . . . she . . . Dave struggled to bring his thoughts back to the conversation. She saved . . . who was she? Oh, Marisa. Marisa saved Sandro's life this morning, yes. Dave clenched his teeth and rubbed his hand down his pant leg, half-afraid he was losing it. "Point taken," he conceded at last. "Okay, tell me where do we meet?"

"I will pick you up in front of the drugstore around the corner from your office. In one hour. Make sure you are not followed."

"I won't be followed," Dave promised. "What are you driving now? Her car?"

"Not her car. I don't yet know what I'll be driving. Keep your eyes open."

"Oh, they'll be open, Sandro. Nice and wide. I won't be caught off guard again."

CHAPTER 10

Dave stood with his back pressed against the outside wall of the large chain drugstore. An ominous looking rain cloud approached with the evening's dropping darkness. Soon enough, the skies opened and fat, cold raindrops pelted the ground. Dave shivered and turned up the collar on his overcoat. Welcome to New York City in the fall. Although snow was in the forecast, the temperature hadn't yet dropped enough for any white stuff to form. Thank God for little favors.

Huddling against the wall under the eaves, Dave fought the feeling he was losing control of this case. He couldn't fail at this. Never mind he'd always wanted to emulate the old man, had gone into the FBI in the first place thanks to his dad, one of the first profilers. Dad's footsteps were hard to follow, but Dave thought he'd done okay. Until now.

Now, it wasn't only his reputation at stake, but Nia's life. Nia, the woman he'd dreamed of marrying, patiently waiting for her to grow up and notice him. But he'd waited too long. She fell in love with a soccer player instead of Dave. Leaving Dave pining after her all these years. While it might disgust him, that he was married to his job and not the woman of his dreams, he'd simply never found a woman to compare.

An older maroon Buick LeSabre pulled to the curb and thankfully saved him from moving further down the path of self-castigation.

The dark-tinted front passenger window cracked. Marisa's flawless face came into view in the opening, but it was Sandro's voice who ordered from the driver's side, "Get in."

Dave quickly opened the back door and slid onto the seat and immediately choked on the smell of cigarettes. "Damn, Sandro! Have you two taken up smoking?"

"Sorry, it is the best we could do." Sandro didn't sound apologetic.

"Whose car is this? I don't recognize it." Dave thought he'd had all the mobster cars under surveillance at one time or another, and this was one he definitely hadn't seen.

Like any aggressive Italian driver—or native New York driver for that matter—Sandro muscled the car back onto the road through the smallest of openings in the traffic. Car horns and squealing brakes sounded behind them. Dave resisted the urge to jump into the front seat and take over.

"I don't know whose car this is," Sandro answered once he was in the flow of traffic.

Dave paused in taking off his overcoat. The car smelled awful, but it was warm and with his wet coat, he felt steam rising from his neck. "You don't know? You saying this car is stolen?"

"I can look at the registration papers if you like." Marisa offered an innocent smile from the front seat.

A glance at the steering column showed no key. "You wired this car?"

"No. She wired it." Sandro nodded his head toward Marisa.

Dave stared, somehow not finding it difficult to imagine Marisa wiring the car. With her sharp intelligence, Dave bet she had all sorts of hidden talents. Immediately, his imagination teased him with images of her in bed, eager to teach him her talents.

"My brother runs the auto-theft ring, you remember. He thought it would be amusing to teach his little sister a few trade secrets."

Her words brought Dave back to focus. He knew her brother Massimo's long list of *talents* as well, which really made him wonder how many of those trade *secrets* she knew.

"She taught me how," Sandro said. "I will do it next time."

"Next time? You taking up stealing cars in your spare time?" Dave's head started a low throbbing in his temples. Whether from the strong, stale smell of cigarettes or the new problems piling up, he wasn't sure, but he had a feeling the throbbing would be a full-fledged pounding before he got out of the stolen car.

"It will be best if I don't use the same car for long," Sandro continued.

"Shit, I can see this on my fucking report . . . Federal witness stealing cars."

"It might look better on your fucking report than, 'Federal witness found dead'." Sandro frowned when he caught Dave's gaze in the rearview mirror.

Tension filled the air, but Dave broke eye contact. Sandro was right. There was no sense arguing with the legality of it, especially since Sandro and Marisa appeared to be operating on their own agenda now. How much farther would Sandro venture outside the law once he found out about his wife? Dave rubbed his forehead.

"I might as well confess about the BMW I stole this morning," Marisa said.

Dave sighed. "Because I look like a priest?"

Marisa's lips turned up slightly at Dave's attempted humor. "So you can recover it and return it to the owners. You most certainly do not look like a priest."

The look she sent Dave was blatantly appraising, like the night he held her in his arms at the bar. Every time they'd met since, he'd struggled to ignore the feelings she evoked. Long, leggy, lithe, she was perfection personified, no argument there.

But his attraction would never move beyond the physical, and at the moment, he didn't have time to even indulge in that little fantasy. Aside from the legal issue of her being an informant, they had grown up in different worlds, both literally and figuratively. Black and white, cop and criminal, total opposites on the spectrum.

Get back to work, Armstrong.

"What went wrong, Sandro?" Dave blurted, jerking his thoughts back to business. "They've kidnapped Nia."

Sandro stomped on the brake. Dave's face slammed into the back of the front seat. Okay, so maybe he should have been a little more tactful. He rubbed his sore nose.

Tires squealed and horns honked impatiently behind them once again. "Damn it," Dave swore, more upset with himself than Sandro. "Don't stop in the middle of the road. Find a place to pull over."

"My wife is . . . Gone?" Sandro demanded as he double-parked in front of a popular local restaurant. "And you wait this long to tell me?" He swung around, his face contorted, the promise of murder in his eyes.

"I didn't think I should tell you on the phone."

"Certainly not," Marisa lashed out. "It is much better to tell us while he's driving so he can kill us in an auto wreck."

Dave gritted his teeth. "And there's a good time?"

"How did this happen?" Sandro demanded, the anger in his voice echoing in the confines of the car.

"Carlo's men ran her down in her car." Dave admitted, mentally replayed his total failure at saving Nia. "I tried to help," he added quietly. "But they shot out my tires and got away."

"Shooting? There was shooting around my wife? They got away?" Sandro thrust his hands in the air and leaned back, looking up as if to speak to the heavens. Or the roof of the car. "*Dio mio!* You are useless."

Dave tensed at the insult, though he wouldn't attempt to defend himself. He had failed, pure and simple, and Sandro was more than justified to be furious.

"Was she hurt?" He met Dave's gaze in the rearview mirror.

By now Sandro's neck muscles were bulging; his eyes like shards of sharp, green glass. Marisa laid a hand on his arm to calm him, which only seemed a marginal help.

"From what we could tell, she wasn't harmed," Dave said, watching Sandro's nostrils flare in the struggle to breathe and visibly bring his raging emotions under control.

"The trunk and tires and back window had been

59

hit," Dave continued, "but we found no trace of blood. From what witnesses said, she was struggling when they forced her into the other car."

"Witnesses? There were witnesses and no one helped her?"

"People get nervous around guns, especially when someone's shooting them. There were five men with guns."

"What of my son? If they got Nia, where is—"

"Danny's fine. He's with your aunt and uncle at a safe house. You need to go there."

"No. No safe house." Sandro slammed a hand hard against the steering wheel, before turning to face Marisa. Dave had no clue what Sandro was spouting in rapid Italian. He was talking much too fast for Dave to pick out any familiar words. As typical of many Italians, Sandro used his arms, punctuating his raised voice and rapid speech with hand gestures.

The sudden attack didn't appear to faze Marisa. She argued back, their voices growing louder until she and Sandro were screaming at each other.

"Whoa, guys." With a hand on each, Dave pushed them away from each other. "This is not helping. And besides, all this Italian flying around, I can't understand a thing. You're going to have to speak English if you want my help."

"We don't want your help." Sandro's face was still flushed, but his voice was controlled, the volume lower. "Get out."

"Sandro!" Marisa scolded.

"You asked for my help, Sandro."

"It was a mistake to trust a *buffone* like you."

The words splattered like hot grease and Dave felt

the burn.

He forced himself to stay calm. "I never intended for Nia to get kidnapped. You know I would give my life for her. We were supposed to get through this without her knowing."

"If you weren't so incompetent—"

"Sandro, blaming me is only wasting time."

"Something went wrong." Marisa said, changing the course of the dialogue. "We all agree. Now, we will have to work together to find Nia."

"No."

"We need each other, Sandro," Dave said quietly.

Sandro ignored Dave and turned to Marisa. This time he spoke in English. "You said she would be safe."

"No one said she isn't safe. Poppa is using this as a tactic. It's you he's after."

"We knew something could go wrong," Dave added. "That's why I wanted to have her under surveillance."

"If Carlo's men had seen you watching my house, it would have tipped them off. Waiting until Nia left for her game in Germany, and she was out of harm's way would have been best."

"No one would have known we were watching."

"Because you are professional, right? What kind of professional let's his office get bugged? Either way, Nia and Daniele were at risk. My way would have been best had Carlo not discovered our plans."

"I suppose she didn't believe you after all," Marisa said.

"She might have believed me. There might not have been time for her to have made arrangements."

"Then why was she in the car?" Marisa asked.

"Most likely she was trying to hunt down answers."

"Believe you about what?" Dave asked. "Hunt answers for what?"

"I needed a plan to get my family out of the way once Marisa told me Carlo had put a contract on me."

Dave turned to Marisa. "When did you find out?"

"Early this morning. But I couldn't get to Sandro right away. I was afraid I'd be too late."

"You should have called me," Dave told her, irritated he'd had to depend on tapes to be translated. He'd been a step behind all day. He hoped it wasn't an omen.

"There was no time," Marisa said. "I heard Gigi on the phone giving orders that poppa wanted Sandro. But I couldn't leave until . . . later."

Because she'd been in bed with Gigi . . . Luigi, Marisa implied. Dave read between the lines. He'd known Marisa and Luigi Conte, the Peruzzo family *consigliere,* or advisor, were involved. It was actually good for their set-up that she was 'sleeping with the enemy.' Still, it didn't stop the swift feeling of envy powering through Dave.

Nothing more than lust, he assured himself. He'd simply been too long without a woman. "What is the plan you are talking about? The plan for Sandro to drop out of sight?"

"No, the plan to get Nia out of the way." Marisa started her explanation with how she drugged Gigi with sleeping drops, slipped out and stole the BMW.

"A cop's coming from straight ahead, Sandro," Dave interrupted. "You're still double-parked. Start driving again and we'll keep talking." Hardened New Yorkers would likely ignore a cop giving a traffic ticket,

62

but for someone looking for Sandro, it would be waving a red flag.

After Sandro merged with the traffic, narrowly missing a bike messenger, Dave turned back to Marisa. "No one noticed you swiping a car off the street in plain sight?"

"Of course not. I know what I'm doing."

"Okay, so you swiped the car, then what?"

"I drove to a place where I could stop Sandro soon after he left his house. I was afraid they might get him on the way to the soccer field or be waiting for him once he got there."

"Good thinking," Dave said. "I know Carlo's men were there sometime before we arrived."

"You went to the field?" Sandro asked, looking in his rearview mirror.

"My translator discovered they knew about you when he was working on the tapes from last night. We rushed to the field, but you were gone. So, what have you two been doing all this time? Why didn't you contact me earlier?"

"Sandro wanted Nia and Daniele out of town before we started working on any ideas to keep him alive."

"We should have put them—and you, Sandro—in a safe house—"

"No. How many times do I tell you no?" Sandro cut him off. "I will be *prigionero* to the Peruzzo family no longer. It is why I offered help in the first place. So you could catch Carlo and get him out of my life."

Sandro switched on the turn signal and turned a corner. "I believed Nia would be safe. Carlo told me years ago he would never harm a woman. Marisa told me the same thing. He lied. She was wrong—"

"You don't know he's going to hurt her," Marisa protested. "He's only trying to use her to get you."

Somehow, to Dave's ears, he picked up that Marisa wasn't as confident as she sounded.

"*Si*." Sandro nodded. "If I stay hidden, what will happen to her? Who knows how she will act as prisoner. She is fearless," he said with loving admiration in his voice. "That is why I wanted her out of town. If I had disappeared, she would have looked everywhere for me. Who knows what trouble she would have gotten herself into?" He caught Dave's gaze in the mirror. "You've known her since she was child. Is this not so?"

Dave agreed. "Knowing Nia, you're right. It's why I okay'd waiting until she left for Germany before we tried to trap them. But . . . " He shrugged, knowing their plan had gone horribly off track. "So what did you come up with to get her out of town so suddenly?"

"*Poca importa*? What does it matter?" Sandro gestured with his hand. "She is a prisoner now."

"It might help to know her mindset. I want to know what you told her and see if I can decide how she is going to react to being a prisoner. If she has even the slightest inkling you are in danger, she's liable to do something crazy."

"In spite of what Marisa said earlier, she has no, what you call it . . . inkling."

"You can be so sure?"

"*Si*."

"What did you tell her?" Dave persisted.

A silence, then, "To go back home to Dallas."

"Just like that? I know better. She would have never gone without a good reason. What made you think

64

she would rush back home to Dallas?" Dave was fighting an increasing urge to throttle Nia's husband. Nothing new about the urge. Dave had wanted to throttle Sandro the moment he swept Nia off to Italy and married her.

Sandro exhaled, then finally answered. "I told her I was leaving her for Marisa."

"Jesus!" The word exploded from Dave's mouth. "Well, no need to worry about her looking for you. Unless she didn't believe you."

"She believed me. I . . ." Sandro looked at Marisa, "was very convincing."

Dave ached for what Nia must have suffered thinking the man she loved so much had betrayed her with another woman.

"Still," Sandro went on, "even if what Marisa says is true, that Carlo will not hurt her, if he doesn't release her soon, she will try to escape to get to Daniele. She thinks I have left her, and there will be no parent for him. She is fiercely protective of our son."

Dave saw a man living with an enormous amount of pain, guilt... and no doubt incredible fear for his loved ones. Damn, this was a mess. He pulled his mind back to focus. "First, we need to find Nia," Dave said. "Bringing Carlo down can wait. When we get her, all of you will have to go into the witness security program."

"No. I must get Carlo."

"We *will* get him. It's going to take more time now. Until then you have to stay out of sight." Dave tried to be persuasive.

"No. There is another way. Marisa and I are working on other plans."

Dave looked at Marisa. "You're still willing to help, knowing attempted murder—make that a likely murder if something goes wrong—will be involved? You found out today how hard it is to make everything go right."

"Murder has been a reality my whole life. This is not like the old days where the women were sheltered from the business. I even know of two women in *Napoli*—grandmothers, both of them—who ran their own families when their men went to jail."

"What of your own life?" Dave asked her. "You're taking a great risk. For now, they believe you're part of them, but what if they find out you're helping us?"

"I want out."

Dave had heard enough in the past weeks to know Marisa was speaking of her father's crime family and not any possible set-up they might devise in the next few days. He still didn't understand her reasoning, didn't totally trust her, but he was smart enough to work with what was offered. Catching Carlo Peruzzo would be one step further up closer to Dave's father's hallowed reputation.

A grim look covered Marisa's face. "If I must die, I have no one to mourn me. Sandro is the one with all to lose."

Dave thought it sad Marisa believed no one would mourn her. But he understood. Sometimes it felt like he stood all alone himself, fighting criminals, managing to put a few in jail, only to have more spring up to take their place. It was an isolating job, a lonely life.

He imagined Marisa probably felt alone as well, surrounded by a family of criminals, trapped, looking for a way out.

He and Marisa could no doubt have a long, meaningful conversation about the many different ways of isolation and loneliness, over a glass of wine, with soft candles glowing on a table—

Whoa, where was all this sentimental crap coming from? Now wasn't the time to get hung up on a romantic fantasy. She'd probably have a nice little stiletto for his back.

Now was the time to convince the stubborn Italian who thought he was invincible he wasn't bullet proof.

"She's right, Sandro, you have a lot to lose," Dave said, hoping somehow Sandro would see reason.

"Exactly why he must be caught for my family to have a normal life. And now we must find a way to get Nia back as well."

"We'll get her back." Dave hoped if he said it enough it would be true. His team was currently going through traffic light cameras hoping to follow the kidnappers' SUV electronically.

"*You* won't do anything," Sandro snapped.

"Let's talk more," Dave urged. They were approaching the parking lot where he kept his car. "Pull over in this next parking lot so you can concentrate on what I have to say instead of driving."

Sandro held silent, once again acting as if he were going to ignore Dave.

"Come on, I'll pay the parking fee," Dave added. "Working together we'll accomplish more."

At the last possible moment, Sandro whipped the Buick into the parking lot, stopping to take the ticket from the automatic machine. He parked, but left the engine running.

"Look, Sandro, after I talked to you, we swept the office, found the bug." Dave looked at Marisa. "Tell me who dropped the device?"

"I don't know his name," she answered. "His son was in a motorcycle accident and is now paralyzed. He needed the money for medical bills."

"Son of a bitch. John Madison. I donated money to help cover the medical expenses."

"Perhaps your donation wasn't enough?" Sandro said.

Dave ignored Sandro's sarcasm. "He's not one of my team, but we'll be watching him," Dave promised. "John won't plant another bug. When we get Carlo, we'll nail John's ass right along with him."

"Nailing asses won't do good now. He has already caused much damage," Sandro said.

"Tell him what we have discussed, Sandro," Marisa encouraged. "He can help."

Sandro shook his head. "No, I do not think so."

"*Che*?" she asked, looking obviously frustrated.

"Why not?" Dave demanded.

"It is dangerous for too many people to know."

"I trust my men, Sandro."

"The trust has done me no good."

"We won't make the same mistake twice," Dave assured him. "I'll tighten security so much—"

"My *wife* is in danger, Agent Armstrong," Sandro interrupted. "I do not think Carlo will hesitate to kill her in spite of what Marisa says."

Dave lost his temper. "Don't you think I know she's in danger! That's why I have to help."

"I know you loved her. Maybe you still love her." Sandro met Dave's gaze. "But I will save her. She is *my* wife."

Heat rose under Dave's collar. Marisa sent him a curious look, which he ignored. "Do you plan to turn yourself over to them?"

"If it becomes necessary."

"One man. Against the mob? You plan to live to tell about it?"

"Marisa will help. We have a plan."

"You could be killed."

"It is a chance I must take. If I am killed, you must make sure my wife and son are safe."

Dave didn't even want to consider the possibility of Sandro's death. It was too tempting, and after working years to get over heartbreak, which right or wrong, Dave had blamed Sandro for, it was a road Dave didn't want to travel.

"You have no authority to act, Sandro."

"Carlo will only recognize authority from someone more powerful. Your laws are not good enough."

"That's bullshit. We have RICO, surveillance equipment. We have men and weapons—"

"You do not have Carlo."

Dave sighed. "You're bound to be planning something illegal."

"Which is a good reason for you not to know. You cannot break your laws. I can."

"I'm not sure I'll be able to keep you out of jail."

"Jail is a minor thing."

Under the circumstances, Dave knew Sandro was right. But still, Dave would do his best to keep their plans within the law, so no one but Carlo and his men would be going to jail.

Dave looked at Marisa. "You're in this with him?"

She studied Sandro's set jaw before she turned back to Dave. She nodded. "*Si*. I am in."

"You want us to secure you a place to stay?" Dave

asked Sandro.

"I will find my own place. I think I will move around often."

"And drive different cars, right?" Dave's attempted humor didn't even evoke a smile this time. He cleared his throat. "My car's parked close, I'll get out here."

In the rearview mirror, Sandro met Dave's gaze. "Keep my son safe."

"I will." Dave laid his hand on Sandro's shoulder. "Take care of yourself."

"Carlo will not get the best of me this time. I will be careful. He will get what he deserves after taking so much from me."

Dave couldn't disagree there. "Keep in touch," he added before he got out of the car.

When Sandro and Marisa drove off, Dave's shoulders slumped as he felt his chance for bringing down the Peruzzo crime family leaving with them. He didn't know what Sandro had in mind, but Dave had firsthand experience that it wasn't easy to outsmart Carlo. Even if Sandro had Marisa's help. Too many things could go wrong. Today's big all around fuckup, proved that.

Dave knew without a doubt he couldn't let them handle this on their own.

CHAPTER 11

Nia didn't know where they had taken her. Once they left New York City and headed north, the roads were unfamiliar. They drove forever it seemed. By the time they stopped in a densely wooded area and the New Yorker with the gun dragged her out of the car, tension and fear had been replaced with a growing exhaustion. Her limbs felt heavy, hard to move. At this point, if he shot her, she didn't know if she'd have the strength to care.

The red brick house rose in straight, narrow lines, three stories high.

"Mikey, take her up to the room," the big Italian whose name she learned was Angelo, instructed the New Yorker.

With the gun poked into her ribs, Mikey, a slimy little man with dark gel-stiffened hair and an acne-scarred face, forced her to walk up all three flights of stairs. He opened a door and waved the gun. She moved inside.

It was a bedroom. Brief panic stiffened her spine, penetrating through her tiredness. She didn't know his intentions. The thought of him touching her made her tighten her muscles, ready to defend herself.

She turned in time to see the door shut, followed by a distinctive click. Alone—thankfully alone—but locked in. Breathing easier, at least for the moment, she walked to the window. A damn long drop to the ground. A quick scan of the room and a useless shake on the locked doorknob promised no escape anytime soon. She needed a plan.

First, rest. She sank into a soft overstuffed chair set up beside a small table. Her brain couldn't function when she was so tired. The bed looked tempting, and she was afraid she'd sleep too long if she lay on the inviting down comforter. It was not a normal condition, this tiredness— usually her energy abounded—but circumstances were not normal.

And being pregnant sapped her strength, as well. That had been her first clue. Not a missed period like most women. As a professional athlete, she trained so much her periods were irregular anyway. But when her energy level dropped off drastically, she knew. It had been the same way with Daniele.

Daniele. A pain hit her heart. God, her sweet son. Was he okay? Would she ever see him again?

Of course she would. No negative thoughts. Positive thinking made her a success. Positive thinking would help her escape. At the moment, her options seemed limited, but she would find a way to get away from these criminals. Then she would find her husband.

She rested her head against the plush chair. Closed her eyes. Just a little rest.

* * *

She was running. Running as if demons from hell were nipping at her feet. If she fell, she was dead. Hurry. Her heart hammered frantically against her ribcage. Her breath labored through her lungs. Move, feet.

Move, move, move.

Safety was close. Just a little further. She had to make it.

Gunshots exploded around her. The noise was deafening.

Instinctively, she ducked, and urged her churning legs to greater speed.

Someone hurled a bowling ball into her shoulder. Another loud crack sounded. She went sprawling. She scrambled to stay on her feet, scraping her knees, her fingers clawing at the ground to push her upright.

Blood dripped from her hand. She followed the red sticky trail up her arm. A bowling ball hadn't hit her. A bullet. She'd been shot—

Nia jerked awake, her heart beating furiously as if she'd tried to run a hundred-yard dash in an impossible two seconds.

The dream. No . . . nightmare.

It had haunted her for years, but hadn't bothered her for several months now. Of all times for it to recur. She had enough fear to conquer without her own mind creating horrible scenarios. Even if it was a recurring nightmare, it still had the power to scare her.

And always before, Sandro had been there to comfort her. Ease the irrational fears. Even the time she first had the dream, he'd been there. The same night she met him . . . .

* * *

Ten years earlier

Italy had been in the states for a friendly soccer match with the USA team. Nia and her former soccer coach Giuseppe Zambrotta had tickets. The day had been magical. Not only did she get to see her soccer hero Sandro in live action, she learned he was Giuseppe's nephew. Giuseppe and Sandro's mother were siblings, different last names, which is why she'd never known there was a connection. That, and the fact that her coach had been mysteriously closed- mouthed about his famous relative.

That night, Sandro would dine at Giuseppe's and she was invited. From the moment she met Sandro, he stole her heart with as much certainty and skill as he'd ever scored a goal. Even more amazing, he seemed to be as attracted to her—later, he told her about the *"thunderbolt"*, an Italian man's expectation of being struck blind with love. For her, he told her, she had been his thunderbolt.

He even persuaded Giuseppe to let her spend the night, upstairs in the guest room of course, while Sandro volunteered to take the couch. Alone in her room, reviewing the day, she knew she'd never get to sleep. But she dropped right off, awakened a short while later by the nightmare.

Too agitated to go back to bed, she went downstairs for juice. Only to be scared for real when Sandro, whom she thought was sleeping, whispered in her ear, "It is dangerous to walk in the dark."

"Yikes! Sandro." Her shoulders slumped as the tension eased from her muscles. "I thought you were asleep."

He turned her to face him. "I pretend. In case it was Beppe or Luciana." He picked up the juice glass from the countertop. "You have trouble to sleep? Drink *latte*…milk." The glass made a soft clink against the marble counter as he sat it down.

"I wasn't having trouble sleeping, not at first. Then I had a bad dream. I don't like milk, but I thought juice would help." Realizing she was inanely chattering, she turned the question to him. "Haven't you been able to sleep?"

She felt him studying her. In the dark, she couldn't clearly make out his features, but she felt his intense look, his warm breath stirring the air between them.

"No. Sleep does not come to me tonight."

She wanted to ask him if he couldn't sleep because he was thinking of her, but to her shame, just the thought made her tremble. *Coward, she scolded herself. He's years older and totally experienced. The last thing he wants is a nervous virgin.*

His hand slid from her shoulder, up her neck to cup her face. "You are shaking. Because the dream frightened you?"

No, not the dream. Her feelings for him. "It was very bad," she agreed, while wondering if she should rub against his hand, which felt so nice and strong against her cheek.

"*Vieni qua.* Come. Tell me. I will hold you." He took her hand and led her to the gray-and-blue plaid sofa, gently illuminated by a lamp turned on dim. He sat on the hide-away mattress, and gently tugged her down beside him, not giving her a chance to resist.

Nestled in his arms, her cheek pressed against his

warm bare chest, she felt safe and secure. The dream seemed less frightening in the telling especially when he kept rubbing her back and dropping soft kisses atop her head as she spoke. She was having more trouble by the minute remembering terror pulled her from sleep.

"Someone shot you? This is very bad."

His whisper-soft kiss brushed her hair. Beneath her cheek, his heart beat strong and steady while hers was bouncing all over the place. "Just a dream though."

"But still enough to frighten."

His warm, masculine scent filled her nostrils. "Yes, it was scary." She finally looked at him. "But I'm not afraid now."

Their gazes locked; the moment dragged out between them. She became aware of the bulge in his fitted boxers growing larger, harder. Unable to stop herself, she glanced down. *Oh, wow.* When she looked back at him, she saw him swallow. Hard.

"It is time for you to go back to bed," he said, his voice tight with strain.

A surprising thought practically knocked her upside the head. "Come to my room with me," she blurted before she chickened out.

He stared at her, the moment stretching to infinity, before he finally said, "This is bad idea. Is better we watch television instead."

She was inexperienced, true, but surely she hadn't misread him that badly. "You don't want . . . ? "

"Si, I very much *want*. You need your sleep."

"I've heard sex makes you sleep better." God, where did that come from?

"Is true then, you are *innocente* like Beppe says." He said it as a statement, not a question.

"Beppe said that?" she gasped. Heat rose up her neck. "How could he?"

Sandro chuckled. "Because he knows the way a man's mind thinks."

Beppe and sex. That was not an image she wanted to consider.

"Is true?" he repeated.

"Does it make a difference?"

"Do you never answer a question?"

"Why should I answer if it doesn't make a difference. Does it?" She held her breath as he stared at her.

"No," he answered at last. "*Innocente* or not, is best we watch the television."

She sighed. "It figures I'd fall for a lady's man with scruples."

He chuckled again. She settled back against him while he punched on the remote, lowered the volume, and flipped channels on the wall-mounted flat screen television, one of the first she'd seen at the time.

"Stop," she said. "I like this movie." It was *The Bodyguard*, one of her mom's favorite movies, and Kevin Costner had workmen ripping up Whitney Houston's estate, installing security measures. She explained the movie to that point, well aware of what would happen later. Hoping the growing attraction between Whitney and Kevin might persuade Sandro to change his mind. Nia never realized she was so devious.

When as a prelude to their love scene Kevin let Whitney's scarf float down to slice in half on his sword, Nia felt Sandro's body tense next to her.

"You are very bad," he scolded, obviously realizing what was coming next.

She looked at him. "I'm trying to be but no one will let me." She slid her hand across the hard ridges on his stomach surprising herself with her boldness.

He grabbed her arm with a low growl.

That's when she came to her senses, aware she was throwing herself at him. "I'm no better than a groupie," she muttered realizing he must have women throw themselves at him all the time. "I'm sorry," she told him, embarrassed by her actions. "I thought you were interested. Beppe's right, I am inexperienced. Sex has never been high on my priority list." She slid her arm from his grasp. "I'll just um . . . go back to my room. Um, now."

She intended to climb off the couch, but he caught her around her waist, and in an unexpected move she was on her back with him straddled on top of her.

Her eyes widened.

Sandro moved closer, closer, so close she felt his breath whispering across her face. Her heart thumped heavy and hard. She was certain he could see it pounding as he lowered his gaze to her chest. As if in proof, he laid his hand between her breasts. Her eyes drifted shut. Anticipation. Fantasy. Need.

Maddeningly avoiding her breasts which were swelling with desire, he trailed his hand up to her neck. There, his thumb brushed the thudding pulse at the base of her throat.

When he pulled back, she moaned.

"You are wrong," he said.

Her eyes snapped back open.

"I am interested. But your first time . . . should be special. Not like this."

"Like this?" The weight of him, the closeness of

him, her brain seemed sluggish and she didn't understand what he meant.

"In a hurry," he told her. "Afraid someone will interrupt."

"There's my room," she suggested.

"And if Beppe wakes up and I am not on this sofa, where do you think he will look? Besides, it would not be honorable to use his house for our pleasure."

Nia knew he was right. She sighed. "Why do you have to be so logical?" She didn't know *how* he could be so logical either, since the thing most prevalent on her mind was finding a way to get closer to him.

"Is not easy being logical, especially when I want to . . ." and what followed was a whole string of Italian words that sounded so sexy she wanted to rip off her clothes, even though she had no idea how to translate.

"What'd you just say to me?"

"I told you what I want to do with you, but I don't know how to say the English."

"Why don't you show me instead, and I'll interpret for you? I know, I know." She cut off the sure protest he would make. "You don't want to do anything here. So you can come to my dorm room with me tomorrow night. I'll kick out my roommate."

He chuckled. "You have one thing on the brain."

"Can you blame me?"

His smile swiftly changed to seriousness. "I would like that very much, but Beppe and Luciana—"

"I know what you're going to say. You haven't seen them in years. And I understand. You don't have enough time with them as it is. I guess I'm out of luck."

"Don't be impatient. You will be at the World Cup."

"World Cup? Geez, that's four months away."

"Will give you time to learn Italian so you know what I say."

"Ha. You're the one making me wait. Better learn those words you need to know in English."

He kissed her then, a passionate kiss that had her pushing her body as physically close as possible. He followed with more whispered words in Italian.

"All right, all right. I'll learn Italian," she gasped. "You just make sure you find a way for us to be together during the World Cup." She hoped he had an idea how he was going to pull that off.

"I'll find a way. I will be your first lover."

"My first lover, hm? That means I'm not supposed to have sex with anyone in the meantime? After you got me all worked up like this?"

"Your first lover," he repeated, all seriousness. "And it will be very special."

When he put it that way, all desire to tease him fled while she fought off a renewed wave of sexual desire. "I better get to bed before I do something you'll regret," she said.

"But we were watching the movie," he protested, before he kissed her again. Teasing kisses, nibbling kisses, then more serious tongue-dueling kisses that had her reeling with dizziness and desire.

Coming up for air endless minutes later, she glanced at the television. "Too late," she breathed. "We missed it already."

His gaze turned to the TV where Whitney sang the last refrains of *I'll Always Love You.* Kevin stood guard next to his new employer. Loving the song, Nia hummed along.

"What happened?"

She stopped humming. "He left her in the end. To move onto his next job." The ending always made her sad, which is why she felt sorry for herself as she added, "Like you'll leave me."

Sandro stared at her, passion still smoldering hot in his eyes. "There is a difference, *carissima.* I will be back. And you will be my woman. For always."

* * *

He came back; he made her his as promised. But now he was gone. And she was alone. No comforting, strong arms. No sweetly whispered Italian words to ease her fears.

No, not alone. There were bad guys. Mob guys. With guns. And she was prisoner—God only knew where. And Sandro had disappeared, running from these bad guys. She was certain of that. No matter the little charade he pulled off this morning, he hadn't left her for another woman or broken his promise that she would be his woman always. He had only been trying to protect her, for what reason she wasn't sure. She only knew they were all in danger now.

He needed her. Her son needed her. Her son would be frightened without her.

She was frightened without her son. She was frightened without Sandro.

She had to fight for her family. No matter what it took, she wouldn't be defeated.

After the nap, her mind was sharper, more focused. Escape foremost on her mind, she scanned the room again. The door lock she could pick, thanks to lessons from Dave when they were kids, but she had no tools. And who knew what waited for her on the other side of the door.

She walked to the window again. Looked out. Her room was three stories from the ground. Much too far to jump, but it seemed her only option. Quickly she searched the room, looking for anything to help her escape, to use as a ladder. She eyed the bed. Could she make a ladder from the bed sheets and slide down?

Working quickly, efficiently, she stripped the sheets from the bed. Keeping an eye on the door, she tied the sheets together, spreading them on the floor to judge the distance. Not enough. But thankfully, the bed was made for winter and had blankets.

She added the two blankets, their bulk making it harder to tie. Jerking the knots as tightly as possible, she took her bundle to the window. A thorough glance outside showed a red pickup truck and the black Lincoln Navigator, but no people. No guards around the perimeter to stop her.

Lucky her. Stupid them.

Now for something to tie her bed-linen ladder onto. The bed itself looked stout enough to hold her weight, but it was too far from the window and would use too much of her precious homemade rope. The dresser was adjacent to the window, and although not as heavy as the bed, it would have to do.

Kneeling, she tied the end of a sheet around the dresser leg. She tugged on it, testing the strength. Satisfied, she tossed the end out the window. It didn't quite reach the ground, but she thought she could drop the remaining few feet with no trouble. She took a quick look around the room but found nothing she needed. Her purse, phone and jacket still lay on the seat of her car.

She was hoping to steal one of the vehicles in the driveway although she didn't know how to wire a car. Unfortunately, Dave had never taught her how. She prayed that someone left keys in an ignition or under the visor or floor mat. Otherwise, it was going to be a long, cold walk.

Taking a deep breath, she swung a leg over the window ledge. The movement reminded her of the time she climbed over the stadium wall at the game where she first met Sandro with his uncle. She paused, gathered her courage. *Sandro, Daniele, I'm coming my darlings.*

Holding onto the sheet, she climbed out the window.

Breathe.

She'd never climbed a mountain—but she'd seen it on TV. She braced her feet against the wall, but she could feel her hands slipping. The sheets twisted and swung, banging her against the rough bricks which scraped the back of her hands. It was harder than it looked. Her strength was in her legs, not her arms...

The texture changed beneath her fingertips. She had reached the blankets now; she was almost at the end. A little lower then she looked to check her positioning.

And froze. They weren't so stupid after all.

"Where do ya think you're going, bitch?"

CHAPTER 12

Running across the parking lot to his car, Dave pulled his phone from his pocket. He punched a number while trying to keep Sandro in sight.

"Hey, Tony. Sandro's no longer cooperating. He and Midnight just left to take off on their own." Dave reached his car. "I'm following."

"Shit," Tony said in his mother hen way. "Guess he got scared off. Can't really blame him."

"No, I can't. But he's too inexperienced to take on the mob alone. It's my job to keep him alive." Dave unlocked the door and jumped into his company Crown Vic, now with two new tires.

"So we lost Midnight, too?"

"Maybe not." The engine roared to life and Dave jerked the car into drive, spinning out of the parking space on those new tires. "I'm thinking I can persuade a little cooperation in that area. If I can separate the two."

"It's a shot. Maybe turn on that charm of yours."

"Watch it," Dave warned. Tony was venturing too far away from their agreement to not reveal Marisa's name or gender. Now that he knew his office had been bugged, he was thankful for the precaution. "How's the rest of them?" he asked, referring to Danny and the aunt and uncle.

"Everything's A-okay," Tony said. "No sign of trouble."

"Good. You keep watch on them, and I'll see what I can do on this end."

"Sure thing, boss."

Dave disconnected the call, stuffed the phone into his jacket and forced his way onto the crowded street, honking and cussing his way through the heavy traffic, all the while keeping his gaze peeled for the maroon Buick.

It didn't take him long to find it. He stayed back several car lengths, while still keeping the Buick in his line of sight. Sandro and Marisa, apparently involved in a deep discussion, waved hands and nodded heads. Sandro was driving as if he didn't have a contract on him, hardly glancing in his rearview or side mirrors to check for tails.

Sandro, buddy, you're going to have to get better at watching your ass if you're going to stay alive.

Just then, Sandro made a quick left turn out of the right lane, and with the unexpected move, Dave lost him. Horns honked and brakes squealed as Dave tried to swerve through three lanes of traffic to keep up.

Italian driving skills apparently came in handy in New York. He growled, slapped his hand on the steering wheel, and drove up another block before he was able to circle back and get on the same road Sandro had taken. Dave drove on, constantly scanning the streets, hoping Sandro hadn't made any more unexpected turns.

In front of him, drivers were stopped, waiting for a car to make a left turn into a parking garage. Dave whipped into the right lane. As he approached the turning car, he saw it was the Buick. Bingo. Sandro turned the car into the parking garage without noticing him.

Dave looked up at the skyscraper. A popular hotel chain. He drove around the block, found a place to park, sprinted to a side door and entered the lobby in time to see Marisa at the front desk. But he saw no sign of Sandro. Dave ducked behind a large potted plant to scan the slickly elegant lobby until he spotted Sandro at a newsstand, reading a magazine. His infamous ponytail was shoved up under a cap.

Marisa walked by Sandro, punched the elevator button. After glancing around, forcing Dave to slide back out of sight, Sandro folded the magazine in his hands and followed a discreet distance behind Marisa, entering the elevator just as it was closing.

Following them was out of the question. The elevators were enclosed and Dave had no way of knowing which floor their room was on. He considered going to the registration desk and intimidating the clerk for the information. But that would make him too public and at this time discretion was the better part of valor and all that.

From necessity, he reasoned, Marisa was going to have to do most of the legwork for whatever scheme she and Sandro, who was too recognizable to be running around on the streets, had devised. Following a gut feeling that she would soon be back down, Dave decided to stay put and watch the elevators, betting if he followed her, he'd find out quick enough what they were planning.

* * *

A sense of déjà vu welcomed Marisa as she used the key card to unlock the second hotel room of the day. Sandro, walking past her, tossed his cap and magazine on the king-sized bed—one bed only—since she would be staying at her apartment. Or if absolutely necessary, with Luigi. She hid a shudder by giving careful attention locking the door behind them. *Not much longer*, she promised herself.

Sandro unzipped his jacket. Her purse joined his things on the bed before she pulled off her short, leather, fur-lined jacket. She took her jacket, as well as his, and hung them on the standard room hangars.

She didn't have to ask him what he was thinking. She remembered all too well the horror of learning the person who gave you the reason to exist was in danger. The memory tightened her throat, cutting off her air. She'd been too late for Paolo. But there was still time for Nia.

"Ho bisogono di una pistola," Sandro said, asking for a gun.

Her back had been to him. She dragged in a breath and turned to face him. As long as Sandro stayed in the room he was safe enough and had no need for a gun, but she could play along. Without a word, she walked to her purse and pulled out her derringer from its snug compartment.

Looking skeptically at the tiny gun she handed him, Sandro said, *"Questo è un giocattaolo, non una pistola."* This is a toy, not a gun.

"Un giocattolo mortale, se sei un buon tiro." A deadly toy if you're a good shot, she told him, continuing in Italian since he was more comfortable with their native language. "And you are a very good shot." She

remembered the times before momma's . . . tragedy, when Sandro joined them on family hunting trips. He'd only been a teen then, but he bagged his shot every time. Birds, a hundred meters in the air. As he grew older, he succeeded in everything he tried. She hoped his luck held with their venture. The stakes were so much higher.

Hefting her derringer in his palm, he bent over and slid it inside his sock. Almost immediately, he pulled it back out and said, "Uncomfortable. I'll need an ankle holster."

Apparently he planned to keep her gun, whether he thought it a toy or not. Of course, she did offer. But now she'd need to get herself a replacement. "I can buy you an ankle holster when I buy your clothes." She'd only had time to go to the software store earlier. Since he couldn't return home, he was going to need at least one change of clothes.

"I need a bigger gun, too. One where I don't have to get so close to use it on the people who want to kill me. The derringer is a good back up weapon, but not as a main weapon."

"I can get you a bigger gun, *si*," she offered. It would be no problem since she was going to buy herself another one anyway.

"I want to buy my own."

He simply was not going to be cooperative, was he? "Getting out is risky," she pointed out, not telling him anything he didn't know. She'd saved his life once already today. Who knew if she would be in the right place at the right time again? And of course, there would be an 'again'. Poppa would be relentless until Sandro was stopped.

"You know I have to look for Nia."

Marisa almost sighed. But truthfully, she'd known there was no chance of talking him into staying hidden and safe. Dave had already tried every version of that tactic. And could she blame Sandro? She would have willingly risked her life, given her life even, to have been able to save Paolo. Sandro, with her help, had a chance to rescue his beloved and stop her father as well. No, she couldn't blame him. Still his insistence on going out would cause them problems. Keeping him safe being the biggest problem.

Needing time to think, she reached inside the small room refrigerator for a cold drink. "Want something?"

He shook his head.

She twisted the cap off the bottle and took a sip. "Georgio's nephew sells guns," she said at last. Georgio was the head chef at Sandro's restaurant. "You can get one from him without having to wait for a background check."

"I'd heard that rumor. That will be the best option. I will go to the restaurant and get the location from Georgio."

"Go to the restaurant? Hello? Ever heard of a *telefono*?" She almost lost her temper, but checked it at the last second. Waste of energy; obviously, he wasn't listening.

"Who knows if the phones are tapped? Even if they can't trace this throw-away phone you got for me, calling could put Georgio in danger."

Ratcheting down her frustration, she stood sipping her soda. She studied Sandro, considering the point he made. It was nice to see his quick intelligence had not deserted him in a crisis moment. "I can swing by and talk to Georgio." She tried one last time, knowing his answer even before he spoke.

"No. I must do something for myself."

Her lips tightened. She expected no less.

"Just get me some clothes so I can get out on the streets," he continued. "I'm too recognizable to everyone in these warm-ups."

He didn't mean 'everyone', of course. Although avid soccer fans would likely recognize him, true, since his image was splattered over sports magazines and the Internet. But the 'everyone' of whom he spoke was the people he would, of necessity, have to be around. The mobsters. They were the ones more likely to recognize him in his customary warm-ups.

She set her drink down on the nightstand and pulled a notepad and pen out of the drawer. "What sort of clothes do you want?"

He gave her a list, and added that he wanted one of those razors to shave his head.

She blinked. "You're cutting off your ponytail?"

"It will help disguise me."

Sadness overcame her, he'd had that curly ponytail for as long as she could remember. But it would grow back. His safety was most important, she agreed.

He unzipped the front pocket on his warm-up pants to pull out his wallet. Surely he did not intend to pay? He passed her a debit card. "I could only get three hundred out of the ATM in the lobby. I need that for a gun. You should have no trouble using my card, I'll give you my PIN."

Shaking her head, she handed the card back to him. "I will pay. You're in this because of my family."

When he refused to take it back, the stubborn Italian, she added, "We're stealing poppa's money anyway, what is the difference?" Stepping closer, she smiled at the grim look on his face. Before he could object, she stuffed the card back into his pocket. "You know I'm right."

CHAPTER 13

Nia released her homemade rope and dropped to the ground. Mikey examined the tied-together blankets and sheets dangling from the third floor window.

"Pretty slick, bitch." He nodded. "I figured you'd try something. You'se got the look of a fighter about ya."

And fight she would, if she thought she'd stand a chance. But that gun in his hand definitely made her think twice. Still. Giving up was a hard thought to process when freedom had been so close.

A black Lincoln Town car pulled into the drive, distracting Mikey's attention for a moment. "Ah, Giovanni's arrived with the foo—"

Nia seized the chance. Swinging her foot up to kick Mikey's wrist, she heard a sickening crack before the gun went flying.

"Fuck!" Mikey screamed cradling his hand. "You broke my wrist, bitch."

With only a vague idea of how to use it, Nia made a mad dash for the gun. Technical know-how or not, she wanted it with her.

She scooped it up and kept on running, heading for the wooded area behind the house. It would soon be dark.

If she could reach the trees, perhaps she could lose them and hide until they gave up searching. Then she could find help.

"Hey, what's going on?" she heard the man named Giovanni ask as he climbed out of the car.

"Stop the bitch. She's getting away. Damn it, she broke my wrist," Mikey whined, but Nia heard him take off after her. He wasn't too injured to run it seemed.

Giovanni, who was at least a hundred yards away, started running at her from the right. She swerved left.

Instinct, honed from years of being chased for possession of a soccer ball, told her Mikey was fast closing behind her. Giovanni still wasn't close enough to be a threat. The trees were just ahead, but what once before seemed a welcome haven, now was a hindrance. Mikey was too close; she couldn't outrun him by weaving and darting between trees. The tangle of branches would slow her too much.

Panic threatened. She forced it down. Stay calm, she told herself.

Just then, she sensed Mikey making his move. He lunged. She twisted and sped away, now running parallel to the trees. He leaped forward again, managing to touch her. He wasn't close enough to grab her, but he shoved at her.

"Shit!" he yelled. "My wrist."

Injured wrist or not, his move had pushed her off balance while she had been running full speed. She struggled to keep her balance, but she stumbled, stuttered, then slammed into a tree.

The impact knocked the breath from her. The gun fell from her limp fingers.

Mikey grabbed her hair, jerking her head back,

twisting her around to face him. She hadn't yet recovered from the collision with the tree. Too much pain. She gasped, trying to breathe.

"You broke my wrist, you fucking bitch." He waved his hand in front her face.

Blinking, she tried to make her eyes focus.

"That hurt, damn it." He slammed his right knee viciously into her stomach.

She cried out in shocked agony. The baby! "No, not my stomach," she whimpered.

He let go of her hair and she slumped forward, clutching her stomach. Before she hit the ground his left fist caught her right cheekbone, snapping her head back. She staggered into the tree again, this time the back of her head colliding with the unforgiving tree. She slid to the ground.

"Mikey, what the fuck you doing?" Giovanni caught up to them. "You ain't s'pposed to hurt her."

"She broke my fuckin' wrist."

Their voices came at her from a growing distance. Over the reverberating in her head, she wished he'd shut up about his stupid wrist.

Mikey jerked her hair again, tugging her to her feet. The pain nearly blinded her.

"Leave her alone." Giovanni stepped between them. "She ain't no good to us dead, asshole." He shoved at Mikey, forcing him away from her.

She nearly crumpled to the ground again.

Giovanni caught her. "Jesus, she can't even walk." He swung her into his arms.

He was a lean wiry man who reeked of garlic and cigarettes. Her head swam, sweat dripped in her eyes despite the cool weather. Her stomach protested over the dull throbbing pain. "No . . ." she muttered. "Lemme . . . go."

Ignoring her, he carried her at a steady pace to the house. "Mikey, get the food out of the car," he yelled over his shoulder.

"My damned wrist's broken. How am I s'ppose to get the food outta the car?"

"Just quit your fucking bellyaching and get the damned food, asshole." While still holding her, Giovanni managed to open the screen and the wooden back door without causing her more injury. They entered into the kitchen. "Hey, Angie, get me some wet cloths and an ice pack."

Angelo, more commonly known as Angie, met them at the entrance to the dining room. "What the—"

"She tried to escape and Mikey got a little too ambitious."

"Mikey? Where the hell is he? I'm gonna—"

"Let's take care of her first." Giovanni carried her into another room and laid her on a sofa.

Angie brought two wet dishcloths and a plastic bag with ice cubes. "Move outta the way," he told Giovanni. He lowered his considerable bulk to the floor beside the sofa. "Ah, *Bella*, what was you doing?" he muttered.

Disappointment, anger, heartache robbed Nia of the ability to speak, if Angie even deserved an answer to such a stupid question. She barely winced when he washed her bruised cheek.

"Not too much blood for such a nasty cut."

She looked dully at the cloth. She hadn't even realized she'd been bleeding.

"But you will have a big, ugly bruise. Already, it is very swollen."

It felt like it. It felt like she had a bag of bouncing marbles sewn inside her cheek, while someone else had another bag and was pounding it on the back of her head.

"Anywhere else?"

"The back of her head hit a tree, and Mikey kneed her in the stomach," Giovanni answered when she didn't.

Angie swore in Italian, and then his gaze settled on her hands still clutched in a shielding gesture across her midsection. He laid his hand on top of hers and made as if to move them.

"No," she said finding her voice at last.

"You hurt here?"

"Don't touch me." She curled her legs protectively inward.

He nodded, made a *tsking* sound. "Let me see the back of your head, then." He helped her to a sitting position. More *tsking* noises. "Yes, a very big knot. What the hell was Mikey thinking?" He spoke in a mild tone, yet Nia could see the anger burning deep in his brown eyes. His sympathy brought no relief.

"She was trying to escape, Angie," Mikey whined from the doorway. "She broke my wrist. I had to stop her."

"You know she is not to be hurt. You were very careless. I told you she is athletic, and grew up with many brothers. She's bound to know how to fight."

Nia's blood grew chilled at the realization that these mobsters knew so much about her.

"You're taking your own life in your hands to hurt her," Angie warned.

"That's a bunch of shit, and you know it. He's gonna whack her, just as soon as he gets Sandro out in the open." Mikey taunted her with his eyes, then

96

awkwardly reached across his body with his left hand and pulled his knife out of its holder. "And when they're both dead, won't be any reason for the kid to live, either."

"No!" She lunged off the couch, going for Mikey's throat. Angie barely caught her in time. She shoved against his restraining grip. "You hurt my son and I'll rip your heart out, I swear I will," she promised Mikey, anger making her voice shake.

Laughing, Mikey popped open the wicked looking knife blade with his left hand. "Won't be a thing you can do about it, bitch. When I slit his little throat, you'll already be dead." He made a cutting motion across his throat. "Just like butter."

She made a growling sound, struggling wildly against Angie. "I'm going to break every bone in your body before I kill you," she promised grimly, never before having been filled with such hatred and fear at the same time.

He laughed again. "I'm really sca—"

"Mikey, you fucking crazy? Shut up," Angie told him. "Get the hell out of here. Go back to town, get your hand fixed. Giovanni, get him outta here." He nodded his head in a dismissive gesture.

Giovanni placed a hand on Mikey's shoulder.

"Yeah, I'll go now, but I'll be back. I owe her."

Nia spat toward Mikey. He took a threatening step closer. She tugged against Angie's grasp.

"Go!"Angie commanded. Giovanni grabbed Mikey's jacket and led him away. "Lie down, *Bella*," Angie told her, wiping the saliva from her mouth with one of the cloths. "Do not upset yourself. Your head must hurt."

Nia only glared at him. The back door slammed.

"Here, hold this ice on your face. Do I need to tie you up, or can I trust you to stay put while I eat?"

She still didn't speak.

He laid a cloth on her face, then propped the ice bag on top. He examined his work. "I will trust you for now. Giovanni, bring the food in here." He pushed up from the floor and settled in a chair across from the sofa. "So, how did you manage to get away from us?"

She refused to answer, instead analyzing all she'd learned, knowing she had to find another way to escape. But her mind was too jumbled and her head hurt too much for her brain to work. And her stomach was sore, too. But fortunately no cramps. Yet. That had to be a good sign. Maybe that brutal knee didn't hurt the baby. She was only a few weeks pregnant after all. Surely the baby was small and safe deep inside her womb. She sent up a prayer.

Giovanni walked in with take-out Chinese and answered Angie's question. "She tied the sheets and blankets together and climbed out the window." He went back to the kitchen.

Angie nodded, looking impressed. "Very resourceful. Of course you know you'll now have to sleep without any linens on your bed."

She started to spout off she didn't plan to sleep until she found a way to free herself from them, but she'd said enough for the night. Threatening to kill a man wasn't included in her everyday conversation. Yet she had meant every word to Mikey.

Discovering the depths of violence she was capable of shocked her. Yes, she was aggressive on the soccer field; otherwise she was pretty easygoing. Never violent. But this was her family they were threatening.

Her very life.

She'd known Sandro was in some sort of trouble, but this kind of trouble she never would have imagined. Having the Mafia calmly discuss wiping out her and the two people she loved most as if they never existed.

Tremors started deep inside her. She fought the helpless feeling, knowing that somehow she had to free herself. Save her family.

Angie sat calmly unpacking the take-out Chinese from the white plastic bag. He looked at her. "Tomorrow I'm going to cook my pasta primavera. But tonight there wasn't time. Giovanni, did'ja get my sun-dried tomatoes?" he called to the kitchen.

Giovanni walked back into the room carrying two cans of beer. "Yeah, I got 'em. That fresh garlic you asked for, too."

"Good thing for you." Angie opened a container and sniffed. "Hm, pork chow mein. Smells pretty good. Here, take a whiff." He held the container across the coffee table. "Hey," he said to Giovanni. "Where's her drink? You want something to drink, don'tcha? You wanna brewskie? Vino?"

The smell of the food made her nauseous. With fear churning acid in her stomach and that knee in her gut, she was already on shaky ground.

She was going to be sick.

"Nah, you're an athlete. You probably don't drink," he continued, apparently unbothered he was talking to himself. "How about a soft drink? Giovanni, what we got?"

"I need a bathroom." She tossed the ice pack aside, interrupting his rambling monologue.

"Angie, she don't look so good. She looks kind of

green."

Angie turned his gaze back to her. "You okay? You gonna be—"

"Please," she interrupted. "A bathroom?"

"Yeah, sure." He pointed. "Right over there."

With one hand splayed on her roiling stomach, and one hand covering her mouth, she stumbled toward the bathroom.

"Giovanni, go keep a watch on her."

"*Minghia!* What the hell for?"

"I haven't had a chance to check out that bathroom, have you?"

"No—"

"There could be something in there she could use as a weapon."

"Yeah, like what? Eyebrow tweezers?"

They laughed. "Yeah, eyebrow tweezers," Angie chuckled. "She's gonna come back out here and kill us with tweezers." Abruptly he stopped laughing. "Get the fuck over there now!"

With a look of distaste, Giovanni went to stand outside the bathroom door.

"Angie, she's really heaving it up in there." Giovanni got a queasy feeling in his stomach. He walked closer to Angie, where the retching noises in the bathroom weren't so loud. "Maybe she got hurt from the knee in her stomach."

"Could be." Angie shoveled in a bite of chow mein.

Giovanni didn't know if he'd be able to eat now. "Or all that talk about killing her and her family could've made her sick. Damn Mikey and his stupid ass big mouth."

"Listen, get back over there and wait for her to stop. Don't give her time to look around."

Reluctant, and still feeling green himself, Giovanni went back to stand by the door. Finally, he heard the toilet flush. He knocked briefly and opened the door. Nia paused in the act of blowing her nose. Her eyes were puffy, her hair tangled, and her cheek swollen and turning purple. She looked like shit.

"Do you mind?" she said.

"Sorry." He shrugged. "Angie said I gotta watch ya."

She finished wiping her nose, then tossed the tissue in the toilet. Ignoring him, she went to the sink and washed her face and rinsed out her mouth. "I don't suppose you bought me a toothbrush when you were at the store?"

He looked blank. "Uh, no. . .guess I didn't. I'll pick you up one tomorrow."

She dried her face, turned off the light. "Don't bother." She walked past him.

"Feeling better?" Angie asked.

"Just peachy." She plopped on the sofa.

"Listen, I know Mikey upset you. I wanna tell you ain't nothing gonna happen—"

"Let me tell you what's *upset* me," she said, leaning forward with a burst of renewed energy. "This morning I found out I was pregnant. And who's the first person I'm telling? You . . . some half-ass mobster. When I should be telling my husband." Was it only this morning? It seemed ages ago.

"Only he's not home," she continued before Angie could say anything. "He's left me. Said our marriage was over and walked right out of my life. But now I'm thinking he was just trying to throw me off track while he drops out of sight. Because for some unimaginable reason you jerk-offs are after him. Wanting him dead. *My* husband. Who has never to my knowledge ever received even so much as a traffic ticket.

"And not only is he supposed to be killed, but one of your asshole thugs beats me up and threatens my life, the life of my unborn baby and my innocent two-year-old son.

"Yeah, I'd say I'm a little pissed, Angie. So, what the fuck are you gonna do about it?" She leaned back and crossed her arms.

Angie gaped at her, his fork frozen halfway to his mouth; Giovanni had the same, stupid open-mouthed look on his face.

Putting his fork down, Angelo closed his mouth and used his napkin to wipe his face. "I gotta keep you here, Nia. I don't got any orders to kill you . . . or your son. Mikey was just mouthing off. As a matter of fact, Mikey's liable to get whacked for what he did to you—"

"Killing Mikey is too good for him." There was that surprising violent streak again.

"Probably." He shrugged. "We're supposed to hold you here and make sure you stay safe."

"But you have orders to kill Sandro."

He didn't answer. She looked to Giovanni, whose gaze slid away from hers.

"But why? What has he done?"

Angie wouldn't give her a direct answer. "Carlo's supposed to be here tomorrow night. Ask him your questions."

"Will he answer?" She divided her attention between them, trying to figure out what they weren't telling her. It was their lack of responsiveness that confirmed her worst fears. Sandro was definitely in danger.

He shrugged. "I don't know. Worrying about it won't help anything. Eat something."

She eyed the food with disinterest, her sudden energy burst short-lived.

"Come on. You got a baby to think about, you said. Eat something. You don't want this, maybe some toast? Milk? Giovanni, we got milk—"

"I don't want milk."

"Okay, forget the milk. A soft drink. Here's a plate. You want some of this?" He pointed to a carton of stir-fried vegetables with noodles.

Reluctantly, she accepted. He was right. She needed to eat. Not only for the baby, but for the strength to escape. Because one way or another, she was getting away from this house.

Alive.

Later, after she nibbled at her vegetables, Giovanni cleaned up the empty cartons, while Angie took a phone call in the kitchen out of her hearing range. She put her plate down and idly picked up a plastic card on the coffee table. Woo-Sung's Chinese Take Out, it advertised. On the back it listed twenty-six places Woo-Sung's was available in the New York/New Jersey area. Nia idly flicked the card around, until a thought occurred to her. She remembered the lock on her door and looked at the card more closely. About the same weight and thickness of a credit card. Perfect.

She quickly slid the card into her pocket before they came back into the living room.

Just in time.

"Giovanni's missing a knife." Angie walked back in the room. A dinner knife lay next to her plate on the coffee table which had been their informal dining table. "Ah, here it is."

"What? Did you think I took it?"

"Wouldn't put it past you. I did hear you threaten to tear out Mikey's heart. I wouldn't want you getting any ideas while I'm sleeping."

"You're not telling me you're going to let me roam around the house while you're sleeping?"

"Not on your life, *Bella*. You'll be locked back into your room again. This time without your sheets."

"It's getting very cold."

"You should have thought of that. And you should be grateful you didn't escape earlier. With no jacket and those flimsy shoes, once nighttime hit, you'd have frostbite in no time."

Frostbite would have been better than being held prisoner with nothing more to think about than her future. Or lack of one.

"I'll leave you the comforter," he finally conceded. "You won't freeze to death tonight."

Great. She wouldn't freeze to death tonight. But by tomorrow night. . .or the next, she might be dead. She didn't for one minute believe Angie about Carlo not planning to hurt her. Once they found Sandro, they had no reason to keep her alive.

She bit back a surge of fear. She was going to have to escape again. Tonight. Frostbite was better than dying.

CHAPTER 14

A clock seemed to be counting down in Sandro's heart. Minutes, hours, days, and Nia could be dead. Did they have days? No, he didn't think so. He pulled on the black leather jacket that matched the black shirt and jeans Marisa had purchased, and wished he could throw off the sense of doom that clothed him as surely as the new clothes. He hoped their plan worked, but he had to take action. Sitting, hiding, worrying, that was not his way. Cautiously, he opened the door and scanned the hallway. Marisa had left minutes earlier and they were counting on anyone watching them following her.

With no one in sight, he slid through the door, closing it quietly behind him. When they arrived at this hotel, he had looked for the stairway. His feet made no sound on the carpeted floor as he strode quickly to the right door. Another quick look showed he was still alone. He pulled the door open and hurried through.

The stairs weren't carpeted. But they were concrete and not metal. His new black sneakers would barely make a sound. He ran down the steps, his legs pumping, his heart steadily beating. Once he heard a door open somewhere above him. He stopped. Listened.

Breathed.

Nothing.

He hurried on. Down nine flights of stairs and into the parking garage.

He found the maroon Buick and slid into the front seat, his nose wrinkling in distaste at the stale cigarette smell. Ignoring it, he located the right wires, touched them together and pressed on the gas pedal.

The car engine started. He twisted the wires in place, put on his seatbelt, and left the garage. He drove around the streets for a while to check if he'd picked up a tail. When he found no one following him, he decided either Dave hadn't had time to get men in place, or else he was giving them some breathing room until he could decipher their plan. Sandro decided it was the latter reason. He knew Dave had had plenty of time to get men in place.

No, Dave wanted to know what they were up to without a chance of another leak. And he wanted a hand in helping to save Nia. Knowing the history between his wife and Dave, Sandro began to suspect the FBI man might be willing to go outside the limits of the law to rescue Nia.

Sandro sighed. If Dave was willing to bend enough to help, perhaps Marisa was right and they should use him. And at the moment, Sandro found it could be reassuring to have one more person on their side. Even if that person preferred that Sandro himself was out of the picture.

He turned the Buick uptown, heading for his restaurant, parking more than a block away. Sliding along the shadows of the buildings, staying alert for Carlo's men, Sandro made it to the restaurant's kitchen door without incidence. He breathed out a small sigh of relief. Unlocking the door with his key, he slipped inside the business he'd bought for his aunt and uncle when they moved to the States to make up for the business his uncle lost in Italy.

Hiding inside a janitorial supply closet, he held the door slightly ajar listening to the noise and chatter in the kitchen. He had to find a way to isolate Georgio so he could get the information he needed about Jason, the gun-supplying nephew. Sandro thought the fewer people at the restaurant who saw him, the less danger for everyone all around.

The walk-in freezer was located almost directly across from the supply closet. Sandro waited, and then opportunity greeted him.

Georgio went to the freezer.

Sandro whispered his name, hoping the slight sound would get his head chef's attention.

Stopping abruptly, Georgio turned, scanning for the source of the whispered voice. Sandro opened the closet door a little wider.

Georgio squinted then said, "Sandro!" not thinking to lower his voice.

"Shh."

Grimacing, Georgio lowered his voice to a whisper. "Your hair! Where is it? And where have you been? You and Giuseppe and Luciana have all disappeared, there are *Mafioso* in the dining room looking for you, and now you're hiding back here?"

"Peruzzo's men are here, then?"

"*Si*, guarding every door. They only check this one occasionally because I refuse to allow those filthy men to dirty my kitchen."

If the situation had been less tense, Sandro would have smiled at his head chef's possessiveness. *Por Dio* that Giuseppe was so possessive. "I need help. Can you get rid of the other cooks for a moment? Perhaps with one of your famous tirades?"

Looking thoughtful, Georgio murmured. "*Si*, I think the tomatoes look too ripe . . . ."

Sandro ducked back out of sight, waiting for the explosion.

Georgio didn't disappoint, and soon tomatoes were flying, Georgio was screaming in loud, virulent Italian and cooks and waiters were scampering for their lives.

With the kitchen cleared, Sandro stepped out of the closet.

"What did you need?" Georgio asked.

"How can I find Jason?"

"My nephew?"

Unlike Georgio who was full Italian, Jason was half-Italian. Georgio had once told Sandro in a disgusted tone that his nephew's American father had a fascination with the Greek myth about Jason and the Argonauts and had named his first born accordingly, which no doubt led him to the wrong side of the law. Fortunately, the rest of the seven children had good Italian names.

"*Si*. I need a weapon."

"He can get you one," Georgio admitted with a nod. "He has many connections."

"*Si, si*," Sandro said impatiently hoping to avoid a long dialogue on Jason's underworld business. "How can I find him?" he repeated.

"I'll call him for you. Set up a meeting." Georgio headed for the wall phone.

"No, no!" Sandro stopped him. "The phone here

might not be safe. Just give me his number, and I will call him."

"He won't see you if he doesn't know you. It's the nature of his business . . . *capito?*"

Sandro blew out a frustrated breath. "Then tell me where he lives. Surely once he sees who I am, he will let me in."

"But you look so different, I'm not sure he'll recogn—"

"Georgio! It's a risk I must take. Please. His add—"

"What's going on in here?" A voice came from the double-door entrance to the kitchen.

"*Merda.*" Sandro muttered. Shit. At least he and Georgio were around the corner and out of sight.

"Quick. In here." Georgio pushed him into the walk-in freezer. "Leave him to me."

"No, don't lock—" Sandro was cut off as Georgio shut the freezer door. He couldn't hear a thing, so he hovered by the boxed frozen food, the chill penetrating even his thick leather jacket. He waited. And waited. And wondered what the hell he was going to do if Georgio stayed gone so long he froze to death.

Finally the door opened. At the first sound on the door handle, Sandro had Marisa's derringer in his hand and ready. He was taking no chances on the wrong person opening the door.

Georgio's eyes widened at the sight of the gun. "You have a gun."

"I need a bigger one."

"You are in much trouble?"

"*Si.* Is best you do not know." Sandro shoved the gun back into his sock and rubbed his cold hands together.

"No, I don't need to know. Here's Jason's address." Georgio shoved a paper into Sandro's hands and hustled him toward the back door. "I wish you luck. I like my job here at your *ristorante*."

With a quick shove, Georgio pushed Sandro out the back door and closed it after him. The sudden thrust made Sandro stumble and unfortunately caused him to bump into a man walking by on the sidewalk.

"Hey, watch it, asshole."

"My apologies. I lost my balance." Sandro recognized the guy as one of Carlo's men. He tried to look unobtrusive as he turned to walk away.

His jacket was tugged from behind. "Hey, who're ya? And whatcha doing coming out of the restaurant that way?"

Sandro thought quickly. "Looking for food." He hunched his shoulders and shoved his hands in his pocket to look down on his luck. Since it was now dark and the only light available was streetlights, he hoped the man wouldn't be able to tell that the clothes he was wearing were too expensive for a beggar. "I have no home, no place to eat—"

"Well, you stay away from the place, you bum."

"Yes, yes, I will. I am sorry." Sandro kept his head down. He hated the placating victim's act, but he didn't want to test if his new haircut really altered his appearance that much. Especially not at this close range. Even if the lighting was dim.

"And you apologize for bumping into me. You're so dirty, you likely ruined my suit."

Sandro didn't point out he'd already apologized. "Yes, I am most sorry. I was very clumsy."

The man grabbed his shirt and tugged him closer with his left hand. In his right hand, he held a gun pointed at Sandro. At the sight of the gun, two men walking by turned abruptly and headed back the other way.

"You look familiar. I seen you around here before?" the man asked, so close to Sandro, even under the shadowy streetlights he could see the acne-scarred face.

"I often come by here for food." Sandro noticed the man's right wrist—the wrist of the hand that was holding the gun—was wrapped in a tight bandage. He hoped that meant an injury that would play to his advantage if this *Mafioso* grew even more threatening. . .or worse, realized his real identity.

"Well, don't you come back here no more. This place's too good for the likes of you. As a matter o'fact I think if you don't kiss my feet, I'll just kill you and put ya out of your misery." He pressed his gun into Sandro's forehead. "Well?"

With a resigned sigh, Sandro bent down as if he were going to kiss the man's feet. While he was bent over, he snatched Marisa's derringer once more. In a quick move, he jerked upwards, knocked the mobster's gun out of his hand and held the derringer underneath his tormentor's chin.

"I don't feel like kissing your feet." Sandro glared at the man. "Perhaps I'd rather you kiss mine."

"Hey, my wrist, man. I broke it today. It put me in a bitchy mood." He swallowed. "I didn't mean nothin' by threatening ya. I was just fuckin' with ya, y'know?"

"Mikey, that you?" Another man stood outside an open car door down the street. "You better come on.

Carlo's waiting."

"Answer him," Sandro said, knowing his position in the shadows hid him from view. "Careful what you say, though."

"Yeah, yeah," Mikey answered the other man. "I'm coming. Be right there."

Sandro nodded. "Now, on your way, little man. And be careful who you're fucking with next time."

Mikey walked two steps, then bent to retrieve his fallen gun.

"No, no," Sandro warned. "Kick it over here."

Mikey stared hard at Sandro. "Ah, fuck it." He kicked the gun toward Sandro, who retrieved it and shoved it in his waistband, all without taking his eyes or his gun off Mikey.

"*Arrivederci*, asshole," Sandro told Mikey. "Have a nice trip."

Shoving his hands into his pants pockets, Mikey walked off, half-watching Sandro over his shoulder. Sandro suspected the man was expecting a bullet in his back any minute. Before Mikey could get to the car, and perhaps recruit extra help, Sandro took off at a run down the street. He turned the corner and slipped out of sight.

* * *

Mikey carelessly bumped into a couple who were walking along holding hands. "Hey, watch it, jerk," the man said.

Fury thrumming his temples, Mikey considered pounding the man, but then remembered his wrist. He had it x-rayed earlier, bitch had broken it for sure. Heading for Joey's car, Mikey obsessed over losing his gun. He couldn't believe a street bum had got the best of him. He hadn't been expecting the cocksucker to come back and attack him. Most street people didn't have those kind of balls when a gun was pointing at them. He walked on, lightly rubbing his aching wrist. Something was unusual about that man . . . .

Mikey frowned, tried to focus. The man did look familiar. Had he seen him around the restaurant before as the man said?

He couldn't remember.

"What the hell took ya so long," Joey asked when Mikey got to the car.

"Ah, just a street bum begging for money. Had to teach him a thing or two." He certainly didn't want his pals to know a nobody got the drop on him.

"Well, get in, let's go." Joey, standing by the back door, slid into the back seat beside Ralphie.

Only seat left was the front passenger. Carmine was driving. Mikey cringed. Carmine made a little old lady look like a speed demon. The car, an old beat up Chevy, didn't look like it would win a race either.

"Why the hell are ya in this car?"

"Gotta make a delivery," Carmine said. "It's crap on the outside but it's still got good parts."

Mikey nodded. Carmine made money off jacking cars and selling them to mob-owned chop shops.

"Man, I'm starving," Mikey said. "Hope this meeting doesn't take too long." He'd been at the doctor's and hadn't had time to eat before Carlo called a meeting. He'd been planning to swing into the restaurant and grab a snack when the bum bumped into him.

"So, what's the boss want?" he asked, ignoring his growling stomach and anger, no time for either now. "I hope it ain't no job. I didn't bring my piece." He didn't want to tell the guys a street bum took it off him. And what was a street bum doing with a gun like that stuck in his sock? Or that fancy leather jacket, come to think of it. Mikey frowned. The guy still looked familiar—

"Why didn't you bring your gun?" Joey asked.

"I broke my wrist. It ain't no good now for shootin' a gun." Though he'd managed to hold his gun on the bum, Mikey never would've been able to pull the trigger with his right hand. "I'm not as good with my left hand," he lied. Actually he couldn't use his left hand at all to shoot with. He needed to get to a shooting range tomorrow and practice.

"So, how'd you break your wrist, Mikey?" Carmine asked as he put on the blinker and turned the corner.

Mikey knew they'd ask questions. He was prepared with his answers. "Ah, I got in a fight with Pauline. I went to slug her one and she moved. I hit the wall instead."

"That's funny. I heard Sandro's bitch broke it, not your bitch," Joey said from the back seat.

An unusual chill went through Mikey. They were contradicting him to his face. "How'd you hear—"

"Then you beat her up," Carmine added, staring intently at the road.

The bad feeling persisted. Mikey fought it. Tried to laugh it off. "Angie! That fat motherfucker's already been talking."

"'Fraid so, Mikey," Joey said, suddenly up close and breathing down the back of Mikey's neck.

Mikey's neck quivered. He slid away and turned to talk to Ralphie, sitting next to Joey. "Well, you know she was one tough bitch. She kicked Carmine's knee, after all." Ralphie hadn't been with them when they snatched Sandro's wife. Then he added to Carmine. "Ain't your knee still swollen and hurting?"

"Sure is," Carmine said. "If it'd been my right leg, I couldn've driven tonight."

"See what'd I tell ya," Mikey said, feeling like he'd just loosened a quickly tightening noose. He settled back into his seat. "So, uh. . . do you'se think that Angie's talked to Carlo already? He gonna chew me out tonight?"

He asked the question as they approached a corner. Carmine turned right. He should have turned left to go to Carlo's place. An ominous silence filled the car. Mikey's heart started to pound as he waited for the answer.

"Yeah, Mikey," Joey finally admitted. "Angie's already talked to Carlo. 'Fraid the news ain't good." The cold barrel of a small caliber gun poked the base of Mikey's skull. "Normally, Mikey, you know I use a wire," Joey said, referring to the braided wire he used to choke a person when Carlo ordered a hit. Mikey swallowed hard.

"But Carlo said since he's known you so long to make it quick," Joey said.

"Wait!" Mikey's forehead broke out in a sweat. "That street bum back at the restaurant? That was Sandro!" He was grasping, he didn't know for sure it was Sandro. If it was, he'd cut his hair. But if he could buy some time, get them to go back and look, maybe he could find a way to get away from them. He'd have to go on the lam, but that was better than dead. "I think he's cut his hair," he added to be more convincing.

"We'll check into it." Joey pulled the gun from the

base of Mikey's skull.

He relaxed a little, thinking he'd bought some time, that they would turn around and go look for Sandro.

Mikey never heard the two shots that killed him.

CHAPTER 15

Instead of returning to her apartment, Marisa headed for her office. Earlier, she had a flash of inspiration where to look for Sandro's wife. Things had happened so fast today that the idea hadn't occurred to her until after she left Sandro getting dressed in his new clothes she'd bought. Her father owned numerous pieces of real estate—houses and businesses alike. He was bound to be holding Nia at one of them.

By now, everyone would be long gone and she could access the company files. And while she was there, she could work on retrieving the passwords she needed from the information she copied off Roberto's hard drive. Even though she could do that from her home computer, might as well try it while she was at work.

Marisa stepped out of the taxi a block away from the office building. It was several minutes before the top of the hour when the security guard left his desk to make the rounds. Being early, she decided to walk the last block. Although she had an office in the building, she didn't want to sign in and leave a record of her being there after hours.

The typical night sounds and smells surrounded

her. Honking cars, street lights flashing, heavy exhaust fumes, people jostling along the sidewalk even at this time of night, which by New York standards wasn't late at all. After living here several years, the sights and sounds barely registered.

At straight up ten o'clock, she peered around the corner of the entrance into the front door of the office building. The guard stood and stretched. He checked his gun, looped his baton over his wrist and walked away from his desk. Right on time.

Waiting only moments, Marisa slipped her passcard into the electronic entry box. Avoiding the elevator, she hurried to the stairway entrance and quietly opened the metal door. She slipped off her black Manolo Blahnik pumps and ran up fifteen flights to the suite of Peruzzo offices. She was gasping for breath as she disabled the office security system and relocked the big wooden door behind her.

Time was of the essence. She had to do her searching and be ready to leave when the guard made his next hourly rounds. Or else be stuck here until his midnight rounds and be late for her meeting with Sandro.

The front of the office had a big glass window, and although the mini-blinds were shut, and the guard only gave a cursory glance down each hallway, she didn't want to accidentally attract his attention by turning on the overhead lights. She pulled out a flashlight from her purse and clicked the on button.

Something about the sudden LED light metaphorically illuminated all the challenges facing her. A sigh escaped, a temporary second of feeling overwhelmed, vulnerable. But only a momentary weakness before she pulled herself back together.

Bringing her father to justice and getting away from this life was much too compelling to even consider defeat. She could no longer be chained to this life.

Years earlier, in Italy, she had planned a different path. To testify against her father and escape with Sandro's cousin, Paolo, who had been willing to leave the *carabinieri* and to go into Italy's version of the Witness Security Program with her.

Those dreams ended when Paolo died.

Now her aspiration of freedom would end yet again if they couldn't change those bank accounts and rescue Nia.

Marisa went into her office, turned on her computer, and pulled up the files of her father's real estate holdings on her computer. She scrolled through the list before her, looking for vacant ones, or ones which had no current rental payment history. She found eleven such properties, some in the area, some in upstate New York, and some in New Jersey. It would take time to check each of them, but she and Sandro could divide the list.

Elation lifted her spirits. It was the best chance they had so far.

She printed the information and slid them into her bag.

Checking her watch, she had time to find those passwords. She pulled the flash drive out of her purse. Inserting it into her computer, she started to search through the information she'd taken off Roberto's hard drive. Marisa's heard thudded as account after account flashed before her eyes. Finally she tracked down the sites for the bank accounts. She debated on accessing the accounts; from her experience many had time stamps from the last time an account holder last signed in to the bank's site. Would Roberto notice? Would he think there'd just been a mistake? Or would he get suspicious and change the passwords? She looked at the information on her computer. There were several bank accounts, and she needed to know if these passwords worked. She'd try one to see how easy she could access the information and hope he didn't notice; she couldn't pass up this opportunity. With a deep breath, she started typing.

"Si, si, molto buona," she murmured. Ten minutes later, thrilled that their plan seemed workable, she began the process of opening new accounts in her name.

Her watch now showed it was a few minutes before eleven. By the time she got back down the stairs, the guard should be ready to go on his hourly rounds again.

Shutting down her machine, she made certain nothing looked disturbed, reset the security system and locked the main office door behind her before heading for the stairway. At the bottom of the steps, breathing hard again, she waited, muscles tense, watching the guard through a small rectangular window in the stairwell door. When he moved out of sight, she pushed open the metal door. Then the security guard's phone rang, and the guard reappeared. She quickly tugged the door shut, and squatted below the window while he laughed, purred and murmured on the phone. At last, he said, "See you at four, lover," replaced the phone in the cradle, then whistling an odd tune, left again.

Cautiously, she pushed open the door once more. With no sign of him, she slipped past his desk and didn't stop, not even to put her pumps back on, until she was outside on the sidewalk. Gathering her reserved, in-control facade around her like a cloak, she glanced at her watch and noted with satisfaction she had timed everything perfectly. She drew a deep breath to slow her pulse.

She still had time to go home and shower before she met Sandro. It had been a long, exhausting day and she was dirty and tired. With the thought of a refreshing shower looming enticingly before her, she hailed a taxi, already able to practically feel the hot water spraying against her skin.

When she opened the door to get in the cab, she was rudely shoved from behind. "Scoot over, princess. I'm going with you." Dave shut the cab door before she had even sat down.

She swung to face him, eyes narrowed, anger crawling up her spine. "This is my taxi. Get out," she ordered.

"Don't think so. And I'll take these, thank you." He snatched the printout of the vacant properties out of her bag before she could react.

She reached for them. "Who do you think you are? Give those to me."

"Where you go?" the cabbie asked.

Holding the papers just out of reach, Dave looked at her. "I'm with you."

Deciding to ignore him, she gave her address to the driver. Dave drew her unwilling attention again when he turned on a pocket flashlight to study the papers. The glow of the light reflected off his patrician nose, chiseled cheeks and strong jaw. He really was easy on the eyes she conceded, once again feeling that unwanted spark. And he was attracted to her, she knew. Even if he still loved Sandro's wife, Dave found her attractive.

Too bad he was a damned control freak.

"Stop reading those. Give them back," she said, as much irritated at herself as she was with him.

She tried to grab the papers, but he easily held her off.

"Hold on, princess. I want to see what kept you up there for an hour." He finished reading the list. "These places where your father might have Nia?"

She glared at him, summoning a shield of haughtiness to protect herself. "Fuck you."

"Now, now, princess, what language. Unless . . . you meant that as an invitation?"

The image of them naked, limbs entwined, slid into her mind, and as much as she hated to admit it, the thought made her mouth go dry while other parts of her swelled and moistened.

Oh, no, don't go there.

Deliberately, she crossed her arms and stared out the window, knowing to reveal her weakness for him would be disastrous.

"Thought not." He looked back at the papers. "It wouldn't have taken you more than a few minutes to get this information off your computer. What else were you doing?"

The man was frustrating beyond belief. And it was easier to focus on that than deal with her attraction.

She decided to answer him. "I had to wait on the security guard, you idiot. He goes on his rounds on the hour, and I didn't want to sign in and leave a record. As if it's any of your business."

His stare burned her. "I think you answered that much too easily."

At least he was bugging her and not Sandro. And

she could handle the sexual innuendos. She could. "Tough. You're not getting any more information about it from me."

"I wouldn't bet on that," he said softly. "Where are we going now?"

"*We* aren't going anywhere. *I'm* going home."

"Good. I've always wanted to see the inside of your apartment."

"You mean you haven't already?"

"No reason to before now."

"There's no reason now either." Oh, no, she didn't want him in her apartment at all. "You're not invited."

"That's where you're wrong. Where you go, I go." He folded her papers and tucked them into the inside pocket on his jacket.

"You can't have those! Give them back," she growled. His high-handedness infuriated her, made her want to scratch out his eyes.

"No can do." He patted his chest. "These papers are going to insure you stay right by me."

"I didn't know you cared," she said sarcastically.

"Wrong again." His voice was grim. His hand slid across his forehead. "I care a lot."

His momentary show of weakness startled her. "Would you care as much if Sandro's wife wasn't missing?" Marisa deliberately brought up Dave's obsession to keep herself from feeing any sympathy for the pain he was trying to hide.

Dave paused, looking momentarily taken aback. "He's been talking, I see."

"I asked." Let him make of that what he thought.

"Now, why's that?" He recovered his smart-ass attitude quickly enough, and leaned closer, definitely intruding on her space. His voice dropped to a husky level. "Could it be you're attracted to me, princess?"

Her heart beat so hard in her throat she had to swallow before she could answer. She covered it with a fake choking sound. "Don't flatter yourself," she said, ignoring the very rapid pulse that denied her words. "And stop calling me princess."

"I would have expected more honesty from you. princess," he added deliberately, running a finger along her jaw. "I saw how you were looking at me earlier."

Of course he would notice. Her skin rippled along the path of his finger. Deliberately, she moved away from his hand.

FBI agents were trained to notice things. No way in hell she'd admit she was giving him the once—or twice—over. "You're imagining—"

"You said I didn't remind you of a priest, I believe."

"A priest wouldn't be so rumpled is all I meant."

He smiled smugly, crossing his arms. "Sure it is."

The cab pulled to a stop. Dave looked out the window. "Your apartment?"

"I told you I was going home."

"So you did. But I didn't believe you."

"I'm disappointed. I would have thought you recognized the address when I gave it to the driver."

"Guess I was too distracted to pay attention."

His sexual innuendo was clear, it made no sense to deny it. But it made no sense to let on it affected her either. "Should I be flattered?"

She said the words casually as she was opening the car door. He still hadn't answered by the time she paid the driver. Instead, he waited for her on the sidewalk.

"You better tell the cab driver not to leave," she warned. "This isn't your stop. But hand me those papers before you go." She held out her hand, proud that she managed to keep it from shaking.

"Afraid I can't do that."

Blood rushed to her head. She curled her fingers into fists while she fought off the childish urge to stomp her foot or throw something at him. She took a deep breath instead. "Doing your job does not include pestering me."

"That's where you're wrong. Following you is my job. Will Sandro be at your apartment?"

"No." She spun away.

"You're meeting him somewhere else then?" he asked from much too close behind, obviously following her.

Resigned to him traipsing after her whether she answered or not, she entered her apartment building, the glass door already held open at her approach by the doorman, a man in his mid-fifties who always had a smile for the tenants. "Hello, Murray."

As usual, Murray gave his trademark welcoming smile. "Good evening, Ms. Peruzzo." His smile changed to a frown when Dave followed through the door. "He with you?"

She turned, looked at Dave, rolled her eyes. "Afraid so."

"Is he pestering you?" Murray let the door shut and took an aggressive wide-legged stance, which looked rather comical. Face lined with tiny threads of wrinkles, thinning salt-and-pepper hair, and spiffy doorman uniform, he was shorter than Dave by more than a head. Yet instead of provoking the urge to laugh, the image warmed her heart.

Marisa sighed. "Yes, but he's a harmless pest. I'll take care of him."

Not looking convinced, Murray said, "I can get rid of him for you."

To her alarm, Dave squared off with the doorman. "Back off, buddy. She said I'm with—"

Hadn't her day been long enough already? She stepped between them and shoved at Dave. Feeling squashed between the two men like a pickle on a pastrami sandwich, she managed to offer Murray a reassuring smile. "Really. He's fine." She grabbed Dave's arm and jerked him toward the small, elegant lobby.

"Why me?" she asked, more rhetorically than anything, stopping beside a Victorian-style wing chair. "Why follow me and not Sandro?"

His gaze scanned over her, his look suggestive. "You have a nicer ass."

His blatant sexual answer, when she hadn't really been expecting an answer at all, made the blood shoot straight through her limbs. Her body tightened from the sudden rush.

Fighting off the long dormant, but rapidly-activating-against-her-will desire, she tried once more to gather anger as a defense. She considered slapping him, but rationalized that would get Murray involved again when the older man didn't need that kind of worry. "You think you can be crude because of who I am?" she demanded.

"Just being honest, princess. And you're lying if you deny it. Anyway," Dave continued, cutting off another protest, "I'm with you because I know you'll eventually lead me to Sandro. You two are up to something, and I plan to find out what it is."

She laughed. "You think."

"I know." He took a step closer, leaned toward her. "And besides . . ." he paused and looked into her eyes, a look that made her suddenly feel faint.

"Besides . . ." he repeated as if he'd lost his train of thought. "I can't do this to Sandro," he whispered before he pulled her into his arms.

And kissed her. The sudden unexpected, yet oddly gentle assault made her head spin. Already close to falling from the dizziness of long denied needs, she wrapped her arms around his neck.

Then she was kissing him back, her lips as demanding as his while their tongues dueled in a mimicry of raw, wild sex . . . until she remembered Murray the faithful doorman was an audience. She jerked away, drew deep breaths, forced a calm back to her limbs she absolutely did not feel. Willed her heart rate to slow.

"So is this a plan?" she asked, her voice husky in spite of her best efforts to sound normal. "Kiss me and pump me for information?"

For the briefest instant, Dave looked as puzzled and disheveled as she felt, but he recovered fast enough. "Is it working?" he asked, with just the right tinge of boyish charm and hope in his voice.

"You have one thing right. You can't do that to Sandro. He'd punch you."

"Are you saying it's okay to kiss you?"

"Only goodnight. And since you've already had your kiss. . .then goodnight." She turned to walk off, concentrating on a dignified retreat. *Get away, get away, get away. Just past the gym door and around the corner to the elevators.*

"Forgetting something?"

She paused, looked back over her shoulder. He patted his pocket where the property listings were. She also caught sight of Murray, who no doubt by now thought they were having a lover's quarrel.

Shrugging, she started forward again, focused on getting away. "Keep them," she called. "I'll get another copy." She remembered enough of the addresses to send Sandro on a search until she could. She glanced at her watch. If she didn't get upstairs soon, a shower was out of the question.

"Where are you going?" He fell into step beside her.

"Isn't it obvious? I *do* live here."

"And then where?"

"No. Where."

"Luigi?"

She clenched her teeth, hating he brought that up. "I never go to Gigi's until later. I have time to nap first."

"Is Sandro meeting you here then?"

They passed the gym entrance, turned the corner and the elevators were in sight. "No."

"You keep looking at your watch. What are you late for?"

"Questions, questions. I'm late for a shower, and then bed. That's all I have on my mind." And bed in more ways than one since his kiss. Unfortunately, Dave was a fantasy and Luigi was her reality. She swallowed a lump of distaste.

"I don't believe you."

"Fine. Wait down here. See if I leave again." She focused on the elevator button, she was within ten steps.

"And let you slip out the garage entrance because you know I'm waiting out front? I don't think so." He rushed ahead and punched the button, which lit under his finger.

She stopped, crossed her arms and stared at him. "What are you doing?"

"I'm going up with you. You lost me earlier. You're good, I'll give you that. And you in heels, too." He glanced down at her feet then back to her eyes. "I can't risk losing you again. You're going to need me."

His words sounded suddenly ominous. "You think so?" she forced out past the sudden chill.

"Trust me. You will."

He didn't know how close to the truth he was; she had to convince Sandro of the fact.

The ding echoed in the quiet marble-lined hall, the elevator doors opened. Dave urged her inside.

She sighed. "Look, Dave . . ."

The doors slid closed. "What time are you going to meet Sandro?"

She punched the number for her floor. "I'm not—"

"Stop lying, princess. And don't think you can pacify me and make me leave by getting in the shower and pretending to get ready for bed."

The elevator surged upward. She tottered on her heels at the motion. Distracted by Dave she forgot what a rocket-like launch these elevators had. "What if I really plan to go to bed?"she asked when she regained her balance.

"I'll sleep on your couch. Unless you invite me to share your bed?"

"Don't get your hopes . . ." she paused and glanced at his crotch before meeting his gaze again . . . "or

129

anything else . . . up." Yes, she thought she pulled that off nicely.

"You have a dirty mind. I like that." He grinned. "What time are you meeting Sandro?"

"Why do you insist I'm meeting—"

"My guess is midnight."

Her gaze sharpened. She had to admit his persistence was wearing on her. "What makes you say that?"

"I've noticed you have a thing for midnight."

She still hoped to get rid of him. "By midnight, I plan on being asleep."

He crowded her into a corner and leaned close. "You wouldn't be lying, would you?"

She couldn't stop focusing on his lips. Lips that moved closer and closer until they touched hers. Again.

And she wasn't objecting. Again.

"What do you think?" she whispered against his mouth, not giving an inch.

She needed to object.

"I think you're definitely lying," he said before he turned the teasing into another real kiss. His hand encircled her throat. She arched into him in spite of herself. He deepened the kiss, and she still didn't object.

No matter how she tried to keep her distance, there was something about him that made her want to get as close as possible. In spite of his sometimes crude behavior which she suspected was just an act to keep his distance. She sensed his goodness, and it had been a long time since she had been close to anything good.

It was that thought which forced her to break away from firm, warm lips that had the power to melt her bones. "Don't. We can't do this." She struggled for control, more obvious this time than the last.

While in contrast he barely looked flustered. But she had felt his erection against her stomach.

"Why?" he asked. "You weren't serious about the goodnight thing were you?"

She knew his composure was an act, just as likely as his jerk routine was an act. He was good at both.

But she could be as composed as he was, she thought, drawing herself together, calling on years of experience to help her. "I don't like it."

A smug grin settled on his face. "You can't tell the truth, can you?" Cupping the back of her head, he pulled her closer for another kiss.

"Dave," she warned when his lips left hers to travel down her neck. He nibbled at the Florentine cross necklace hanging around her neck, her breasts swelled as if in hope his mouth would move lower.

"I like this necklace," he whispered.

She blinked to catch up through the haze of desire. "It was my grandmother's. She gave it to me when she was on her death bed." Marisa fingered the cherished necklace. He kissed her hand, making her grip the necklace more tightly. "I never take it off."

"Never?" The word hung heavy with meaning.

The elevator stopped, saving her from having to answer. She slipped out as soon as the doors opened. At her apartment, she paused. This whole incident with Dave was repeating a familiar, ominous pattern. She couldn't get involved with a law enforcement official again. The results last time had been tragic.

Better cut it off now. "Dave, follow me if you must. But stop trying to seduce me. You're not going to throw me off," she said bluntly.

"Is that what I'm doing?"

"Yes, I know you're not really interested—" at his raised eyebrow she amended, "maybe you're interested but you won't act on it. You know you'd be breaking all sorts of rules."

"No doubt." He nodded. "But I bet I'll be breaking a few when I help you and Sandro with whatever you have planned."

Did he mean what she thought? "Nia means that much to you that you would risk your career?"

"I've known her since she was a baby. I'd do anything to keep her alive."

"Including sleep with me?"

"You think that'd be torture?"

That was the answer she wanted to hear, she told herself. "Is that why you'd do it, though? To save Nia? She's Sandro's wife, you know." Marisa didn't want to hear he wanted her for herself. It was easier that way.

And she really tried to believe it.

"You sound as if her life isn't important. Do you still love Sandro?"

"What?"

"You two were once engaged."

"How—"

"I have my ways, you know that."

She opened her apartment door. "I've known Sandro many years. I love him like my . . . like a brother." She was compelled to share part of her life with Dave as with no other aside from Sandro. "It was my father's idea for us to become engaged. My father loves soccer." Most of what she'd done in her life had been her father's . . . idea.

"Yet you didn't marry Sandro." Dave followed

her inside and shut the door behind him.

She dropped her bag by the accent table and switched on the Tiffany lamp. "I met. . .someone else."

Dave's eyes narrowed. "Luigi?"

She was startled. "No. Gigi . . ." She raised her hands, searching for a good answer. "Is useful."

"This someone else . . . you didn't marry him either?" Dave stepped closer.

"He's dead."

Dave stopped.

"He was a policeman," she added, careful to keep the pain tucked away.

"Oh. I'm sorry."

"I didn't tell you for sympathy."

"Was it a warning then?" Dave moved closer. "You think you're bad luck for cops?"

Instead of answering, she made a point of looking at her watch once more, noting the time quickly slipping past. It was becoming obvious she wasn't going to get rid of him.

"I've had a long day. I'm going to shower." She turned away, walked toward her room, all the while wondering what Sandro would say about Dave tagging along.

"Marisa."

She stopped and turned to face him. The lamplight crested a halo about his dark hair—but he was obviously no saint.

"If we have sex," he said boldly, "it will be because we both want it. Not because I'm trying to use you for information."

Her heart sprang to her throat, and she couldn't make a sound, couldn't swallow. Couldn't even think of an answer.

Dave moved closer. She would have stepped back, but he took her arms and held her in place. "If I want information, I'll just ask you," he said softly before adding, "And if I want to have sex with you, I'll just ask you."

Somehow that seemed far scarier to her than if he used sex as a way to get information.

"Go." Dave turned her back toward her room when she didn't answer. "Get your shower."

While Marisa showered, Dave explored her apartment. Exquisitely furnished, but cold, he thought, like a magazine ad, the only splash of color was the Tiffany lamp. No pictures, no memories. He felt the apartment was a cover, maybe even from herself. From their kisses, he knew a fire smoldered underneath the cold, beautiful exterior she presented to the world.

Buried with the dead boyfriend, perhaps. Buried too deep? He thought not. But having loved and lost himself—he could certainly understand her need to protect herself.

Marisa's strength and independence reminded him of Nia, but Marisa had vulnerability lurking beneath the surface that he'd never seen in Nia. It almost made him feel protective toward the Mafia princess, something he'd never experienced with a woman before.

Twenty-five minutes later she walked out of her bedroom, looking refreshed in designer jeans and a casual, expensive sweater.

"You always blow dry your hair and wear makeup and jeans to bed?" he asked.

"I'm in a hurry," she said. "I don't have time to fool you, and you're too stubborn to leave. So, follow me if you must."

She walked out the door.

"No need to follow you. I'll just go with you." He glanced at his watch. "Yep, almost midnight."

She shook her head. "Men. Why must they always act like such know-it-alls," she said to the elevator doors.

"Where are we going?"

They entered the elevator and she punched the button for the first floor.

"You don't need to know everything. Just keep quiet and stay out of sight. Sandro's upset enough as it is."

"So what's new?"

"He's armed this time."

Dave blinked. "He bought a gun?"

"I gave him mine, but he went to buy another."

"You carry a gun?"

"Of course."

"You know that's illegal."

She shot him a *you've got to be kidding* look.

Yeah, stupid thing to say, Armstrong. "And Sandro has it and is buying another?" When that sank in, Dave looked heavenward. "Another inexperienced hothead with a score to settle, loose on the streets of New York."

Marisa narrowed her eyes. "He is not a hothead. He is even-tempered. And as for the weapons, he is very familiar with guns. A crack shot."

"I'm in awe," Dave mocked. "Is there anything the great Sandro can't do?"

She granted him a look and a sly smile as they left the elevators. "Jealous, Dave?"

He didn't answer. He didn't want to admit, even to himself, that he'd been jealous of Sandro for way too many years.

Instead, Dave nodded his head at Murray as they walked past.

"Goodnight, Murray," Marisa said to the surprised looking doorman.

On the sidewalk, Dave took her arm. "I have my own list of great qualities, too."

"Do you?"

"I can tell you some if you like."

She slid her look provocatively up and down his body. "I can see a few . . . imagine a few others. That's enough for now."

Her words sent heat straight to his groin. She obviously knew how to play with fire. But for the moment, he couldn't have the flames stoked. Later, though . . .

"Tell, me," he said, "where are we supposed to meet Sandro?"

"I'm meeting Sandro," she pointed out. "You're waiting out of sight."

"I never agreed to that. For the safety of you and Sandro, I think I should know what you two are planning."

"Sandro wants no more leaks." She turned into a schoolyard.

"And that's why we're meeting here at the . . ." he waited a moment until her direction became obvious. ". . . at the school playground. I'm alone. Just you, me, and him. Nobody but us, and we're all trustworthy."

"How do I know that? You could be wired."

Dave held out his arms, raised his eyebrow and gave a smug little grin. "Feel free to pat me down."

She hesitated, then ran her slender hands over him,

carefully avoiding the part he most wanted her to touch. Holy Mother, help him.

"You missed a place," he managed to choke out, sudden need burning away any previous smug thoughts.

She followed his gaze downward. "I can see there's something definitely there." She brought her gaze back to his face. "But I don't think it's a recorder."

"What's he doing here?" Sandro stepped out of the shadows.

Marisa whirled, her normal calm seemed a little ruffled.

The need to play hero came on strong. "I didn't give her a choice," Dave said, placing his hands protectively on Marisa's shoulders.

Sandro gave him a stone-cold look, taking in Dave's protective gesture.

"He's alone," Marisa said, her voice breathier than usual. She cleared her throat. "He's willing to work outside the law to help us—"

"To help Nia," Dave corrected, her outside-the-law comment somewhat cooling his ardor. Marisa stiffened under his hands.

Sandro's cold look didn't waiver. "We wouldn't want to forget that you are doing this to help *my* wife."

"But Sandro, whatever his reasons, he can help—"

"We don't need his help."

"What about Roberto?" she asked.

"Yeah, what about Roberto? The accountant?" Dave wondered aloud. What would Roberto have to do with anything? Of the mob guys, Roberto seemed the least threatening.

Sandro shook his head. Dave released Marisa and pulled the papers from his pocket. "Then what about these?"

Sandro's narrow gaze barely concealed the anger and frustration boiling under the surface. As ridiculous as it sounded, Dave found himself fighting not to squirm under the deadly, probing look.

"What are those?"

Marisa glanced at Dave before telling Sandro, "A list of my father's properties—places he might be holding Nia." She turned back to Dave. "I told you I could get other copies."

Sandro took two steps forward and pulled Marisa to stand beside him. "If she can get others, then we don't need those." The message was clear. *We don't need you, either.*

Marisa hadn't even given a squeak of objection to standing beside Sandro. And there Dave thought he'd made progress with her. He supposed her loyalties couldn't be shifted easily. That was a good thing, he told himself.

Still, Dave couldn't squelch the urge to taunt."No?" Unreasonably jealous or not, Dave twisted his point to a sharp threat. "Perhaps you can get other copies, but if you don't let me help you, I'll have to bring my Task Force up-to-date. They can help me search these properties."

Sandro, his face even more hard and menacing, if possible, stepped forward and squared off with Dave. "The last help your task force gave me nearly got me killed and it did get my wife kidnapped. I will not let you risk her life again."

His angry response made Dave feel he'd evened the score. He softened his tone. "Then let me help you. Work with me here."

Sandro slowly shook his head. "You have obligations to your job. You can't go off on your own and keep your task force uninformed."

"I can tell them what they need to know without jeopardizing my career."

"No."

"Damn it, I have resources you don't have."

Marisa turned to Sandro. "I think he's being truthful."

"At some point you're probably going to confront her father," Dave said. "How do you plan to walk away alive?"

Sandro remained silent.

"You know he'll never meet you alone, and even if you hold some sort of information that will let you walk away, he'll have his mobsters follow you and kill you after they get what they want. I can have men in place to help you."

Marisa said something to Sandro in Italian. He answered, and they went back and forth for at least two minutes. Dave stood, waiting, trying to remain patient. Still, he clenched and unclenched his fists, fighting the urge to wrap his hands around them both and shake some sense into them.

Finally, he moved between them and broke into their conversation. He laid his hands on Sandro's shoulders, in a begrudging offer of friendship. "Sandro, you're right. I put her at risk. Let me work with you now. Let me correct my mistake." He swallowed a feeling of distaste and added, "Please."

Sandro's gaze searched Dave's face. Time hung suspended between the three of them while Sandro made his decision.

At last he spoke. "All right, Dave Armstrong. You will help us. But take this to your heart. If you fail again, and my wife is harmed, you will pray to the blessed Virgin for a quick death. If you make another mistake and we lose, you will die a tortured fragment at a time until there is nothing left of you for anyone to remember. And then I'll kill you a little more."

CHAPTER 16

She was running . . . .
Move, move, move . . . .
Safety was close . . . .
A gunshot . . . .
Someone hurled a bowling ball into her shoulder.
Another loud crack sounded.

Blood dripped from her hand. She followed the red sticky trail up her arm. A bowling ball hadn't hit her. A bullet. She'd been shot . . . .

Nia bolted upright, eyes wide open, heart pounding. She hadn't meant to fall asleep; she needed to work on her next escape plan. But her exhausted body had claimed her unwilling mind.

Concentrating on making her heart rate slow to normal, she breathed deeply and stretched. Stiff and sore muscles made her moan. Mikey had really done a number on her. She owed him for that. She wasn't a vengeful person, but she could learn fast.

For a moment, the real nightmare, not the dream one, that had become her life threatened to crush her. Alone in a strange house, with dangerous men guarding her, she had a brief urge to crumple in despair.

Oh, Sandro, where are you?

Mental toughness honed from years of relentless physical conditioning, pitting her wits against an opponent's, along with being raised with five brothers, lent her strength. Resolve stiffened her spine and her will. She would not be defeated. She would escape, get to her child then find her husband. Wonder Woman, move over. Here comes Nia Crocetti, the newest Superhero.

The thought forced a chuckle. Yeah, right.

At least the whimsical idea of her soaring through the air with a red, white and blue cape whipping behind her dispelled the last of her uncharacteristic feelings of hopelessness. She climbed out of bed.

Her watch read just past two in the morning.

She took a bathroom break, relieved to find no blood, no spotting, and she was experiencing no cramps. Mikey's beating hadn't robbed her of her unborn child. Proof the universe was on her side.

Slipping the plastic Woo-Sung's Chinese Food advertisement card from her pocket, she listened against the wooden door for sounds of activity beyond. Everything was quiet. Time to put her plan in motion.

She eyed the ordinary bedroom door lock—it had been turned backward, where the locking part was on the outside. She supposed they had been in a hurry and holding her prisoner had been a makeshift plan. Whatever the reason, she was grateful for such a simple lock which wouldn't call for more intricate lockpicking skills with tools she didn't have.

Taking a breath, she whispered a prayer for luck, then slipped the card into the doorjamb and jiggled the door, trying to force the card past the latch.

"Come on," she muttered to herself. After only

moments, the door slipped open. She bit back a gasp and stifled a shout of excitement. In her mind, though, she was jumping up and down and screaming for joy.

Cautiously she peered into the hall. Angie sat at one end in a wing backed chair between her and the stairs.

Damn.

Quickly she unlocked the door from the outside then quietly closed it back. Pressing her forehead against the hard wooden door, she debated what to do. Angie looked as if he were asleep. Perhaps she could slip past him. Pulling the door open again, she poked her head out into the hallway and studied him. Should she risk it?

She glanced the other way. Nothing more than a window at that end, and she wasn't going that route again. Her gaze lit on a dark green clay vase that sat on a decorator table beneath the window. It was filled with artificial blue, orange and purple flowers arranged in artful disarray.

Unconcerned with the artistic qualities of the vase, she debated whether to risk using it to knock Angie unconscious. He was between her and freedom. Between her and her family. Would the vase be heavy enough to knock him out?

But what if Giovanni or someone else was still here? Would the noise alert them and hamper her escape plans? She strained to listen for other sounds of life, but heard nothing other than Angie's deep breathing.

It was a risk she would have to take.

Quietly, she sneaked to the end of the hallway and lifted the vase. It was heavier than it looked. It must've been made of pure concrete. All the better to knock him out cold. Or kill him. She paused with distaste at the thought, but there was no guarantee they'd leave her alive. And her family needed her. So she had to use any method she could. If she killed someone, she'd deal with the fact later.

Determination steeling her spine, she jerked the flowers out, dropped them on the floor, and hefted the vase into her arms. Tiptoeing down the hall, the vase securely in her grasp, she held her breath, afraid to make any noise. At last she stood next to Angie. Carefully, she forced the heavy vase over her head. One hard swing ought to—

"Hey, Angie, it's time for me to take over. You asleep up there?"

Damn! Giovanni was climbing up the stairs. Trapped!

No! She'd take them both out.

Angie stirred, beginning to awaken. He opened his eyes, sleep, then confusion as he saw her, clouding his gaze.

Now or never.

She brought the vase down. She felt a dull thud at impact, like the time she'd busted a pumpkin. Angie's eyes widened, then blinked out.

She hurtled down the stairs, rushing Giovanni, using the vase as a battering ram. He stumbled from her onslaught, losing his balance. Tumbling backwards, he rolled down the stairs. He didn't move once he landed. After a fall like that, he could well be dead.

Nia never slowed to contemplate his condition. Dropping the vase, she jumped over Giovanni's body and barreled out the kitchen door into the night.

She ran to the Town Car and jerked open the door. No keys. She flipped down the visor and looked on the floorboard. No luck there since she hadn't learned hotwiring with lockpicking 101.

She repeated the process with the red truck parked in the drive, but no luck there either. The SUV and silver Lexus were gone. There was a jacket and some dollar bills lying on the truck bench seat. She grabbed the jacket, the money, and a flashlight she'd found under the seat.

Nerves threatened to overwhelm her at the obstacles still facing her. But she had to be clearheaded. She pulled her thoughts together and focused. Earlier, she had thought it best to make her escape through the woods. Now, that it was pitch dark, she changed her mind, not wanting to risk getting lost in the dark.

The best plan would be to follow the road. If Giovanni was still alive and managed to come after her, she could hide on the side of the road. The darkness would work to her advantage. By first light, if she ran most of the way, she should have covered a good distance. Perhaps even found a sign of civilization.

Good thing she was in prime physical shape despite being pregnant.

She sprinted toward the road.

Breathed in freedom.

CHAPTER 17

"She got away."

"How the hell'd that happen?" Joey asked, still groggy from the ringing phone jerking him out of sleep.

"Shit, I don't know. I checked that door," Giovanni answered holding an ice pack on the back of his neck. He ached all over. "It was locked. But now it's open. I shoulda got a deadbolt when I was at the store."

"Or you shoulda been guarding her. You know she's smart."

"We was guarding her . . . well, Angie was and I was on my way to relieve him. But she's not only smart, she's one mean bitch, too. She got the jump on him and laid a vase upside his head. Cracked his skull open, then she shoved me down the stairs."

"You okay?"

"Yeah, I'm fine, but Angie's still out cold, bleeding all over the fuckin' floor. No way I could move him, heavy ass shit. I got some towels piled under his head."

Joey made a disgusted sound. "The fat son-of-a-bitch must've fallen asleep for her to catch him like that. You called Carlo yet?"

"Fuck, no, you think I'm crazy? I wanna get her back before he finds out," Giovanni answered. "Especially after you took care of that piece of business earlier. I ain't goin' on no ride with you guys."

"So, what's your plan?"

"Get ahold of the dog trainer that trains our guard dogs. Doesn't he have a team of tracking dogs?"

"You want to bring dogs out?"

"There's lots of places in the woods for her to get herself lost where we can't find her."

"Okay. But what if she takes the road?"

"All the better for us if she does. The dogs will let us know. Right now, I'm gonna drive down the road— south first, she'll likely head back to the city—and if I don't see her, I'll stop at every little store that might be open and insure their cooperation."

Joey sighed. "Sounds risky; someone might know who she is, but I guess it's the best you can do."

"Anyone gives me trouble, I'll just whack him." Giovanni felt like murder considering all the trouble this was causing him.

"We don't need a bunch of dead bodies to account for," Joey warned.

"Then you better get here fast. And bring Carmine and Ralphie along with the dogs. More of us working, more likely we are to find her. And one of you needs to take Angie to a doctor. He's likely got a concussion or something."

"Okay, yeah, good idea. Give me a little time to get the dogs—I'll have to bring the trainer, too, I don't know how to work tracking dogs."

"As long as he keeps his mouth shut."

"You know it."

Giovanni hung up and leaving Angie lying on the floor with a wet cloth over his head, the best he could do at the moment, Giovanni took off for the car.

* * *

With his warning hanging in the air, Sandro stood still in the dark night, watching through the glimmers of moonlight, the effect of his words as they fell on Dave.

Marisa's gaze was riveted on Dave, while Dave's eyes still locked with Sandro's.

Then Dave nodded, relaxed his stance and asked, "So, what's the plan?"

His easy acquiescence surprised Sandro, made him more wary. But Marisa seemed to think Dave was trustworthy. Her instincts were usually good, while Sandro admitted his own opinion of the FBI man was skewed by their long, personal, and contentious history.

Glancing sideways at Sandro, Marisa answered Dave's question. "We're stealing the money from my father's overseas accounts. Which is most of it."

Dave's eyes widened and he turned to Sandro. "Whoa, that's ballsy. You don't like living much, do you, buddy?"

"Carlo loves his money more than revenge. To get it returned, he'll give Nia back," Sandro said with forced confidence, ignoring the sarcasm. The plan had to work—they had no other options. And if force of will alone could make it work, then Sandro would do it.

"You have access to the accounts?" Dave asked Marisa.

"Yes, I'm actually on the accounts, but I didn't have the passwords. It's a need-to-know system. I needed to know so I have them now."

"What's that supposed to mean?"

"I'm on the account in case of an emergency, if I ever needed to access them, Roberto would give me the passwords. That only happened once when he was sick, and then he changed the passwords as soon as he got back to work."

"So you now have the passwords how?" Dave asked.

"I copied the information on his hard drive. I accessed one of the accounts tonight. It works."

"Mirror imaging software."

Obviously, Dave knew the technique. Sandro had no concept that such a thing existed and was thankful Marisa was the computer whiz.

Marisa nodded. "I then started the process of creating new accounts to transfer the money."

"So you're going to transfer the money out of your father's accounts and into another one in your name?"

At Marisa's confirmation, Dave quickly zoomed in on the most obvious problems, and Sandro conceded the man was no dummy.

"What will your father think when he realizes the account is in your name?"

"We hope he'll think Sandro forced me. It might not matter by then."

"Possibly. But it takes time to transfer the money, what do you have planned to keep Roberto from noticing the money is moving?"

Marisa moved closer to Dave. "We have a few ideas, none very good. The best one is . . ." she paused and touched Dave's chest, the starlight glittering off her diamond bracelet. "You."

Sandro admired that Dave made no outward move when Marisa touched him, but he couldn't hide the reaction in his eyes. He cared for Marisa. The better for them, Sandro thought.

"Me?"

Dave must have an idea of what they needed, but for whatever reason, he seemed intent on making Marisa spell out what they wanted.

"I'm hoping since my name is on the accounts at the same banks, the transfer won't take but a few hours. But just in case . . . you can pick Roberto up for investigation, no?" She inched her hand up closer to his shoulder. "Keep him a few days without charging him?"

Sandro smiled when Dave placed his hand on top of hers to keep it still. No doubt Marisa's fingers were quite distracting. And no doubt Dave was aware that Sandro was carefully watching the entire exchange.

Dave sighed. "Why do I feel like I've been set up?"

"What?" Marisa asked.

Sandro understood her surprise, she'd worked hard to convince him that they needed Dave's help; there would have been no need to set Dave up without Sandro's cooperation.

"Don't be coy," Dave told Marisa, moving away from her touch. "There's no other way for you to change those accounts without me taking Roberto into custody."

"Yes," Sandro spoke up. "We could kill him, or take him prisoner."

"Yeah, I can see you two taking Roberto out," Dave said wryly, obviously not realizing the lengths Sandro would go to save his family.

"And you don't have enough manpower to hold

him prisoner," Dave continued, pacing a short distance across the grass.

"I could poison him." Marisa shrugged. "Maybe not enough to kill him but to put him in the hospital."

Dave stopped suddenly. "You play with poison, princess?"

"I have many hidden talents," she admitted.

He cocked his head and studied her. "Somehow, I can see that. Still, it's risky. Bottom line, basically there is no sure way without me. So you pretend you don't want my help, make me beg and bam," he paused to clap his hands together. "You have me."

When put that way, Sandro conceded perhaps Marisa set them both up. She knew they couldn't do it on their own. She was a very clever woman.

"Will you help?" Marisa asked, neither denying nor confirming Dave's accusations.

Dave ignored Marisa and turned to Sandro. "You're way out of your league here. What happens when you give him his money back? You think he won't come after you then? Let me have the information on those accounts, and we'll get him with RICO. The AUSA on our team is just chomping at the bit to bring a case against Carlo."

"The . . . what?" Sandro asked.

"Assistant U.S. Attorney," Dave clarified.

Sandro started shaking his head; Marisa interrupted.

"Who said we're giving it back?" she asked.

"Sandro said to get it returned—"

"Your RICO laws are worthless," Sandro interrupted, not wanting to get too detailed with their plans about the money. "It would take so long to prosecute him, he would have plenty of time to kill us."

"So you agree, your idea is too dangerous."

"Of course the idea is dangerous," Sandro said abruptly, already irritated with Dave's persistent doubts.

"Then what . . ." Dave paused, frowning, obviously confused how the exchange could be made and how Sandro planned to come out of it alive. Until at last his face lit with understanding. "You're going to kill him first."

The man's instincts were good, Sandro allowed as he purposely held silent.

Dave turned to Marisa and demanded, "Am I right? Is he planning on killing Carlo?"

Marisa didn't answer either.

Dave grew frustrated. "Stealing money or information I can see. But murder? I want Carlo as badly as you do, Sandro, but I can't let you murder the man."

Sandro's temper snapped. He grabbed Dave's shirt and jerked him close. There was no way Dave could want Carlo as badly as he did. "I don't recall asking your permission," he growled, bringing Dave's face down close. "You're the one who wanted to be here. If you want to help rescue Nia, then help. Otherwise keep quiet, or get out." Sandro pushed Dave away, daring, hoping he would come back at him. Sandro ached with the urge to release the fury and fear boiling inside him.

Dave stared hard at Sandro, then ran his hand through his hair. He turned his gaze back to Marisa. "You're going to let him kill your father? Help him even," he spread his hands wide, "by getting the information to bait Carlo?"

Sandro saw the pain enter Marisa's eyes, though there was no outward sign. He knew what she'd endured at the hands of her father, the years of being auctioned off, what Carlo did to her mother when she objected. Sandro hurt for Marisa, yet with quiet dignity she stood up to the censure.

"There are things you do not know," she said quietly. "You are not in a position to judge."

Finally, Dave seeming no closer to comprehending their reasoning, at last relented and turned back to Sandro. "I'll do what I can. I'll help with Roberto and with searching the properties. I draw the line at murder though."

By agreeing to stay in and help, Sandro wondered if Dave realized he'd just committed to insuring Carlo's death as he had accused Marisa of doing. But he seemed not to judge himself the same way. Or he refused to acknowledge Carlo would really be killed and hoped Sandro would still turn over the information. Whatever the reason, Sandro would take the help and let Dave worry about the morality of it all later.

"Just don't get in my way," Sandro warned, still not trusting Dave, but reluctantly admitting he needed him.

"I want you to rethink giving me that information. If you kill Carlo, and it's not in self-defense, I'll have to take you in."

Yes, so that was Dave's plan—to convince Sandro to turn over the information, not believing Sandro capable of murder.

"When my wife is safe, you do what you have to do," Sandro told him. Let Dave think what he would, threaten what he could. Sandro would do what he had to do.

Dave looked at Marisa again, maybe sensing he

hadn't reached Sandro. "You understand that, don't you? I'll have to arrest him."

"Sandro will do what he thinks is necessary to keep the woman he loves safe. To keep his family safe," Marisa said firmly. "Would you do any less?"

It was Dave's turn not to answer.

* * *

After Sandro left with the list of properties to search for Nia, Dave took Marisa's arm. "Come on, princess, time to get you tucked in. We've got a busy day tomorrow."

She jerked her arm away, but the anger stemmed more from where she had to go than at Dave's take-charge attitude. "If you know so much about me, you should know I'm not going home."

"What? You're going to Luigi's? Mr. Useful himself?"

"He *is* useful. The information I got from him saved Sandro's life." But the thought of going to Luigi was getting more distasteful, no matter how important.

Dave frowned. "True enough. But we don't need him anymore."

"Maybe. Maybe not. If I don't show up tonight, he might get suspicious. It could ruin all our plans." Even though going to Luigi's tonight was the last thing in the world she wanted to do.

"Why do you think he'd get suspic—"

He broke off as she started to walk away. If she didn't make herself move, she'd never go.

"Hey, wait," he said, following her. "Why do you think he'd get suspicious?"

154

She paused to outline the reasons. "Very simple. One," she held up a finger, "I was there when he gave the order to go after Sandro. Two," she raised a second finger, "Sandro disappears, and then three," the third finger in the air, "If I were to disappear? Sounds pretty suspicious to me." She took off again at a brisk pace. Chances were good that Luigi would be suspicious regardless. And even an idiot would know he was going to be in a bad mood. Not a good night before her, but still necessary.

The frown deepened on Dave's face, but he kept up with her this time.

"You're acting like a jealous lover, Dave." The thought sent a little tingle of anticipation down her spine. For a moment she wished it were true.

He pulled her to a stop. Again. "As much as I might want to, I can't get involved with you."

Marisa froze as the past repeated. Paolo had once said those same words. And her reaction had been the same. *If only you knew.* That he did not know how warped she was, how her father had destroyed her innocence. It was a memory that never left her, never strayed far from consciousness. The fear, the pain, the humiliation and most of all the feeling of betrayal as her father sold her virginity to the highest bidder.

There was an old saying that Italian men valued their family above all else. Lies. At least for her father. Power and prestige was all he valued.

No, Paolo had not known the truth. With him she pretended a reality that didn't exist. Yet it all ended badly.

And so while her arm pulsed where Dave's fingers touched, and her body tightened in anticipation of what

155

could be, she knew that she was broken. Unfixable. And dangerous. Especially for Dave. She wanted no more bad endings.

A car exploding. Another image that never left her mind.

She would do anything—anything—to erase that image. And since that wasn't possible, she would do anything to bring her father to justice. For herself. For her mother. For Paolo.

With no more innocent lives lost.

Marisa hardened her voice and her resolve. Her plans would not fail. "You're right, Dave. You can't get involved with me."

"I want to apologize . . . for earlier . . . for my loss of control. I was out of line then. You're a witness, and I know better."

She stared at him, surprised and relieved, she told herself, by his unexpected apology. "A witness for what?"

"If I can talk Sandro into turning over that information, we can build a good case against your father."

"You really think you're going to have a case?" She gave a short, abrupt laugh. "You don't know Sandro very well then. He always gets what he goes after. The opportunity to build a court case has passed."

Dave looked thoughtful, and instinctively Marisa knew without a doubt he had to be remembering how Sandro had gotten Nia instead of Dave. As Marisa expected though, he didn't say a word about it.

Instead he changed subjects. "And you. You're really going to stand by and let him kill your father?"

"I'm sick of this life. I want out."

"Do you always get what you want?"

"No. I never have before," she said, and Paolo's beautiful brown eyes flashed in her memory. "But I will this time."

She turned and walked away.

This time Dave didn't follow.

* * *

"You got anything of hers for the dogs to sniff?" Eddie DiMarco asked. He unloaded three bay bloodhounds from the kennels in the back of his Ford truck.

"No, but we got these sheets and comforter that was on her bed." Giovanni handed the folded bundle to Eddie, before he took out a cigarette.

"Don't light that," Eddie told him. "Not until the dogs get her scent. She lay on these?" He indicated the bundle of bed linens.

The unlit cigarette dangled from Giovanni's mouth. "She used the sheets as a rope, probably laid on the comforter after we caught her the first time. She wasn't feeling too well."

"This is the second time she escaped you, then? Must be pretty slick."

"Vicious, too." Angie stumbled out of the house with a makeshift ice bag on his head, his shirt and suit jacket blood stained.

"Jesus, look at you." Joey stepped away from Eddie's truck to remove the ice bag and look at Angie's head. "That's some big fucking gash. You better let Carmine take you to the doc, get it sewed up."

"Doc's getting a hell of a business thanks to her.

She sent Mikey there earlier." An uncomfortable silence descended at Angie's observation.

Eddie sensed the unease, but not the reason. "Better catch her before she harms anyone else," he said lightly, trying to ease the suddenly somber mood. After all, one woman. How bad could she be? So she got lucky once. Or twice.

"Giovanni, you check out those places along the road?" Joey asked.

"Nothing open. That convenience store about six miles down the road—won't open until five. Gives us a couple of hours. If she's even headed that way."

"Let's see if she is." Eddie held the bundle in front of the dogs to smell and gave them the command to find.

Immediately, their noses dropped to the ground and they took off baying. At first they headed for the woods but began circling by a big tree. Changing directions, they headed for the road. "Looks like she took the road after all."

"Good." Giovanni finally lit his cigarette and blew out a puff of smoke. "Let's go then. Before the morning commuters start to work. Don't want any witnesses."

* * *

While Marisa searched in the bathroom for headache medicine, Luigi looked at the sparkling diamond engagement ring he'd bought. Beautiful ring for a beautiful lady who, if he were lucky, would soon be his beautiful wife. He placed the ring case into the top drawer of his chest of drawers, in the compartment next to his keys and cell phones. Luigi always kept his things neatly compartmentalized and organized.

"C'mon, *Bella*, what is taking you so long?" He tried to pull back his impatience, yet already he felt the pill he'd taken earlier surging the blood to where it was supposed to go. He was anxious to take advantage while it lasted. And then . . . he'd propose.

He and Marisa might have gotten together in the first place because Carlo encouraged her to be *nice* to Luigi for his promotion from *capo* to *consigliere*. Of course he had heard the ugly rumors of how she'd been used in the past as a reward until she became proficient with the use of a stiletto, and later a gun. But she'd been exclusively with him from that time, no more favors. He credited himself for keeping her with him.

She had to say yes. Hadn't she been seeing him all these months, and didn't she tell him she loved him? Yet he constantly fought insecurities. He was fifteen years older than her, approaching middle age. And although he was careful with his appearance and exercised, his hair was thinning and his middle spreading no matter how much he worked out. But his age never seemed to make a difference to her.

And with the help of the little blue pill, he was able to keep her satisfied.

At last she came out of the bathroom. He frowned. She had not changed into one of those sexy nightgowns she usually wore for him. "Excuse me, love," she murmured. "I must lie down. My head..." She waved her hands helplessly then collapsed on the bed. Usually so elegant and refined, her dishevelment surprised and then confused him.

He felt the minutes ticking, realizing that soon the effects of the pill would be worthless. He reached for calm. He wanted the night to be memorable although it was starting out less than perfect.

"Let me rub your shoulders," he offered, proud of himself for thinking of it. She would like that, no? "Roll onto your stomach."

He straddled her back. She tensed when he rested on the curve her ass, she couldn't miss that he was aroused, but when he started massaging her back, she relaxed and murmured in the pillow, "Ah, *si*, that feels wonderful." But his fingers were tired within two minutes and his erection rubbing against her was growing painful. He bent over to nuzzle her neck and whispered. "I have a surprise for you . . . later."

She turned her head to give him better access to her neck. "Hmm, I'm sure I'll love it."

That was all the encouragement he needed. He turned her over, allowing him to reach her lips, her body. He kissed her. She stiffened, muttered a protest.

He brushed off her complaint, knowing she'd give in, she always did.

Then his phone rang. He froze. He would have ignored that as well, too, but it wasn't his regular cell phone ring. It was the throw away phone, the ones they used in an emergency. Or in other words, a fuck up. He couldn't ignore this call.

"Get the phone, *mi amore*. I'll go . . . change," Marisa murmured.

He would have been satisfied she was giving in if it wasn't for the damn ringing phone. He scrambled off her and pulled open the drawer to snatch the irritating damn phone.

The caller ID read *unknown caller*. No surprise there. He wasn't sure who was on the other end, but it would not be good news. Luigi punched the button to connect. "What?"

"Got bad news," Angie said without preamble. "She got away."

"What the fuck!" He'd expected bad, but not that bad. The chemically-induced heat drained like water out of a tub after the plug had been pulled, leaving him shriveled and useless. "Tell me you got her back?" he shouted before he remembered Marisa was still here. He glanced around. Still in the bathroom with the door shut, but he needed to keep a lid on his anger. Growing up in the business, she knew to keep her mouth shut. But there was no need to involve her in this mess.

"No, we haven't found her yet."

"And you're the lucky bastard who gets to call me." Which meant Luigi was the one who got to tell Carlo. His plans for the evening had just been blown to bits.

"We got the dogs out," Angie continued, his words sounding strangely slurred. "They caught a scent."

"That's some good news, at least," Luigi said. "You okay? You sound funny."

"Yeah, yeah, I'll be okay. She busted me upside the head with a vase, but I'm here at the doc's now to get sewed up."

"Sewed up? Damn."

"I gotta go. Doc's ready for me. But, well . . . we were thinking . . . maybe you could hold off reporting this until we—"

"Are you kidding me? He'd whack us both if we kept this from him. I'll take care of it, keep me updated."

Marisa came out of the bathroom then, dressed in a filmy red negligee with a sheer red robe. Unfortunately, no matter how hot she looked, his penis didn't care. Damn it.

"Problem?"

"Yeah," he said. "Gotta go out for a while." Did he see relief in her eyes? Oh, yeah, she had a headache. "You get some rest."

He gave her a distracted kiss before he changed his clothes. He slid the phone in his jacket pocket hoping Angie would call him soon with some good news. As he grabbed his keys out of the drawer, the black box with the ring mocked him. Not tonight.

With a frown for his ruined plans, he slid the drawer closed. He didn't worry that she would find the engagement ring. Marisa wasn't a snoop. That was another reason he wanted to marry her. He could trust her.

Before he got to his car, he called Carlo. Luigi's evening hadn't been the only one interrupted, he heard a woman in the background while he was talking to Carlo. No question it was one of Carlo's latest *comares*. Carlo's wife had been an invalid since before they came to the States. Carlo never let that slow down his love life. Luigi envied the boss for his stamina.

Once at the club, the night went from bad to worse. Carlo gave orders that Luigi couldn't help but question.

"The kid? You really wanna do that?"

"Hell, yeah." Carlo wagged his finger in front of Luigi's face. "Don't you go fucking questioning me. Sandro betrayed me and he's fucking gonna pay. Get that bitch back and the kid will keep her in place. She gets away, the kid will bring them both running."

Like other made guys, Luigi had tortured people. Killed them. But nothing gave him the willies worse than messing with kids. Babies were sacred. He wanted a bundle of them with Marisa.

While Carlo had little regard for any human life. Old, young, in between. His reputation was built on his ruthlessness. Back in Italy, before Luigi was part of the family, Carlo supposedly wiped out a whole family, dad, mom, kids; one child as young as two. Without blinking. Just because he suspected the dad of being a rat. No one was ever brought to justice for the crime, but rumors among the *Mafioso* pointed to Carlo. If anyone knew for sure, no one talked.

In an effort to stave off the inevitable, Luigi presented the best argument he could. "Agent Armstrong's gonna have him squirreled away somewhere. And now we've lost our inside man—"

"Find the kid." Carlo's words were final.

No argument against that.

CHAPTER 18

Snowflakes floated onto Nia's face, melted, leaving wet spots for the cold night air to freeze. She pushed to her feet out of the damp ditch. With each breath, the biting cold stabbed her lungs, pierced her throat, and brought reality into sharp, bitter focus.

A car and a truck had passed. She took off running again, though the wind cut through her flimsy slacks and her feet felt like blocks of ice. She'd been jogging steadily for the past hour, pacing herself, until the occasional car sent her flying to her belly, heart pounding, waiting in the ditch.

The cars that drove by might hold possible rescue. But just as likely one of them held the mobsters. She had no doubt they were looking for her, and she wasn't going to risk making contact with anyone. So far, other than the rare passing car, she hadn't seen a sign of life—no houses, no businesses, just acres and acres of farmland, but she was bound to come upon something soon.

Far off, but fast approaching headlights sent her heart rate spiking and her scurrying to the ditch again. Lying flat on her stomach, she pretended it was Sandro driving the car, scouring the state of New York for her. No matter what he'd tried to make her believe earlier, she knew without a doubt now he was in serious trouble.

Regardless of his own troubles, she knew once he learned of her kidnapping, he would be out searching for her, no matter the risk to himself. She knew him well. Fear for him, fear for herself and her son made her muscles tighten and she wanted to curl into a ball and pretend none of this was happening.

To dispel the freezing fear, she pictured how happy he would be when he found her. How he would cover her face, her lips, with warm grateful kisses. The strong image was so real, she almost jumped up from her hiding place to wave down the passing car.

Last minute sanity prevailed. She knew she couldn't take the chance no matter how tempting. The cold and fatigue must be making her lose it.

She forced herself to stay still, returning to her daydream of Sandro's soft, soothing kisses, and that he would soon be awakening her from this horrible nightmare. He would hold her, whisper sweet Italian words in her ear, and when she was calmed, he would lay her back and make slow, passionate love to her.

The car finally passed. Nia realized her cheeks were wet with more than snowflakes. She wiped the tears away, dragged herself to her feet, and made herself start running once more.

* * *

Sandro had made a wrong turn, and ten miles down the road, he still couldn't find the smaller street that should have been there. He pulled into the parking lot of a closed convenience store and put the stolen Honda Accord in park. The bright security lights surrounding the store made it easy for him to look at the map he'd bought before he left the city. Now, he wished he'd taken time to buy a GPS.

He turned too early. The road was still at least five miles ahead. If he'd been concentrating more on driving and worrying less about his missing wife, he wouldn't have gotten lost.

To some, to chastise himself for worrying about his wife, who was in the hands of the mob, might seem heartless. It partially came from his belief to live in the moment. Worry was a waste of energy. But mostly, he knew his wife, and had confidence in her abilities. She would find a way to stay alive until he found her. He had no doubt if a chance to escape presented itself, she would take it. By now, she would have realized his leaving was a set up, and she would know he would come after her.

Making her think he left her for another woman had been a last minute plan, the best he could do under the circumstances. If it had gotten her out of town and back home to Dallas, that would have sufficed. He hadn't counted on Carlo moving so fast.

It made no sense to lament fate though. Once again he would do what he had to do. He always had. It was a code he lived by.

Sandro had been manipulated like a puppet for too many years. More than once, doing what he thought he had to do meant violating his honor. Missing the all-important free kick in the World Cup game that would have brought honor to his whole country, being forced into laundering money in the restaurant business he'd built for his family.

Now, doing what he had to do meant drawing the imaginary line to regain his lost honor as well as his wife. He would settle for no less. Once and for all, he wanted the Mafia out of his life, and his family together and safe again. He wanted a normal life. One not haunted with distress and deceit and danger.

Sandro remembered when once everything looked so hopeful. A time of sweetness and innocence. A time when the future promised a life brimming with happiness. A time before Carlo had brought the Mafia into his life . . . .

* * *

Ten years earlier

"I feel like words aren't adequate, but I had a wonderful time. Like a dream come true." Nia wrapped him in a hug as he prepared to board the long flight home to Italy after their passion-filled night. Where she had, as he promised, retained her virginity, even if she had lost some of her innocence. Never would he have imagined that a trip to the States for a friendly soccer match would result in his *thunderbolt*, finding his true love.

"Email me." He refused to let her go though the attendant had called for his flight to board. He prayed all he had done, all they had shared, was enough to last in her memory until they could meet at the upcoming World Cup in the summer. If she promised to write, then at least he'd be on her mind part of the time. *Dio*, he hoped most of the time. All the time. He knew she'd be on his mind.

"You want me to email?" She seemed so amazed. Why was she amazed? He was the one most blessed to have met her.

"Every day."

"Every day? Sheesh, what would I put in an email every day?"

"Anything. Everything. What you do during the day. . ."

"So, you mean like a journal?"

And that's what she'd done. Her first email arrived in his inbox eight days later, a typed account of what she had done every day for a week. Not exactly what he had in mind, even if that's what he'd told her.

He called her. Her roommate answered the phone. Anxious to hear Nia's voice, he decided at that moment, he'd get her a cell phone. They were smaller than they used to be, maybe small enough that she'd carry it with her.

"Hey, Nia, your Italian stallion's on the phone." Although the roommate had obviously moved the mouthpiece away, he heard her. He walked to his bookshelf and as he checked the translation of what she'd called him, he heard Nia express disbelief. "What? No way."

And then she picked up the phone. "Hello?"

"Why does your friend call me a horse?"

"Sandro! My, God, it's really you. Remind me to kill you, Kelsie," she called off into the room. "Sandro!" she said again, happiness bubbling in her voice. "I can't believe you called."

"Did I call too early?"

"No, I have a class soon."

"I won't keep you then—"

"That's all right. I mean . . . is something wrong?"

He made his voice deliberately firm. "*Si,*

something is wrong."

"Oh, God. What? You're injured! You can't play! What happened?"

"I am not injured. I play on Sunday. Will you be watching?"

"Of course. I always watch. If you're not injured," she continued, "why—"

"It's this email."

"Email?"

"The one you wrote me."

"Oh." She sounded puzzled. "What's wrong with it? I did as you asked."

"*Si*, you told me what you did day-by-day. But where is the recounting of the passion we shared? Or a mention that you miss me? That you dream of me at night and awaken with my name on your lips?"

"Sandro," she breathed, her voice low and intense. "I can't put that kind of stuff in an email—"

"Why not? Was the passion we shared only imagined? Are we not lovers?"

"Well . . . I mean . . . you know . . . anyone could read it . . . and, um, like Giuseppe said, you're known as a lady's man."

"And you think I would share our private emails, that I just play with your affections?"

"Well . . . you know . . ."

"Did you not promise me your virginity?"

"Of course, but—"

"Were you playing with my affections?"

"No, I was serious, but—"

"So you think I'd take your gift lightly? Use you then leave you?"

"I don't know. For all I know you have a hundred

lovers over there, and I would be one of many. You could even sit around the computer with someone else and laugh at what I wrote."

He managed to control his temper by reminding himself Giuseppe was right. She was stubborn. "Remember what I told you?"

"Every word."

That was better. "Remember when I told you I loved you, and I would marry you?"

"Of course I remember. But you couldn't have been serious."

He didn't comment.

"You weren't serious, were you? We barely know each other."

"Perhaps we've just met in this lifetime, but our souls have known each other forever."

"You're really serious?"

"I am an honorable man. You may trust what I say . . ."

* * *

An honorable man. Once Sandro had been honorable and trustworthy. Until he was left with no choice.

But the time had come for new choices. New promises to keep. He would be honorable again.

A dark-colored, long-bed Ford truck slowed and turned into the parking lot as Sandro checked the map one last time. Three dog kennels sat in the back of the truck. Probably early morning hunters waiting for the store to open to get hot coffee or gas for their truck. He barely had time to make note of that when a big black car drove by and passed the store. Unusual for two vehicles to be so close together this early and in this weather. The further north he'd driven, the more deserted the road became. At times the isolation and darkness was so complete, he felt totally alone in the world.

He put the Accord in gear and pulled out of the parking lot.

One man searching for his missing wife.

* * *

The black car that Sandro saw pass by the store after the truck pulled in, slowed, made a u-turn and headed back to the convenience store.

Giovanni parked next to the truck where Joey and Eddie sat. Giovanni hit the switch to roll down the window. "What'd you think? That guy who just left. He gonna be a problem?"

"Nah, some out-of-towner," Eddie said. "Looking at a map, probably lost. Most likely he thinks we're hunters."

"So, you think she's headed here?"

Eddie glanced around thoughtfully. "Since she definitely took the road and there aren't any houses or turn-offs before this store, this is the most likely place. And there's a phone inside, something she's no doubt looking for. If she's walking fast or jogging, she should be here before daylight."

"Hell, she's in great shape, she's probably running, probably already here and just hiding out—"

"Maybe not." Giovanni interrupted Joey. "She's pregnant."

"You serious?"

"That's what she told Angie. And she was throwing up earlier." Giovanni grimaced at the memory.

"Shit. I don't like this," Joey muttered. "At any rate, she'll push herself as hard as she can. She could still be here."

"The snow's letting up. I'll get the dogs out and prowl around. If she's hiding, they'll find her." Eddie opened his door.

Joey climbed into the Town Car to wait with Giovanni while Eddie set his dogs to search. They disappeared around the back of the building.

"Killing a woman's bad enough, but I don't want to whack a pregnant woman," Joey said.

"You think Carlo's gonna want her dead?" Giovanni pulled out a cigarette and lit it.

"Don't see any other way. Sandro shows and he's dead. She's a witness. Carlo never leaves loose ends."

"Damn, you're right." Giovanni puffed then blew out the smoke. "I don't think I can whack a pregnant woman either. Mikey could've done it."

"Yeah, but he's no longer with us. Carlo's pretty fucking crazy over this whole thing. I think he must've loved Sandro like a son. This betrayal has cut the boss deep."

Eddie came back with the dogs, stomping a light dusting of snow off his boots. He stopped by the car window as Giovanni rolled it down. "No sign of her."

"We better get out of sight then," Giovanni said, tossing his cigarette out the window. "We can go down that road that runs beside this place. We'll be able to watch it from the back."

"Or I can go down further on this road, then turn around and park on the side and watch the front. We'll cover two angles that way and she won't likely think of me as anything more than a hunter."

"Okay. We got binoculars. You see her, you signal us and we'll move in on her together."

"Store opens in an hour. If we haven't seen her by then, we'll have to backtrack. Get the dogs out again."

CHAPTER 19

Dave lay on his battered sofa sleeper staring at the light patterns created by the TV on his tiled ceiling. He'd hoped the droning of the all-night cable-news channel would drown out his thoughts, or at least cover up the sound of the rats scurrying in the walls of his fifth floor studio apartment. It hadn't helped in either case. His mind was a sticky mass of hot black tar, the kind mixed with rocks and spread on the cracked Texas roads on a blistering summer day.

Nia. Marisa. Sandro. Marisa. Nia. Marisa. Sandro. Mar—

Straying too often to the Mafia princess, Armstrong. Not good business, that.

And yet it was a struggle to pull his thoughts away. Was Luigi home yet? Were they together? In bed?

"Damn it!" Dave squeezed his eyes shut. Focus on the business at hand. Nia. He must do his job. He must make sure he was safe. He owed her.

Forcibly he pulled his memories to exactly why he owed Nia. Aside that they grew up next door to each other, and he'd loved her for as long as he could remember. He needed to remember that he'd made that one huge mistake in his life. He, who always strove for perfection. He'd made a total ass of himself, and for a time, he thought he lost his reason for existing.

His memories were painful, humiliating. A good distraction from Marisa. He deserved the punishment letting himself entertain inappropriate thoughts for even one second. From contemplating making another huge mistake . . . .

It had been a decade earlier, he remembered, and he was home for Easter. The holiday fell late in April that year, and Dallas was suffering an early heat wave. It was at least twenty degrees hotter than it was back in D.C. where he'd been living the last couple of years.

Which is why he was outside, de-winterizing the pool. His parents hadn't hired the pool service to do the job yet, and he wanted to swim. So, he'd do it himself. Perhaps by tomorrow he would be able to get in the water.

"Dave, are you here? I saw your car out front. Where are you?"

Nia. She was back from school, home visiting for spring break. His heart rate accelerated. "I'm out here."

She stopped at the double French doors that opened onto his parent's patio. He'd never forget how she looked in her wind shorts and baggy soccer jersey, her hair in a ponytail and as usual, no shoes on her feet. Little girl look in an all-woman's body.

"Dave, you're home," is all she said before she launched herself into his arms. "I knocked but no one answered. I just let myself in."

"You know you don't have to be invited." Her curves felt more womanly. She felt good in his arms. "Mom's grocery shopping and Jared's out in his art room, working on his latest masterpiece." His voice became sarcastic, and he winked. "Most likely he has a naked girl out there and he's painting dirty pictures."

Nia slapped his shoulder. "Don't make fun of him. He'll be famous someday."

"Famous, my ass. He's almost thirty and still lives at home. He needs a job."

"You know it's my older brother who talks like that about my younger one, not the other way around." She pulled away.

Reluctantly, he let her go. "Which brothers?" She had two younger brothers, two older.

She shrugged and grinned. "Well, any of them. Name one. How long are you going to be here?"

He told her, and they chatted while he finished the pool, but soon it became obvious her mind wasn't totally on the current conversation. He wondered if it had to do with her new "boyfriend". Dave couldn't believe how she'd hooked up with the same Italian soccer star she'd had a crush on for years. But now the dude was back in Italy. He was bound to have dumped Nia, or would soon. And when he did Dave could pick up the pieces. He breathed a sigh. He'd almost waited too late.

He decided he couldn't go back to D.C. without letting her know how he felt. "The pool will be ready to swim in tonight. You want to come over?"

"Sounds great. We haven't fixed ours yet. You want the two brats to come?" She jerked her head toward her two younger brothers who were outside playing ball.

No, he didn't, not at all. "Sure, they can come."

"Hey, guys," she called to them. "Want to go swimming tonight?"

"We can't, Nia. We're going over to Tim's house."

She looked back at him. "Guess it's just me. But I can't stay too late; Sandro's supposed to call me about midnight."

The Italian player was calling her from Italy? Dave forced a smile. "I guess I can survive if it's only you who makes it over," he said, thinking how perfect it would be. It was his parents' bridge night, and his brother had a hot date with a new model. He and Nia would be alone with plenty of time for him to convince her he would be better for her than Sandro, the soccer player.

And if she couldn't be convinced, he'd let her know he would be there when Sandro dumped her and left her broken-hearted.

Early in the evening, as time drew closer for Nia to come over, Dave started thinking about Sandro. The more he thought about competing with an international soccer star, one she'd had a crush on, no less, the more Dave's confidence waned. Nia had been in lust with the guy for too many years. Maybe Dave couldn't compete.

He went to the bar and poured a drink. Bourbon on the rocks. Somehow the drink disappeared so he made another. He was on his third glass when Nia arrived. By now he felt better, much more relaxed, confident even.

They played in the water like old times. She was a strong swimmer, so they could play tag games without fear of her drowning. Finally, she pleaded defeat.

"You win." She got out of the swimming pool, grabbed a towel from the table, and plopped onto the lounge. He watched her from the water, waiting for her request.

"Swim for me," she said.

He was on the swim team in high school and college. She'd always loved to watch his butterfly stroke.

"If I won," he joked, "how come I'm the one who has to swim?" In truth he was flattered and would have been disappointed if she hadn't asked.

"I'll juggle a ball for you if you want, but I don't swim as prettily as you do. Go on, stop stalling. You know you want to show off."

He swam for her.

"You look so wonderful when you do that. You still practice don't you?"

He pushed up out of the pool, dripping water. He took her towel and rubbed it over his body before he sat on the edge of the lounge. She scooted over and made more room for him.

"Yeah, I still practice." He let his gaze roam over her, taking in her lithe muscular body, barely covered by a bikini held together with flimsy ties. The cooling night air had her nipples pebbled beneath her wet top, and goose bumps raised over the exposed parts of her body. Which was most of it. His Speedos grew uncomfortably tight while silence stretched out between them.

"Dave, why are you staring at me like that?"

He pulled his gaze from her body. "I want to kiss you."

She tried to get up.

He took hold of her shoulders. "Stay."

"No. You know about Sandro."

"Yeah, I know. But I'm here, Sandro's not."

"Dave, I'm involved." She tried to squirm away.

"You really think he's being faithful?"

She stopped squirming. "Yes. Why wouldn't I?"

"Oh, I don't know. He's in Italy. He's a superstar who no doubt has a legion of groupies... Besides, you've never kissed anyone besides him."

"I . . . "

Her blush told him she regretted confessing that tidbit.

"You need something to compare, don't you think?" He reached behind the chair and lowered it to the reclined position. His confidence was building . . . from the liquor he'd earlier consumed or from her heady admiration of his swimming. He didn't know. He just knew he'd loved Nia years longer than Sandro even knew about her.

Nia tried to scoot away. Dave laid a leg across her body, holding her trapped.

"Dave, I don't know. Wait. Please don't."

He ignored her and kissed her anyway. She lay pliant and unresponsive in his arms. "Kiss me back, Nia."

"I . . . "

"Just once. This can be an experiment. You don't plan to kiss only one guy in your life, do you?"

Her gaze grew thoughtful. In all his bourbon-laced confidence, he knew he could win her over. He had to. He kissed her again, using slight force to urge her lips apart.

She didn't struggle. But she still didn't return his kiss.

"Please, Nia. Kiss me. I love you. I've waited all these years for you to grow up."

"You love me?" She froze and something that could have been alarm, if he'd been in the mood to analyze it, entered her eyes.

"I've loved you forever, Nia."

"Oh, Dave . . . I had no idea . . ." She drew a breath. "Just a kiss."

She had the look that she hoped a kiss would pacify him and then she could make her escape. He could have agreed; he didn't remember. He just knew that when she stopped fighting and started kissing him, he lost control. Somehow he had her naked, and he was naked. He was fingering her. Of course, by that time she was fighting again, but he easily overpowered her. He had to get inside her.

He forced himself between her legs.

She squirmed and fought harder. "Dave, no!"

"Nia—" He tried to ignore her panicked cries. He didn't want to stop now. He couldn't. He pushed against her.

Suddenly, he was shoved backwards and off the lounge. He flailed trying to save himself from splashing into the pool. He heard Nia's scream as he went under water.

He came up sputtering, ready to kill.

"Hey, asshole, I distinctly heard her say no. That means stop. They forget to teach you that in FBI school?" His older brother Jared stood glaring at him.

Nia wriggled off the lounge, grabbing the towel and her bikini before she dashed inside the house.

Jared marched forward. "What the fuck are you doing, you jerk off? You're the example mom and dad keep throwing up in my face, following in dad's footsteps. The big successful FBI man. About to rape a woman. Not just any woman, but Nia, the girl next door that we all love. Jesus H. Christ, she's the most famous woman soccer player in the world, and you're treating her like a whore."

"Shut up, Jared. Just shut the fuck up." Dave laid his head against the tiled pool ledge. He felt sick inside.

Jared left his date, who he'd brought over for a swim, cooling her heels in the living room, while he walked Nia home.

She wouldn't speak to Dave any more that week, even though he'd gone over and tried to apologize. She refused to come out of her room, leaving him in an uncomfortable conversation with her mom.

A month later, he got her to take his call and accept his apology. Then in a whirlwind romance after the World Cup, Sandro had whisked her off to Italy so fast, that Dave never saw her again, until they moved to New Jersey and into his jurisdiction. He never had to heal her broken heart.

Even now, years later, the memory of the near-rape had the ability to make Dave's stomach twist in knots so painful he wanted to hurl. He slowly drew in a long breath of air, releasing tense muscles.

When she and Sandro moved back stateside, a desire to see her, to see if her marriage was working, to see if she perhaps hated him, had him seeking her out. Nia welcomed him with open arms. Still crazy in love with her Italian superstar, and proudly showing off her new son.

The visit was painful, but he deserved the pain. He thought he'd never love again.

And now Nia was missing, in the hands of hardened criminals who wouldn't hesitate to kill her. Dave would do everything in his power—and beyond—to rescue her. He couldn't afford even the slightest mistake. He wouldn't fail—disappoint—her this time.

* * *

Nia saw lights ahead. Not lights moving in from a distance like headlights. But bright, tall lights. A building. Hopefully, people—good guys. If there were no people, at least a phone. Please God let there be a phone. Hope blossomed within her. She forced the blocks of ice masquerading as her feet to move faster.

As she drew closer, she saw it was a convenience store, and even from a distance she could see it was dark inside. Closed. At the last moment, she veered off into the field surrounding the store. Perhaps the mob guys thought she'd gone into the woods by the house. But perhaps they hadn't.

Until she had her bearings—knew whether the phone was inside or outside, had an escape route mapped out—she wasn't approaching the store.

Taking care to move slow and stay low, she circled the perimeter. No phone outside. But she saw one through the windows, just outside the women's restroom door. A good thing. Now that she had stopped running, nature called. She hoped the store opened soon. She didn't want to answer the call out in the open fields.

Fat, fluffy flakes started falling faster than before. She sought shelter between the dumpster and the back wall and huddled down to wait. But it was difficult to control her shivering.

A car door slamming startled her awake. Amazingly, she must have dozed. Slowly, she stretched stiff, frozen muscles, fingers and toes tingling painfully. Forcing herself to move despite the pain, she shook her head like a wet dog to knock off accumulated snow, and then peeked around the corner.

A man in uniform was unlocking the front door. Yes! She wanted to rush the door, but she made herself wait. It might not be as safe of a haven as it looked.

Ten minutes passed before she scanned the area again. She didn't note anything suspicious though the now-heavy snow limited her view. She decided if it limited her view, it would also limit anyone watching, too.

Bells hanging from the door tinkled as she entered. Quaint. The warmth inside made her popsicle-like body parts ache even more.

"Good morning," she said to the skinny red-haired clerk who was staring at her. She must look a fright with her black eye, bruised face and wild appearance.

The clerk nodded his head, questions clear in his blue-eyed gaze. "Cold enough for you?"

"Certainly is." She considered telling the man a bunch of bad guys were after her, but she hesitated. She didn't know if the mobsters came here for their morning coffee. Or if this guy and the mob guys were good buddies, as they'd say in Texas. Maybe he was even a mob guy in disguise. Mentally, she cringed, realizing she was close to losing it.

"Got coffee going," he added. "Should be ready in a few minutes."

"Sounds great," she said, deciding to keep quiet. It was best to trust no one, call for help, and be ready to bolt if that plan failed.

"Out awfully early this morning?" Although the clerk was friendly enough, the suspicious look had never left his face.

She thought quickly. "I . . . uh, had car trouble. A . . . blowout. I hit my face. On the airbag." She touched her bruised face, courtesy of Mikey. "I've been walking an hour. My cell's dead. I need to use your phone to call for help." A makeshift story, but it would do. She pulled the dollars she'd gotten from the truck out of the jacket pocket. "Can you make change?"

His suspicious look softened as he handed her coins in exchange for a couple of dollars. "Sounds bad, my wife was in a wreck about this time last year. She was on the way to the doctor, she was pregnant. Icy roads always a danger. I told her she should reschedule."

Nia felt an immediate bond with the unknown pregnant woman. Yep, definitely losing it. She pulled her thoughts together. "I hope she and the baby were okay?" She noticed a wedding band on his left hand. She would have thought him too young to be married. Especially married with a baby. *Didn't matter. Find the damn phone.*

"Ah, yeah. We got us a nine month old little girl. It'll be our first Christmas with a baby."

Right now, Nia didn't want to consider Christmas was only a few weeks away. Feeling the clock ticking, she was getting impatient with the chitchat but she felt herself smile and say, "That will be wonderful."

He seemed to remember what she needed. Maybe it was her pained smile. "Oh. Sorry. Phone's right around the corner," he added.

"Thank you." She hurried to the phone, looking at the surroundings. While windows lined the wall, they were plate glass, not the kind that opened. She peeked into the bathrooms—only one high window in each. Very tiny high windows. No way could she fit even if she could reach one by standing on the toilet. She didn't like not having an escape route, but she had no choice. She had to use the phone. Now that it was almost daylight, it would be that much easier to find her if she set out to look for another phone. She would just have to hurry.

First she called Sandro's cell phone. His voice mail picked up. "Sandro, it's me. I got away. I'm—" Where was she?

"Excuse me, sir, what is the name and address of this place?" she called to the clerk. He told her and she repeated the information. "Oh, Sandro, where are you? Why do they want you?" She rested her head against the phone. The cold metal helped her collect herself. "I'm calling Dave, Sandro. He knows something." Another pause, then she added in a whisper. "I love you. Keep safe."

She dialed Dave's office and asked for him.

"He isn't in yet. Can I help you?"

"Will you give me his cell phone number?"

The nameless voice on the other end immediately took on a suspicious tone. "Who is this?"

"My name is Nia Croc—"

"Nia! Shit!" Then he calmed. "Nia, where are you?"

It was her turn to be suspicious. "Who are you?"

"I'm Frankie. I'm on Dave's team—"

"Where's Dave?"

"Scouring the country for you. Where are you?"

"Sandro. Where's he?"

"I don't know—"

"Daniele?" Tears welled into her eyes as her panic grew.

"Now there I can help you. Danny's in a safe house with his aunt and uncle."

Relief warred with confusion. "Giuseppe and Luciana? Are they in danger, too?"

"Possibly. We wanted to be cautious. And we

figured Danny would feel better with someone he knew. How about you? Are you safe?"

"For the moment. I got away."

"Where are you now, Nia? Tell me, and we'll come get you."

"I'm—"

"Hey, what are you doing?" The clerk's fearful voice startled her into silence.

"Sit down and shut up," a man instructed. She heard a ripping sound.

She knew that voice. She glanced around the corner, then quickly pulled back. "Oh, dear God," she whispered, heart pounding. Giovanni was wrapping duct tape around the clerk who was sitting in a chair. She remembered she was on the phone. "They found me. I've got to go."

"Honey, no. Nia, don't hang up." Frankie's voice tinged on frantic. "Tell me where you are. We can help you."

She whispered the information. "I've got to leave now, or I'll be trapped."

"Stall them. I'll get someone there as fast as I can."

"The phone's toward the back and around that corner," she heard Giovanni say, his voice growing closer. Her gaze darted frantically as she crept forward, intending on dashing down a back aisle and circling around. At the last second she pulled back. They were too close. No way out.

Trapped. Her body started shaking.

No. She couldn't be trapped. She couldn't. Not when she was so close. Choosing her only option, she ran into the women's restroom. She decided that was too obvious and backtracked into the men's restroom instead.

She locked the door. Even though the flimsy lock would only buy her seconds.

She needed a weapon. On first glance, there was nothing obvious to use. She tore open the cabinets under the sink. Jackpot. Plumber's tools. She hefted a large pipe wrench and slid behind the door just as the knob rattled.

"She in there?" A voice she didn't recognize.

"Has to be. No one's in the women's bathroom. She never left the store, so there's no place left for her to go. Get the key from that clerk."

"There's no need for a key. Step outta the way."

Nia was prepared for the sound of the door busting open. She wasn't prepared for the gunshot or wood shattering. She jumped in shock, but stifled the surprised scream threatening to burst forth. She adjusted her grip on the pipe wrench. Ready for them.

"Watch it, she's—" Giovanni's voice cut off suddenly as if he'd been motioned to silence.

Nia raised the pipe wrench. She knew there were at least two men. Her hasty plan was to disable one, and rush the other as she'd done earlier.

A gun appeared. Followed by an arm. Her heart was pounding hard enough to jump out of her chest, but if there was one thing she'd learned from soccer, it was patience. One more second and . . ..

She aimed for the wrist and brought the wrench down. Obviously expecting the move, he slammed the door into her.

She stumbled back. He whirled on her. She recognized him from earlier in the day. The tall thin one with a big nose called Joey. Before he got his bearings, she kicked his gun hand then rushed him, swinging the pipe wrench like a bat. The heavy metal tool connected with his stomach. He grunted. Staggered.

Running past him she barreled through the remains of the wooden door prepared to batter her way through Giovanni. But he wasn't there. She paused. Then Giovanni's arms came from nowhere and wrapped tightly around her. He'd been out of sight, waiting for her. He had her now. She twisted uselessly to get free.

"I know your tricks now," he said, turning her so his tobacco-laced breath was hot on her face. He forced the wrench out of her hands. Ignoring her throbbing wrist where she'd tried desperately to keep her grip on her weapon, she kicked him in the shin.

He groaned. "Shit. I fucking forgot that one."

Though she managed to hurt him, he didn't release her. She cupped her hands and bopped him in the ears with all the strength she could muster.

Along with a cry of pain, his grip finally loosened.

She kneed him in the groin, broke free and sprinted for the front door. Only to skid to a stop. A short, fat man with three big dogs blocked her path to the door. This man she didn't know.

Cautiously, she edged forward, figuring once she passed the dogs, she could easily escape the man. His very plumpness gave him a kindly look. Despite the company he kept.

His words told a different story. "You don't want to go no further, *signorina*. These dogs, they are not my trained attack dogs, but they will hold you in place. To them, you are no more than the squirrel in the tree."

Surely his warning was a bluff. The dogs were big, but they didn't look mean. They looked like Jed Clampett's sweet old hound dog on the Beverly

Hillbillies. She kept inching forward knowing any second the two other men would recover and come after her.

But with a command from the dogs' owner, they assumed an aggressive stiff-legged stance, growling low in their throats, teeth bared.

Nia stopped. "Let me go. Please. I have a small son. He needs me—"

"I admit Eddie has a weakness for pretty ladies, but he can't let you leave." Giovanni came up gasping behind her and grabbed her arms tighter than necessary, she thought.

Joey, holding his stomach in obvious pain, joined them. "You are one mean bitch—"

"Didn't I try to tell you?" Giovanni questioned.

"Wouldn't you have done the same if you were in my position?"

Joey stared at her. "Yeah, I guess so. No hard feelings."

"I'm sorry I don't share your sentiments."

"Listen," Giovanni cut in. "We don't have time for this lovey-dovey kiss-and-make-up stuff. We gotta get going before the Feds are on us. Who knows who she talked to on the phone." He looked at her. "Who'd you call?"

"I don't know what you're talking about. I was trying to use the restroom."

"Sure you were. C'mon. Let's go. Joey, you take care of the clerk."

She didn't like the sound of that. She glanced at the white-faced clerk, his red hair standing in stark contrast. He was bound and gagged in a straightback chair. His eyes were wide with fear. He really couldn't be old enough to be married.

Giovanni continued giving orders. "Eddie, put the dogs in the truck and I'll settle with you when I get her tied up." Giovanni tugged her toward the door. She knew if she left with him, there would be no hope of rescue.

Stall them.

Frankie's words came back to her. She dug in her heels. "I still have to go."

"Go where? What the hell you talking about?"

"To the bathroom. I never got the chance."

His look said he wasn't buying her story.

"I'm not lying. I'm pregnant, remember? You know about pregnant women? We have to pee every five minutes."

Giovanni sighed.

"You better not let her out of your sight," Joey offered.

Oh, God, she didn't want them watching her in the bathroom, but she really did have to go. "I don't need any help."

"You think I'm stupid? You just tried to kill Joey with a chunk of steel. I can't trust you."

"Then let the dogs watch me. Otherwise, I'll wet the seat in your car and it'll smell—"

"Okay, okay. I get the idea. Eddie, can your dogs do watch?"

"Sure, why not?"

She took as long as she could. It wasn't hard considering they made her leave the door open and let the dogs guard her.

"Nice, doggies." It was hard to relax when three formerly innocent-looking turned vicious-looking dogs showed their set of big, sharp, white teeth.

"You need help in there? What's taking you so

long?" Giovanni called through the doorway.

"Pipe down. I'm doing the best I can."

"Maybe I need to come hold your hand—"

"Sure. If you're brave enough to come through these dogs." She zipped her slacks and washed her hands.

"Finished yet?"

"Yes, no thanks to you." The smell of freshly brewed coffee made her stomach growl. Had it only been a few minutes earlier the clerk had put on a fresh pot? "Call off these dogs if you want me to come out there."

The dogs trotted out at Eddie's command and followed him out the front door. They looked as sweet and innocent as a lap dog again. Amazing Jekyll-and-Hyde performance.

Giovanni took her arm and led her toward the door. "Okay," he said to Joey, who stood next to the clerk. "We're going."

Nia looked back as Giovanni dragged her along. Joey put his gun next to the clerk's head and calmly pulled the trigger. Blood splattered over the cash register. She jumped at the sudden violent act. Though the gun had made little sound, the lack of noise didn't erase the horror of what had just happened. She suddenly found herself screaming.

Giovanni shook her. "Shut up. You shouldna looked."

Slowly, her brain started functioning again. "You shouldn't have killed him! What the hell did you do that for?" she screeched, panic lending her strength to jerk an arm free and swing a fist at him. "What did he do?"

He grabbed her flailing arm. "He saw too much."

"You think the Feds don't know who you are?"

"Can't prove nothing without no witnesses. This

ain't no fun and games, Nia. Do what we say, so more people don't get killed." He dragged her toward the car, calling over his shoulder."Take out that security camera."

The horrid scene replayed itself in her mind. Bang. Just like that, a man was dead. And for no more reason than he saw too much. He was a witness.

Another horrifying thought made her legs go weak.

She was a witness.

She could identify them. Tell what they did.

Put them in jail.

The world started spinning. Bile rose in her throat.

She was as dead as the clerk.

CHAPTER 20

"Mornin', princess."

Lost in her thoughts, tired from too little sleep, Marisa jumped and whirled at the sound of Dave's voice. He sat on the couch in the lobby of her apartment building, looking calm and collected as if he'd had a full night's sleep, which she knew he hadn't because it was barely after five a.m. and it had been nearly one when she had left to go to Luigi's.

Detouring from her path to the elevators, she walked toward him, her pulse skittering. Just jumpy from lack of sleep she told herself.

"Didn't expect you this early," Dave commented when she stopped in front of him.

True, it was earlier than she had expected to be back as well. But Luigi had never returned. It wasn't unusual for him to get called away at night. Usually he came back; sometimes he didn't. She'd dozed off while waiting on him. When she woke up after a short nap and saw he still wasn't back, she left.

"How'd you get in here?" she asked, trying to regain her composure over her shock at seeing him.

"FBI credentials come in handy once in a while."

Dave stood, then smiled and nodded at the doorman currently on duty, which was not Murray.

She narrowed her eyes, curious, hopeful even, yet not wanting him to know. "And just what are you doing here so early? It's still dark outside."

"I could ask you the same thing. Makes me wonder what you're doing home so soon. I thought I'd have to wait hours. Glad I came when I did."

"Why are you here?" she repeated.

"I filed the papers to pick up Roberto. I thought we should get started on those accounts."

She swallowed a groan; she was exhausted. "Don't you ever sleep?"

"Sleep is overrated."

Yeah, if he spent the night with her, she could see how sleep could be overrated. Since that wasn't going to happen however . . . she sighed. "Will he be picked up today?"

"Should be."

He followed her into the elevator. The doors shut, and she pushed the button for her floor before she leveled him with a look. "What are you really doing here? I don't need to you to help me transfer the accounts."

"Rumor has it I'm a control freak."

"I'm *certain* that must be a false rumor."

"Ha. Ha," he said, catching her sarcasm.

He moved closer. She stepped back, bumped against the wall. He reached out his hand. Her breath caught. Lifting her necklace off her neck, his thumb playing with the delicate Florentine cross hanging from the chain, he said softly, almost to himself, "Luigi must've had an early night."

Marisa released her breath and sighed. "So that's

it." The elevator door opened. She didn't say anything else until she entered her apartment.

"What's it?"

Tossing her purse on the couch, she turned to him. "Come on. Don't be coy. Go ahead and ask."

"Ask what?" He tried the innocent routine once again, and once again she saw right through him.

"Whether I slept with him."

"That's none of my business," he said stiffly.

She got the distinct impression he wished he'd never said anything about Luigi. "You still want to know, don't you?" she pressed, not willing to let him off, trusting her instincts that he was suffering from this unwanted attraction as much as she was.

"What you do or who you do it with is your own business."

"True enough." She stepped close to him, definitely invading his space. "But you want me enough to be jealous if I did."

"I told you last night—"

"I know what you told me. And apparently you don't remember what I told you. Everything has collapsed. My father will never be brought to trial now. Therefore, I will never be a witness."

She ran her finger under his collar. He drew in his breath. Yes, she was right. He wanted her. And the strangest thing of it was, she wanted him, too.

It was the first time she'd felt even an inkling of true desire since Paolo's death. Maybe it was just the law enforcement types that attracted her. They were so much the antithesis of what she was normally surrounded with. And that's why she knew she needed to stay away from him. But she couldn't seem to help herself.

She was so tired of using and being used.

Just for a short time she wanted to desire and be desired. It had been so long.

Standing rigid as a statue, Dave grabbed her wrist before her hand strayed any further. She didn't let his feigned reluctance deter her. A half step and her body pressed against his. "I didn't have sex with Luigi," she whispered, turning her face up to his, her body pulsing with anticipation.

His lips were inches from hers. "What'd you do? Plead a headache?"

"It was my plan. But he was called away on business."

Dave froze. "Anything I should know about?"

She gave a small shake of her head. "I don't know, I was in the bathroom looking for headache medicine when he got the call." Actually, she was in the bathroom changing into the lingerie that Luigi liked, but there was no need for Dave to know that tidbit.

His lips curved upward ever so slightly.

"I didn't think anything about it." She'd been too relieved to give it much thought. "It's not unusual for him to get called away."

She moved her hands up to his shoulders.

Dave finally gave in, wrapping his arms around her. Whisper soft words brushed against her lips. "A headache wouldn't work for an excuse with me."

"Oh, forceful. I like that in a man." She kissed him. Just for a short time, she repeated to herself.

He kissed her back, moving his hands up from her waist to her ribs, thumbs resting beneath her breasts. He only had to stretch those thumbs up a bit to rub across the nipples.

But he didn't.

Instead he pulled back and gazed earnestly into her eyes. "I'm sorry. I can't believe I did that again."

She saw true regret in the depths of his dark gaze. "Why fight it, Dave? I want you. You want me."

He shook his head. "There's no future for us. When this case is closed, you'll go into witness security and never see me again."

She was no longer sure that witness security would be necessary, but she wasn't going to argue with him. If everything went according to plan, her father would be dead and his organization destroyed. "Did I ask for a future?"

"All women want a future." He lifted his hand and ran his thumb gently across her lips. "A commitment."

She nipped at his thumb, then kissed the small wound. "We have no idea what the future will bring. All we know is now. And now is all I want."

Dave watched her lips close over his thumb as she drew it between her lips, making gentle sucking motions, leading his mind immediately to other things she could do with her mouth.

Thoughts of right and wrong warred, but desire made his blood run heavy, and his thoughts were fleeting. With an effort he forced himself to remain detached, so he could think as logically as possible given the circumstances.

What game was she playing? Did she really want him, or was she using sex as a means to an end as she did with Luigi? But for what purpose? He'd already agreed to help them. Did she perhaps think if he were involved with her she could somehow save Sandro from jail if he did murder her father in cold blood? Questions hounded

Dave as relentlessly as he had ever hounded a suspect.

Seconds ticked by with Marisa studying his face expectantly. At last he moved his thumb again, this time smoothing the moisture from her mouth still on it across her lips. Her eyes darkened in anticipation before she closed them in surrender.

At that moment he was lost. He slid his hand across her soft, silky cheek, down her slender throat, to the back of her neck, pulling her closer. She came willingly, turning her lips up as an offering. He gently touched them with his own. Desire flamed when she eagerly opened her mouth, accepting, encouraging, drawing his tongue in to deepen the kiss.

Then his phone rang.

He jerked away, heart thumping. "Damn," he muttered, yet he was almost grateful to have been stopped from doing something extremely stupid.

Taking a step back from Marisa, he fumbled with his phone, not even taking time to look at the caller ID. "Armstrong."

"Boss, this is Frankie. I just got off the phone with Nia."

"Nia? Was it a ransom demand?"

Marisa met his gaze, hope flaring in hers.

Frankie continued, "No. Somehow she got away—"

"Where is she?"

"At a little store up in Orange County, somewhere between Montgomery and Walden."

"Orange County? That's where Sandro was headed. What's the address?"

Frankie gave it, then added, "But boss, they've found her again. I told her to stall and we'd get someone there, but I don't know how long she can hold them off."

"Montgomery and Walden, northern Orange County," Dave said, trying to picture the map in his mind. "It'll take us a couple of hours to get there," Dave said, thinking aloud.

"Can you get us a helicopter?"

"Snowing too heavy."

Dave hadn't even thought to check the weather, his mind had been so jumbled. Snow would mean it would take longer to drive, as well. "Get ahold of the Hudson County Resident Agency." Hudson County was a satellite office of the New York Field office. After thinking for a second, Dave added, "And call the state troopers, the local police, anyone who'll have jurisdiction there—"

"Already done. We're just heading out ourselves."

"I'm on my way, too." He disconnected, then met Marisa's gaze. "C'mon."

He strode quickly to the door, leaving her scrambling for her purse and hurrying after him. Dave punched the button on the elevator.

"What's happened?"

"Nia got away. But they found her again. She'd made it to a convenience store outside Montgomery." Dave stood aside and let Marisa enter the elevator before him.

She pressed the button for the lobby. "Sandro's supposed to be in that area."

"I know what you're thinking. But we shouldn't call him. If he shows himself, they'll kill him."

"He'll want to know." The elevator doors shut and she added another argument. "He can protect himself. He's armed, remember."

"God, don't remind me. That's all I need is a bunch of dead bodies." Dave sighed, then gave in under her relentless stare. "Call him then." He thrust his phone at her.

Marisa dialed the number. "Sandro? She got away."

* * *

Sandro slammed the car into gear and spun out of the driveway. He'd found the house, but a thorough search proved it vacant. He'd been kneeling by a blood puddle on the floor at the top of the stairs, struggling to breathe, hoping it wasn't Nia's blood. He'd sagged in relief when he took Marisa's call.

His windshield wipers slapped at the snow. He cursed the weather. Visibility was poor at best. Heedless of the dangerous road conditions, he sped on.

He remembered the time when he'd sped to the airport, anxious to fly back to the States to be reunited after months of carrying on a long-distance relationship.

Her father had objected to his and Nia's romance. By her own right, Nia was a soccer star in the United States. Her father didn't want to see her lose her status over a love affair with an Italian.

"Believe me when I tell you I won't ask her to give up soccer," Sandro had told him. "But she will have to live in Italy when we marry. There is no other way. At least while I'm playing soccer. My schedule is more demanding. But she can fly back for her training and games."

"You've got that much money that you can afford to fly her back and forth?"

"I am the highest paid soccer player in Italy. She will be well cared for."

Well cared for. His words to her father had been arrogant, and seemed like a sick joke now. Maybe her father had been right and Sandro should have never asked her to make that choice. Then she would be safe now. Married to some American—maybe even Dave.

Who would have thought that after Sandro had given up his career in Italy to escape the Mafia's clutches—with the excuse to Nia that he was ready for a less demanding career—that Carlo would land in America, and in New York, too. Many of the mobsters fleeing ahead of Italian justice had run to South America. Just his luck that Carlo already had ties to New York.

Sandro wasn't running again. This time there would be a face off. And this time, he would win.

He whipped his car into the convenience store parking lot, the same one he'd used earlier for the light. The irony of it did not amuse him.

A man staggered out of the store as Sandro parked the car. The man weaved along, holding his stomach. He dropped to his knees and threw up in the snow.

Sandro got out of the car and hurried over through the slushy parking lot. "What's wrong? How can I help you?"

With a shaking hand, the man pointed to the store. "Dead. Blood everywhere."

Sandro's horrified gaze shot to the store. He pulled out his gun. "Someone's dead?" A cold hard lump settled in his stomach. "A woman?"

Sweat glistened on the man's bald head in spite of the freezing temperatures. "A man. The store clerk—"

Not Nia. Relief. Then sadness for the person who

had been killed. "Is there anyone else inside?" Sandro moved toward the door, gun ready.

"I don't think so." The man pushed to his feet. "I stop by here every morning on the way to work. To get coffee and a bagel."

The poor unlucky customer had lost his appetite today.

"Did you see anyone when you got here?" Sandro asked as the man followed him back to the store.

"Yeah. Some men were leaving as I pulled up." He squinted in thought.

"*Merda.*" This came from Sandro as he entered the store and took in the scene. The clerk slumped in a straightback, chrome chair, duct tape wrapped across his chest holding him upright in the chair. His mouth taped shut. Blood spattered on the cash register and counter behind him. It was obvious there was no need to feel for a pulse.

Sandro walked back outside. "Did you see anyone else with the men? A woman?"

A light dawned in the man's eyes. "Yeah. A woman was with them. Sitting between them."

"What kind of car?"

"There were two cars—or one car and a truck rather."

"A truck?"

"A big dark blue truck with dog kennels in the back."

Sandro's interest immediately sharpened. He'd seen that truck earlier. What kind was it? He wracked his brain. At the time, his mind had been on other things.

"Is there anything else you remember? What kind of truck? What color was the car?"

202

"The car was black—a Lincoln Town Car. And I think the truck was a Ford, one of those kind with four wheels in the back."

"Which way did they go?" Sandro tucked the gun back into his holster and pulled out the throw away phone. He punched in Dave's number.

"South, toward the city," the man answered at the same time Dave did.

"Armstrong."

"Dave, it's me. She's not here. The store clerk is dead—"

"Shit."

"There's another man here. A customer. He was driving up as they left. They've got Nia with them again." Sandro told Dave the rest of the information.

"Sounds like DiMarco's truck. He trains security dogs, but he has a tracking team, too. I'll update the local law enforcement. Someone should be there any minute. Make sure that the witness doesn't leave."

"I'll tell him to stay, but I'm going after them," Sandro said. "They can't be too far ahead. The witness said they were heading south. I found the house, but it was north of here, so they're probably taking her back to the city."

"True. They'd want to distance themselves from the crime scene."

"I've got some of those downtown addresses with me. Get me more."

"Sandro, it's dangerous. Wait on us."

"I've got to find them. I was so close—"

"They want you dead, you know."

"Screw what they want. Give me those damned addresses."

CHAPTER 21

"*Bella*, you shouldn't have hit me so hard." Angie had a square white bandage and an ice pack tied to his head. He was sitting behind a desk in a warehouse office, pulling stuff out of the drawers and packing it into a box sitting on the floor—most likely packing up anything she could use as a weapon because she figured this warehouse office was going to be her new prison.

Nia sat in the only other chair in the office, a straightback wooden chair. She shrugged at Angie's words, too tired to feel any compassion or remorse that she had severely injured another human being. Maybe later she would be shocked—if she were alive later. But now she was tired. She slumped in her chair unable to hold herself upright.

"You were in my way," she told him glumly. "Get in my way again, and I'll do the same thing."

Angie made tsking noises. "Such a sweet *donna*. I am sorry it has come to this."

"You're sorry? You're not the one who is contemplating his own imminent murder."

"Murder? What are you talking about? I told you we mean you no harm."

"Quit bullshitting me, Angie. I saw your pal Joey kill a guy today. Am I going to suddenly forget that?"

"Many people have forgotten minor facts such as who pulled the trigger in a shooting. You could forget."

"Oh yeah? Once you have my husband, you're just going to let me go? Walk away? And you think I'll keep quiet when Sandro shows up dead? What reason would I have to keep quiet then?"

"You have your son," Angie said quietly.

The blood drained from her face. She shot out of her chair. "Don't you even threaten—"

With surprising speed and agility, Angie stood up and pushed her firmly back to her chair. "I have made no threats. I have just reminded you that *you* are in no position to make threats. Remember that when Carlo comes to talk to you."

"And when will the sleazy coward be here?"

"That is no way to talk," Angie scolded her. He picked up a fat roll of duct tape on the desk. "You will do better to keep your tongue in your head. Powerful men like Carlo are very dangerous when angered."

Helpless rage poured through her. "He might be powerful, but he's still a— What are you doing with that?"

He had the roll of duct tape in his hand. She remembered the sound ripping duct tape made when they tied up the clerk. Was he going to tie her up?

"I must tie you up," he confirmed.

Her blood chilled. She tried for bravado. "You're kidding. I'm too tired to even think about escaping again."

"I cannot trust you. Carlo's orders are to keep you tied up until he gets here."

"When will that be? And where is 'here'?" They had arrived back in New York, going to a warehouse area she'd never seen before. From a back alleyway, they hustled her into what was obviously some sort of storage facility—probably full of illegal goods, but she still had no idea exactly where she was.

"Sit in this chair here, you'll be more comfortable." Angie indicated the padded desk chair.

Great, he wanted her comfortable while she was tied up. "Are you avoiding my questions?"

After she switched chairs, Angie taped one arm to the arm of the chair, then repeated with her other arm. "I don't know yet when Carlo will be here," he said at last. "And obviously, we are in the office of a warehouse."

"*Obviously*. I can tell by the plush decor. I meant the location. Ouch." The tape had pulled the hairs on her arms—she knew it would hurt to get it off.

"Sorry." He finished with her arms. "How is that? You are comfortable?"

"Just great," she answered sarcastically.

He lowered his considerable bulk to the floor with a grunt. Wrapping her ankles with the tape, he told her, "I won't tie your feet to the chair. That way you can prop them on the desk if you want to lie back in the chair, but you still can't get away." He seemed pleased as he heaved himself back to his feet.

"You've got me taped up tighter than a calf ready for branding. I don't think I'll be going anywhere for a while."

"Good." Angie patted her on the head. "That is what we want."

"That may be what you want. What I want is for Carlo to get here so he'll answer my questions."

"Just remember when he does, *Bella*, watch that tongue of yours." Angie wagged a fat bejeweled finger at her.

* * *

A grim scene faced Dave and Marisa. By the time they arrived, the locals had already cordoned the crime scene and Sandro was long gone. Marisa, dressed for the cold weather in a ski jacket, toboggan and gloves, took an offered cup of coffee from one of his men and made herself scarce while he set his team to work.

"Any of those phone calls you've been taking from Sandro?" she asked sometime later, with a worried expression she couldn't quite hide.

So, she had been watching him even while avoiding the unpleasantness of the work he had to do. "No. He hasn't had time to make it downtown yet. Even if he'd been speeding."

"No doubt he was speeding. I'm surprised we didn't pass him on the way here, though."

"More than likely he got a car we didn't recognize. It's also possible he took another road in." Dave wrapped his arm around Marisa's shoulders and led her toward his government-issued Crown Vic. "Come on, I'm finished here. Let's go."

"Where are we going?"

Beneath his arm, she felt tense, brittle. Her teeth were chattering; he suspected it was from more than the cold. The sooner this was over, the better. "We're going to your place. I'll drop you off, then go to the office to check on the paperwork for Roberto. When I know something definite, you can get those accounts transferred."

"Yes," she agreed, a hard set to her face. "It's time to end this."

Dave pulled into the underground parking to her apartment and rushed around to open her car door.

"Thanks." Her voice cracked on the word.

Alarmed, he took her arms. "Hey, what's wrong?"

She cleared her throat. Attempted a shrug. "Nothing, I told you. Just—"

"Don't give me that bullshit." He wasn't fooled in spite of the way she pulled herself together.

She looked at him, then sighed. "I can't stop thinking about that murdered man. What if the same thing happens to Sandro? To you?" She gritted her teeth and sniffed, obviously still fighting for control

"Ah, princess." He pulled her into his embrace. "I didn't even think how that must have affected you."

She rested against his chest. "Do you know what it makes me feel like? Knowing my father is responsible for that innocent man's murder. He had a wife. A baby girl. Now you know why he must be stopped." She pulled back and looked at him. "By any means necessary." Her words were firm, although there was a bit of moisture in her eyes she tried to hide by blinking.

Dave felt his control slip. Compassion was not something he experienced. He strove to be analytical. Aloof. Professional. There was no room for emotion with his job. And yet . . . he pulled her close and brushed his lips in her hair. Then found himself saying, "Come on, I'll take you upstairs. Make you some coffee, something to eat. You haven't eaten all day, you know."

"I don't think I can eat." She stepped away. "Besides, I don't have any food."

He led her to the garage elevator. "I'll order in, then. And you'll eat or I'll force feed you."

She gave a thin-lipped smile, and attempted humor. "There you go being forceful."

He shrugged and pushed the button to the elevator. "Sorry, it's just my nature."

She seemed fascinated by the elevator doors closing. "Sometimes a woman likes a forceful man."

The statement said in a thoughtful monotone, almost as if she were only talking to herself, left Dave at a loss to answer. He knew how he'd like to answer, but he'd crossed the lines of impropriety with her enough already. He suddenly found the elevator doors fascinating as well.

"I have coffee," she said once they were in her apartment. "I'll make some." She slipped into the serving role; he knew it was an act. He'd seen his mom do the same thing in times of stress.

"No, I'll make it, and I'll order something to eat. Do you want to shower or something?"

"A shower would be nice," she agreed.

Her quick acquiescence clued him that she was off-kilter. Marisa never gave in so easily. "Where's a close place to order food?"

"A deli's around the corner. The number is on my refrigerator."

When she came out of her room again, she was wearing a fluffy maroon robe and towel-drying her hair. Dave had the table set, food arranged neatly on the plates.

"I called about Roberto, we're good to go. He should be picked up within the hour. We'll eat, then get to work on those accounts."

She gave a quick nod. "That was faster than I expected." She pointed at the table to indicate she meant the food and not Roberto. It was almost as if she were shutting down about the realities confronting her.

"I paid them extra to hurry."

A half-smile spread her lips. "It isn't as if I'll waste away if I miss a couple of meals."

He stared at her, glad to see some of the worry lines ease in her face. "You'll feel better once you eat. I hope you like roast beef."

"Roast beef is fine."

He pulled out the chair for her. "How do you take your coffee?"

"Dave, I can get my own—"

"Sit down," he ordered. "Eat."

When he returned with her coffee, she was absentmindedly playing with her food. Picking at the crust and rolling it into little balls, not noticing her robe gaped open offering him a small view of naked skin. Whoa. He definitely needed not to go there. Setting the cup on the table, he hunkered down beside her chair, putting him below her eye level and out of sight of naked flesh.

"You don't like it?"

"What?"

He nodded at her plate.

She blinked. "Oh, sorry, I didn't realize."

He picked up a sandwich half and held it in front of her mouth.

"Really, Dave, I'm just not—"

"Open."

She stared at him, then the sandwich in his hand. He thought he had her, when suddenly, she pushed the chair back and ran from the room.

Dave heard her crying and sighed. "Damn." He slowly put the sandwich down and pushed to his feet.

He found her in the bathroom, splashing her face with water. He had the hand towel ready when she reached for it. She wiped her face.

"I'm . . . sorry." The crying made her hiccup. "I . . . I just—" She wiped her face with the towel again. "I just couldn't stop thinking about that man and how he'd never eat again. How Sandro or you might never eat again. How . . . how Paolo will never eat again. How can my father be such a monster?" The last words were a whisper.

"Come on, princess." Dave swung her into his arms. He carried her to the living room, ignoring the stark, utilitarian wing chairs and chose the sofa—still staid and stiff, but more comfortable. Cradling her, he let her cry her tears, thinking it interesting that twice now, she'd worried about his safety or Sandro's safety, but never her own.

Did she think she was immune from being killed? Would a father kill his daughter if he found out she betrayed him? Something told Dave no, or he hoped not. More than likely Carlo would send her off to another country. Maybe. Dave frowned. The thought of her risking her life didn't set well with him.

Finally her tears slowed, and he used the towel to dry her face. He kissed her forehead. In the silence, the only sound was their breathing. Absentmindedly, he stroked her hair, almost dry now. He noticed some hair was caught it in her silver-cross Florentine necklace. He pulled the hair free. "Did you shower with your necklace?"

She turned watery, big brown eyes on him. "I told you I never take it off. It was my *nonna's*. She never took it off either—until the day she died. On that day, she gave it to me. She must have known."

"It must be very special to you. I like it. It looks good against your skin."

"*Grazie*," she murmured. She held onto the cross pendant and smiled.

He let her calm a few more moments, then asked something he knew he shouldn't. It was none of his business. But he found he was wanting to know more about her. "Was Paolo your cop?"

She stared off toward the kitchen. "*Si*."

"Tell me about him. Where did you meet?" Perhaps talking about the past would help settle her, distract her from today's problems, Dave told himself.

She seemed willing enough. "I knew him already. Or knew of him, more truthfully. He was Giuseppe's son."

"Giuseppe? Sandro's uncle? Paolo was Sandro's cousin then?"

"*Si*." There was pain in that one word.

"What happened, princess?" he asked softly. "Tell me."

"Paolo approached me one day. He worked for the police, I knew this. He tried to convince me to testify against my father." She took a breath. "What he offered was tempting, but I was afraid.

"So, he started seeing me more often—in secret of course. After the first couple of times he stopped trying to convince me to testify, and we just talked. Got to know each other. And fell in love. I broke the engagement with Sandro long before that point. I knew I wasn't in love with him. He didn't love me. It would never have worked between us."

Dave wasn't sure how he felt hearing her talk about someone she once loved. Instead, he tried to piece the timeline together. "Was Sandro involved with your father then?"

She shook her head. "No. It happened as he told you. My father never approached him with family business until that World Cup when Italy made the finals and poppa forced Sandro—and others, of course—to throw the game. He'd bet heavily against Italy. He had something on each of the players, he always had something to make sure he got his way."

Dave didn't like the sound of that. Carlo had something on Sandro? "Define what you mean by something? Something they'd done wrong to hold over their head?" There was a time Dave would have loved that sort of information to discredit Sandro with Nia.

"Sometimes, it was information," Marisa revealed. "More often it was people."

"People?"

"*Si*, you know, he threatened their family. With Sandro, he threatened his Sandro's *zia y zio*, his aunt and uncle, as well as . . . Nia and her family."

She cut a look at him. He was sure she saw shock in his gaze. "Nia?" he choked out.

"*Si*. Poppa knew all about her. Her brothers."

She'd been at risk? And then Sandro took her to Italy? Carlo had still been in Italy a decade ago. Dave's blood pressure soared.

"After that, my father tried to bring Sandro into the business, he wanted Giuseppe's business, but Sandro refused. Poppa ruined his soccer career in Italy in retaliation. Forced Sandro to flee to America. The rest you know. It is only fate that we all ended up in New York together."

Dave struggled to bring his spinning thoughts back to the story, when in reality, at the moment all he wanted to do was strangle Sandro. It was his fault Nia was in danger now. Sandro kept her in his life knowing she would be in danger. He could have broken off their relationship, flown back to Italy and left her to Dave. Yeah, he'd royally screwed up, but she would have forgiven him. And he could have made her happy. Without endangering her life.

Marisa watched him as if she knew all his thoughts. That idea made him uncomfortable. Then again, was she not baring a part of herself to him?

He swallowed his frustration. "And Paolo. What about him?"

Marisa picked up her story. "As I got to know him more, he told me about my mother."

"Your mother?" What could he tell her about her mother? As far as Dave knew, her mother had a stroke that left her not much more than a vegetable. It happened back in Italy, when Marisa was still a young girl—which had to be hard on an only daughter. "What could he tell you about your mother? I thought she had a stroke?"

"This is what my father tells the world. To me, he said that she had overdosed."

"Overdosed? As in drugs? Why would she do that?" Was there abuse involved? Did the woman have a moral dilemma when she realized she was married to a mobster? Did she try to leave and couldn't escape? But no, what sort of mother would abandon her child? Was Marisa a child? He tried to calculate the years, how old

214

Marisa would have been, but his thoughts were a jumble.

"How old were you?"

"Twelve."

"Was it an accidental overdose? Is that it?"

Marisa shook her head.

Dave guessed again. "She tried to kill herself then? Why would she do that when she had a young daughter who needed her?"

Marisa dropped her gaze and was silent so long that he thought she wasn't going to answer him.

But Paolo had known. Dave felt a twinge of jealousy that this cop, the one who died, the one who she loved, knew the truth and Dave didn't. No, wait. Paolo told her the truth, Dave realized. She hadn't known.

A truth that she obviously didn't want to share with Dave. "I'm sorry, I'm over—"

"She didn't overdose."

"No? And she didn't have a stroke? Then, what—"

"She had a lobotomy."

Dave went rigid. "A . . . a . . ." Surely he didn't hear correctly. "A *lobotomy*?"

Marisa's nod was barely perceptible, but tears silently leaked out of her eyes.

Dave automatically passed her a tissue from the box on the end table, while his mind struggled through the chaotic jumble of his thoughts. It was an old procedure, once quite common to treat mental illness and other conditions, of cutting the frontal lobe of the brain. "Do they even do those anymore?"

"Obviously." She sniffed. "Yes, they still perform them occasionally if that's the only treatment the doctors feel they are left with."

"Your mother, she was crazy then?"

215

"No." Marisa's head shake was emphatic. "My mother was vibrant. Fun. Maybe a little selfish, but she had a good heart. People liked being around her, they all wanted to be her friend."

"Then . . .this was done as some form of punishment at your father's wishes?"

Surely he was wrong with that guess, but Marisa's nod said otherwise.

"Did she . . . cheat on your father?" He was reaching for motivations for such a barbaric action. "Try to leave him?"

Another slight nod. "She tried to leave him, yes. But not for another man."

"Another woman?"

Marisa laughed, a quick, startled sound.

"It's been known to happen," Dave defended.

"True. And maybe in a way . . . " She sighed, then stared off again.

Dave waited.

While Marisa warred with herself. Should she tell him? Not even Paolo had known the truth; the police, of course, had the same theories as Dave. But once Paolo told her what had been done to momma, Marisa knew the reason why. And she couldn't tell him. No, she'd rather pretend it never happened, be happy that Paolo loved her and believe that a new life was possible.

Now, she knew fairy tales were lies and only nightmares were true.

She needed Dave to stay away. She wasn't going to make the same mistake twice, endanger someone else. Laying here in nothing more than a robe was a really bad idea. It was too hard for her to fight her attraction and his, too, and nothing good would come from it if they

216

gave into temptation. When all was said and done, he would despise her, so it was best to keep him away now. The few minutes' pleasure would not offset the pain later. And there would be plenty of pain.

"Marisa?" he said gently.

She glanced at him and braced herself. Steadying her nerves, she began, "From the outside, we looked like the perfect family. Sunday mornings we went to mass. And Sunday afternoon we had a big family dinner, typical Italian. Poppa would sometimes entertain friends during these dinners. I was precocious as a little girl. Poppa's friends, all men older than him as he was still working his way up in the family, delighted in bouncing me on their knee."

He smiled slightly. "I bet you were an adorable little girl."

"Maybe." She shrugged. "But that was not a good thing."

Confusion clouded his eyes, and in a minute she knew she would see horror, disbelief. She plunged ahead.

"My father was ambitious. He would do anything to get ahead. Anything."

Dave opened his mouth. To question? To object? She didn't know. She placed two fingers across his lips to keep him silent.

"Anything," she repeated. "I was nine when my father struck the first deal. My virginity was the price."

Dave squeezed her arm tightly, almost painfully. She didn't mind. No matter how much the pain, it was nothing compared to the terror of a wrinkled old man stripping off her clothes, roughly fingering her and then shoving his penis inside her. His slobbery, smelly tobacco-and-espresso breath mouth cut off her scream.

She clenched her teeth. "Afterwards, the fat old pig had patted me on the head as my reward."

"My God," Dave exploded. "I can't bel—"

The look she shot him silenced him immediately. Clamping down on every bit of emotion, she continued, "My father wasn't the only one to sell my favors. My brother Massi learned of my new talents and sold me to his friends. When I was twelve, I stole a stiletto, and no one ever touched me without my permission after that. No one. The first boy who tried, I stabbed."

Yes, it was there, the look of shock. Horror. She expected revulsion next. But she should have known better. No, Dave the good Boy Scout, the pristine FBI man, had anger in his eyes, not revulsion.

"I—"

"Poppa sent me off to school, then. And paid off the boy's family. No, I didn't kill him," she answered the question she saw in his eyes. "But he did spend time in the hospital."

Dave visibly reined in his anger. "Your mom, did she know then?"

Marisa shook her head. "No, I don't think so. I do think she found out. She had the . . . surgery while I was off at school."

"But you thought it was a drug overdose?

"Yes. Poppa told me it was my fault that she overdosed. That she found out what a whore I was, and that I'd stabbed that boy, and she was overcome with embarrassment." Knowing how fiery and passionate her mother used to be Marisa couldn't believe she'd fallen for her father's lies. "She hadn't wanted me to go off to school. So, I think she pushed and found out what was going on, and then planned to leave my father." That's what Marisa chose to believe anyway.

"Your father wouldn't let her divorce?"

"Bosses don't get divorced. And my father always wanted to be boss."

Dave swallowed, his face now smooth and hard to read. "And you came back . . . to the family?"

"I thought I needed to be here. But momma is no more than a child most days. Most time she doesn't recognize me." That was most painful of all.

"I'm sorry," Dave whispered.

"Before I could decide what to do with my life, I met Paolo, who suggested I make myself invaluable to my father with my computer skills.

"I did as he asked, although at the time I thought there little need. My plans were to turn *peniti*. Witness. And after I testified, Paolo was going to leave the police. And marry me. We were going to live in the protection program together. We were going to take momma, too."

"How did Paolo die?" Dave asked, although it looked as if he already knew the answer.

She told him anyway. "He was murdered."

"Your father?"

Her lips flattened. "My father ordered the hit, but my brother carried it out."

"Had they found out you were helping Paolo?"

"At first I thought so. But then—that morning—I learned differently. Giuseppe had witnessed a crime outside his restaurant committed by one of poppa's *Mafiosi*. I don't know why Paolo never told me. Maybe he was trying to protect me somehow.

"But that morning, I overheard my father talking to my brother. I figured out what was happening. As soon as I could, I rushed to Giuseppe's house. But the traffic. I couldn't get through. I was too late. The bomb—"

Dave flinched as if he'd been hit. "Your brother set a bomb?"

Marisa nodded. "Paolo was there to pick up Giuseppe and take him to court. Beppe was just reaching for the car door when it exploded. Paolo was already inside."

She felt herself on the edge of tremors. She sat up, gathered her robe tightly around her.

"And you know it was your brother who set the bomb?"

"Oh, yes, he's very talented in explosives. He taught me how to make a couple of different bombs. Even if I hadn't heard my father talking to him, I would have recognized Massimo's work."

"He taught you how to wire a car. He taught you how to build a bomb." Dave's eyes asked the question while his lips held silent.

"*Si, la mia famiglia* is the definition of dysfunction, no?"

"Remind me not to make you angry," Dave joked.

His words brought a faint smile to her face.

Dave continued, "But . . . Giuseppe's still alive . . ."

"It was a remote control device—Massimo likes that kind, he likes to watch—it wasn't meant to kill Giuseppe, just give him a message. Still, the blast injured him. He was in protective custody at the hospital until he recovered from his injuries."

"And then he fled to the States," Dave concluded. "And didn't testify, did he?"

"No, he didn't testify. I don't blame him." She sighed. "He lived in Dallas coaching soccer until Sandro asked him to join in the restaurant business. Sandro knew Luciana always wanted her own restaurant again after they were forced to leave Italy."

"And after Paolo died, you were still stuck with the *family*, and . . . all that entailed."

"*Si*. Once we moved to America, poppa made me help at the company. By that time I was very good with computers. "

Dave pulled her into a comfortable hug. "You are amazing."

Her eyes widened. She certainly hadn't expected words of praise.

"We'll get you out, Marisa," he continued. "Trust me."

She shook her head and said softly,"I've found out the hard way there is no one to trust but myself." She looked at him. "But sometimes, I get tired. And I need someone to lean on. Thank you." She touched her lips to his.

Just a soft, sweet kiss of thanks. They both knew this wasn't the time for them, that there might never be a time for them. But in this moment, they were two people offering and sharing comfort.

"We need to get on those accounts. I'll get dressed. You get my computer booted up."

Once dressed, and in front of her computer, she became all business. Dave stood behind her, watching, when his phone rang and Frankie told him the accountant had been picked up.

"We're good to go," Dave said when he disconnected the call. "Roberto's in custody."

Marisa typed in more numbers.

Dave gave a low whistle. "Princess, your father is

loaded."

She barely glanced at him. "He likes to save for a rainy day, and all that. His parents were children of the Depression."

An hour later, she finished, closed the web browser and took the last bite of her sandwich. "I'm hoping with my names on both accounts that they'll transfer quickly. The faster this is over with, the better."

"Couldn't agree more." Dave's phone rang again. "What now?" he muttered, clearly not expecting another phone call. "Armstrong," he answered, and then didn't talk. Immediately, a frown formed on his face. At last, he said, "I'll be there as soon as I can."

Alarmed, she tried to catch his gaze.

At last he looked at her and snarled, "Son of a bitch!"

"What? What is it?"

He punched the phone off and slammed a fist against the table.

Heart pounding, she demanded, "Is it Sandro? Have they caught him?"

"No, but we've got a shitload more trouble. Grab your jacket. Let's go."

* * *

Earlier

Carmine drove down the long street of row houses, each home looking like the other only with a different paint job. He slowed the truck, coming up to a sandy peach house with brown trim. "This better be the right one, we're at the corner."

Joey checked the address. "Yeah, this is it."

"We going in now, or we gonna wait until dark?" Ralphie asked.

Joey would've liked to have waited. He'd had a busy damn day. Waiting was not an option though. "Carlo said now. I'll take the front door. You two stay over there out of sight. Make sure you got on your ski masks." He pointed over to the side of the front porch by the shrubs. "And remember, don't hurt the kid. Anyone else sees your face or gets in your way, whack 'em."

The three men exited the stolen four-door city utility truck. Joey adjusted his phony uniform, went to the front door and knocked.

"Who is it?"

"City worker. We got to get to that gas line in your back yard that's leaking. Could be dangerous."

The door opened a fraction, the chain obviously still on. "A gas leak—"

The Fed never finished his sentence. Joey kicked the door, easily busting the flimsy chain. He pulled the trigger on his gun and shot the FBI agent twice before pulling on his ski mask.

"Freeze."

A man with a gun came around the corner. Another suit. Joey shot in reflex. The man went down. Carmine and Ralphie ran inside the open front door.

"Find the kid," Joey told them.

Carmine ran up the stairs, Ralphie went to the left.

"What's going on?" The old man came around from the dining room on the right, took in the situation in a glance. "*Cara*, get the baby. Run!" he shouted before he picked up a fireplace poker and came at Joey.

Joey shot him.

223

"Find the old lady," he yelled. "She's got the kid."

In less than a minute, Joey heard her screeching. "No, you can't have him!" Joey found Ralphie and the old lady in the kitchen. She had a death grip on the child. The little boy set up howls of his own as Ralphie struggled to pull him out of her grasp.

Joey came up behind the elderly woman and tapped her on the head with the butt of his gun. She dropped like a log. Ralphie caught the kid before he fell to the floor.

"Shut him up, we'll have the whole fucking neighborhood calling the cops."

Ralphie jiggled the boy helplessly. "Shh, *bambino*. Shh, shh."

"Carmine, bring that truck around to the back so we can hustle him in and go."

Carmine ran out the front door, while Joey unlocked the back door and the fence gate across the driveway.

Moments later he directed to Ralphie. "Get in. Hurry. Let's go."

The truck doors slammed shut. The three men drove off with little Danny Crocetti.

CHAPTER 22

"I love you, Sandro."

He heard her message too late. Sandro wearily rubbed the back of his neck and disconnected the throw away phone from his voice mail on his cell phone. If he'd had his phone, he would have gotten her call. He had been at the very same store where she had been, only right down the road when she called. They might be together now.

But his phone had been in his SUV. He'd only just now thought to call and check his messages remotely. Too late.

Nia was back in Carlo's hands.

He slammed his hand against the Honda's steering wheel. Frustration ate at him. How much longer? In reality he knew they could put the plan into effect within the next twenty-four hours. Not that long.

A lifetime.

No. Soon, Carlo would be dead and Sandro would be free. Soon, he would have his wife back. A happy ending.

Simple.

Anything but simple.

Too many things could go wrong.

Faith.

Faith would help him survive until his family was reunited.

He pulled out the addresses again. Checked with his map and put his car in gear. Yes, it was a long shot that he would find her like this. But it was something to do. Something to keep the fears pushed away.

He'd been driving for hours when the throw away phone rang.

"Sandro. There's been some trouble," Dave said without preliminaries.

Sandro's heart stuttered. "What trouble?"

"Are you driving?"

"Yes, of course."

"Pull over."

"What's happened? Is it Nia?" Sandro's erratic heart rate jumped to triple time. He couldn't bear to ask if they'd found her body dumped on the side of the road somewhere. Of course, that would make no sense for Carlo to kill his bait. Unless he counted on Sandro coming after him to kill him. Yes, Carlo was warped enough to use that reasoning. Because it would be right—

"No, Sandro, it isn't anything about Nia. We need to meet."

"What's wrong, damn it?" Sandro demanded, growing tired of trying to guess what Dave didn't want to say.

"Where are you? I need to bring you in."

"Tell me now, Dave. Right now," Sandro growled, his patience gone.

Dave sighed. "They got Daniele."

"Nooooo." An animal-like shriek of pain ripped through the car. Sandro realized it came from him. He jerked the steering wheel hard toward the curb and slammed on the brakes, barely aware he missed a parked Mercedes by mere inches. "Ah *por Dio*, no. No," he said again. "No, no, no." He demanded answers. Threatened Dave's life.

"Damn it, Sandro, speak English. I can't understand you."

Sandro drew a ragged breath. Tried to remember the English words. His mind failed him.

Marisa came on the phone. "Sandro. *Caro, calma, per favore*." Her Italian words sank through the thick fog surrounding his brain.

"What happened?" he demanded in Italian.

"Poppa's men found the safe house. They broke in—Daniele will be all right, Sandro," she soothed when Sandro broke out in a string of crude Italian. "Poppa will not hurt him, this I promise."

"You cannot make those promises, Marisa. He does not play by the same rules now. I do not play by the same rules."

"*Si*, I understand. Sandro, there is more. Your *zio y zia*. They were injured."

"Injured? *Dio*! Can't the FBI do anything right? How badly were they hurt?"

"They are both in the hospital. Giuseppe has been shot. He is in ICU. Luciana was knocked unconscious. She has a concussion but she's awake now."

"Beppe . . . will he live?"

"They don't know, *caro*."

"What hospital?"

"Sandro, you cannot think to see them. It is too

dangerous."

"I must."

"Sandro, no—"

"Tell me, Marisa."

With a sigh, she told him.

The phone went dead in her ear. She handed it back to Dave. "He's on his way to the hospital."

Dave nodded grimly. He punched some numbers on his phone. "Sandro's coming in. Get our men in place."

* * *

As Sandro sped to the hospital, he asked himself how things could have gone so terribly wrong. But he knew the answer. It was his fault. Had he been a stronger man, he would have taken a stand against Carlo from the beginning. Found some way to not get under the Mafia's control.

Yet to this day, he didn't know what he could have done differently. Except perhaps abandon Nia, leave her behind in America. Instead of making her his wife.

But no, impossible. She had been the most precious thing to enter his life. He had been too selfish to give her up.

And then she had given him a son.

How could it be wrong for him to have the woman he loved, a son he adored? Every man had that right. And he had done what he thought necessary to preserve his family. Preserve his happiness.

In so doing, he had risked everything and everyone.

It was up to him, and him alone, to right his

wrongs.

First, he would check on his aunt and uncle. Promise to get Danny back. Give his uncle a reason to live.

Afterward, he and Dave and Marisa needed to talk, to plan.

No, to take action.

The time for planning had past. Now, it was time to rescue his family. And right the old wrongs.

Darkness had fallen by the time he pulled into the hospital parking lot. White snow reflected the parking lot lights. He pulled up the collar of his jacket and tugged on a beanie cap he'd bought for the bad weather. He hoped no one recognized him. Scanning his surroundings for possible threats, he kept one hand inside his jacket, firmly gripping the Browning 9 mm he'd taken off that mobster. There'd been no need to buy another.

Still, the three men came from nowhere. He pulled the gun out of the shoulder holster he'd bought and aimed.

"Hold it, Sandro. We're FBI." With their hands raised in the air, they appeared to have no weapons. Sandro leveled his gun at one. "You. Prove it. Toss me your ID. Carefully."

"My name's Frankie," the man said as he removed his ID and slid it across the ground.

Sandro bent to pick it up, holding it under the parking lot light to read it. "I have a friend named Francesco. We call him Frankie sometimes."

"Yes, I know. Francesco Berti. He plays goalkeeper for Italy, as well as *Internazionale Milano.*"

"You watch Italian *calcio*?" Sandro looked over the ID. It looked authentic. Still, it could be fake. What did he know?

"Of course. I'm Italian. I watch soccer every chance I get."

"Let me see your driver's license."

"Huh?"

"How do I know if this is real? Let me see more."

Frankie took his wallet out of his pocket and slid it across.

"What is your birthdate? Your address."

Frankie answered the questions. Sandro tossed him back the wallet. "Okay, now the others."

"Sandro, you saw I'm for real—"

"Yes, you are FBI. But they could be Mafia. There has been at least one leak and now my wife and son are in danger."

"We're wasting time here, Sandro. You're out in the open, putting yourself at risk. Already your aunt and uncle were injured, and two of our men lost their lives trying to protect your family."

Shock stabbed him. Marisa had mentioned no deaths. "Then your men better hurry and show me their IDs." He swung the gun to the next man who slid his ID and driver's license across the snowy parking lot.

Then Sandro checked the third man's information.

"Satisfied now?" Frankie asked.

Sandro stuck his gun into his shoulder holster. "Why were you waiting for me?"

"Dave sent us to keep you safe."

"I'm going to see *mio zio y zia*."

"We'll escort you."

"I need no escort."

"Yes, you do. You're taking a big risk coming here. You know it."

Sandro didn't want protection, didn't trust anybody other than himself. Trying to depend on others, to do things the proper way had only made matters much worse.

"They'll be watching the hospital," Frankie reminded him. "They could be watching now."

Sandro knew Frankie was right on that point at least. "You cannot take me into protective custody."

"I won't try," Frankie promised. "We'll just walk with you."

"Okay."

"You need to give me your weapon."

Sandro stiffened. "Why would I do that?"

"There's a metal detector and guard at every door. I can get your weapon inside for you."

Sandro didn't want to be without his guns in the hospital, even with supposedly honest FBI men protecting him. There was no choice but to turn over his guns. He pulled the Browning 9mm back out, released the clip, then handed the unloaded weapon to Frankie. Sandro handed the clip to another agent.

Frankie's lips tipped in a small smile as he pocketed the gun.

"Wait," Sandro said. He pulled up the leg on his jeans and took out his back-up weapon, Marisa's derringer. He unloaded it, too, before he handed it to Frankie and the bullets to the last agent, making his weapons and ammo spread out among them. Perhaps overly cautious. Better that than dead, though.

"A back-up." Frankie nodded his approval. "Good precaution."

Sandro entered the hospital with the three men, waiting while they got clearance to enter with their weapons. Down the hallway toward the elevator and out of sight of the guard, Frankie stopped Sandro and handed him back his guns. The other two agents gave him his ammunition. Sandro breathed a sigh of relief.

"It is almost ICU visiting time. You wanna see your uncle first? There aren't restricted hours on your aunt." Frankie punched the button on the elevator.

"Yes, my uncle first. How is he?"

Elevator doors opened and the men stepped on.

"He's holding his own. He took the bullet in his chest, but it missed his heart by an inch or so. He regained consciousness pretty quick after surgery, and the docs say that's a good sign." Frankie led the way off the elevator.

Sandro followed him down the hallway. The other two men stuck close, forming a protective barrier around him.

Frankie pushed open the door that said ICU waiting room. "We wait in here and then they'll announce when it's visiting time."

"Is there someone watching him?"

"Yes, we have a guard posted. But we really don't think Giuseppe's in any more danger. He told us he was trying to protect your son. The men were wearing masks so I think their only intent was to take Danny. They only shot those who got in the way. Except for your aunt. She told us she was trying to run with Danny when one of the men stopped her and tried to get Danny. She fought with him until someone tapped her on the head. After that, she doesn't remember anything."

The thought that men in masks snatched his son and the terror Danny must have felt being ripped from *Zia's* arms, nearly sent Sandro crashing to the floor. He clenched his muscles and forced himself to remain standing.

Frankie stared at him. "I'm sorry about your son, Sandro. I don't think Carlo's going to hurt him. What I think is he snatched Danny because Nia was so close to escaping. He's just trying to keep her in line until he can get to you. That's why Dave wants you guarded now."

"I don't need—"

"Sandro, *caro*, you are safe." Marisa hurried to embrace him when he entered the waiting room. "I have been so fearful for you snooping around the warehouses. Afraid someone would recognize you."

He accepted Marisa's condolences, but put her aside and squared off with Dave as he approached.

"Sandro, I'm sor—"

Sandro slammed his fist into Dave's face. Dave stumbled back into the wall. Sandro advanced, all his anger and frustration of the past two days targeted at Dave. He grabbed Dave's shirt. Oblivious to his throbbing hand, he reared back to hit Dave again.

Two strangers in the waiting room gasped at the scene unfolding before them.

"Sandro, no!" Marisa cried.

Frankie and the other two agents rushed him, pulling at him. "Let him go, Sandro," Frankie ordered.

Sandro had no choice but to release Dave. "You told me my son would be safe," he growled.

Marisa hurried to Dave and helped him as he pushed away from the wall. Blood dripped from his nose.

"My aunt and uncle were injured; my uncle might die because of your incompetence." Anger was still pounding through Sandro.

"I lost two men today," Dave said, holding a tissue

that Marisa had given him to his bleeding nose.

Sandro felt little sympathy. "I lost my son. My wife." Everything was getting worse, spiraling out of control.

"We'll get them back."

"No, I'll get them back."

"You can't go against them alone."

"I won't be alone. You will help. And if you make one more mistake to risk my family, I will kill you."

"Calm down, Sandro," Frankie ordered.

"Let me go," Sandro demanded.

The men holding him waited until Dave nodded before releasing Sandro's arms.

He walked to Marisa, who turned her attention from Dave to face Sandro. Her wide-eyed gaze locked with his. With sure movements, Sandro lifted her Florentine cross necklace and jerked. The chain broke off in his hand.

She barely twitched.

Sanity returning, more mindful of the people who were watching the drama unfold, he spoke to her in Italian. "You are my prisoner now, *Principessa*." He smoothed her hair, pleaded with his eyes to soften the blow. "I know you want away from your father, but your freedom may have to be sacrificed."

"I understand." She didn't blink.

"No," Dave said, after Frankie quietly translated what Sandro had said. "That's not acceptable."

Sandro approached Dave, not stopping until he was face-to-face with the taller man. "Then you better make sure everything works just right, Dave. Because I will sacrifice whoever is necessary to rescue my family."

A disembodied female voice came over the loud

234

speakers in the waiting room then. "It is now visiting time in ICU. Please limit your visits to no more than two people at a time. Visits will be limited to fifteen minutes. Thank you."

Sandro stepped away from Dave. "Which room?" he asked Frankie.

"Come on, I'll take you."

"When I return, we will talk more," Sandro told Dave and Marisa.

Frankie and Sandro walked out together, the other two people who had been in the waiting room following at a safe distance, off to see their own friends or family members after having witnessed the unfolding drama.

Marisa wondered about the tragedies in those people's families. Wondered if humankind was destined to suffer together forever. She shuddered.

Dave took her hand. "You okay?"

"*Si*, I am fine. But you look like shit. Sit down and wait here." She went to the small waiting room restroom and wet some paper towels.

She wiped at the dried blood on his face, trying not to grimace. "Looks like it hurts."

"Hurts like hell," Dave agreed, talking like he had a bad cold. He gingerly touched his swollen nose. "Feels like it's three times bigger than normal. I can imagine what it must look like."

She tilted her head, then chose not to comment. "I can go to the cafeteria, get some ice," she offered.

"No, stay with me. I don't want you out of my sight."

Marisa nodded and dabbed at the blood that had dripped onto his shirt. "I don't think there is much we can do for this shirt while you are still wearing it."

"I've got a change of clothes in my car. It'll be fine until then."

"I am sorry." She laid her fingers against his face, his cheek warm beneath her touch.

"I can't blame him," Dave admitted. "Now, if he hurts you—"

"I understand. He has no choice."

"Yes, there must be a choice. I won't let you be sacrificed."

"I will pray that everything will work out right." She reached for her necklace, then remembered Sandro had it. She let her hand drop as tears welled in her eyes. "I never take it off," she whispered uselessly.

"I know." Dave pulled her into his arms. "I'll get it back for you," he promised. "I'll get it back."

* * *

Tubes and wires ran out of every part of Giuseppe's body. Sandro's uncle looked pale and frail and a little out-of-this-world against the stark white sheets and steel-and-tile room. The whole experience reminded Sandro eerily of death and he wanted his uncle out of this place. He wanted him back healthy and laughing and arguing with the head chef. Sandro vowed to make it happen.

He bent close, ignoring the antiseptic smell. "Beppe, it's Sandro. Wake up, *Zio*."

At Sandro's command, Giuseppe slowly opened his eyes. His normally sparkling green eyes looked dull and lifeless. "Sandro—" He clenched his eyes shut as if a spasm of pain hit him.

Sandro was alarmed. "Do you need a *dottore*?"

"Daniele. They took our little Daniele."

Sandro gently squeezed his uncle's hand. "I will get him back, *Zio*. I promise you. I will get him back."

CHAPTER 23

"Wake up, *Bella*."

"Hm?" Nia fought against the voice urging her from the sweet escape of sleep.

"You see, I told you she is so tired."

"You are very generous, Angie, since she tried to take you out with a flower vase."

The new voice snapped her eyes open. How could she have slept in that damned chair—hands and feet bound, even if her feet were propped up on the desk?

"I would have done no less in her position."

"More likely, you'd have killed the person. Ah, now she's awake."

Nia eyed Carlo warily. He was dressed in an Italian designer suit, same as Angie. Instead of a tie, Carlo wore his pale blue shirt with the top button open to expose a gold cross necklace resting in his dark chest hairs. Trimmer than Angie, Carlo had a hard-edge, air-of-vanity around him.

"Good evening, *Signora* Crocetti." His voice was heavily accented.

Her voice held contempt. "So, you've decided to show your—"

"Bella."

She shot Angie a look. Caught the pleading in his eyes. Carlo must truly be powerful to make a big man like Angie so nervous. She bit back her insults.

"She looks worse than you, Angie."

"I told you Mikey roughed her up good."

"Dear cousin Mikey. I told him she was a guest. But no manners. That side of the family always was a rude bunch."

"Rude?" Nia burst out angrily, drawing Carlo's attention back to her. She couldn't hold her tongue as Angie cautioned. Too much had happened. "You call what Mikey did to me rude? Untie me for five minutes, and I'll show you rude."

"Bella!"

Carlo waved Angie off. "I've already seen some of your handiwork," he said to her nodding toward Angelo. "And I was told you broke Mikey's wrist. I believe I will pass on a sample for myself."

"I'm glad his wrist is broken," she said. "If I see him again, I'll break his head."

"She is very good at breaking heads," Angie commented rubbing his, obviously trying to dispel the palpable tension.

Carlo smiled. "Too late for you to have the pleasure, I'm afraid."

He could mean one of two things. One, that she wouldn't have a chance to get at Mikey again because she was going to die, or two . . . it was too late because Mikey was already—

"Yes, I see you understand," Carlo said. "Mikey met with an unfortunate accident. A gun to his head." He made a gun image with his forefinger and thumb.

That he seemed to read her mind gave her chills. "You had him killed because he beat me up?"

"I had him killed because he didn't follow my orders."

The cold grew within her. Just like that, Mikey displeased Carlo, and he was dead. Just like that, a man was an unlucky witness, and he was dead. How many others had been murdered? Would be murdered?

"Man, if you kill all your employees who screw up, your turnover rate must be sky high." She was really too tired to think of minding her mouth.

Angie made a funny noise, and at a glance, Nia saw him frantically shaking his head at her. But her attention quickly refocused on Carlo who was approaching her. He pulled up a chair before her, diamond and gold rings glittering on his well-manicured fingers. She wondered how much blood was on those fingers.

"*Si, Signora* Crocetti," he said softly, his flat eyes blinking like a shark. Cold, dead eyes. "Sometimes my turnover rate is sky high as you say. But it's a peculiar thing, there is always someone waiting to take their place. Ready to follow my every command. And is it for the money? No. It is for the power, the prestige, they get from being a part of the Peruzzo family."

Nia realized she was dealing with something way outside her realm of existence. Something sinister and evil. These people didn't have any sense of right and wrong other than what they deemed fell within that realm. How did Sandro, someone so honorable and upstanding, ever get involved with these people?

Worse, would she and Sandro die because of these warped men?

No!

That was defeatist thinking, and she wouldn't be defeated.

"My mistake," she said. "I didn't realize there were so many sleazebuckets in the world."

Carlo laughed as he stood back up. "Angie, I don't think she likes us."

"You can't blame me, can you? You haven't exactly rolled out the red carpet for me here." She tried to lift her tied hands and feet to make her point.

"Ah, you don't like the bindings? Or is it the surroundings?" He indicated the sparsely furnished office with its bare wood and glass walls and cold concrete floor. "You started out in a nice country house. Who wouldn't have loved it? But you kept running off, determined not to accept our hospitality. So, *Signora* Crocetti, you can say you brought your circumstances upon yourself."

"Forgive me if I find your logic skewed."

Still chuckling, Carlo told Angie, "She is very much like my Marisa, *si*?"

"Who's Marisa?" Nia played carefully dumb, though she was pretty sure she knew.

He pulled out his wallet, removed a picture. "My daughter."

Nia kept her face blank, although the picture was clearly of the woman who was with Sandro—

"You know her?" Carlo was as perceptive as ever.

Her instincts screamed that Marisa was somehow helping Sandro. "No, I don't know her personally," Nia answered truthfully. "But I've seen her at the restaurant." That much was true as well.

Sandro was a faithful husband. The only

reasonable explanation was that Marisa, for whatever reason, was helping him. Surely that gave Sandro an edge to have the Mafia don's daughter helping him. Nia just had to make certain not to reveal what she knew. Or thought she knew.

Carlo was still probing her with a look that said he wasn't certain he believed her. She had to change the subject.

"Tell me, since I'm here for this enforced vacation, what do you want from my husband?"

"To talk to him of course."

"Of course. Ever heard of a telephone?"

Carlo turned to Angie and smiled. "I like her." He faced her again. "To answer your question, telephones are so impersonal, especially when there's business to discuss."

"I can see how a gun wouldn't reach through the phone lines."

"You think I want to kill your husband?"

Nia tossed him a phony coy look. "I don't think you went to all this trouble so you could invite him to dinner."

"I love your husband like a son. Yet—"

"You're crazy! I've never heard him mention you."

Carlo's eyes narrowed. "Now, you are being rude." He adjusted his suit jacket. "As I said, I loved him and yet he was set to betray me. Of course, if he apologizes, I may forgive him."

"Betray? Apologize? I'm not following you."

"We are in business together."

"Sandro's not in business with you!"

"Of course he is. With the *ristorante*."

"No. I was there at the lawyer's office when all the legal work was done. You have no connections to our restaurant. I know you frequently eat there, but you certainly don't own part—" She broke off. "Oh, God. You're laundering money through our restaurant. How?" She shook her head. "That makes no sense. Sandro would never agree."

"You never know what makes a man say yes, do you?"

"I know Sandro. You must have threatened him somehow . . . threatened us. That's it, isn't it? You threatened his family."

"Threats. Now, that is such an ugly concept, *signora*. I just presented a business proposal that was mutually agreeable to us. He couldn't refuse."

Nia felt sick. Worse, her reserve of courage was wearing thin. At the moment, she could see no way out alive. For her or for Sandro.

"*Signora* Crocetti, do not look so sad. I am a fair man. Once Sandro shows himself, I'm sure we can resolve our differences."

The only resolution she saw was for someone to die. She stiffened her spine. That someone certainly couldn't be a member of her family.

"There, now you look better. And to show you I'm not heartless, I have brought you a present."

"Just get this tape off me and keep your present."

"I will do better. I will loose your bindings, and I will give you your present, too."

Unease skittered through her stomach. His present couldn't be good for her. He was too pleased with himself. Sandro! Had they already found him and were just torturing her before they killed them both?

"Angie, get that tape off her. I will return *un attimo*."

"*Bella*, you are too fearless." Angie cut through the duct tape on her arms with a wicked-looking pocket knife.

Fearless? She was scared to death. It was only through a supreme effort that every muscle in her body wasn't visibly shaking.

"You are lucky he is in a good mood," he continued.

"Angie, he's going to kill me. Surely you see that? It doesn't matter what I say to him."

"No. He said he has you a present."

"Yes, as warped as he is, I can only imagine. Do you know what it is?"

"No."

"Probably a .357 Magnum tied up with a pretty bow."

"I cannot believe that, *Bella*. Carlo is not heartless to kill *la madonna*."

She rubbed the circulation back into her wrists. "You think being pregnant's going to keep me alive? No, as soon as Sandro shows himself, Carlo plans to kill me. You know it. I see it in your eyes."

Angie bent down, concentrating on the tape around her feet. When he finished, she said, "Don't get in my way next time, Angie. I don't want to have to hurt you again."

Looking unhappy, Angie was saved from comment when Carlo's voice sounded outside the office. He was singing an Italian children's song.

Nia frowned. "What the—"

Carlo opened the door and entered.

"Oh, God!" Nia's chest caved in. "Daniele!"

Angie caught her before she rushed Carlo.

She turned on Angie. "Let me go." She swung at him, kicked at him. Without food all day and with the physical demands she'd put on her body, her blows were weak and ineffectual.

"*Calma, Bella*. Be calm." Angie wrapped her in a tight bear hug.

The moment he saw her, Danny started screaming for her, squirming in Carlo's arms.

She strained against Angie's hold. "He's got my son." Hot tears burned her cheeks. "He's got my son." Nia lunged, but Angie's grip remained firm and secure. "Give me my baby, you son of a bitch. Let him go."

"Really, *Signora* Crocetti. Such language in front of your child. You are upsetting him."

"I'm not the one upsetting him. Let him go!"

Danny's screams matched hers as they reached for each other. Tears flowed out of big hazel green eyes that were so much like his father's.

The pain hit her like fierce blows. "Please," she whispered, hating herself for begging. "Let me have my son."

The pleading seemed to please Carlo. "Certainly. I'm a thoughtful man, see? I have brought your Daniele to you."

His 'thoughtfulness' felt like sharp shards of glass piercing her skin. She wondered how Carlo had gotten him, what had happened to the babysitter?

He released Danny. Angie let her go. She sank to her knees to embrace her son. "*Mio bambino, mio bambino*," she crooned over and over until he quieted and all that was left of his tears were soft little hiccups.

"Such a beautiful picture. Mother and child. Your son looks very much like his father." He touched Danny's curly hair.

"Stay away from him," Nia hissed as she pulled her son protectively closer.

"He could have been my grandson."

The thought of that man as Danny's grandfather was too horrible to contemplate.

"Ah, you won't ask. But I will tell you anyway. Your husband and my daughter were once engaged."

Another blow. Carlo was a malicious man despite his claims.

"Don't look so distressed. It was many years ago. He is several years older than you, no?"

His question didn't need an answer and he continued with his monologue. "She broke off the engagement long before he met you in the United States. Yes," he said to her shocked look. "I know all about when he met you. How Beppe was your coach. And I know all about your family and where your parents and each of your five brothers live now."

She felt sick. It was like he was an octopus with tentacles everywhere.

"It is a good thing in my business to know all about my family."

"We're not part of your family."

"Oh, *si, signora*, you are. Are you not here as my guests?"

She stood, pulled Danny into her arms. "Really, I think we've imposed enough. We can leave now."

"Ah . . ." he chuckled again. "You have the sharp wit. Because you must stay with us, I have brought you your son. As long as you behave, he can stay with you. If you continue with your persistence in trying to escape, I will take him from you. You will know nothing about him then."

She squeezed Danny. Kissed his curls. Tears clogged her throat. She couldn't lose him.

"I know you must be hungry. I will have food brought to you, a bed. Some toys for Daniele. If you cooperate, your stay will be pleasant." He stepped toward the door. "If you don't, remember that I warned you."

Angie followed Carlo out of the office.

They were alone. She and her little boy. Nia held her son. Just held him. Relishing the warmth and weight of his little body. She hadn't known if she would ever see him again.

Daniele squirmed. "Momma, you have owie." He gently patted her bruised face.

"*Si, bambino*. Momma has an owie." She moved to the desk chair and sat down. "Where have you been, little one?"

"*Zio. Zia.*" He bounced in her lap. "I've been with *Zio* and *Zia*."

"So your aunt and uncle have had you?" She wondered where they were now. She prayed they weren't hurt when Carlo's men snatched Daniele, but in the pit of her stomach she feared they were. She'd known Giuseppe and Luciana longer than she'd known Sandro. She knew without a doubt they would fight to the death to protect their family.

She was tempted to question Daniele about how Carlo's men got him, but she didn't want him to have to live through it again.

Frustration chewed at her stomach, making it difficult to eat when Angie brought in food from the local deli.

"I thought perhaps the little one would like chicken. All children seem to like chicken."

"That's fine."

"And you, *Bella*, you eat something, too."

"I'll try."

"No. You must remember the *bambino*."

Sudden tears sprang to her eyes. If she died, there would be no baby. And Danny would without a mother. Perhaps without a father, too. An orphan. Or worse, what if Carlo kept him and raised him to be a crook? Unthinkable.

Angie's brow knit in concern. "Look, just for you I order vegetables and juice." He took the items out of the bag. "I remembered you don't like milk." For such a big man, he seemed awkward and eager to please. She wondered how he got involved in such a sordid life.

She sniffed away her tears. "Thank you." Of them all, Angie seemed to care whether she lived or died. Of course, she could be hallucinating from fear and fatigue.

Once he left, she laid the food out on the desk and helped her son to eat. She ate a few bites herself, knowing she needed food now more than ever. For nourishment, but more importantly for stamina to face whatever would happen. There was bound to be an opportunity to escape again—even though Carlo thought that Danny would make her hesitate. If anything, having Danny made her more determined to get away. And she would need her strength to succeed.

She opened her mouth and shoved in another forkful of green beans.

Later, Angie brought in a cot, a couple of blankets and two pillows. Nia used the small office bathroom to wash Danny's face and ready him for bed. She climbed onto the cot with him.

When Sandro wasn't traveling, he tucked his son into bed at night, telling him some Italian fable or another. Nia wracked her brain to remember one of the stories.

"Where's poppa? Why aren't we home?" Danny asked when she finished the story.

"Poppa's gone right now. And we will be home soon."

"Don't like these men. Want to go home."

"I don't like them either, my sweets, but we'll all be home soon and we can forget them then."

After Danny fell asleep, she kissed him, then closed her eyes and prayed. "Let us all be home soon." She had to believe. Soon. They would be together again.

* * *

The lock rattled. Nia tensed and sat up as the door opened and Angie walked into the office.

"You are still awake."

"Are you alone?" Her gaze searched for any sign of Carlo.

"I am alone."

She relaxed her guard a little.

"The *bambino*," Angie said. "He is sleeping?"

She smiled down at her son, smoothed her fingers over his curly hair. "Yes, he's sound asleep."

"You should be, too."

"I can't sleep."

Angelo nodded, looked thoughtful. "Wait here, I will be right back."

"Not as if I could go anywhere, Angie," she said after he shut the door behind him. When she didn't hear him turn the lock, she considered grabbing up Danny and making a run for it. But no, he said he would be right back. She doubted there would be—

He opened the door again. Ideas of escape flittered away.

Angie had an old-fashioned boom box in one hand, a stack of CDs in the other. "Listening to music sometimes helps me sleep at night."

"Yeah, I bet with all you have on your conscience, it is hard for you to sleep."

Angie didn't defend himself. He looked through the CDs. "Here, I like her. Do you?" He held up a Celine Dion greatest hits CD.

Nia's heart clenched as memories hit her. She'd sung Celine's songs at their restaurant. "Yeah, she's okay."

"Will it wake the *bambino*?"

"No. He can sleep through anything."

Angie nodded. "The sleep of the innocent."

Nia bit back another insult. Angie had tried to be nice, all things considered. She mentally shook her head. Geez, she must be losing it. Making excuses for a mobster.

Celine's voice came softly out of the speakers. Angie settled his bulk in the desk chair. "I've heard you sing at the restaurant before. You are very good."

"Thanks."

"Why have you not gone professional?"

"I have soccer. And my family. There's been no time to pursue a singing career. The music business is very demanding. Very competitive."

"You are blessed with much talent. Perhaps after this next *bambino* you will think it is time to retire from soccer. Then you can sing."

Nia gave a rude laugh. "You really think I'm going to be alive that long, Angie?"

A sad look filled his face. He ran his hand through his salt-and-pepper hair, obviously conflicted. "If I have anything to do with it, *Bella*, you will be alive. And so will your husband."

Tears burned her eyes. She sniffed. "Thanks, Angie."

He pushed his bulk to his feet and awkwardly patted her head. "Try to sleep, *Bella*." He shook his head and muttered, "A bad business," as he closed and locked the door behind him.

* * *

A federal agent led Roberto out of the holding cell to a secure meeting room. His lawyer, waiting at the table, stood when Roberto entered. Roberto had an odd sense that he was on a television drama, because this stuff only happened on crime TV. But there was no bright lights and cameras, just a security camera mounted high in a corner. Strangely, it did not make him feel secure.

Roberto shook his lawyer's hand. Like all men high up in the Peruzzo family, the lawyer dressed well. Three piece designer suit, gold jewelry, manicured fingernails. Roberto had seen the lawyer at the office, but never had much contact with him. Roberto's main focus was his job. He knew he worked for the mob, but he wasn't involved with the seedier side. His job was to find legitimate investments and keep track of the money. The ethics never bothered him, and he never thought he'd be the one arrested when there were bigger crooks than him who worked with Peruzzo.

"Why am I here?" he asked, when they took seats at the table, one on each side.

"I don't know," the lawyer said. "They don't have to formally charge you for seventy-two hours."

"That's three days! I have to sit here that long not knowing why I'm here?"

"Listen, Mr. Torino." The lawyer leaned over the table, closer to Roberto. "I've seen this kind of thing before. I think they have you in custody to give you time to think."

"Time to think? What does that mean?" Roberto demanded.

"Yeah, you know how it goes." The lawyer sat back, shrugged. "You sit here, think, worry, get scared, and when they offer you a deal, you'll be more willing to help."

"A . . . deal? You think they're after Mr. Peruzzo then?"

The lawyer shrugged. "Or one of his associates. It's possible."

A chill skittered down Roberto's spine. His job could be at risk. Worse, if he became a rat, his life could be at risk. But if not, could they keep him locked up? What did they have on him? His thoughts were moving at lightning speed with one scenario after another.

"What can I do?" he whispered, fear stealing his voice.

"Best thing is just to sit here and keep quiet. They'll have to make a move soon, and then we'll know what to do. I just came here to let you know that Mr. Peruzzo is thinking of you."

Somehow, knowing that did not offer Roberto any comfort.

CHAPTER 24

Dave headed to the Crown Vic to get it warmed up while Sandro visited with his aunt and uncle. At Sandro's insistence, Marisa waited inside until he was ready to leave. Dave supposed Sandro thought he was calling the shots now, but Dave didn't see any reason to challenge him over Marisa waiting behind. There was no reason for her to be cold.

But Sandro was not going to steal another woman from him, Dave vowed, knowing Nia would have been his if Sandro hadn't entered the picture.

At first, Dave believed Sandro was no more than a passing infatuation. It hurt to see Nia so obviously crazy for the guy. It hurt to think of her climbing into Sandro's bed. Yet, Dave's goal had always been long term, and he could live with a passing fling.

After the World Cup, Sandro would return to Italy, this time for good—and Nia would return home heartbroken. Dave had planned to be there to comfort her. Which was exactly why he had taken more vacation time at the end of the World Cup games that summer, prepared to be the shoulder that Nia would need.

Only Sandro hadn't returned to Italy alone. He

came to the States, and then he took Nia home with him.

Just remembering made Dave's heart hurt. He had never expected her to leave her family, school, the United States. Although she hadn't given up her spot on the national soccer team. She flew in for training and games.

But that fateful summer before she left for Italy, Nia had come back to Dallas after the World Cup, and Dave was prepared to step into his role as comforter. Only she was still holding him at arm's length. Given time, he was confident she would forgive him for what had happened by the pool over the Easter holidays.

Especially now that she was home—alone—and after Sandro had missed that final, all-important penalty shot to send his country home in defeat. Dave gloated, knowing Sandro's pedestal would be crumbling and quickly crashing.

The jealousy, the envy, the enjoying someone else's downfall was not normally in Dave's personality, but when it came to Sandro, Dave couldn't help himself. His need for Nia was an insidious thing, truly awakened only when he realized he might lose her. He had taken her for granted, he realized. But now, he could make it up to her. Help her past her heartbreak and turn her love toward him.

But days past, and she refused to see him. With his vacation days slipping away, hoping to prod her, he called and invited her on a picnic at the lake. While she took the call, at least, she turned him down, claiming she had errands. She left soon after, driving off in her little yellow Volkswagen bug.

A couple of hours later, Nia pulled back into her driveway. Much to Dave's shock—he'd been outside kicking a soccer ball with Nia's two younger brothers—

Sandro had climbed out of the passenger seat.

"Wow, Sandro's here." Nia's brothers ran over to greet him. Dave hadn't realized they knew Sandro.

Laughing and shooing her brothers away, Nia took Sandro's arm and led him over to Dave. "Hey, Dave, I'd like for you to meet Sandro."

It was a clear message.

Reluctantly, Dave stuck out his hand and said the first thing that came to mind. "Sorry about the World Cup. How's your leg?" Sandro had played over two hours on a severely injured hamstring muscle during the last game. The injury no doubt played a part in the missed goal.

"It will heal." Sandro's words were given in an offhand manner, while his gaze intently probed Dave's.

In that moment, he knew Nia had told Sandro what he'd done. Told that he'd pushed her to have sex that one crazy night. Dave refused to drop his gaze, yet he felt the bitter sting of shame all over again.

"Sandro, how long are you going to be here?" Nia's youngest brother asked.

"We'll talk about it later, brat," Nia said. "Go inside and tell mom we're home." She turned back to Dave. "Sandro's got a few days before he has to head back to Italy. I'm going to show him around town. Maybe take him to Six Flags."

Dave mentally collected himself, forced a smile. "Sounds great. Enjoy your stay."

"*Grazie*," Sandro said before Nia said their goodbyes and led Sandro to her house.

Dave's fake smile faded from his face.

For three days he watched Sandro and Nia come and go. One day she and Sandro came back loaded with sacks from the mall. Dave was on his way out.

"You buy out all the stores?" he teased. When he ran into them he always made a point to be friendly, even though inside he was burning. His vacation days were drawing to an end, and frankly he was glad. It was torture staying around, watching the woman he loved with another man. No matter how temporary the situation might be.

"Guess what? I'm going to Italy!" Nia announced.

All the air sucked out of Dave's lungs. "Great," he somehow managed to say.

She turned to Sandro. "I'll shower first. Then you. We've got to hurry though, we're supposed to leave for dinner in an hour. Bye, Dave." She waved at Dave over her shoulder.

"Sandro, wait," Dave said, knowing on a deep level that what he was about to say was none of his business, yet he knew he was going to say it, regardless.

Throwing a puzzled look Dave's way, Nia kissed Sandro's cheek and went inside.

Dave waited until Sandro approached him, then he plunged right in. "I know this is none of my business, but you're dragging this out aren't you? Wouldn't it be a cleaner break if you just cut it off right now?"

Sandro frowned. "I don't know these terms "cleaner break" and "cut off"."

"It means why continue this affair? Why not leave her now and go back to Italy alone so she can start to get over—I mean so she can forget you."

"Why would I want her to forget me?"

"You can't mean to have a long distance affair? That wouldn't be fair to her."

"Long distance?"

"You know, with you living in Italy while she lives here. It's hard to keep a romance going like that."

"*Si*, I agree. These past few months were difficult for us."

"Then let her go. Let her move on with her life."

"Ah." A knowing look came into Sandro's eyes. "You want me out of the way. But do you not live out of town, too?"

"There's a little difference between Washington D.C. and Ita—"

"I intend to marry her," Sandro interrupted. "There will be no trouble with our romance. The next time she comes home to visit the United States, she will be my wife."

"Your—" Dave couldn't say it. The words felt like bullets ripping through his body.

"You love her," Sandro said, nodding as if just reaching the conclusion.

"Yes," Dave admitted, in too much shock to protect himself.

"I thought so." Sandro paused. "You must let her go for her own happiness."

"Have you asked her then? Has she said yes?"

"No, I have not asked her. I will ask her in Italy, after she has a chance to fall in love with my country. Ah, I see hope in your eyes. Do not get hope, Dave Armstrong. She will marry me. And she will be very happy."

From that moment, Dave hated Sandro with a smoldering rage.

In shock and despair, he retreated to his house and started drinking, although the last time he drank too much, he had made that colossal mistake with Nia at the pool.

The bourbon bottle was nearly empty, but that didn't stop him. When he drank the bottle dry, he moved on to tequila. The old song *Wasting Away In Margaritaville* came to mind, but he was too intent on getting drunk to waste time making margaritas.

When his brother came home about ten o'clock, Dave was sitting on the couch, crying. He hadn't realized he was crying until Jared said something.

"What's wrong with you, man? Someone die?"

Dave mumbled an answer.

Jared knelt down in front of him. "What'd you say? Something about Nia? Is she okay?"

"No, sheeee'sss not 'kay. She's gonna be Italian."

"Man, you are making no sense. I'm calling her to see what's going on."

"No. Don't. She doesn't know."

Jared only raised an eyebrow and picked up the phone. "Oh, you're going to Italy. That must be it," he said a few minutes later. "I just thought something had happened to you the way he's bombed out of his mind over here."

"Shu' up, 'sshole," Dave demanded.

"Yeah, that might be a good idea. I'll see you in a few minutes."

It seeped through Dave's soaked brain that Nia was coming over. "No!" He tried to stand up, but his legs collapsed and he fell back on the couch.

Moments later, the doorbell rang. Jared let her in. "He's in there."

Dave closed his eyes, tried to will himself away since his legs weren't working.

She touched his knee. "Dave? Geez, what have

you done? You smell awful."

He opened his eyes and she gasped. "Look at your eyes." She gazed around and found the empty bourbon bottle and near-empty tequila bottle. "My, God, did you drink all this? Are you trying to kill yourself?"

"Don't leave me, Nia."

"God, Dave, why are you crying?" She knelt in front of him and wiped at his face. "I'm just going to visit. I'll be back."

"No, you won't."

"Of course I will."

"Don't go."

Finally, he got to hold her. But she was the one offering comfort, not him. "I know it's not the smartest thing in the world for me to go, Dave. I know I'm gonna be hurt when I have to come back. But I have to go. I love him."

Dave buried his face in her neck, a part of him mortified that he'd turned into a sniveling fool, but unable to help himself. "I know you love him. That's what he told me."

She hesitated. "Is that what has you so upset?"

Dave shook his head, then wished he hadn't, belatedly realizing she was going to probe for more answers.

He was right.

"What, then? What else did he tell you?"

Dave pulled away from her, lay his head back against the couch and refused to answer.

"Is Sandro the reason you're drunk? What did you say to each other?" A noise behind her caught her attention. Sandro had followed her apparently. He and Jared stood side by side. "What did you say this afternoon, Sandro?"

Sandro stared at her without answering. She turned back to the couch. "Dave? What?"

"I can tell you what they said, and I wasn't even there," Jared offered. "They were both staking a claim."

"A claim? Over me? Dave, I told you last time—"

"Go home, Nia. I didn't call you." Dave couldn't take one more moment of humiliation. "Take him with you."

Sandro touched her shoulder. "Come, *cara*."

She bit her lip, touched Dave's knee again, sadness in her eyes. "God will bring someone special for you one day." Then she stood and took Sandro's hand.

Dying was nothing, Dave thought, watching them with bleary eyes leave hand-in-hand. Sometimes in training, the FBI students would discuss among themselves the real possibility of dying on the job, whether it would be painful. But that was a useless worry, Dave realized. The real pain came from living and losing the woman you loved.

That wouldn't happen again, Dave vowed, pulling himself from painful memories, heart pounding. The snow began falling again, melting on the heated windshield. He turned on the wipers.

Nia and her child were important, but even for them Dave wouldn't let Sandro sacrifice Marisa. There had to be a way—to rescue Nia and Danny—and help free Marisa.

The woman he was growing to love.

* * *

The snow continued to fall, leaving the late

afternoon sky as dark as evening. Dave glanced at Marisa as he turned the car into the underground garage of her apartment building. Sandro sat behind her, muttering in Italian. They'd left the stolen Honda behind.

As Dave parked, Sandro said to Marisa, "Hurry, I want to leave again in five minutes. Grab your computer. We'll come back later for anything else."

"I'll go," Dave said.

"No," both Marisa and Sandro said at the same time.

"I'll go," Marisa said.

"I'll go with you."

Marisa shook her head.

"You'll slow her down," Sandro explained.

"What if she runs into someone, what if—"

"I'm a big girl, Dave, and anyone who might be here thinks I'm still on their side. Don't be silly."

Dave tightened his lips, unused to being overruled. His gaze glued to her shapely behind as she hurried off.

"You care for her," Sandro said. It wasn't a question.

"Yes." Dave watched Marisa until she was out of sight.

Sandro nodded. "That is good."

"Good?" Dave turned to face Sandro. "It's a bitch. She's a Mafia princess; I'm a Fed. Not the best foundation for a relationship."

"All relationships have problems that must be worked through. Yet men need a partner beside them. To share their life."

"Is that why you married Nia? You wanted a partner, and you were selfish enough to put her at risk?"

"Marrying me was not a risk—"

"You were involved with the mob—"

"No."

"I know you missed that goal that sent Italy home in second place because of Carlo. Marisa told me you gave in because he threatened your family, your girlfriend's family. Are you denying that's true?"

"That was a one-time thing, he said."

"Once is never enough with the Mafia."

"*Si*, I was very naïve." Sandro nodded. "The next time instead of giving in, I gave up my career in *Serie A*, closed my soccer school, and fled Italy. Now, I run no more. I stand and fight."

"If you had been honorable, you would have never married her."

"She would never have married you, Dave. Even if I had gone to Italy and left her, she wouldn't have married you. And she would have been very unhappy. Did you wish for her to be unhappy?"

"I could have made her happy."

"You can't force another person to be happy, Dave. Like you tried to force her to have sex with you. It doesn't work."

Dave rubbed his hand across his face. "I always suspected she'd told you."

"Marisa is a good woman, Dave. Get her away from her father and she will be a good partner for you."

Dave gave a bitter laugh. "You're handing her right back to her father."

"If things go the way I plan, Marisa will be free. I will be free. My family will be free."

"You're just as likely to be dead."

"If that is the case, Nia still will not marry you. You are dear to her, yes, like a brother. She will accept help from you, but even if she is alone, she will not marry you. When all this is over, marry Marisa and find happiness. It doesn't come around often in a lifetime."

Watching for Marisa out the windshield, Dave said, "I'll take your words into consideration."

Fifteen minutes later, the three of them sat in a hotel room, Sandro on the bed, Dave in the chair by the table, and Marisa at a small, serviceable desk. She booted her laptop and plugged in her USB Internet card, not wanting to risk the hotel's unsecured Wi-Fi.

She pulled up the accounts. "Two are clear, the other three are still in process. They'll clear soon."

Sandro nodded. "I want to go to Carlo's tomorrow then. He should be at his club after lunch."

"How are you going to get away, Sandro? Poppa won't let you walk out of there alive."

"He will have no choice. I have his money and his daughter."

Marisa answered, "He can have his men hold you, torture you—"

"I don't think he'll do that," Dave interrupted. "He will let you walk out, but he'll send men to follow you. Once he finds out where Marisa is, then he'll have his men nab you."

"I can lose his men."

"Don't be so sure. I can have men stationed to help you—"

"No. I trust no one."

"Don't argue, Sandro." Dave held up his hands. "I know you want to do this on your own, but nothing will be accomplished if you're captured. Carlo won't let you go until you return his money to him, then he'll kill you and Nia both."

It was clear frustration was eating at Sandro. "But I have Marisa. He won't hurt me as long as she is my prisoner—"

"I think you overestimate his affection for me," Marisa cut in. "He loves no one."

"Love doesn't have much to do with it, princess," Dave said. "It's a pride thing. Look, Sandro, if his men follow you, then they'll find Marisa. All I want to do is station men to keep Carlo's men from following."

Sandro clearly wasn't buying Dave's offer of help. Dave couldn't blame him. He added one last tempting morsel. "He already knows that you're working with the FBI. I think he'll look at it as a challenge to outsmart us all."

"All right," Sandro conceded. "We'll talk to your men. Only your most trusted men," Sandro warned. "I like Frankie."

"Frankie's a good man," Dave agreed, relieved the troubled Italian was seeing reason. "So are Tony and Steve."

As Marisa shut down her computer, her phone rang. The three of them froze. Another ring and Marisa snapped to action.

"*Por Dio*, it's Luigi" Marisa said. "He is looking for me. I should answer."

Sandro pulled the phone out of her hand. "No. You are my prisoner now. I want your father to know you are missing."

"It might be too early to play that card," Dave suggested. "If they think Marisa is missing, then they may tighten their security. We don't have everything lined up yet."

Sandro thought for a moment. "You are right." He

gave her back the phone.

"What do I tell him?"

"That you are out with friends. You went to an opera and coffee afterwards, and now you are headed home."

"He'll check up on me."

"By then it will be too late."

Marisa took the phone. "Hello. She listened for a moment, then repeated the story Sandro suggested. "No, no. Not tonight. No, please. I am very tired. I will see you tomorrow. Promise." She hung up.

"Did he believe you?" Dave asked.

"I don't know. He wanted to meet me at my place, but I talked him out of it."

All three felt the noose tightening as they stared at each other. So far so good, but one little misstep—

But no, failure was not an option.

CHAPTER 25

She was running. Running as if demons from hell were nipping at her feet. She knew if she fell, she was dead. Hurry. Her heart hammered frantically against her ribcage. Her breath labored through her lungs. Move, feet.

Move, move, move.

Safety was close. Just a little further. She had to make it.

Then she heard it. An echo of a gunshot from behind her.

Instinctively, she ducked, and urged her churning legs to greater speed.

Someone hurled a bowling ball into her shoulder. Another loud crack sounded. She went sprawling. She scrambled to stay on her feet, scraping her knees, her fingers clawing at the ground to push her upright.

Blood dripped—

"*Cara*, you are dreaming." A strong hand brushed against her hair.

Nia blinked her eyes, struggling from the depths of the nightmare. "Sandro?" Then her gaze focused. Her heart dropped. Not Sandro after all.

A strange man knelt beside her, touched her. She had been sleeping on the small cot, curled protectively around Daniele's warm little body. She sat up, careful not to wake her son.

"Good, you are awake. You were having the bad dream."

"You're new. Who are you?" A gold cross hung around his neck, large diamond and gold rings adorned his fingers. An air of importance surrounded him, and she knew she had seen him at the restaurant, like the others. The nights she performed, she always studied the audience. Like most of the other Mafia guys, he had olive skin, big dark eyes and a somewhat familiar face, but she couldn't specifically place him.

He seemed insulted she didn't know who he was. "I am Carlo's son, Massimo."

Her heart stuttered. The big guy's son. Was this a good development, or bad? "Why are you here? Have you found . . . found Sandro?"

"Your husband is still missing."

"Thank goodness," she murmured under her breath.

"You sigh in relief. But do not be too happy, *cara*. I imagine Sandro has some grand plan to rescue you, but it will never work. He will have to give up sooner or later."

Nia detected his gloating, superior tone, and decided she liked Massimo even less than his father.

He turned his attention to Daniele, touching her son's hair. "Curly hair, like his father."

Deliberately, Nia moved his hand away from Daniele's head.

He met her gaze and smiled. The smile didn't reach his eyes. "*Il caprino*."

She sent him a sharp look. He had repeated the childhood nickname for Sandro—the goat boy—the one Giuseppe had told her to call to Sandro the first time they met.

"Yes," Massimo nodded. "I knew Sandro when he was a boy."

"Of course you did. Apparently everyone around here knew him when he was younger."

"We played on the same team," Massimo continued. "From the first, it was obvious he was destined for greatness."

The sound of jealousy rang clear in his voice. Nia prodded him, unable to help herself. "What about you? You didn't go professional?"

The look he sent her said he knew what she was doing, and she had better beware baiting him. "A knee injury." He stood; his knee popped as if to prove his point. "I never made it out of *Serie C*."

Serie C was a third division league. One where the soccer players had talent, but not enough to make it with *Serie A*, the elite Italian league. Every professional soccer player in Italy—indeed many the world over—aspired to the Italian *Serie A* teams. First class. Big money. Lots of prestige. Sandro had made it. At one time, he was the best of the best. Until he gave it up to come to the United States for her.

Thoughts of Sandro and how his life was in jeopardy made her angry. That anger made her speak before she stopped to think. "I'm surprised with your father's money and *influence*, he didn't buy your way into *Serie A*." As soon as the words left her mouth, she realized she might have pushed too far. She held her breath, wondering how he was going to take her dig.

This time his evil smile actually reached his eyes. "I've heard you have a smart mouth."

"Oh, yeah? What else are they saying about me?"

"That you have a big set of balls." He made an obscene gesture. "Get up. I want to see these balls." He took her hand.

She refused to stand until he started squeezing her fingers. She squeezed back, a useless game, she knew. It was soon obvious he was much stronger. Finally, realizing he wouldn't stop until he broke her fingers, she stood.

"Ouch, you son of a bitch." She tugged at her hand, but he wouldn't release it. "What the hell did that prove?"

"Careful, do not wake your son." He jerked her closer, let his gaze roam over her. "I do not see these big balls."

His close scrutiny made her distinctly leery. Deliberately, she straightened her spine. "They only inflate when I'm pissed off." She used bravado as a defense tactic. At the moment, it was all she had.

"Fearless, I see. It will do you no good here. As a matter of fact, your fearlessness has caused you much trouble." He nodded at Daniele.

She wanted his thoughts nowhere near her son. "What'd you do to get stuck with babysitting duty, Massimo? I'd think your father would have something better for you." She said it with the tone that perhaps he wasn't trustworthy enough for anything more important.

He was sharp and didn't miss her insult. His eyebrows lowered. "Actually, I'm here on my own, *cara.*

I've always thought you were very beautiful, talented. I've wanted to meet you, but Sandro was very protective of you."

She didn't know what he meant, but whatever Sandro did to keep Massimo away from her, she was grateful. His presence was no more welcome than a poisonous snake.

He leaned close, his breath hot on her face. "But now, Sandro isn't around."

"You might just be making a mistake," she warned him, not backing down though she desperately wanted to.

"I don't think so. Sandro's not here now, and frankly, *cara*, I don't think you'll ever see him again. But don't worry, I will be happy to take care of you."

The terrifying thought that she would never see Sandro again temporarily held her frozen.

"Of course, I will let you keep your son," Massimo continued. "Angie tells me you are expecting another *bambino*, too. Perhaps one day you will have a child for me." He rubbed her stomach.

Taking advantage of her shock, he brought his mouth down to hers. No gentle touch of lips or persuasion from him. Instead, his mouth was open, his exploration bold. Invasive.

At the first unwelcome touch of his tongue, Nia, no longer immobile, sprang to action. She bit his tongue and stomped his foot simultaneously. "I have never needed a man to take care of me," she grunted.

He jerked away. Quickly, before he moved completely out of reach, she slammed her knee upward into his crotch. He yelped in pain and grabbed between his legs with one hand while touching his tongue gingerly with the other.

His fingers came away bloody. "I'm bleeding, you vicious bitch." He grabbed for her. She sidestepped him, scooted past him. Knowing she had to choke him unconscious to avoid the beating she read in his eyes, she jumped on his back. Grabbing a handful of his hair, she yanked his head back, wrapped her arm around his throat and squeezed with all her strength.

He was just as determined to make her lose her grip. He clawed at her arm, but she wouldn't release her hold. Massimo stumbled backwards, found his footing then rammed her against a wall. Pain shot through her bones, but she held on.

Anger vibrated through his every muscle. Nia knew if she lost her grip, she would pay heavy consequences she might not survive.

The noise had awakened Daniele. "Momma." He sat up and saw Massimo trying to violently dislodge his mother and promptly started screaming.

Nia couldn't go to him, though she ached that her young son was fast growing hysterical. There was simply no help for it.

The office door burst open. Angie came in. "Nia! What is going on?" He grabbed her and tugged.

She was losing her hold. Her muscles strained to keep her arm around Massimo's neck. "No, Angie," she said through gritted teeth. "He'll hurt me, hurt my son—"

Angie tugged her off. He held her by the arms while Massimo coughed and gasped and caught his breath.

Nia struggled and twisted frantically against Angie. "You gotta let me go." She angled her head behind her to plead.

But Angie didn't release her. His gaze flitted

between her and Massimo. "What are you doing here?" he asked Carlo's son.

Massimo massaged his throat, slowly regaining his breath. "Just getting acquainted with Sandro's soon-to-be widow," he answered in a scratchy voice.

Nia still struggled. "Let me go, Angie."

"Don't let her go. Hold her." Massimo finally regained his breath and stalked toward them. "You made me bleed, bitch."

He pulled his arm back to hit her.

"No!" Her arms were imprisoned, but her feet weren't. She shot out with her right foot, catching Massimo in the face with a front snap kick. His head popped backwards. Blood blossomed under his nose.

His hands went to his face. His fingers came away bloody once again. When Massimo saw them, his eyes narrowed. He reached for his gun.

At last, Angie shoved Nia out of the way, shielding her with his body. "What are you doing? Get out of here, Massimo!"

"Momma!" Daniele screamed hysterically from the cot, his little arms outstretched, his fingers curling, reaching toward her. Nia stumbled to Daniele, picked him up and wiped his wet cheeks. Though she was shaking, she made soothing noises to help him calm down. It ripped her insides that her little boy had to witness such ugliness.

"Move, Angie. Get outta my way," Massimo ordered.

"She is not to be hurt."

"You fat fuck, I said get outta my way."

"Listen to me, Massimo." Angie walked toward him, his arms held wide. "Your poppa had Mikey killed after he hurt her. I can't let you hurt her."

Massimo swiped at the blood running down his nose and waved his gun. "I'll shoot you, goddamn it."

In a quick move, so surprising because of his bulk, Angie knocked the gun out of Massimo's hands, sending it skidding across the concrete office floor. "I can't let you hurt her," he repeated. "Now, go."

"You're making a mistake, Angie."

"I'm just doing my job like Carlo told me. He changes his orders, he has to tell me. I don't take orders from you."

Massimo recognized defeat. "You'll get your orders, all right." He turned his angry gaze to Nia. "All I have to do is tell my father I want you, and you're mine."

She narrowed her eyes and raised her chin. The whole time her muscles were quivering. "I'd rather die."

"That is a very real possibility, *cara*. If I decide I don't want you. Think about your little *bambino* without his momma or poppa." With that threat hanging in the air, Massimo walked out the office door, slamming it behind him.

Nia drew a deep breath and tried to stop shaking for Daniele's sake, but she couldn't stop the tears that slipped down her cheeks. He was still crying and she knew he sensed her fear. Be strong, she chastised herself. Your son needs you.

Angie turned to her.

"He started it. I was just defending myself," she told him.

He stared at her with sad brown eyes. "I did not expect this to be so hard," he confessed.

Nia sensed a moment of weakness. "Let me go, Angie. Please," she begged. "Just look the other way and let me and Danny walk out of here."

He shook his head. "I can't do that, *Bella*." He scooped up Massimo's gun and slid it into his waistband. "I can't just let you go. As much as I might want to. My loyalty is to the family." With that, he turned around and walked out, closing the door behind him.

Nia sank onto the cot and cried with her son.

* * *

Luigi tossed and turned for hours, unable to sleep. He missed having Marisa beside him. He was fifteen years older than she, and lately, he'd been worried she was pulling away from him. She seemed distant— distracted when they were together. That was why he'd gotten the engagement ring. But he hadn't been able to give it to her since he had to leave in the middle of his planned evening with her last night. And tonight, she had not come to him at all. Had not even called him.

What could he expect? She was young and beautiful. But he'd always thought age hadn't made a difference with her. Especially since he was her father's right hand man.

Although there was a point not long ago, when Luigi thought he was going to be a very dead right hand man.

He and Carlo had been in the private meeting room, the one the Feds didn't know about, waiting on Angie and the *capos* to arrive.

Carlo leaned forward across the table. "There's a question I want an answer to, Luigi."

"Sure, shoot." A bad choice of words though he hadn't realized at the time.

"You and my daughter still together? You a thing now?"

Luigi and Marisa had first gotten together when Carlo had offered an evening with her as a reward for his promotion. Luigi thought back to the dirty deeds he'd done which won him the *consigliere* position. The one with acid was especially horrendous. It had taken seven hours for the man's hand to dissolve. He hadn't thought someone could scream for so long. In the end, he'd given the information, but the shock had killed him anyway.

So yes, he was happy to take Marisa when she'd been offered. And even happier she seemed to want to stay with him. To his knowledge, Carlo had never offered her to anyone else since then.

But why was Carlo asking now? Luigi's heart pounded so hard he felt it in his throat. "I think we're a thing now. Is that against the rules?"

Nodding to himself, Carlo laced his fingers across his stomach. "Since you two obviously have something going, I want you to marry her. You are an important man in the family. Be good to have you married to my daughter. Good for you, good for me, know what I mean?"

Relief sank through Luigi when he realized what Carlo meant. If he were married to Marisa, Carlo would always be sure of his loyalty. Not a bad idea. A Mafia don never knew who was plotting a takeover—which most often meant a violent, bloody death for the boss. "I have bought her a ring, I plan to ask her soon."

"I will talk to her."

An absolute seal of approval from Carlo. Luigi was pleased. "I would prefer you not. I would like to take care of it myself."

Carlo rose from his chair and came around to Luigi to kiss his cheeks. "You're a good man, Luigi. My son Massimo could learn a few things from you. Massimo sometimes has too hot of a temper, even for an Italian." Carlo shrugged.

And that was just the sort of attitude Luigi hoped for from Carlo. In the family, the don's son didn't necessarily inherit the title when the old man died. It was up to the other families' bosses to vote and approve the heir when a family needed a new boss. Luigi had his eye on the spot. Of course, he knew that Angie did, too. Angie was the underboss, equal in rank to Luigi. Angie was old and fat though. He'd probably die of a heart attack before Carlo did. Unless somebody whacked Carlo out . . .

Yes, Luigi needed to be married to Marisa. Soon.

Which was why he was going to check up on her. See if she had really been at the opera with her friends. Nothing like a personal visit to see if they were going to lie. He shoved aside the bedcovers and picked up the phone to call for his car.

CHAPTER 26

The next morning, Dave showed up at the hotel with Frankie, Tony and Steve, coffee, a city map, a notepad and a small printer.

"I thought it would be better if we printed those accounts with their zero balances."

While Marisa hooked up the printer to her computer, the rest of the group piled around the table in the room. It would have been easier to plan at headquarters, but Dave didn't want to risk Marisa being seen or their conversation overheard.

"This will be the easiest route to defend." Frankie sketched pencil lines on a city map lying in the middle of the table. "We can have men situated here and here." He circled two different places.

"You are certain they will be following me?" Sandro asked.

"Oh, yeah," Frankie nodded. "Carlo wants you bad, and if it's like you say, and you've got something to bargain with him over, something that takes away his advantage, he's going to want to stop you dead. He doesn't believe in compromise."

Silence. Then Frankie seemed to realize his choice

of words. "Uh, sorry."

Sandro waved him off. "That's all right. I know Carlo wants me dead."

"And you better believe he'll kill you, too," Dave said.

"Yeah, his takeover was one of the bloodiest we've seen," Frankie added. "All that hard work cleaning up those scumbags and in waltzes Carlo fresh from Italy. He whacks out anyone who might be a threat and set himself up as boss—"

"Frankie, we can finish with the history lesson another time," Dave said.

Sandro realized Dave was aware of Marisa sitting there listening to Frankie talk about her father. Frankie finally realized it himself.

"Yeah, sorry, boss."

"The trick is to get you in and out alive, and then keep them from following," Dave continued to Sandro. "We'll set up men where Frankie says, plus two will accompany you and wait in an inconspicuous place outside the club. Sandro, since you'll be wired, they'll be the first on the spot if something goes wrong—"

"I want Frankie to be one of those men."

Dave stared at Frankie, then Sandro. "Yeah, good choice."

"But I can't be wired."

"It's too dangerous without—"

"It's dangerous with a wire. I'm sure they will search me."

"He's right, boss," Frankie said. "We'll keep a close watch and get him out alive."

Dave nodded. "Seems I'm outvoted."

"You're in charge of Marisa," Sandro said. "I want

nothing to happen to her."

"Nothing will happen to Marisa," Dave promised.

Sandro hoped Dave was right. Enough wrong had happened. It was time for things to go right.

"Okay, guys, here's the plan . . ." After they worked out the details, Dave told them, "You two take Sandro and get set up. Make sure you're wearing vests, they'll be shooting live bullets."

Dave turned to Marisa. "Got the accounts printed?"

She handed them the papers. "They all went through without a hitch."

Dave looked them over, nodded, and passed them to Sandro.

"I want Marisa's phone as well," Sandro said. "Along with the necklace I have, I hope to convince Carlo I have her."

Marisa retrieved her phone from her purse and handed it to Sandro, who pocketed it and headed toward the two men waiting by the door.

Dave turned to Marisa as the others prepared to leave. "Stay here, I'll get food and bring it back."

"No."

Sandro stopped at the door and looked at Marisa, who up to this point had been silent.

"I have to go to my apartment," she told Dave.

"Princess, there's no reason to go to your—"

"Yes, there is. There's something I need that I didn't have time to get yesterday. And you said I could go back later. Now is later."

Dave stared at her questioningly. "Now is a really bad time. Would you care to elaborate on what you need?"

She hesitated. "Personal . . .things."

"We can buy whatever you need. It's too danger—
"

"I have to go to my apartment. With, or without you."

"I can't allow it," Dave said, crossing his arms.

"You can't hold me here—"

"Marisa," Sandro spoke up, intent on putting an end to the argument, "I forbid it. You are my prisoner. You cannot be traipsing all over New York." He crossed the room and took her shoulders, then loosened his grip when he saw her flinch. But he didn't release her.

"If I lose you, then I lose bargaining power." Sandro earnestly pleaded, knowing that he could restrain her, but not wanting to resort to violence when she had been so willing and helpful.

"Sandro, *caro*, I'll be careful, I swear. But I *have* to go back to my apartment."

Something in her gaze appealed to him. "Will you not tell me what it is that you need?"

She shook her head. "It is best you do not know," she answered quietly, regret in her soft brown eyes.

"I can get what you need," Dave said.

"No." She shook her head. "You'd never find it."

With reluctance, but trusting his instinct, Sandro relented. "Then Dave must go with you. Be quick."

"I will."

Sandro pulled her into his embrace, kissed her forehead. "Be careful."

"I will." She hugged him back.

Looking at Dave over the top of Marisa's head, Sandro said, "You will keep her safe."

"I will."

* * *

Luigi's driver pulled the car in front of Marisa's apartment building. Luigi got out, pulling his coat tighter against his neck as a burst of cold wind hit him.

"Hello, Mr. Conte. How are you today, sir?"

"Freezing," Luigi snapped, his temper short from lack of sleep.

"Well, yes, sir, it is unseasonably cold this year. Makes me look forward to summer again."

Luigi turned off the doorman's idle chatter. "Have you seen Ms. Peruzzo this morning?"

"No, sir, I haven't." He looked at the wall clock. "Funny. By now, she's usually left for work."

The doorman's comment snagged Luigi's attention, gave him a bad feeling in the pit of his stomach. On top of everything else, Roberto had dropped out of sight yesterday morning. Very unlike him. It flashed through Luigi's mind that maybe Marisa ran off with the accountant.

"I'll go up and check on her," Luigi said, more anxious than ever to figure out what the hell was happening.

"Sure, go right up, sir."

As manager, Luigi was a well-known figure at the apartment building. He didn't visit Marisa often, she was quite protective of her privacy, but he was at the building often enough to make sure things were running smoothly. Every employee, unless they had been hired yesterday, knew this.

Luigi got onto the elevator and pushed the button for her floor. At her door, he paused, straightened his coat, then knocked.

No answer.

He knocked again. Still no answer.

The bad feeling in his stomach became persistent. She had said she would be home. If she wasn't here, and wasn't at work, then where was she?

His cell phone rang. Thinking it was Marisa, he answered so quickly the caller ID didn't have time to come through.

"Yes?"

"Mr. Conte? We learned what happened to Roberto."

"What?" Luigi braced himself.

"The Feds have him."

"What?" He blinked. "What do those assholes need with Roberto?" And why would they even be after him? "Have they pressed charges?"

"They've sequestered him and are holding him with no charges right now."

"I'll be right there, we'll see what we can do." Luigi headed for the elevators. Talking to Marisa would have to wait. He still wanted to know where she was, but he wouldn't be able to look for himself. As he exited the building, he punched a number into his cell phone.

"This is Luigi," he said after his *capo* answered. "Marisa has dropped out of sight. Watch her apartment; call me when she gets home. Or if anyone sees her around town, let me know and follow her. Keep me informed."

She had better not be with another man. The persistent feeling in his gut told him that was most likely where she was—and where she had been last night.

He would just have to make her see reason, take measures to curb her independence in the future. A man in his position needed a wife to stay home and take care of wifely duties, not running out on her own with God knows who. True, she wasn't his wife yet, but with Carlo's blessing, it was only a technicality as far as Luigi was concerned.

CHAPTER 27

Sandro left Frankie and Tony blending in with the people on the crowded sidewalk and entered Carlo's private club and retreat. Like old-time American bosses, Carlo had adopted the habit of conducting his mob business there, though he had offices downtown where he ran many legitimate businesses. And some not so legit.

Although the snow had stopped, the temperatures outside were still chilly and Sandro hadn't thought to have Marisa buy an overcoat to cover the gray Armani suit he'd worn. The warmth inside the club was welcome.

Two men stopped Sandro before he had walked three feet inside the door. "You're in the wrong place," one said. "This is a private business."

Sandro looked him in the eye. "I'm here to see Carlo."

The second one, Sandro recognized as Joey, stared hard. "Hey, Carmine, that's Sandro. He's cut his hair."

Carmine stared, then disbelief covered his face. "Well, I'll be. I guess Mikey was right." Carmine grabbed Sandro's arm. "Carlo will be pleased you've decided to pay a visit," he said, sarcasm clear in his tone of voice.

"Wait, Carmine, we should probably search him. He might have a piece on him."

Carmine looked incredulous. "Him? He's a soccer player, whatta they know about—"

"If you was in Sandro's position, you might start packing, don'tcha think?" Joey explained to Carmine, who obviously wasn't too bright.

The light dawned in Carmine's gaze. "Oh, yeah." He patted Sandro down, found Marisa's cell phone in Sandro's pocket, determined it was okay, then continued his pat down. "He's clean," he said smugly.

Sandro adjusted his suit jacket and followed Carmine and Joey to a back room. Carlo hunched over a table, talking on his cell phone, surrounded by the remains of a take-out lunch. Sandro recognized the boxes from his restaurant.

At first, Carlo only gave a passing glance, then his gaze came back, his eyes widening. He quickly ended his call. Stuffing the phone in his jacket pocket, he stood and walked toward Sandro. With a wave, and an "outta here," Carlo dismissed his two men.

"Sandro!" Carlo kissed Sandro on each cheek, then wrapped an arm around his shoulder and led him toward the table with all the enthusiasm as if he were a long lost relative. "Nice to see you looking so well."

Sandro didn't buy the friendly act and knew any moment Carlo's boisterous and fake enthusiasm would turn deadly quiet. Sandro didn't allow his guard to lower.

"Sit down, sit down," Carlo said, taking his seat, expecting Sandro to do the same, though the order had been couched in the most polite tone.

"I like the new look." Carlo nodded, referring to Sandro's short hair. "No wonder my men have had trouble locating you." He took a sip from his wine at his right hand. "Ah, where are my manners? Would you like a drink?" He held up the glass as an invitation. "Or join me in Georgio's excellent ravioli?"

Sandro only shook his head.

Carlo set the glass down, then leaned back in his chair with his hands folded over his stomach. He stared at Sandro. "I never would have guessed you'd give up your ponytail. Like that guy in the Bible, Sampson, who got his great strength from his hair—

"Samson," Sandro corrected.

"*Si, Si.* I suppose I thought you might be suspicious and think your great soccer skills came from your hair."

"I no longer need my skills for soccer, so it doesn't matter if my hair is gone."

"A pointed reference, I note. And a sound of blame, perhaps? You think you've had to give up soccer for me? If you'd only done what I had suggested, you would still be at the top of *Serie A.*"

Suggested? It had been out-and-out death threats. First in Italy. Then the same here in the United States—this time with nowhere else to run. "There is nothing honorable about following a criminal. I achieve my success on my own."

"Sandro! Are you saying I am not an honorable man?" Carlo asked, ignoring Sandro's reference to calling him a criminal. "Am I not a good husband to my poor invalid wife, a good father to my children? Do I not take good care of my 'family'?" He spread his arms to indicate all the people around him. "Did I not take care of you? Is your restaurant not prosperous?"

The so-called good husband, the man responsible

for making his wife an invalid, had a new mistress every month. And, because her father deemed it necessary, his children—at least Marisa—had been brought into the life of crime against her wishes. As for Sandro's restaurant—

"My restaurant was successful before you ever came here."

"Yes, it was," Carlo conceded. "But I could have ruined it. Any business I want destroyed in this city—all I have to do is say the word. But because we were old friends, and had done business together before, I made you a part of my new family."

"I want nothing to do with your 'family'. Never have, never will. I want nothing to do with you."

"You wound my soul, dear boy." Carlo laid his hands dramatically over his heart. "I, who have loved you like a son, would have done anything for you."

"Your price is too high, Carlo."

"And what are you going to do about it?" Carlo asked, narrowing his eyes at Sandro. "I'm asking myself a question," Carlo continued as if he didn't expect an answer. As if Sandro had no way to defend himself. No weapon to fight with. "'Why is he here?' I say to myself. If not to *dishonor* himself to work with me, then why?" He cocked his head inquiringly. "Do you wish to plead for your life? Plead for your family, your very young son and lovely wife?"

"I do not come here to beg."

"Then why do you show yourself? Ah," he continued once again not allowing Sandro a chance to answer. "You must think you have something to bargain with. Some deal you want to make."

Sandro knew Carlo was shrewd. A quick mind had kept the mobster in business and one step ahead of the legal system all these years. Still it was fascinating to watch Carlo's brain work.

For once, Carlo waited expectantly for Sandro to answer.

Dragging out the moment, Sandro knew just how he wanted to jab the knife into Carlo, an inch at a time. He planned to start with Marisa.

But Massimo walked into the room before Sandro could speak.

He stopped behind Sandro. "I heard Sandro's here."

So much the better. Sandro could watch both their faces. He turned to face Carlo's son. Massimo's eyes widened. "It's you! Your hair. It is gone."

"*Si*, Massimo, we have already had this discussion," Carlo said. "Very smart of Sandro I think, to cut his hair. But we knew he was intelligent."

Massimo pulled out a chair at the table. Sitting down, he said, "I can't believe you came here. You certainly have balls." He turned to his father. "What's he have that he thinks will keep him alive?"

"I don't know," Carlo answered. "We were just getting to the bargaining stages I think. Isn't that right?"

"*Si*, I have a proposition for you."

"I saw Nia earlier today." This from Massimo, and obviously designed to throw Sandro off guard. From the look on Carlo's face, Sandro suspected the news was just as much of a shock to him. But Carlo quickly recovered.

Sandro struggled to resist the urge to rip off Massimo's head, while Carlo nodded as if the news were expected.

"And how is she feeling?" Carlo asked.

"She is *feeling* just fine." This was said in a lewd

tone to match Massimo's wolfish grin.

With the deliberate emphasis on "feeling" and the self-satisfied grin, Sandro knew without a doubt Massimo had been touching Nia.

Sandro saw red. The whole world in front of him went fuzzy then burst into the brilliant bright color. He clenched his jaws and cautioned himself to patience. Self-control lay at the heart of a good soccer player. All his plans would do no good if they were forced to kill him now.

"I am glad to hear she is feeling well," Carlo said to Massimo, then turned to Sandro. "I understand that congratulations are in order."

Having no idea what Carlo meant, Sandro tried to keep his face blank and waited expectantly for Carlo to continue with his revelation. A revelation, no doubt calculated for the most emotional response. Carlo didn't disappoint.

"It is always joyous to learn you are going to be a poppa again, don't you agree?"

A poppa . . .again? *Dio*, was Nia pregnant? The idea slammed into Sandro's gut. He searched his brain for any remembered sign. Had her breasts been fuller? Had she been more tired lately?

He couldn't remember; he had been so caught up in his own problems of working with the FBI to rid himself of Carlo, he must have been neglectful. Remorse tore through him.

"Are you feeding her properly?" he asked, hoping to cover his lack of knowledge.

Carlo looked offended. "Of course we are feeding her properly. We wouldn't defy *una donna incinta* proper nourishment."

"Is she eating the food? Has she been sick?"

"Such concern is wonderful to see. Yes, I believe Angie said she is eating well. And she was rather ill one time, but none since, I don't believe."

Suddenly, Sandro had to know more. "What of my son? Is he safe?"

Carlo smiled at the desperation Sandro had unintentionally allowed to slip into his voice. It was like a cold stab of reality. Sandro forced himself back under control.

"Daniele is safe and happy with his momma. As long as she behaves herself, he will stay with her."

Sandro allowed an inward smile that Nia had so obviously caused them trouble. Though he regretted the trouble that led to his son's abduction and *zio y zia's* injuries, and deaths of Dave's men, in no way did Sandro blame her. Carlo was the one to blame. This whole disaster would not have happened without Carlo's orders.

And even though so much tragedy had come as a result of his son's abduction, perhaps Daniele was safer with his mother. Sandro knew she would die before she allowed harm to come to their child.

"Of course, how long they are safe is up to you," Carlo pointed out. "And whether you decide to cooperate."

"I rather hope he doesn't cooperate," Massimo said to his father, then turned to Sandro. "Nia is a beautiful woman. I have offered to take care of her—and your children, of course—once you are dead. With her fiery temper, I bet she is *magnifico* in bed."

Sandro came up out of his chair and went after Massimo without a conscious thought other than to stomp the last breath out of the little bastard's body.

Massimo jumped out of his chair, but Carlo moved quickly to intercept Sandro, shoving against his chest. Almost in his face, Carlo said in his deadly quiet voice, "Perhaps you see how much risk your family is in now. My son . . . well, he's my son and I love him very much, of course, but sometimes he is rather . . . *rough* with his women. You understand?"

Brilliant stars burst in Sandro's head, blurring his vision. Nose to nose with Carlo, Sandro's breath came heavily as if he'd just run the length of a soccer field, flowing hard through his widened nostrils. He gritted his teeth, and forced control back into his body. As his vision cleared, he noticed at a glance that Massimo had wisely backed away from him.

Sandro turned to Carlo. And said deliberately. "I have your daughter."

Carlo backed away. "Is this a threat?"

"If you love her, it is. Earlier you said you were a good father, no? A good father loves his children." He pulled out Marisa's necklace and dangled it in front of Carlo. "Recognize this?"

Color faded from Carlo's face. "*Si.*"

"I want my family back. If you want your daughter back, you will be willing to make a trade."

"Do you honestly think I believe you will hurt her?" Carlo quickly recovered from his initial shock.

"Do you honestly want to find out?" Sandro deliberately mimicked Carlo's words.

"No, Sandro, you are a good boy." Carlo smiled. "I do not think you would harm my daughter."

"I am a desperate man, Carlo. Surely you know not to underestimate a desperate opponent. You know of what great lengths I go to on the soccer field when the situation is desperate." Sandro had never hesitated to sacrifice his body if it meant a win for his team.

Carlo's smile had not wavered. It was time to present him with the second part. "I have your money as well."

Carlo's smile dropped off his face. "*Che*?" Then he laughed. "You have my money? You are talking nonsense."

"Unfortunately, you are wrong. Your money in your overseas accounts…I'm afraid it's quite gone." Sandro reached into the inside pocket on his suit jacket and pulled out the hard copy of Carlo's accounts with the balance at the end of each account summary printed as a big fat zero.

"You see, you have no more money. Poof. No more. I have it all now."

A red so bright it almost looked purple rushed into Carlo's face. His eyes bugged as he stared at the papers. "Let me see." He snatched the papers from Sandro's hand. After studying them a moment, he reached into his pocket for his phone. He punched a number.

Nearly successful at regaining his composure, Sandro stood by and watched Carlo sweat.

"This is why they got Roberto," he mumbled, when apparently no one answered.

"Roberto was understandably in the way, of course," Sandro conceded.

Carlo's eyes narrowed.

"In case you don't believe me, though, I'll give you time to think about it. I'm sure you might even want to put in a call to the bank managers. Let's see, your banks are six hours ahead of us, so they are closed now, of course. You should be able to reach someone by two a.m. I'll expect to hear from you after then. If not before.

"I have Marisa's phone." Sandro pulled the cell phone from his pocket to show a stunned and surprisingly quiet Carlo. "Call me on it."

"What do you want, Sandro?" Carlo finally found his voice. "What do you hope to gain?"

"It's very simple. I want my wife and child back. Your daughter for my son. Your money for my wife."

"I can have you all killed when this is over."

"Oh, Carlo, such a threat." Sandro's gaze narrowed. "It is not good to threaten an enemy when he's holding all the cards. Perhaps then, you'll be the one to die.

"I see in your eyes you do not believe me capable of murder, do you? Remember what I said. I'm a desperate man. I'll do anything to keep my family safe. Including murder.

"So perhaps it will be better for us all to make this deal and live happily-ever-after, each going our separate ways. Remember, I've gotten the best of you once. I can do it again."

Sandro turned to walk out. At the doorway, Carlo called to him.

"Sandro! While you are waiting for my answer, think about my son . . . and your wife. Together."

Rage poured through Sandro as he turned back to Carlo. In his own deadly quiet voice, Sandro promised, "If Massimo touches Nia, I will rip him apart piece by piece."

* * *

In the seconds after Sandro's departure, Carlo

stood stunned and silent.

Finally, Massimo spoke. "Poppa, let me go after Sandro. We can hold him hostage, too, torture him for the information. Do you not think he will talk as he watches me with his wife?"

A new respect entered Carlo's eyes. "Very good, son. Very smart of you. Yes, yes, get him."

Eagerly, Massimo took off running, pulling the gun Angie had taken away, then returned to him, out from beneath his jacket. He stormed into the front room. "We have to stop Sandro!" he ordered.

Instantly, three of his men were with him as he burst through the front doors. To be met with two men armed with semi-automatics.

"Going somewhere?" one of them asked.

Massimo and the other three stopped in their tracks. Pedestrians scattered away from the unfolding deadly drama.

"Drop the guns and hands up," the man said. "That's right."

In frustration, Massimo raised his hands as he saw Sandro enter the passenger side of a car down the street. Massimo made mental note of the make, although the car was too far away for him to see the license number.

He turned his attention back to the men in front of him. "I know you," he told the man who had been doing the talking. "You're Frankie."

Frankie only nodded.

So, the FBI was still helping Sandro, Massimo thought. Bad news for now. Good news for later. If Sandro was working with the law, then he wasn't going to carry out the death threats he made. Massimo smiled to himself. Sandro was going to suffer. Massimo would make certain.

Frankie glanced down the street and saw Sandro drive off. "We're just going to leave now." He nodded to the other man who backed his way to a car parked out front and got into the driver's side.

"And just in case you're thinking of following us, Massimo . . ." Frankie turned to Massimo's car and sent a spray of bullets into the tires. " . . . You'll have to change the tires first, or find another car, I'm afraid."

Frankie backed toward the car as his partner started the engine.

Massimo heard a noise behind him, from right inside the club. "Drop Massimo," Joey whispered from the doorway.

Keeping his gaze trained on the agent getting into the car, Massimo yelled, "Now," and he and his buddies hit the ground while Joey sent bullets flying toward the two agents.

* * *

"Shit." Frankie stumbled backward from the onslaught, then sent more bullets toward Carlo's club. "Haul ass," he told Tony, diving into the car.

Tony stomped on the gas and pealed out of the parking place. Frankie covered them with bursts from his semi-automatic, not wanting to think of all the paperwork this shoot-out was going to cause him.

When they were out of range, he leaned back in the seat, his heart pounding. "Man, that was close."

Tony looked at him. "Jesus, you're shot."

Frankie glanced at his shoulder and laid a hand over his wound, squeezing. "Just in the arm. I'll be okay.

My vest saved me from anything worse. Hurts like hell, but I'm okay.

"Think they'll follow?"

Tony looked in the rearview mirror. "Oh, yeah, they're following."

"Let's lose them, then."

"Pedal is to the floor." With that, the car jumped forward.

Frankie clicked the mike on his walkie-talkie, then turned to look behind him. "Sandro's away, but they're in pursuit. I'm sure Massimo got a good look at the car Steve and Sandro are in. We're ready for phase two."

Phase two was "Stop the Bad Guys."

Frankie waved at the driver of a garbage truck as they sped by. A minute later, with perfect timing, the big truck pulled out and parked across the road. Tires squealed and then a crash rocked the big truck.

Frankie leaned back and grinned.

* * *

Luigi hurried toward the elevator of Marisa's apartment building, not stopping for idle chit-chat with the doorman this time. He punched the button and waited impatiently for the doors to open. Traffic had been a bitch, there had been some wreck with a garbage truck and it had taken him almost twenty minutes to detour around the snarl.

Impatiently, he waited to reach her floor. Grim determination lay in every step as he exited the elevator and walked toward Marisa's door.

Marisa was helping the FBI. As incredible as it seemed, it was the only scenario that presented itself given the evidence. Carlo hadn't made the connection yet. He still believed Sandro was holding her, but Luigi could see no other way for Sandro to pull off his stunt without Marisa's help. Even if she claimed to be a prisoner of the FBI.

And nothing could have been more devastating to Luigi. He loved Marisa. He felt incredibly grateful that she gave an old fart like him the time of day. He knew it wasn't his power that attracted her like it did some women. Her father was the most important man in the family; by now, it was likely he was the most important man among all the families in New York.

So Luigi had thought although her father offered time with her as a prize for a job well-done, that she'd stayed because she had really been attracted to him. Had slept with him and appeared on his arm in public because as incredible as it seemed, she desired him.

She'd played them both. She had been using him for information to help the FBI make a case. It was the only explanation possible.

Head throbbing, with rapid, impatient taps he knocked on her door.

No answer.

Then like some low-classed common person, he pounded on the door and yelled. "Marisa, I know you're in there. Open up." He knew she was there. He had men watching both exits and she hadn't left. Neither had Dave Armstrong.

Still no answer, so he banged on the door again. "If you don't open up, I'm going to shoot the lock."

Surely by now, the other tenants had noticed the disturbance. Any moment, he expected security to barrel up the stairs and come after him. And if they weren't, he'd fire their asses.

The door opened. Marisa left the chain on and peeked her face through. From what he could see, she had on her jacket as if she were about to leave. He knew she'd been there less than half an hour, he'd come as soon as his men saw them pull up. Why did she have her jacket on, ready to leave again?

"I need to talk to you."

"So talk."

"Not out here in the hall. Open the door."

She glanced sideways. "What do you want?"

Luigi suspected that Dave was right there with her, listening. "We need to talk."

"Now's not a good time," she said.

"That's too bad. Open up." He wanted her where he could grab her; he wasn't stupid enough to just waltz inside her apartment and let Dave ambush him.

She shut the door to release the chain. Unfortunately, at the same moment, security chose to act. A guard came up, his hand hovering over his holster. "Excuse me, sir. Is there a problem?"

Luigi shook his head. "Took you long enough."

"Oh, Mr. Conte, it's you." He relaxed his gun hand. "This was a test?"

"You can consider it a test, yes. You were too slow. You're going to have to work on it."

"I'm sorry, sir. It's just so rare that we have any problems."

"You get paid to take care of problems. I suggest you practice."

"You're right, sir, we'll do that."

Marisa watched through the crack in her door.

"Open up, Marisa," Luigi said as the guard left.

"Let me in."

She opened the door a little more. "I don't know why you didn't call."

"I did call. There was no answer. I've had my men watching the place until you returned." Before she could turn and re-enter her apartment, he grabbed her arm and jerked her toward him. "I know Dave Armstrong is here with you." He spun her around, wrapping his arm around her neck to shield his way into the apartment. Once he got rid of Dave, he could find out what was going on, talk her out of this craziness.

"Luigi, what are you doing? There's no one here with me."

"We'll just see about that." Luigi pulled his gun free then kicked the door wide open with his foot. He pushed his gun under her chin and forced her to walk forward.

As he expected, Dave stood inside the entrance, his gun pointed at them. "Drop it," he ordered.

"So there's no one here, huh, Marisa?" Luigi said in her ear. "Drop your gun, Agent Armstrong. You don't want nothing to happen to this pretty lady here."

"You won't hurt her," Dave said, not lowering his gun. "You're planning on marrying her. She's your ticket to step into Carlo's shoes."

Luigi's eyes narrowed. "Did you go snooping and find that ring I got you?"

She gasped. "I didn't—"

"Don't blame her. You forget, we're always listening. I heard you tell Carlo you planned to ask her to marry you. Got the big guy's nod of approval. Pretty smart of you."

Dave sounded smug, but underneath it all Luigi

sensed a rage in the FBI man. An anger provoked by jealousy perhaps?

Luigi decided to test his theory. "There are worse ways of getting to the top. It's been no hardship to take her to my bed." He moved his hand from her neck downward to slip inside her open jacket and grope her breast.

Marisa gasped but otherwise stayed still, apparently all too aware that his gun was still shoved into her neck.

As Luigi suspected, his actions made Dave livid. His face, set in rigid lines, flushed a dark red while his narrowed eyes promised certain retaliation. So, if Dave hadn't fucked her already, he definitely wanted her.

Luigi controlled the rage that thought caused. "You're right though. I'm not going to shoot her. I'll punish her my own way later." He pointed his gun at Dave. "After you're out of the way."

"Are you crazy?" Marisa screeched, more out of control than he'd ever heard her. "He's a federal agent, you can't shoot him."

Luigi chuckled. "You're not so innocent that you don't realize people disappear all the time. Even feebies. After today, no one will see Agent Armstrong again." Luigi's finger tightened on the trigger.

"No!" In a sudden surprise move, Marisa rammed her elbow into his gut and slung her hand to knock his gun arm aside.

The gun went off with a deafening bang, but the bullet zinged harmlessly past Dave. Before Luigi could recover, Marisa brought her clenched hands down on his wrist, making his fingers go numb. The gun dropped and she kicked it hard, sending it sliding under her sofa.

"You fucking whore!" Luigi grabbed for her.

She spun out of the way.

Dave attacked him then. Slammed him into the wall.

Fury gave Luigi strength. He slugged Dave twice in the stomach. Though it was at close range, it was with enough force to make Dave gasp and stumble backward. Luigi advanced.

For a moment, indecision held Marisa immobile. She couldn't risk letting the fight play out and hope Dave won the battle. Too much was at stake.

Luigi must have realized it, too, for he was fighting like a wild man.

Frantically, heart thundering in her ears, Marisa's gaze searched her apartment for a weapon. Luigi's gun was under the sofa and she had no idea where Dave had put his gun.

Dio, why did Dave have to attack with his hands? Why couldn't he have just shot Luigi? Some sort of man thing she was certain, having sensed his rage when Luigi was fondling her.

At last her gaze landed on a small statue of Atlas holding up the world. It was small, not over a foot tall, but it was solid marble. It would have to do.

She snatched it up and brought it down on Luigi's head with such force the statue's arms broke off and the world dropped and rolled across the floor.

Luigi fell to the floor, out cold.

CHAPTER 28

The only sound in the apartment was Dave's heavy breathing—and Marisa's thudding heartbeat. Dave looked at Luigi on the floor in front of him, then at her.

"Damn, don't you do anything like that again," he gasped.

"Like what? Saving your life?"

"Like being taken hostage in the first place. I told you to let him come into the apartment."

"Dave, he knew you were here. His men are watching the place, he showed up not long after us. He wasn't going to come in unless I let him use me as a hostage."

"When I saw that gun at your throat, I just—"

Marisa laid a hand on his arm. "I'm used to taking care of myself."

He pulled her into his embrace and squeezed her tight. "I know you are. You took care of me, too. Even though it wasn't necessary."

"Ungrateful man, he was going to shoot you," she murmured against his chest.

"Look at me."

She looked up and saw unfamiliar emotions

swimming in his eyes. Her heart fluttered in her throat. "Dave?"

"Thank you." He kissed her forehead then rested his head against hers for a few calming moments. Finally, he spoke again. "I better check on Luigi."

"I think I killed him." She shuddered, looking at the unconscious man on her floor.

Dave moved her gently aside and knelt on the floor to check her former lover. He laid his fingers on Luigi's throat. "There's a pulse."

"Thank goodness," she breathed. "I wouldn't want to go on trial for murder." She cringed. "Oh, that sounds cold."

"Hey, he brought it on himself. It would've been self-defense." Dave looked up at her, then back at Luigi. "He must have a damned hard head considering you broke this piece of marble—" Dave picked up the statue and his eyes widened. "This guy is damn near naked."

"Don't say it as if it's pornography." She took the statue from him and clutched it to her chest. "This is art. It's a statue of Atlas. Zeus made him hold up the world as punishment for supporting Cronus in a rebellion. I like him very much."

"And do you like him because it symbolizes your life?" Dave stood and walked to her. "Do you feel like you hold the world on your shoulders?"

She smiled faintly, but didn't answer.

"We need to do something with Luigi. He complicates things." Dave sighed. "We should've never come here in the first place."

"Don't you dare say I told you so. There was no choice. There are things here I need."

"I don't know what the hell you need so bad that

you would risk—"

"You don't need to know, so don't ask."

With lips clamped tightly together, Dave chose to focus on Luigi. "I've got handcuffs, but I want him tied in a chair until I can get someone here to pick him up." Dave pulled his cuffs out of his jacket that was lying across the sofa and snapped them onto Luigi's wrists.

The cuffs made Luigi look like a prisoner. Like she was a prisoner. Had always been a prisoner. "I don't have any rope—" Her voice trembled as delayed reaction set in. This whole ordeal was more nerve wracking than she planned and she was very close to losing it.

"Perhaps chains? A whip?"

With a boyish grin on Dave's face, Marisa realized he was joking with her, trying to calm her. She attempted a smile of her own but it faded away. "Fresh out of chains. Sorry."

"Stay with me a minute, princess. There has to be something." His gaze scanned the room. He got up and walked to her computer center. "Maybe some of these wires. This wire looks perfect if there's enough—"

"Wait! Don't mess with my cords." She went to the front closet. "There's some extra wire left from when I had another phone line installed. Of course now I have cable internet and don't need two phone lines. But the wire is still here." She pulled out a small roll of gray wire.

Dave nodded. "Handy." He went back to Luigi. "Help me get him into a chair. Bring one of those dining table chairs. I don't think there's enough wire to tie him into one of these fancy wing chairs of yours."

Marisa brought the chair, then struggled to help Dave lift and settle Luigi's dead weight into it. She held

Luigi while Dave wrapped the wire around him several times, securing him to the chair. Luigi's head slumped forward.

"He looks uncomfortable," she said.

"He's going to be more than uncomfortable when he wakes up with that knot you put on his head."

Marisa fingered the knot and cringed. Luigi had never been anything but good to her. Even if he was her father's right hand man.

"I'll call for back up now." He had just pulled out his phone when it rang. They both jumped. He recovered and answered, "Armstrong." He listened. "Shit, how bad is he?"

How bad was who? Marisa wondered. Sandro? Her heart sputtered. She prayed her father hadn't caught up with Sandro.

"Everything else went okay, then?"

Marisa relaxed a little. Even if Sandro had been injured, it couldn't be bad.

"Listen, I've got a pick-up for you at Midnight. Yeah, Mr. Right-Hand man himself."

"Wait, Dave." She tugged on his arm.

He paused to look at her.

"Don't forget about Luigi's men watching the place."

"Oh, that's right. On second thought there might be a problem here," Dave said. "There are some old friends visiting who need to go home now. Yeah, both exits at least. You think you can make them? You'll take care of it then?" Dave nodded. "Okay, call me back as soon as it's clear." He punched the button to disconnect.

"Who was hurt?" she asked.

"Frankie."

"Is it bad?"

"Not too bad. A shoulder wound."

"And Sandro?"

"He got away just as planned."

That was good, right? It was okay to feel relieved, she told herself. Everything was working as planned. Well, except for the little glitch with Luigi. But now he was contained. She pulled off her jacket and collapsed on the sofa. "Guess we'll be waiting here for a while."

"I'll call Sandro and see what he has to say," Dave said, pulling up the number. When Sandro answered, Dave said, "Are you safe?" A pause. Then, "How'd it go?" Dave listened for a few moments, had several more questions and suggestions for Sandro before he glanced at his watch and ended the call with, "We'll see you before then."

"Before when?" Marisa asked as Dave slid his phone into his jacket pocket.

"Sandro is giving your father a chance to call the banks to check on his now non-existent accounts. Only trouble is, the banks don't open for another five hours."

"How is Sandro holding up?"

"Better than I expected considering that Massimo has taken a sudden interest in Nia."

Marisa sat up straighter and sent Dave a piercing look. "What sort of interest?"

"Mostly bullshit, I think. You know, threatening that he'd be happy to take care of the grieving widow."

"Oh, no," Marisa whispered. "Massimo has been infatuated with Nia since he first saw her, but Sandro would never let him close."

It was Dave's turn to send her a sharp look. "Infatuated? You don't think . . ."

Marisa shrugged. "My brother has never been one to deny himself what he wants."

"Damn." Dave's chin sagged toward his chest.

Marisa knew the guilt he must be feeling. The worry Sandro must be feeling. "How is Sandro reacting?"

"Typically," Dave told her. "I think he's got your brother's murder planned right along with your father's."

"No!" Marisa blurted. She caught herself before she added, *Massimo belongs to me*. Massimo was the one who planted the bomb. She owed him.

Dave misunderstood her reaction. He knelt in front of her and took her shoulders. "We won't let your brother or your father die."

Taking a deep breath, she tried to make Dave understand. "If my brother and my father live, then Sandro and his family will never be safe. No matter where they go."

"It's not too late, Marisa. Turn over that information on those accounts and we'll haul their asses into jail so fast—"

"They won't stay in jail. My father is very smart, has the best lawyers. You know there'll be some technicality—"

"We've learned a lot of lessons over the years. Many former mob bosses are living out their last years in prison."

"Even if they go to jail, my father can run the family from his cell. At least for a while, and especially if Luigi and Angie stay loyal. Sandro will still be in danger."

"Then we need to find a way to limit your father's power. Possibly have him deported if the Italian authorities were after him—"

"I don't know how much information the Italians have. We had just gotten rumors that they were starting an investigation. After having seen what they did to the other families, we decided to not risk capture. For all I know, the Italians gave up on investigating us after we left."

"I wouldn't count on it," Dave said. "But if that's not a route we can go, then perhaps we can get Angie or Luigi to turn. If they won't help us, then at least we might put a bug in their ear that this is their chance to be boss. If we're real lucky, they'll kill each other."

Shock zapped Marisa, she knew she couldn't hide it from her face.

"What?" Dave asked. "You can calmly speak of your family's death, but is possibly losing Luigi too much for you?"

A bitter smile replaced the shock. "Jealous, Dave?" She ran her fingers along his collar.

He caught her hand. "Maybe."

Not the answer she wanted to hear. She slipped her hand free and changed subjects. "You don't think he's hurt seriously, do you?" She moved over to kneel in front of Luigi, she took his wrist. "His pulse seems strong enough."

"You do care for him," Dave accused.

"I feel guilty for using him," Marisa corrected him, then stood and tried to get his focus off Luigi. "It won't work. If you arrest my father. For all we know he has some trigger in place to kill Nia and Danny if he's arrested. We have to get them safe first."

"I can't imagine you continuing to be caught up in this life."

"I won't," she answered. "I'm finished."

Dave turned away and walked to a window, staring out on the street below. "So you wouldn't have married Luigi if things had turned out differently?"

Marisa hated that Dave had heard that conversation between her father and Luigi. She hadn't even known about it.

"No," she answered Dave at last, moving beside him to look out the window. "My goal has always been to get out of the Mafia. I would never marry a member."

Dave continued to stare out the window."Would you marry someone in the FBI?"

The question came out of nowhere. Stunned, Marisa turned to stare at Dave's profile since he was still watching the traffic below. She wasn't able to look into his eyes. She didn't know if he was serious.

Then he looked at her, and his gaze said dead serious.

Her heart beating fast, she decided to be cautious, yet truthful. "I don't know. The FBI is like a "family" itself. Look at you, for example. Your father before you was in the FBI. Your son after you will probably be in the FBI. After growing up in just such a hierarchy, I don't know if I can handle it for the rest of my life."

He turned back to the window. "The FBI is slightly different from the mob, princess."

"Just because it's a legal organization, doesn't mean it still doesn't control your life."

"There's another difference. An agent can quit the FBI without having to die."

She shrugged. "Point taken." She smoothed her hand over his back to hide her uncertainty, then asked before she could stop herself. "Would you quit?"

He turned and wrapped her hands with his own,

holding them against his chest. His gaze held hers. "Would you ask me to quit?"

"There's no use in this discussion. I shouldn't have asked." She broke eye contact, her stomach sinking.

"Why?"

"We barely know each other."

"I feel like I know you. Very well."

"You know what I told you. You have to realize it affected me." She stared at his chest, just above where he held her hands.

He moved his right hand, and with his finger, he tilted her chin, forcing her to meet his gaze. "I respect you just for surviving, Marisa." He kissed her. Gently, softly.

Marisa's head spun with possibility. But she had to pull herself back to reality. She knew what lay ahead. Dave didn't. There was no way he'd want to be with her when he knew exactly what she was capable of doing. Of what she would have to do. Still, she wouldn't shut the door permanently. Not just yet. "When it's all over," she told him, "if you can honestly tell me that you respect me—"

"I already told you—"

"No, I mean when it is *all* over, if you can tell me that you still respect me, then maybe there is a chance for us. Whether you leave the FBI or not."

Dave pulled her closer for another kiss, but this time a moan interrupted them.

Marisa turned from Dave to look at Luigi. "He's waking."

"Maybe now is a good time to suggest it would be wise to cooperate with us."

"He will never cooperate, but I will try." She

walked over and knelt down. "Luigi? Gigi, can you hear me?"

He moaned again. Then slowly, he opened his eyes. They were clearly out of focus. He blinked and squinted, a pained frown covering his face. "Marisa? *Por Dio*, my head." His awareness coming back, he realized he was restrained in the chair. "What's going on?"

"I'm sorry I had to hit you."

His sharp, narrowed gaze told her he remembered everything now.

"You." Luigi spat the word. "Are you trying to kill me? What are you doing with the FBI? Are you plotting something against your father?" He was a whole fountain of questions now that he was cognizant. He also had his own answers. "Of course. You must be. Why would you turn on your father, Marisa?"

"I am helping Sandro."

Surprise momentarily erased the pain from Luigi's face. "Sandro? Do you love him still, then? Are you trying to win his gratitude if not his love?"

"I'm trying to do what is right—"

"Since when has what's right and wrong ever bothered you?"

The jab hit sharp and true. Marisa looked to Dave and sent him a silent message. *See, I told you. I'm not worthy of respect.*

"It was wrong of my father to take Sandro's family to make him cooperate with something illegal."

"And to make it right, you stole all of your father's money?"

Marisa was experienced at concealing her emotions, but Luigi's accusations were so unexpected, she couldn't hide her surprise.

312

"Oh, yes, I know it was you, Marisa. I know your skills with the computer. And your alibi didn't pan out since your "friends" failed to back up your story about the opera."

"Did you hurt my friends?"

"It took a little coercion."

She felt sad for her friends, who by now would want nothing more to do with her. "Gigi—"

"You didn't answer my question. Do you still love Sandro? Is that why you are willing to destroy your father?"

"No. I've never loved Sandro as more than a brother. I broke off the engagement."

"Then why, Marisa? Hasn't your father always given you everything you wanted?"

"No. He never gave me my freedom."

"You're an Italian. Italian women don't have freedom."

She shook her head, knowing they wouldn't get far if they argued. "Luigi, if you'll just help—"

"Help? What kind of help do you possibly expect from me?"

Marisa didn't answer. In her mind, there was no way Luigi could help except by staying out of the way. She looked to Dave.

"You can testify against Carlo when we bring him in," Dave spoke up.

"You want me to be a rat? Are you outta your mind?"

Marisa pleaded, because if Luigi agreed to help, at least he'd be out of the way so she and Sandro could go through with their plan. "Gigi, *caro*, if you ever loved me—"

"You're an ungrateful bitch. I may have loved you, but I realize my mistake now."

His anger only hardened her resolve. She and Sandro were doing what was necessary. Dave's way would not work at all, but he would never believe it. He still naively believed in the justice system. When true justice only existed for those who took a stand.

"If you don't help," Dave said, anger outlining every feature as he moved closer, "then I'll have to take you in."

Marisa wondered at the anger on Dave's face. Was it because Luigi insulted her?

"What's the charge? Running into a heavy object wielded by a traitorous bitch? I don't think it'll stick," Luigi taunted. "As a matter of fact, I'm the one who should be pressing charges. I could have your badge, Fed."

Marisa wanted to hit him again.

Dave nearly did. He twisted Luigi's shirt with one hand and had the other pulled back in a fist before he stopped himself. "Actually the charge would be attempting to shoot a federal officer. You're on your way to jail, buddy."

He released Luigi and stepped away. "So until my men get here to pick you up, enjoy being tied to a dining room chair." Dave made himself comfortable on the sofa, stretching his long legs across the coffee table. "Join me, Marisa?"

"Can I have a drink?" Luigi said. "Maybe some pain killer for my head?"

"Certainly," she answered.

"I'll get it," Dave said, moving to get up.

Marisa had a flash of inspiration. "No, stay there.

I'll get it. I have some in my medicine cabinet." In the bathroom, she took the pain killer and another, smaller vial from the shelf. Concealing the smaller vial, she went to the kitchen for a glass.

Once she filled the glass with water, keeping her back to Luigi and Dave, she made a show of opening the bottle, while in reality, she was counting off drops from the vial into the water.

Shoving the sleeping drops out of the way behind a crockery of cooking utensils, she took two pills and the water to Luigi. She realized with his hands cuffed behind him, he couldn't take the medicine himself.

"Open," she told him. "You want one at a time or both?"

"Both."

She placed the pills in his mouth then held the water to his lips. He nodded his head when he'd had enough.

"Damn, those taste like shit."

"Yes, they do, don't they?" she calmly agreed, then sat the glass back on the counter. "I'll gather all my things now," she told Dave and disappeared into her bedroom.

* * *

"Hello, Markie. Guess today is your lucky day," Steve, the big Texan on the task force, was hard to miss as he walked up beside the parked mobster car. He opened the door.

"Hey, what're you doin'? Can't a guy sit in his car without being hassled?"

"Not in this neighborhood, partner."

The guy in the passenger seat next to Markie went for his gun but his door suddenly flung open and he found a gun pressed to the back of his skull. "You don't want to do that," Tony told him.

Steve sent Tony an appreciative look, then turned back to Markie. "You two need to come with us."

"What for?" Markie asked.

Tony reached into the glove compartment and rummaged around. "Oh, maybe for these parking violations you haven't paid."

"You two ain't cops. You can't hassle me about no parking violations."

"But we can give you a ride to the police station. I'm sure they'd be very appreciative." Steve reached in and pulled Markie from behind the wheel, while Tony pulled his guy out of the car on the passenger side.

Quickly and efficiently, the two FBI men disarmed the two mobsters.

"Hey, what the hell do you think you're doing?"

"You got a permit for these?"

"Sure I do."

"Good, I think the police are going to want to see it." Steve took Markie's arm and led him toward the gray government-issued sedan.

* * *

Nicola needed some fresh air. The car reeked of cigarette smoke. They'd been sitting in the confined vehicle, doing nothing more than watching the garage exit of Marisa's building and puffing one cigarette after another. Now, Nicola's head was hurting.

"I'll be back, man," he told his companion.

"Where you going?"

"Just up for some fresh air. Honk if you see anything, I'll come back down." Nicola opened his door and climbed out. His eye caught a furtive movement between two cars behind them. It was there, then it disappeared. He peered hard between the cars.

"What's wrong with you?" his companion asked.

"Shh," Nicola warned. "I think something's up." He stared harder. He saw nothing, yet an uneasy feeling had settled in his chest. "Start the car, we're getting out of here."

"Luigi's gonna be pissed if we let Marisa get away—"

"Fuck, Luigi. Something's not right."

The man started the car. At the sound of the engine, two men came from between the parked cars, running toward Nicola.

"Freeze, FBI."

"Shit," Nicola swore then dived into the car. "Get out of here now." Nicola nearly tumbled out of the car as the tires spun on the concrete garage floor. He managed to pull the door shut as the car sped away. He looked behind them. The two FBI men were chasing on foot. One fired his gun. Nicola ducked.

"Wait, man, there's an old lady, don't shoot again," Gregg told his partner.

"Oh, hell, they're gonna run her down." At the last minute, the car swerved and missed the old woman.

Gregg and his partner Bobby, still the newbies on the team, ran over to check on her. "You all right, lady?"

"Get those damned hoodlums." The old woman wielded her walking stick like a weapon.

"Yes, ma'am, we're after them."

"You cops?" she asked.

"Something like that." Gregg and Bobby ran for their car. The engine barely started before Gregg was spinning out after the two mobsters who got away.

CHAPTER 29

When Marisa came out of her room with a duffel bag and a wooden box ten minutes later, Dave was standing at the kitchen counter, examining the glass she'd used for Luigi. A quick glance told her Luigi was out cold.

"Dave?"

He turned. He held the vial in his hand. "You drugged him?"

"Sleeping drops. I thought it would be more convenient if he were unconscious."

"Your own special concoction, I presume?"

She dropped her gaze and shrugged.

"My God, the man most likely has a major concussion and you're giving him sleeping drops."

She looked at Luigi with alarm. "You think it'll kill him?"

"I don't know. I'm not a doctor." Dave sighed. "But if he survived that damned knock upside the head you gave him, he'll probably survive this."

"I'm sorry, Dave. He made me mad when he threatened to press charges."

"Remind me not to make you mad."

The intercom by the door buzzed. Marisa walked over to press the button.

"Ms. Peruzzo," the doorman said, "there's two men down here who want to come up. A Gregg and Bobby—they wouldn't tell me their last names, said you knew—"

She glanced at Dave who nodded. "Yes, yes, I'm expecting them. Please send them up, Murray. Thank you." She turned to Dave. "You better start untying Luigi."

"I'm right on it."

She pulled on her jacket and gathered her stuff. An overnight duffel and a wooden box she'd kept hidden in a secret hollowed out place in her bathroom.

"What's in the box?" Dave asked.

"It's what I needed to come back here for."

"You're not going to tell me."

She shook her head, knowing he'd be stunned. "When it's important for you to know, then I'll tell you."

There was a knock on the door. She hurried to open it. "Come on in."

"Shit, what happened to him?" Bobby asked, referring to the unconscious Luigi.

"I thought he needed a nap," Marisa said, deadpan.

The two men eyed her warily.

"Come on, get over here and help," Dave snapped. "He's dead weight."

"Are you sure he's not just dead?" Gregg asked.

"He's still alive. Come on."

Between the three men, they managed to carry Luigi into the hall. Marisa locked the apartment door behind them, then hurried to press the button on the elevator.

320

It was an uneventful ride down. At the bottom, Dave pushed the "hold" button. "Bobby, give me your handcuffs, mine are on Luigi."

Without question, Bobby turned them over.

Before Marisa could figure out the strange request, Dave ordered her, "Hold out your hands."

She couldn't believe it. "What?" Anger blossomed, heating her face. "You're going to cuff me?"

His gaze, filled with regret, pleaded for understanding. "If anybody sees us, I want them to think you're a prisoner. Trust me, princess."

She sighed, trying to keep her nerves steady at the way things were progressing. "No one carries my box but me," she warned, needing to hang onto some measure of control.

"Since it has a handle, you can still carry it. I'll come back for your bag after we get Luigi into the car."

She set her load down and held out her hands. "All right."

The cold metal snapped around her wrists. She swallowed, took a breath, then picked up her box.

It didn't take long for them to stuff Luigi in the back seat of Gregg and Bobby's car.

"Listen, I don't want you to take him in yet. He'll be squawking too loud when he wakes up. I want him quiet until we get this all pulled together."

"You think we oughta take him to a hospital?" Bobby asked. "He looks like he's in pretty bad shape. That's a big knot on his head."

"That bump on his head's nothing. He already woke up from that. Marisa gave him some sleeping drops to shut him up so we didn't have to listen to him," Dave explained. "Just take him to a hotel room and watch him until I call you," Dave instructed.

"He's gonna be royally pissed when he wakes up again," Gregg predicted. "Maybe we should take those drops with us."

"Just keep a close watch on him," Dave ordered. "He'll probably be out a good while yet."

With a nod, Gregg put the car in gear and drove off.

"I'm taking Marisa to the hotel to wait with Sandro," Dave told Tony and Steve, who'd been in the parking garage watching for any more of Luigi's men. "We'll set the rest of the plan in action soon. You two be ready for my call." The men gave their okays, then left for their car.

Dave went back for her duffel bag. "Come on, princess."

He hurried her to his car and helped her in. She tried to ignore how much she felt like a prisoner.

"I'll take those cuffs off as soon as we are down the road a bit." He reached for the box.

"I'll hold it," she said, tightening her grip on the handle.

From the look on his face, it was obvious he was very curious about what she had in her box, but he shut the door without a word and hurried to the driver's side. As he started the car, he pulled out his phone. "I'm calling Sandro and telling him we're on the way."

They drove up the ramp out of the underground garage; her heart rate speeded. This was it, not too much longer before it was all over. After so many years . . . .

At street level, there was some sort of commotion causing a traffic jam. "Hold on, Sandro," Dave said, then turned to her. "I've got a bad feeling about this. I'm going to see what's going on."

"Dave." Marisa grabbed for him with her bound hands, a surge of worry that he was worried making her nervous. "Be careful."

He nodded, stepped out and walked to the front of the car to scan the road. Quickly, he hurried back and opened his car door to tell her, "There's a big wreck ahead. We'll go another way."

The man ran out from behind a concrete post so fast she barely had time to call, "Dave, look out!"

Her warning came too late. The man running up hit Dave on the back of the head with the butt of his gun. Dave stumbled and fell against the car.

At the same moment, Marisa's door flew open and another man grabbed her. She screamed and fought.

"Calm down, Marisa, we're trying to rescue you."

Oh, Dio. She shut up. Luigi's men were trying to save her from Dave. She had no doubt they'd engineered the snarled traffic jam to allow them to get to her. *Merda*, what was she going to do? If she fought, then they'd suspect she wasn't a prisoner. But if she went with them, it would blow Sandro's plans wide open.

Dave grabbed his head, obviously stunned, but not unconscious. She saw him reach for his gun. She needed to distract the man beside her. "Just a minute, I'll get out," she told him. She scooted to the edge of her seat, then prepared to climb out.

In that instant, Dave whirled and fired his gun at the man behind him. Once. Then in a quick move, Dave spun and fired a second shot. Blood splattered on Marisa as the man beside her fell to the ground.

Adrenaline spurted through her but caught in her throat. She wanted to scream but all her fear was balled up, trapped, unable to escape. She tried to swallow. She tried to breathe.

"Shut the door," Dave ordered, his voice coming from a long distance.

Her head spun.

"Marisa!" he snapped in an authoritative voice. "Shut the door."

Somehow she made herself obey, then he jerked the car into gear. He barreled out into the traffic.

Finally, Dave looked at her. "Damn, you've got blood all over you. Were you hit?"

She looked down at her clothes. Her stomach rolled with queasiness. "You shot that man," she said, her voice breaking in funny ways since her breathing was jagged, uneven. "He was. Right. By me. Shot him." She turned to face him. "You could have hit me."

"Did I?" Dave demanded. "Did I hit you?"

She shook her head, and swallowed, struggled to get more air into her lungs than the jagged, gaspy breathing was allowing.

"I'm sorry. I had to. You know that." Concern etched his face.

She nodded once.

Seeming satisfied, Dave turned his attention to driving then, ramming into cars stuck in the traffic, forcing an opening where there was none. Soon, though it seemed an eternity to Marisa, they burst free on a side street.

Then Marisa heard it. A faint, far off yelling sound. She looked around, puzzled. "What . . .is. . .that. . .noise?" Her brain was still functioning at slow speed.

Dave glanced around then down at the seat between them. He picked up his phone. "It's Sandro. I never disconnected the call."

Putting the phone to his ear, Dave said, "Yeah, they tried to snatch her, I'm sure the whole traffic jam set up was just to grab her. But we're okay now. We'll be there in a few minutes."

Dave disconnected and immediately started punching in numbers again.

"What about Luigi?" Marisa asked. "I didn't see the car he was in."

"I'm calling them now," Dave said.

"What if Luigi's soldiers got him? He could ruin everything."

"Damn, they're not answering." Dave spared her a glance. "If they somehow managed to nab Luigi, then I'm damned glad you gave him those sleeping drops."

CHAPTER 30

They called him a playmaker. A man who could make something happen out of nothing. Time and again, Carlo had watched Sandro take a game that everyone had given up as lost, and somehow—magically—slip through a tight defense and find the back of the net. Or find the perfect pass for another player on his team to score. Providing a victory where there had been no hope.

And now Sandro was playing him. Carlo thought he had the game won, his defense tighter than a young virgin, his offense effective and sure as a Romeo intent on deflowering her. When he captured Nia and little Daniele, Carlo thought there was no way Sandro could refuse to cooperate. Yet suddenly, here Carlo sat, at a distinct disadvantage, his game plan scattered.

He took his cell phone and punched in Luigi's number. There was no answer. Carlo called the office next. "Is Luigi back? No? He's not answering his phone. Where the hell is he?"

Massimo came back then.

"You lost him?" Carlo asked, already knowing the answer from the look on his son's face.

"He has the Feds helping him. They expected us to

go after him and had a trap to stop us."

"Hmm." Carlo pondered a moment.

"That's not a bad thing, I don't think," Massimo went on to explain. "That means that Sandro's promise to kill us were just threats. The FBI won't let him go around murdering people, even if we are on their most wanted list."

"Sandro wouldn't murder anyone anyway." Carlo waved his hand in a dismissive gesture. "He's a crack shot, I know, but he doesn't have what it takes to harm a person."

"He loves his family very much," Massimo pointed out. "If the Feds weren't involved, I'm not sure I'd agree with you."

"Obviously, if he's been cooperating with the FBI, they are still planning to trap us somehow. Since he's accessed our accounts, they may have found a way," Carlo said thoughtfully.

"I thought Roberto had all the money well accounted for."

"So he says." It was true Roberto had an elaborate money laundering system set up.

"Have you talked to our contact at the FBI?" Massimo asked. "Maybe he has some information."

"Other than letting us know what happened to Roberto, Mr. Madison has been very quiet lately. I believe the task force is on to him and he's no use to us now. I can check and see if they've taken Luigi into custody."

"Yes, do that." Carlo tapped his fingers on the table, pondering. Then he picked up his cell phone again. "Angie, I need you down here. *Si, si*, I know you're watching Nia, but Giovanni can handle it a little while. If not, get Joey to help him. We've had something new come up."

Carlo turned back to Massimo. "Find Luigi, and if he's not in custody, get him here."

Massimo nodded, then left his father sitting at the table, deep in thought. Massimo went to Carmine, a trusted soldier, but more importantly Massimo's friend. "Luigi seems to have dropped out of sight. Contact some of his soldiers, see if you can locate him. Carlo wants him down here asap."

Not for the first time, Massimo was disregarding his father's orders. Knowing Angie—Nia's watchdog—would be out of the way, Massimo had more important things on his mind than locating the missing *consigliere*. "As for me," he added to Carmine, "I'll be out of touch for a while. I've got someone else I need to see."

* * *

"Try another bite."

"Don't want another bite." Daniele slammed his fork down on his plate.

Sighing, Nia grabbed the green bean Daniele refused to eat and stuck it in her mouth. She wasn't hungry either, but she knew she had to eat. Not only for the baby growing in her womb, but for the strength it was going to take to escape with Daniele when the chance came. With that in mind, she hadn't been resisting her urge to sleep either, and took a nap when her son did. It was almost nap time. Remembering how she had been awakened earlier today, though, she was a little leery of going to sleep. Surely Massimo wouldn't come back. Or if he did, Angie wouldn't let him in to see her again.

Daniele clambered off his chair and picked up his scattered blocks and toy car—both presents from Angie. Using the blocks, he constructed a ramp for his car to jump. After fifteen minutes of that, he was bored. "Cartoons, Momma."

Angie had also provided a small color television, but unfortunately it didn't have premium cable channels with cartoons. She could only find game shows and talk shows.

"There's no cartoons on yet," she explained, though he couldn't grasp the concept. "Let's sing songs."

"Don't want to sing."

"All right, how about a nap?" She knew how well that would go over.

"I want to watch TV."

Since the incident with Massimo this morning, Daniele was fussier than usual. The whole situation had to be incredibly hard for the boy to process.

"Okay, okay, we'll watch TV." She flipped through the channel and discovered that the television received a PBS channel, too. "The Mob In America" was on. As if she needed lessons. She had up close and personal experience with the mob. Too up close and personal.

She flipped the channel, but Daniele started crying. "Oh, sweetie, you don't want to watch that show, do you?"

"Change it, change it, change it." He ran to the television, attempting to change the channel himself. Hoping he'd sleep soon, she flipped the channel back to PBS.

He quieted and she sighed. "All right, we'll watch this, but come sit and let momma rock you." The comfortable wooden rocking chair with the padded seat was courtesy of Angie, too. Since her son had been brought to her, Angie had gone out of his way to make things bearable for them. She was beginning to appreciate all his efforts.

Daniele climbed into her lap, settling comfortably. Nia rocked him, relishing the feel of his warm little body snuggled against hers, yet hoping he'd go to sleep quickly. Then she could turn off the television and take a nap herself.

It wasn't long before the show focused on the infamous John Gotti. Back in the 80's the media had dubbed him the Teflon Don because no matter how many times the FBI brought a case against him, he slipped right through the system without being convicted.

Physically, John Gotti reminded her of Carlo. Except Carlo's hair had more gray and he was heavier. Yet their manner and bearing were almost identical. Both assured to the point of arrogance as if they were above laws that governed common men. And both fashionably dressed, their expensive suits tailored to look sharp even on frames that were beyond a youthful physique. And watching both men made chills crawl along her spine.

Nia remembered when she first saw Carlo. Not at the restaurant. No, years before that. It was the day after the spectacular night with Sandro, after a night on the town to celebrate Italy making the World Cup finals.

Sandro had gone to see the trainer about his injured leg. It wasn't long after he left that a knock came upon her hotel room door. It was Francesco, the goalkeeper.

"Did you enjoy last night?"

She smiled as memories surfaced. "It was great, a

fairy-tale night. I felt like a princess."

"You certainly sang like a princess."

There had been karaoke, and she took her turn on stage. She was touched and her smile spread wider. "Why, thank you."

"I couldn't find you to tell you last night. You disappeared soon after."

Her smile fell away. "Sandro's leg was bothering—"

"Ahhh. Sandro. His leg. That is why I'm here."

"You're here because of his leg?"

"*Si*. The doctor, he sees my hand, when Sandro came in—"

"Your hand? Are you okay?" She grabbed both his hands in hers, turning them over, looking at them closely.

He pulled his right hand loose. "Not too bad. Just a little strain on the wrist."

"You'll be able to play?"

"*Si*."

"Thank goodness."

"The trainer sent me after you so he can show you how to keep Sandro's leg wrapped."

"Oh, okay. Let me grab the key card, and I'll go right down."

"I'll come with you."

The hotel management had temporarily converted the exercise rooms to training rooms for the soccer teams lodged there. Francesco punched the elevator button for the basement.

When the doors opened, he said, "This way," and took her to the left.

"Which room is it?" Nia asked.

"It is right around the cor—" Francesco stopped

abruptly.

Two men in expensive suits stood in front of the door.

"What's wrong?" Nia whispered, feeling suddenly nervous for no explainable reason.

"Sandro's there." Francesco nodded toward the door. "But I do not recognize those men."

Another man dressed in wind shorts and a blue "Italy" t-shirt stalked toward the door. After exchanging heated Italian—words that Nia couldn't quite hear—with the men in front of the door, the man in shorts stomped toward them.

"That is the trainer coming toward us," Francesco said quietly.

"What's wrong? Why isn't he in with Sandro?" Nia kept her voice lowered as well.

Francesco stopped the trainer and asked him. He spoke in Italian, not knowing that Nia could understand most of what was being said as she'd used the time away from Sandro to study Italian with a computer program.

The man in shorts stomped away from them, obviously pacing the hall.

"What did he mean about the stupid Mafia?"

Francesco sent her a sharp look. "You understood? I did not know you could—"

"I didn't understand much of it. Just something about them running him out of the room. Those men are Mafia? What do they want with Sandro?" Her voice lowered to a mere whisper.

"No, no," Francesco hurried to assure her. "It is just the insult to call someone *mafioso* in *Italia*."

Yet the nattily-dressed man with gray hair who came out of the room certainly looked like a Mafia guy to her. Or how she imagined a Mafia guy would look. And though he smiled pleasantly and nodded to her as he passed, he and his two companions still gave her the creeps.

And as it turned out, she was right. Carlo was not only a Mafia guy, but a head honcho.

She hadn't thought of the incident in years. And now that she had, she wondered what Carlo had wanted then. Had it just been one loyal Italian fan wishing Italy's soccer star luck, as Sandro claimed? Or even then, had there been something more sinister going on?

She couldn't think of what it might be.

And she didn't have to think of it anymore, since Daniele's body was now relaxed in sleep. Carefully, she adjusted him on her shoulder, pushed out of the chair and turned off the TV. Too much of a bad thing was depressing.

Laying her son on the cot, she curled up beside him, ready for her afternoon nap. At least in sleep, as long as she didn't have the nightmare, she forgot the bad things. If she was lucky, sometimes she even dreamed about the good things . . . .

* * *

"Open it."

Nia's hands were shaking visibly as she reached for the small, ring-sized box. "Sandro, is this . . ." She couldn't finish the thought. It would be too disappointing if— She stopped that thought, too, and opened the box.

A solitaire diamond glittered at her. "Sandro, is this . . ." she began again.

"I want you to stay in Italy as my wife."

She'd been the last weeks in Italy, touring his country, falling more in love. "But—"

"I could not bear it if you returned to the States."

"I can't believe this. We haven't known each other for very long."

"For me, the time we've known each other does not matter. I have explained to you about the—"

"Yes, the thunderbolt. I remember. God, Sandro, I just can't believe—"

"You have not given me an answer. Do you need time to think about it?"

"Think about it? It's been my fantasy since we first met."

"And has being with me so far not turned out well?"

She gave a little laugh. "Well? It turned out better than my wildest imaginings."

"Perhaps to be my wife would be better than your wildest imaginings, too."

"I don't know, I think my imagination has gotten better lately."

He smiled and pulled the ring from the box, dangling it in front of her face. "Will you marry me, then?"

"Yes, Sandro. God, yes."

He slipped the ring on her finger.

In her sleep, Nia smiled and stretched.

"Ah, *cara*, something makes you happy."

She frowned. The voice didn't sound as if it belonged to Sandro.

Something cold pressed under her chin. She opened her eyes.

Massimo hovered close to her face and she

334

frowned. "This is twice that you have awakened me," she snapped, trying for bravado though a chill had settled over her. Where was Angie? Why was Massimo here again?

"Lucky you, I would say."

He shifted and she became aware that the cold metal under her chin was a gun. *A gun!* All bravery fled her as a heavy lump settled in her stomach and tremors shook through her body.

Had they found Sandro, and Massimo had been sent to kill her?

Her thoughts must have showed on her face.

"No, we still do not have your husband. This is between you and me." Massimo nodded to someone over his shoulder. "Take the kid."

CHAPTER 31

Angie fidgeted in his chair while Carlo ranted and paced the floor of his private dining room.

"I can't believe he outsmarted me."

Irritation ate at Angie. He felt antsy being away from Nia and her son. If Massimo showed up at the warehouse, Angie didn't think Giovanni could be trusted to do the right thing. Still, Angelo managed to keep impatience from his voice as he answered his boss respectfully. "You always knew Sandro was a very smart man."

"This goes beyond smart." Carlo pounded his fist in the air. "He was diabolically clever, stealing all my fucking money like he did."

"And he nabbed your daughter, too."

Carlo stilled. "He won't hurt Marisa."

Angie looked his boss in the eye. "You have his wife and son, can you be sure of that? A desperate man will do anything."

"Yeah, that's what he said." Carlo sounded thoughtful. "But still, other than hunting, he's always been so non-violent. I've never even seen him lose his temper and he's Italian!"

336

"I'm sure a man might abandon any values he might have when his family's life is in danger. Isn't that how you got him to cooperate the first time?"

Carlo frowned at his underboss. "I never expected he would try anything so underhanded. He's been like a member of my own family. I watched him grow up, for God's sake."

"Frankly, Carlo, I don't think this is just some rebellion. He is serious about wanting away from the 'family.' Why can't you make an exchange and—"

"I can't let him call the shots!" Carlo exploded. "I'm the boss of this family; I've outsmarted the cops in two countries. No way a soccer superstar with a big ego is going to bring me down."

Carlo paced to the wall and banged his fist, rattling the framed pictures of past hunting trips.

Angie didn't back down. "That's just it, Carlo. He is a soccer star—he has a worldwide following. You can't just whack him out."

"I can take out his wife and kid—"

Angie's blood ran cold. "I'm sure there'd be some sort of retaliation. You'd have the FBI crawling all over us."

Carlo snorted. "As if they aren't already. Their deaths can be made to look like an accident."

"As much as Sandro loves his family, if you kill them, he won't stop until you're dead."

Jerking up his cell phone, Carlo jabbed in a number. "Then he'll have to have an 'accident', too." Apparently, there was no answer on the phone. Frustrated, Carlo pulled the phone away from his ear and punched in another number. "Why is no one answering their goddamned phone?" He threw the phone on the table. "Where the hell is everybody? First, Luigi disappears and now Massimo—"

The chilled blood in Angie's veins turned to ice. "Massimo is missing? I thought he was here when you called me."

"I sent him to find Luigi. Now I can't find either one of them. They don't answer their phones. Fuck."

"How long's Luigi been missing?"

"I was talking to him when Sandro showed up and interrupted my lunch." Carlo splayed his hand over his stomach. "I still have indigestion. It's been hours."

"You think he's in on this?"

"Who's in on what?"

"Luigi. Surely you've figured Sandro had to have inside help. What if Luigi's the one who helped?"

"What! That's ridiculous—" Carlo broke off and frowned. "Luigi wants to marry Marisa. He has no reason to plot against me."

"Maybe he doesn't want to wait for you to die. You know ambition has ruined many men."

Carlo shook his head. "Not Luigi. He's as loyal as you are, Angie. I'd trust you both with my life."

"Then where is he?"

"I don't know, but Massimo is missing, too. Are you gonna suggest my son is plotting against me, too?"

Angie had a nasty suspicion Massimo had something else on his mind at the moment. Yet he couldn't get up and walk out on Carlo without his permission and check the theory. The mood Carlo was in, he'd likely shoot Angie.

"Been known to happen in other families, Carlo. A man never can be too careful." At Carlo's thunderous look, Angie wished he'd bitten back his response. Worry

338

was addling his mind, making him speak before thinking. "Of course, that's not the case with Massimo. He's loyal," Angie soothed. "Call the office, see what's happening there."

"Yeah, that's a good idea." Carlo picked his phone up and punched in a third number. "Julia," Carlo said to his assistant, "you found out anything yet? What? You got the bank president out of bed and he's going to the bank now? Good thinking. Let me know the second you find out. And remind me to give you a little extra something." Carlo disconnected the call and looked at Angie. "You heard."

"That was brilliant, Carlo. Julia's as tenacious as a bulldog, she'll find out about those accounts for you." Angie stood. "I better get back to Sandro's wife and kid. They may be too much for Giovanni—"

"What? A woman and a little kid? Don't you have them locked up?"

"Yeah, but—"

Carlo waved his hand dismissively. "She'll be fine."

"You know she's escaped before."

"You think I'm stupid? I think she's tired and worn down now, and too worried about what I'll do to her kid if she tries anything."

"What *would* you do with her kid if she tries to escape?"

Carlo looked thoughtful. "I don't know. I figured just threatening her would keep her in line. Maybe we'd have to shoot her if she does it again."

"What!" Angie tried to rein in his dismayed reaction. "There was a time when we didn't hurt women."

Carlo snorted. "That's old school."

Angie found himself inclined to believe those rumors about Carlo's wife. "But if Nia's dead," Angie argued, "she won't be much use to us."

"I didn't say we'd kill her. Aim for her legs. Can't run with shot up legs."

Angie wasn't going to be aiming his gun at any part of Nia's body. He didn't want anyone else aiming a gun either. "She's a soccer player, Carlo. You shoot her legs and you ruin her career."

Carlo shook his head and gave Angie a look. "Then she shouldn't try to escape, should she?"

Just then, Carlo's cell phone chirped. He picked it up. "Yeah?" His face turned a pasty white. "You're sure? All gone and nothing they can do?" He paused. "Of course, they're gonna look into it. You're goddamned right they're gonna look into it. How could that have happened?" Carlo laid the phone on the table and sat down hard.

"You okay, Carlo? You don't look so good."

"It's gone. All the money is really gone."

"Can't they find it?"

"They can look where the deposits went, but if it's a legitimate account, legitimate bank, and it looks like a legitimate transaction, I'm screwed. He said, of course, they would launch an investigation."

Angie shook his head and whistled.

Carlo tapped his fingers on the table, then looked up. "Someone had to give them the password to get into those accounts in the first place."

"Maybe Sandro persuaded Marisa to talk."

"Marisa's on the accounts for an emergency, but she doesn't know the passwords to them. Just Roberto, me and Luigi . . . Now, Luigi's missing." Carlo frowned. "Maybe he is looking to take over the operation like you said. Why'd you say that? You heard something?"

Angie held out his hands. "Just a thought, Carlo. No, I haven't heard nothing. You know I'd've told you."

Carlo slapped a fist on the table. "Well, I got no choice now. I'm gonna have to deal with Sandro." He jerked up the phone once again. "All right, Sandro, where do you want to meet? And who are you bringing?"

Angie looked at his watch impatiently. He'd been gone way too long.

"Okay, Dave and Marisa and nobody else. I'm bringing Angie and Massimo and your wife and son . . . what do you mean, you're gonna bring someone else, then? I got you outnumbered? All right then. One more man. What's his name?"

CHAPTER 32

"No!" Nia flew up off the cot after Giovanni as he stripped Daniele away from her. Her cry woke her son and the boy promptly started screaming. "Don't take my son!"

Massimo knocked her back down. The brushed steel on the gun gleamed under the artificial lights as he pointed it in her face. The door shut behind Giovanni. Daniele's screams faded as Giovanni walked away.

Rage shook through every muscle in Nia's body. Yet the deadly looking gun in her face kept her from any rash moves. "What are you doing with my son? Tell Giovanni to bring him back!"

"*Cara*, you are in no position to be giving orders."

"Hurt him, and I'll kill you." Her chest heaved and her voice shook, but a calmness descended upon her.

Massimo smiled at that. "You make big threats with my Beretta shoved in your face."

"You don't have the balls to shoot me." With a quick move, she knocked the gun aside and rolled off the cot. She sprang to her feet, preparing to battle.

Fury in his face, Massimo rammed his fist against her jaw, his hand still wrapped around the black grip of his weapon. Pain exploded in her head, forcing her to stumble backward. She landed against the wall, and worked hard to keep her footing.

He didn't shoot her, but that was little consolation with her jaw throbbing like electric volts were arcing through it. She tasted blood in her mouth, felt it dribbling past her lips.

Massimo advanced upon her. She knew she'd have to take him out fast. Her strength would never last against his. She blinked, trying to clear the pain away, but he was too fast.

He pinned her body against the wall, the cold barrel of his gun stroking against her throbbing face. "You will see soon, *cara*, just what kind of balls I do have." With his free hand, he grabbed her right breast.

Her legs nearly gave way. She locked her knees to keep herself upright. Any weakness on her part would add to his power.

She glared. He was too close for her to knee in the groin or stomp his foot. She'd have to wait to make her move. "Show me your balls and you'll wish you hadn't," she ground out, imagining squeezing, biting, twisting . . .

He took advantage of her helplessness. Keeping her pinned against the wall with his body and the Beretta pressed just under her ear, he used his free hand to explore her body. Her flesh shrank away from his touch. A loud roaring swelled inside her head. She closed her eyes, striving for calm. If she couldn't stay calm, she might miss her chance.

She looked for the peaceful place deep inside, as Sandro had taught her with meditation practice. She'd gotten used to using meditation to settle her nerves before a game. It didn't take long for her body to respond. Her breaths came deeper. Her heartbeat slowed.

Massimo grinned. "This is more like it. You must like the rough stuff. We will get along just fine."

Like hell. Her heart speeded again; she concentrated on breathing to slow it once more.

His hand freely roamed over her body. He cupped between her legs, rubbing a finger against her crotch. The seam on her pants pressed against her flesh.

She concentrated on breathing.

When his intimate touch brought no response from her, he studied her face with narrowed eyes. "Where are you going, *cara*? You are not here with me, are you? You think I desire to make love with a cold fish?"

Make love? She nearly gagged at the thought.

She was distracted soon enough when he slid a hand inside her collar and ripped her shirt open. Buttons clattered onto the concrete floor. He jerked her ruined shirt off her body, then yanked off her bra. Her exposed flesh quivered, yet other than that involuntary action, she showed no response.

He lowered his head and took a breast in his mouth. He suckled hard, his teeth bruising her flesh. She gasped with pain. Breathing no longer helped.

She exploded into action.

Curving her hands into claws, she grabbed his head and thrust her thumbs into his eyes. She dug deep. He screamed with pain and stumbled away from her, giving her room to operate.

Grabbing his injured eyes with his left hand, he swung the gun in her direction with his right. Knowing he was still blinded, she rushed him, grabbed his wrist and twisted her body until her back was to him. She slammed his hand against her knee, forcing him to lose the Beretta. It clattered to the floor and she kicked it aside. It skittered into the small office bathroom.

He grabbed her hair forcing her head back. She swung her fist downward and into his crotch. That loosened his grip enough for her to swing her elbow up and backward to ram into his cheek. He let her go and bent double with the pain.

She didn't have enough time to search for the weapon. He was hurt, but not down for the count. Quickly she looked for another weapon, knowing even with him injured, she was no match in brawn.

Of course, Angie had removed anything that could remotely be used for a weapon. Except the boom box on the floor and the small, skinny television sitting on the desk. Quickly, she darted past Massimo and hefted the television set into her hands. She brought it down across his neck.

He collapsed, falling to the ground. She sidestepped and lunged for the door, but he grabbed her leg as he fell. His hand was like a vise and she couldn't free herself. She fell with him.

Throwing the television to one side, she saved herself from a hard crash. The television landed with an explosion. She covered her face.

Massimo pulled himself over her body and reached for her neck. She squirmed and fought, the cold concrete floor rough against her bare back.

He reached her neck, and squeezed. "You bitch," he muttered.

He was weak, but she was weaker. She couldn't break free from his grasp. She clawed for his eyes, but he stayed out of her reach. She struggled for air, but black swirled behind her eyelids. Oh, God, she couldn't pass out. Would he stop choking her and let her live, or would he continue until she was dead?

Her limbs grew heavy and her struggles ineffective. Still holding her throat, he dragged her up onto the cot. She was nearly unconscious when he released her, her strength gone. She couldn't fight against him as he pulled leather strips from his pocket and tied her hands together. It was all she could do to suck air past her bruised, aching throat. Roughly, he jerked her arms overhead and she felt him tie the strip to the leg of the cot, rendering her almost useless.

She still had her legs. Forcing air into her lungs, she bucked, trying to shove him back enough so she could get in a good kick. A good thrusting kick with her heel to the right spot on his solar plexus and hopefully he would pass out. Or be incapacitated enough so she could free herself and escape.

She couldn't buck him off. He lay over her, mashing her with his weight, as his hands reached between them to fumble with the fastener on her pants. Knowing he intended to strip her, she rolled from side to side, trying desperately to knock him off. Her struggles were useless. He jerked her slacks and underwear off in spite of her best efforts. She lay naked beneath him.

Not satisfied to have her simply naked, he pulled more leather strips from his pocket and using his body weight to hold her in place, he forced her legs wide and strapped each ankle to the cot frame. He tied her so tightly, she could feel the leather cutting off her circulation.

Now, she was spread open and naked before him, and there was nothing she could do. She had made every effort to escape. And she had lost.

She focused on her breathing again, determined to retreat inside herself. If he was going to rape her, he was only getting her body. Her spirit, her soul, would be in a safe place deep inside her, where he could not reach.

She was nearly shaken from her calm breathing when he unzipped his slacks and his engorged erection sprang free. Her stomach flipped over.

Quickly, she closed her eyes and counted her breath.

He covered her body, pressing against her.

She didn't react.

Apparently not liking her non-response, he pulled back and looked at her. "Oh, no, *cara*, you are not disappearing on me again. Come back." He yanked her hair. Still no response.

He kissed her swollen tender lips, bit her breasts, roughly fingered her.

Still no response.

"You and your damned heathen tricks," he swore angrily.

Amazingly, she felt him growing soft against her.

He put his mouth next to her ear and roughly told her, "If you do not come back to me, I will bring your son in here and hurt him. Perhaps I will break both his little arms while you are watching."

A gasp of air filled her lungs. "No! You son of a bitch, don't you dare hurt my son."

He smiled evilly as she lost all calm and frantically struggled against the leather bindings. "That's better," he said triumphantly, his erection swollen and throbbing again.

She fought like a wild woman as he covered her body once again. If he wanted her to fight him, then by

God she would fight him if it would keep her son safe.

Oh, God, God, please help me, she prayed, knowing her strength was almost depleted.

His stiffened penis probed between her thighs. She squeezed every muscle she had against his invasion.

The office door flew open and Nia realized there truly was a God who heard and answered prayers.

Angie came in like an avenging angel.

"Thank you," she whispered as Angie ripped Massimo off her and threw him to the floor.

Massimo came up raging mad and ready to fight. Angie had his gun drawn and was ready for Carlo's son.

"You fat bastard, who the hell do you think you—"

"I am in charge of the prisoners." Angie cut him off. "We are exchanging them in a few short hours. She must not be hurt."

"You are too stupid if you think for a minute we're going to let them live. There's no harm in having fun with her before she dies—"

Angie kept his gun trained on Massimo. "You are the stupid one! They are not to die. They are too famous. And they have all of your father's money. Every last penny. You will be begging on the streets—worth nothing—no apartment, no car, no girls, no restaurants, no respect."

The bruise she'd given him on his cheek was the only splotch of color as the blood faded from Massimo's face. He zipped his pants. "There's no way to get it back?"

"Not without Sandro, and even then, I'm not certain he doesn't have something else planned. We must walk very carefully now to get out of this unharmed. Your father is looking for you. And Luigi. Did you find him?"

"No, not yet," Massimo said sulkily.

"Someone had to give Sandro the password for him to get to the money. Luigi is missing. Perhaps you should have been searching for him more diligently instead of concentrating on your fun."

Massimo flushed. "You think Luigi is trying to take over the family?"

Angie shrugged. "Seems likely. You should go to your father so you can get caught up on the plan before we leave."

"Where are we going?"

"Upstate New York. It will be a long drive."

Massimo nodded and approached Nia.

"Don't touch her again," Angie warned.

"Just a simple goodbye, Angie." Massimo held out his hands. He turned to Nia. "One day, *cara*. One day you will be mine."

She wanted to spit at him, but she was too tired and weak to make the effort. She closed her eyes and ignored him instead. To be ignored seemed to bother him more than anything else, anyway. She had proof, as if she needed more, when he slammed the office door on his way out.

When she opened her eyes again, Angie had slid his revolver into his shoulder holster and was removing his jacket. He knelt beside her and covered her nakedness before untying the binds that held her. "I'm sorry, *Bella*, I should have let you go."

"Let me go now."

Angie shook his head. "It is too late now. A time has already been set for an exchange. You will see your husband again tonight."

Nia didn't trust they would let her live. "Please, Angie. Let me go anyway."

"I can't. If we have nothing to trade, we will go to jail."

"Don't you deserve jail, after what you've done to my family?"

"Maybe I do, Nia. But I'm an old man. I don't want to spend my last years locked in prison." He went to the small bathroom, wet a cloth and brought it back for her. "Your poor face has taken a beating."

She took the cloth from him, hardly aware of the pain in her face. "And what about what Massimo said, that Carlo will kill us anyway."

"You will not be harmed. Your friend from the FBI will be there, too."

"Dave?" She wiped the blood away from her lips, knowing between Mikey and Massimo, it would be a while before her face looked normal again.

Angie nodded.

"Your men have shot at Dave before. Why would I believe you don't plan to kill us all?"

"You have my word, Nia. I will take care of you. You are innocent in all this."

She frowned. "Sandro is innocent in all this, too. Why are you after him?" When Angie didn't answer right away, Nia pressed him. "Why do you want Sandro?"

Angie sighed. "Carlo was using the restaurant to launder money—"

"No," Nia protested as Angie repeated Carlo's words. "Sandro would never allow it," she insisted.

"He had no choice, *Bella*. Actually it started several years ago . . ." And as Angie untied Nia's restraints, he told her about the World Cup and how

Sandro, along with others, had been forced to throw the championship game for the sake of lining Carlo's and other Mafia families' purses.

"I can't believe it," she murmured, sitting up and pulling Angie's jacket around her to cover her nakedness. "Carlo threatened Sandro's family? He threatened me?" No wonder Sandro hadn't seemed himself right after the World Cup. She'd thought it was because he was depressed over losing. Or that his leg was bothering him. But he was more likely depressed he'd been forced to lose.

"Sandro thought it was a one time thing. But it is never a one time thing with the family, *Bella*. Sandro learned his mistake too late. By the time he discovered that, he had married you. He had a family to protect."

Angie went on to tell her how Carlo ruined Sandro's career in Italy, then by the strange twist of fate, ended up in New York, the same city to which Sandro had fled.

"So, Sandro was working with Dave to set up Carlo, yet somehow it backfired."

"We have informants everywhere," Angie told her. "Even in the highest levels of government."

"But Sandro must've learned you were on to him."

"He must have had an informant, too. He now has Carlo's money and Carlo's daughter to bargain with."

"Carlo's daughter?" When Angie said that, Nia remembered Marisa was the same one who Sandro had left with.

"*Si,* somehow he was able to take her prisoner."

Nia knew without a doubt Marisa was the one who had been helping Sandro. But no way would she tell Angie. Let him think Sandro really held Marisa prisoner.

351

Whatever Sandro planned, Nia had to be ready to help him. "Where is my son?"

Angie called for Giovanni. He came into the room carrying Nia's son, who had stopped crying but had a case of hiccups. He passed her child to her; she cradled Daniele in her arms, and he shuddered before laying his little head on her shoulder.

Angie brushed his hand over Daniele's soft curls and patted Nia. "I will get you some clothes. We will leave soon."

* * *

"I have to leave now if I want a chance to get the team in place," Dave said. "Most likely Carlo will be early and I don't want to get caught setting the trap."

"You make certain your men are well hidden," Sandro said. "Only you and Frankie are supposed to accompany me." Carlo had only agreed to the extra man because Frankie was injured with a bullet wound and wasn't even supposed to be out of the hospital. But good agent that he was, he'd insisted on helping.

And Dave was still operating under the illusion that when all was said and done he was taking Carlo into custody. Let him think whatever he wanted as long as he left soon. Marisa was quickly running out of time.

"You two don't leave until I've let you know it's safe," Dave said. "I don't want you walking into a trap." He turned to Marisa. "You won't have to go back to your father, I promise," he told her.

She gave him a quick kiss while mentally urging him out the door. "It will all work out, she promised. "Be careful." Under the guise of patting his shoulder, she practically pushed him out the door. "We'll be waiting for your call." She blew him a kiss, shut the door before he'd even turned to walk off. Leaning against the door, she said, "Finally, he's gone."

Sandro watched her as she headed for her box. "You seem in a hurry."

"I am. I have things to do." Dressed in black jeans and a black sweater, she slipped on a black jacket, as well, and picked up her box.

"What are you doing?"

"I have an errand to run. I'll be back before Dave calls."

Sandro's face registered shock. "No, you will not leave." He grabbed her arm and held fast. "I need you at that meeting. It must look as if I plan to exchange you. They are capable of killing my wife and child if they suspect a trick."

Marisa tugged her arm free. "I know exactly what they are capable of, Sandro. That's why I must leave for a while."

"What do you have there?" Sandro nodded at the box she was hugging like a child.

"It is best you do not know."

He frowned. "You are not leaving this building."

She felt the clock tick. Tock. Tick. Tock. "I have to go," she said urgently. "There is no debate in this."

"Tell me why. What are you planning?" He narrowed his gaze. "Is that material to make a bomb?"

She leveled a hard stare at him, she knew chances were good he'd guess. "You have your back-up plan, and I have mine. Neither of which includes Carlo or his associates going to jail."

"You are planning to make a bomb?"

"I must plant it on my father's car before they leave. I have little time."

"Have you built it already?"

Marisa shook her head. "There hasn't been time."

"Where were you going to build it?"

"I'd plan to rent another room in the hotel. Sandro, you don't need to be involved."

He looked at her as if she'd lost her mind. "Are you crazy? I already am involved. Your father holds my entire life in his hands."

She studied his face, then finally conceded. "All right, we'll build it here." She sat the box on the desk and pulled off her jacket. She opened the box and quickly started assembling parts.

Sandro watched intently. "You've done this before?"

"I've practiced many times. Hand me that wire, please." She indicated a small roll of blue wire. She frowned, intensely focusing.

"There," she said at last. "It is almost ready. I will set the trigger device when we get there." She packed the nearly complete bomb back in the box.

Sandro slipped on his jacket. "Come, I will drive you. We must hurry so we'll be ready when Dave calls."

Speed—and caution—were on both of their minds as they left the hotel. Sandro drove to Carlo's club, parking a block away and on the opposite side of the street. They stealthily slipped through the dark, heading for his car. While Sandro kept watch, Marisa stole through the night to her father's limousine and planted the bomb. With quick, sure movements, she connected the trigger device.

It took her less than ten minutes, then they were

hurrying back toward the car. Marisa sank into the passenger seat, nerves just now making her shake. Over an hour since Dave left. He should be calling any minute.

Almost on cue, her cell phone rang. Checking the caller ID, Sandro passed the phone to Marisa.

"My men are almost in place. I have to set up the final details. Are you ready to go?"

"*Si.*"

"I'm sending Frankie for you two. He'll be there in a few minutes."

"I'll tell Sandro."

A movement down the street drew Sandro's attention and he nudged her arm. She glanced up. Her father and brother were leaving the club. Massimo got in on the driver's side.

She ended the call with Dave and told Sandro, "That is good. I was hoping Massimo would drive instead of poppa's driver."

"We were specific on who could come."

"It looks as if he plans to stick with your terms. That is good."

"Should we follow them? Perhaps we can swipe Nia and Danny from wherever they are being held," Sandro said. "We can forget our whole scheme if I could get them back."

"And where would you go? It's as I told Dave, if poppa is arrested, he can still run business from jail. You will never be safe as long as he and Massi are alive."

And she would never be free if they were alive. She thought about all the times they had used her and hurt her without a second thought. How her mother's life was destroyed without a second thought. How Paolo was murdered without a second thought. Now she would pay

them back.
　　Without a second thought.

CHAPTER 33

Luigi moaned.

"I think he's waking up," Bobby said, glancing at the mobster lying on top of the flowered tan hotel bedspread.

Gregg stood up from his chair at the round table, standard in practically every hotel room. He yawned and stretched. "And I think I'm going to sleep. How long did Dave say we had to watch him?"

"He didn't. We just wait until he calls. It could be hours yet."

"This is damned irregular."

"Whatever it takes," Bobby said.

Gregg pulled out his wallet, checked it for cash. "I'm going out to get coffee. You want some?"

"Yeah, sure. Good and strong." Bobby pulled some bills out of his pocket. "Maybe bagels too."

Gregg nodded his head toward Luigi. "If he's waking up, you better get him secured with more than those cuffs. Of course, with a knot on his head like that and those drops she gave him, he won't be too active for a while."

"Yeah, sure. Okay."

Gregg left the rented hotel room. Bobby pushed up out of the chair, where he'd been watching "Cops" on the small, ancient television. He took some rope out of his duffel, intending to hog tie Luigi. He paused long enough to slap at a roach scurrying across the table.

A high-speed chase on TV made Bobby pause. He stared at the cops speeding along in their cruisers on the open freeway in Abilene, Texas. They sure had wide-open spaces there. Hard to imagine.

Still half-watching the show, Bobby bent over the bed and did his own brand of hog tying around Luigi's legs. He took the extra rope intending to loop it through the cuffs to hold Carlo's *consigliere* immobile.

Bobby jumped when he saw Luigi's eyes wide open and alert. Then everything happened so fast—

Luigi lurched up, grabbed the Fed's Glock from his shoulder holster. Using his feet, he launched the man away from him. Holding the gun awkwardly with cuffs on, he still managed to pull the trigger twice. The shocked Special Agent slammed against the wall before sliding down to land in a heap on the floor.

The bone-cracking pounding in Luigi's head knocked him back over when he tried to get up. His stomach rolled. Damn that fucking bitch Marisa.

Ignoring the throbbing, he crawled off the bed and stumbled toward the fallen man. No blood. The FBI man wore a vest. Since he was unconscious, most likely had several broken ribs as well, he wouldn't be coming after Luigi any time soon.

Luigi wouldn't finish the guy off. Attempted murder was enough to be charged with for one day. He fumbled in the guy's pockets, found the keys to the cuffs. Working quickly as he could manage, he freed himself.

Snatching the gun up, he hobbled out the door, pain limiting his speed. He avoided the elevator, knowing the other cop would likely be back soon. Instead he found the stairway. Each step made his head pound like a drum, his stomach threatened to explode out his throat.

As best as he could, Luigi ignored the pain. With a quick scan of the lobby, he headed for the street, hiding in the shadows of the building. He felt his pockets. His cell phone was gone. Fuck. He needed a way to reach Carlo and warn him.

There was a pay phone on the corner. He stumbled to it, dug for change in his pocket, dialed the club number. Only to discover Carlo had already left. He then called the warehouse and Giovanni told him Carlo had come and gone from there as well. Too late. Figured. Definitely made his life more difficult. At least Giovanni told him the meeting place where Carlo was headed.

Luigi knew it was useless to try to reach Carlo on his cell phone while he was enroute. Carlo had an unbendable rule of no phone calls in his car. He had a fear of bugs, with good reason. And no matter that he had his car swept every day, they all knew by now that the FBI had remote controlled listening devices which could be deactivated during a sweep.

No, no way would Carlo answer his phone. Angie or Massimo either. Luigi was going to have to go after them. He sagged against the phone, tried to concentrate. He needed a car.

He could call his men to pick him up, but waiting on them would take too long. Time was something he didn't have if he was going to save Carlo from walking into a trap set by his daughter.

Better to snatch a car and drive to the meeting

place himself, stop by the club and grab some of his men. Before Luigi could leave in search of a vehicle, a rattletrap car pulled up to the curb. Inside were two guys wearing gang colors.

The muscular one stepped out of the driver's side. "Hey, asshole, get away from that phone. I gotta use it."

Luigi raised the Glock. "Fine. Use the phone. Give me your car keys."

"What? No way, you jerk off." The man went for his gun. Luigi shot him point blank, then whirled and fired at the other man climbing out of the passenger side with his gun drawn. Luigi missed, and the other man ducked and ran.

Quickly, Luigi searched the dead man's pockets until he found the keys. Wasn't the first time he had to toss a dead guy.

Hobbling to the car, he slid into the seat, stuck the key in the ignition and pulled the car in gear. He pressed the accelerator and jumped when the car backfired. Luigi hoped the piece of junk lasted long enough to get him to the club so he could get his men and a better car. He had to make that meeting in time.

* * *

Gregg was whistling as he waited for the elevator to reach his floor number. He held two coffees on a cardboard tray in one hand and a sack with two bagels in the other. The doors slid open, and he headed down the hall hoping this job would be over in time for him to catch his wife awake. Sex would be welcome tonight. A good change of pace.

When he found the door to the hotel room standing

half-open, he pulled up short, all thoughts of sex forgotten.

The hairs raised on the back of his neck as his alert signals kicked in. Quickly, he sat the coffee on the floor and drew his weapon from his shoulder holster. Scanning the hallway for a possible ambush, he approached the room with caution. He used his free hand to shove open the door.

When no bad guys or gunshots greeted him, he swung around the door ledge, leading with his gun. At first the room looked empty.

Then he noticed Bobby on the floor.

"Holy shit." In case Luigi or some of his soldiers were hiding, Gregg did a sweep of the room. It was empty and Luigi appeared long gone.

Gregg dropped beside Bobby, felt for a pulse. Found it, strong and steady. Relieved, Steve dug out his cell phone and called for help.

Bobby jerked, came awake swearing a blue streak when Gregg tried to remove the vest.

"Take it easy, buddy." Gregg laid a hand on him. "You likely got a few broken ribs."

Bobby lay his head back down. "Luigi must've been conscious, faking he was out. He snatched my gun and shot me while I was trying to tie him up."

"Thank God you still had on your vest."

"And thank God he didn't take time to kill me. Wouldn't have been nothing to pop me in the head."

"He just wanted to get away. Murder's not on his mind. At least not yours. I bet he's pretty pissed with the Mafia princess."

Bobby nodded. "Yeah, I hope Dave can save her. Call him, hope this doesn't ruin everything."

Gregg grimaced. "Yeah, you're right." He picked up his phone again.

* * *

"Hurry, wash up," Sandro urged Marisa when they were back in the hotel room. "Frankie will be here any minute." She had dirt and grease on her hands from planting the bomb under Carlo's car. Fortunately, no dirt showed up on her black clothes. There was no time to change.

A knock on the door. Sandro literally breathed a sigh of relief which almost made Marisa smile. They had been lucky to have timed it so well.

Sandro opened the door.

Frankie's arm was in a sling, and Marisa marveled he was moving around after being shot earlier in the day. It wasn't his wound that concerned her though. His face was clearly lined with worry, not pain. His eyes looked grim.

"What's wrong?" Sandro asked before she could.

Frankie stepped inside and closed the door behind him. "Bad news."

"More bad news?" Marisa asked, her shoulders slumping. She couldn't help it, she felt so tired.

"Luigi's escaped."

Marisa heard her heartbeat thudding in her ears, a loud boom, boom, boom. "How?" she managed to ask over the noise.

"Apparently he regained consciousness, but he pretended to still be out . . ." Frankie went on to explain what happen and concluded, "Now, our whole operation's screwed. If Luigi contacts Carlo and tells him about Marisa—"

"How long ago did he escape?" Sandro questioned.

Frankie shrugged. "Not more than fifteen or twenty minutes ago. They found a man, a gang banger, who'd been shot outside the hotel. His friend said Luigi stole their car."

Sandro and Marisa looked at each other. They knew that about that time, Carlo was just leaving his club. There had been no sign of Luigi, but the *consigliere* could have reached his boss by phone. However, if that had been the case, then surely Carlo would have left with more men than Massimo.

"Do you know if Luigi made contact with Carlo?" Marisa demanded.

"Dave had Tony go over the club tapes for the last few minutes. Luigi called, but Carlo had already left. Still, he can reach Carlo on his cell phone. We have to assume that's what he's done."

"No," Marisa said, feeling slightly more calm at the information.

Both men turned to look at her.

"My father has a strict rule. No phone calls in the car. No business in the car, period. He knows his car is wired.

"If Luigi missed him at the club, the only way he'll be able to make contact with my father is if he catches up to him or discovers the meeting place."

"The man he spoke to didn't know where Carlo was going, but then Luigi asked about Angie. The other man told Luigi that Angie was at the first warehouse, whatever that means." Frankie said, then looked at Marisa.

She shook her head. "I don't know how they label

the warehouses among themselves. There are so many."

Frankie sighed. "All we can do is go ahead with the plans and be extra cautious. We have back up, and all of us will have to be ready for anything. If you say that Carlo won't answer calls in his car, though, that's a good thing. Unless Luigi does catch up with him . . ."

* * *

Silence. Complete silence reigned in Carlo's stretch limousine. She'd been given a strict warning not to talk, but even without it, no one would have said anything at the risk of having getting his head snapped off. Earlier, Carlo had been royally pissed about his *consigliere* gone missing, spouting threats and promises to murder when they stopped by the warehouse to gather Nia and her son. Nia hoped the missing man was helping Marisa and Sandro.

She sat in the rear-facing seat holding Daniele in her lap. Angie was driving, Carlo sat across from her, and Massimo sat beside her with his arm around her shoulder. She'd tried to scoot away, but he dug his fingers into her skin, holding her in place. So now she concentrated on making herself as small as possible. Still, every once in a while, he slid his hand beneath the coat that Angie had provided her, and pinched her nipple.

Knowing it would be useless to protest, she deliberately ignored him, watching the road disappear beyond the glow of the taillights.

Fortunately, Daniele went back to sleep, which left Nia to reflect on what Angie had told her earlier about Carlo, and what was about to happen. In less than two hours she would be reunited with her husband.

Apparently Sandro had something valuable and Carlo was willing to trade.

Or else it could be an elaborate ruse, the mobsters could have agreed to the meeting in order to spring a trap, and in less than two hours, she could be dead.

She squeezed Daniele and kissed his curls.

CHAPTER 34

Headlights turned onto the gravel road. A light snow fell, more of an irritation than a hindrance.

"Everybody ready?" Dave whispered into his walkie-talkie. His muscles tensed. Adrenaline poured through his veins. This had to work. Had to.

"Ready, boss."

Men scattered all over the property, hidden in sight of the old three story farm house. Dave didn't intend on letting Carlo walk off unless he was being led away with a set of cuffs on him. With the information Sandro and Marisa could provide, Dave planned to lock up the murdering mob boss for a long, long time.

"Showtime." Dave slipped his walkie-talkie into his coat pocket.

Sandro took a high-powered rifle from the back seat of the car he'd arrived in. He propped it carefully against a nearby tree.

"I've got sharpshooters ready," Dave reminded him.

"They won't shoot to kill. I will."

Dave shook his head. "Sandro, if it's unprovoked—"

"I know. You'll arrest me. But I'm not standing by to wait while you attempt to rescue my wife and child."

Hoping Sandro didn't screw everything up, Dave turned his attention to the approaching vehicle, his mouth set in a firm line.

The car slowed to a stop less than a hundred yards away. The headlights stayed on, although a faint orange light glowed dimly through the snow clouds. It would soon be sunrise.

The driver's door, and the back two doors on the same side, opened. Angie climbed out of the driver's side, while Carlo exited the back rear door. He held a notebook computer in his hands.

Sandro, taking two steps toward the car, watched it all with as stoic of an expression as he could manage.

Massimo climbed out from the other rear door, then leaned inside. When Nia slid out with a sleeping Daniele in her arms, Sandro's heart constricted so much he could barely draw a breath. His cherished wife. His precious son. His life would not be worth living without them.

Sandro gritted his teeth and stayed focused.

As soon as Nia was out of the car, she jerked free from Massimo. Sandro frowned. Obviously his wife did not like Carlo's son. Sandro intended to get her away from the man as soon as possible.

Stepping forward three more steps, Sandro held his hands wide and called to Carlo. "How do you want to do this?"

"I want the account information first. I brought a laptop so I can check." Carlo held up the computer. "I will send your son."

Carlo nodded at Massimo who reached to take

Daniele from Nia's arms.

She jerked away, exchanging heated words with Massimo. She refused to release Daniele. Sandro tightened his lips. He knew in his gut that Massimo had somehow earned Nia's wrath. Sandro squeezed his eyes shut and tried not to think about what Massimo might have done. Not now. If Nia had been harmed, it was all Sandro's fault, he knew. And he would have to make it up to her.

When he opened his eyes again, Angie had walked around the car and was reaching for Daniele. Nia turned the child over to the older man who gently cradled the sleeping boy and walked toward Sandro.

It took less than two minutes to cover the halfway mark at fifty yards, yet time dragged out with every agonizing step. Finally, Sandro reached Angie. He held out a flash drive to Angie. Angie passed Daniele to Sandro.

Sandro hugged his sleeping son. "*Grazie Dio*," he whispered.

Daniele woke up. "Poppa?"

"*Si, bambino*. It is Poppa." Sandro's throat clogged.

Grabbing his neck, Daniele squeezed tight. Sandro held on and planted kisses on his son's head and face. Tears leaked from Sandro's eyes.

"Momma?" Daniele asked, looking around.

"Momma will be here soon," Sandro promised, blinking hard. He met Angie's gaze, noting the big man looked relieved. "The password is princess," Sandro told Angie, then turned to take Daniele to safety while Angie returned to Carlo.

Sandro stopped beside Frankie. "This is Frankie,"

he told his son. "You must stay with him while I get momma. Frankie will keep you safe."

Sandro tried to set Daniele down, but his son clung to his neck. "*Bambino*, you must let me go," he spoke in Italian. "I cannot get momma unless you wait here."

Daniele's grip loosened slightly.

Frankie spoke to him in Italian. "Come, Daniele, we will watch over here by this tree while your poppa gets your momma."

Reluctantly Daniele let go and went to Frankie. He was fascinated by Frankie's arm sling. "Arm hurt," he said.

"Yes, my arm is hurt."

Surprisingly, Daniele leaned over and kissed the bandaged arm. Sandro swallowed down the emotion. His son was safe, and he was grateful. But he mustn't let that make him careless. He still had to free his wife. This part could get tricky.

He walked up to wait beside Dave and Marisa. Carlo, holding a flashlight in his mouth, was typing on his computer. He nodded and said something to Angie, who stood beside Nia. Carlo turned to Sandro's small group. "It all seems in order. I will send your wife now. Bring my daughter."

Beside him, Sandro heard Marisa sigh.

"Don't worry, princess," Dave said.

She looked up at him, but didn't speak.

Sandro took her arm and led her away. "When you get close," Sandro told her, "if I signal to you, I want you to grab Nia and pull her to the ground. I have my gun ready." He patted his jacket. "If I think I can take them out without anyone getting hurt, I will. If there's not a chance, I'll use my rifle when I get back. Make sure you stay out of the way."

"Dave will arrest you."

"I know. I hope a jury sees this as self-defense. You know as well as I do, that Carlo will never let me live."

"Dave plans to arrest my father."

"Like that would stop Carlo. He'd just put out another contract on me."

"I know. Kill him. I will testify for you."

Sandro squeezed her arms. "*Grazie*. Just be sure to stay down so you'll stay alive."

She nodded and Sandro took a breath. His heart leapt up to his throat. He knew if he managed to kill Carlo, that a very long and high-profile trial awaited him. Yet it would be worth it because his wife and son would be safe.

They started forward. Step after step after step drawing closer to life. Or death. Sandro kept his eyes on Nia, his heart thundering in his ears. The snow fell harder. The cold wind bit through his thick coat. Time crawled by one agonizing step at a time.

Suddenly, another pair of headlights swung onto the gravel road. Everyone stopped and watched. Sandro squinted through the increasingly heavy snowfall.

The car slammed to a stop, throwing up gravel from beneath the wheels. Four men jumped out of the car, armed with semi-automatics.

Luigi popped out of the driver's side and shouted. "Stop! The bitch's a traitor. It's a set up."

"*Merda*," Marisa swore.

"Back to Dave," Sandro commanded and dropped to his knees, his Browning hi-powered pistol already drawn. Before he could fire, he watched in amazement as

Luigi crumpled by the car. Quickly, he scanned the area and saw Angie with a gun in his hand. Angie had killed Luigi. Why? Was he on their side?

Sandro didn't have time to ponder longer as gunshots exploded through the early morning. Angie whirled and shoved at Nia, urging her to run. He was running after her. Sandro automatically squeezed off rounds for cover. At such a distance, it was hard for his shots to be accurate with only a handgun. He needed his rifle.

"Sandro." He turned and Dave tossed him the rifle. "Move, men, move," Dave screamed into his walkie-talkie, his own gun drawn.

Sandro whirled back and aimed his rifle. Too late. A shot hit Angie in the back and he fell to his knees. Sandro watched in horror as Nia stopped to help the fallen mobster.

"Nia!" he yelled. "Get down."

The noise was horrific. She obviously couldn't hear him. She tugged at Angie trying to help him to his feet, but it was obvious the man was telling her to run and save herself. She kept tugging, but Angie took another hit and fell forward out of her grasp.

She screamed and stared in horror. Sandro aimed and killed the man who had shot Angie. "Get down," he shouted again at his wife. Still, she stood staring at Angie's fallen body.

She must be in shock, Sandro thought, springing to his feet, running toward her. He stopped long enough to squeeze off another round from his rifle, and another mobster fell to the ground.

He was almost to her when she finally started running.

She was running. Running as if demons from hell were nipping at her feet. She knew if she fell, she was dead. Hurry. Her heart hammered frantically against her ribcage. Her breath labored through her lungs. Move, feet.

Move, move, move.

Safety was close. Just a little further. She had to make it.

Gunshots exploded around her. The noise was deafening.

Instinctively, she ducked, and urged her churning legs to greater speed.

Oh, God, it was the nightmare. It was really happening. Had her dream been predicting her own death all these years? But she had a child to raise, another baby on the way. She had to live!

She ran faster . . . she had to outrun the danger.

Round after round, Sandro fired at the mobsters. It was hard to see in snow-darkened sky. Sometimes his shots hit, sometimes they missed. But slowly the good guys seemed as if they were gaining on the bad guys.

Then through his scope Sandro eyes caught Massimo armed with his own high-powered rifle. Massimo aimed at Nia. Sandro adjusted his aim, but Massimo squeezed off his round before Sandro.

He pulled the trigger a split second later and watched Massimo crumple.

Sandro's gaze swung to his wife. In slow motion, he watched as she flew through the air then fell face down.

"No!" Sandro dropped his rifle, running to her. Blood seeped onto the ground, turning the white snow into a red slushy liquid. He knelt beside her, and Dave was there, too.

"We need a medic," Dave yelled into his walkie-talkie. "Get me a goddamned medic now!" He probed Nia's back. "I think it's just a shoulder wound," he said. "I saw her take the hit. I think it was in the shoulder."

Sandro touched Nia, searching for the wound through the layers of clothes and blood. She moaned, and he felt her pain as his own.

Someone touched his arm. Tears blurring his gaze, he looked up.

"Carlo is getting away," Marisa said. She held out his rifle. "Do you want this or do you want me—"

Sandro snatched the rifle from her.

"The car is not bullet proof," she said.

"Sandro," Dave warned, then frowned at Marisa.

"That man is responsible for this," Sandro told Dave. "Killing him is justified." He raised the rifle to his shoulder and took aim. Carlo was just making a u-turn. A minute longer and he would be out of range.

Sandro took a breath. Aimed. Squeezed off the shot. Carlo's body jerked.

The car careened crazily out of control and smashed into a large tree. Sandro released his breath, shuddering.

It was over.

He handed the rifle to Marisa and went back to Nia. Two medics with a stretcher between them rushed up and jostled him out of the way.

Efficiently, they stripped off her jacket and shirt and checked the gunshot. They bound the wound and turned her carefully onto the stretcher, covering her with a thermal blanket.

Sandro hovered over them, his throat tight with

emotion. Her face was swollen and bruised but the gunshot worried him more. "How bad is it?"

"It's a shoulder wound. If we stop the blood loss, she should be fine. Is she a free bleeder?"

"No."

"Any allergies to medicine we should know about?"

Nia moaned then.

Sandro moved to her side, trying not to gasp at her bruised and swollen face. A murderous rage filled him. He would kill Carlo and Massimo again if he could. "*Carissima*," he said softly, belying his churning emotions.

She opened her eyes. "Sandro?"

"*Si, amore mia*. It is Sandro." His heart swelled and warmed, thankful she was alive.

"What happened?"

"You were shot, ma'am." A medic spoke up. "We're taking you to the hospital."

"Daniele?" she asked.

"He is safe, *amore*."

She smiled.

"Ma'am are there any drug allergies we should know about?"

She frowned. "No, but—" she hesitated and looked at Sandro. He knew what she wanted to say.

"She is pregnant," he said for her.

Surprise registered in her eyes. "You knew?"

"Carlo told me."

That brought another frown. "Carlo? Where is he?"

"Dead."

She nodded. "Massimo?"

"Dead, too."

"Good."

At her firm approval, Sandro realized Massimo had harmed her somehow. His wife was not a vindictive person. He was fiercely glad he had killed them for her. In some small way perhaps he had atoned for all he put her through.

"Sandro, what about . . . Angie?"

"I don't know, *carissima*."

Dave heard her. "I'll check on him." He walked off, and the medics continued to work on Nia.

Dave knelt by Angie, felt for a pulse, then stood and shook his head.

With sad eyes, Sandro looked to his wife. "I'm sorry."

Silent tears rolled down her cheeks. "He was nice to me. He tried to take care of me and Daniele."

"We're going to take her to the ambulance now, sir," a medic told Sandro, carrying her away.

"Momma, momma."

Frankie carried Daniele toward them.

Sandro took his son from Frankie's arms. "Momma's got an owie. Like Frankie's." Sandro pointed to the man he considered a new friend.

Daniele touched Frankie's arm. "Frankie's hurt."

"That's right," Sandro said. "And momma's hurt, too. She has to go to the doctor and get it fixed. Let's tell her goodbye."

Sandro walked to the ambulance where they had transferred Nia to a raised gurney. They were preparing to lift her into the back of the ambulance.

"Momma, momma," Daniele said again. "*Ti amo,* Momma."

"I love you, too," she said, "Both of you." Then she turned her attention to Sandro. "Are you excited about the baby?"

He smiled in spite of the grim circumstances. "You know I am." He gave her a kiss.

"I had a special meal planned to tell you, then you . . ." she frowned as her voice faded away.

"I'm sorry, *carissima*. I was trying to keep you safe. If I'd thought for a moment this would—"

"Shh," she interrupted. "I understand what happened. You did what you had to."

"But the pain I caused."

"Not you. Them."

"They hurt you." He touched her bruised face.

"They're dead now."

"I would kill them again."

"Yes, I know, Sandro. But now there's no need. They're dead and we're free from them."

"We need to get her to the hospital, sir."

"*Si, si*. I know. We will be at the hospital, *amore*. I will see you soon."

She smiled. "Yes, I expect you there." The medics pressed the button on the lift and guided the gurney into the ambulance.

She watched him and saw his frown. "It's over, Sandro. Don't think about it anymore. It's over."

"Over, Poppa. It's over," Daniele repeated.

Yes, it was over. It wasn't his way to reflect on the bad. Instead he chose to focus on the good. His enemies were dead, his son was safe, his wife would be fine and in a few months they would have a new baby to celebrate.

For Sandro and his family, it was over.

* * *

Dave looked around and blew out a breath. It was easy enough to tell what went wrong. He was just thankful none of his people had been killed. Two of the men with Luigi were injured but still alive. It was still uncertain if they'd survive though.

It could have been so much worse than a bullet wound to Nia's shoulder. Massimo could have had a better aim. Dave shuddered.

Marisa stopped beside him.

Dave felt his heart soften and swell with relief. She hadn't had to go back to her father, after all. He hoped now they could work on a future together. He turned and pulled her into a hug. Held on tight. He wanted to hold her forever. "How are you?"

"This is for the best, you know." Her voice was heavy with tears.

Dave used his thumbs to wipe away the wetness on her cheeks, only able to guess at the pain and frustration she must be feeling. "I didn't mean for anybody to die."

"Even if you had arrested him, my father would have never stopped until Sandro was dead."

Dave nodded, smoothed her hair back from her face. He wanted to go on touching her, feeling as if he could never touch her enough, happy there was no reason for him to stay away. "Maybe you're right," he agreed. "Are you going to be okay?"

She nodded. "I expected this outcome. Prepared myself. Perhaps not this way, and certainly not with Sandro's wife hurt. But I expected my father to die today." She breathed deep then pulled away. Her voice sounded stronger when she said, "You have a lot of work to do, I know."

"I'll have someone escort you to your apartment." He dropped a kiss on her forehead, feeling more calm and hopeful than he had in a long time. "I'll see you soon." He knew whatever the future brought, he wanted her in it. He wanted to tell her, but not now. "We'll talk."

"Perhaps," she said softly.

Dave felt his mood drop, but then excused her somber mood, knowing it had to be one of the worst days in her life. He'd never lost a family member, didn't even want to imagine such a tragedy.

But she had him now. If she wanted him. He hoped she wanted him. He wanted to give her the world, since so much of her world had been stolen from her. She'd never had a childhood.

Dave could show her a much better place, a different kind of world than she'd grown up in. If she'd let him. And he had to believe she'd let him.

She reached into her jacket pocket. "As you move my father's car, your men need to be aware of this." She handed him a small black remote control device.

He stared at it; at first, not comprehending. A small black remote control was so far removed from the happy place he'd been imagining. As suspicion took over, his triumphant, hopeful mood tried to evaporate. He clung to the thoughts of happiness desperately, hoping his instincts were wrong.

He took a deep breath, released it, and asked her, "What's this?"

Her face was sober, serious. "Insurance."

"Insurance?" he questioned, hoping he misunderstood her meaning. Please let it not be what he thought.

"It's under the back axle, by the gas tank," she told him. "Cut the blue wire."

With so few words she'd effectively burst the fantasy world he'd been creating. He felt the blood drain from his face. A sick feeling swirled in his stomach.

Dave's gaze slammed into hers. "You wired his car?" His voice came out first as a whisper, then grew stronger. "You wired a fucking bomb to your father's car?"

"I owed him. And my brother. I wanted justice." She held his gaze, her chin tilted up, as if daring him to say something.

"You wanted vengeance," he said, still working hard to process what she'd done. Find a reason to deny it. Or find a reason to justify it. Because God help him, he'd wanted her, wanted her in his life, wanted to believe they could overcome all the obstacles in their way. Had convinced himself it could happen.

And now.

She shrugged, her actions belying the emotion suddenly swimming in her eyes. "Do you respect me now?" She swallowed thickly, then whispered, "Do you want me now?"

She'd tried to warn him once. Dave remembered. She'd tried to tell him their worlds were too different. The cynical, jaded FBI man had dared to hope, to believe. . .

Without giving him a chance to answer, she turned and walked off, back straight, head high.

The remote was still in his hand. Dave looked at it, and then looked back at Marisa.

Dave watched her walk away.

Dear Reader:

Thank you so much for purchasing The Good Daughter. *I hope you enjoyed reading it as much as I enjoyed writing it for you. If you liked getting to know Dave and Marisa, you'll be happy to know that they will be making appearances in my upcoming Vista Security suspense series novels. Dave will be making a cameo in my next suspense novel,* Trust No One *(excerpt included here), the first book to introduce Vista Security, a private security company which is a front for an agency that handles jobs off limits to U.S. Intelligence agencies, and its team members.*

I would be appreciative if you took a few minutes to leave a review of The Good Daughter. *Reviews are a helpful way to help authors gain new fans, and are always welcome.*

If you want to keep up with news on my writing, please visit my website and sign up for my newsletter. www.dianalayne.com

I always love hearing from readers. dianalayne@yahoo.com

Sincerely,
Diana Layne

For more information about me, to connect on a social network, and to sign up for my newsletter, please go to: www.dianalayne.com

(Turn the page for a preview of another Diana Layne book, **Trust No One**.*)*

Coming Soon: *Trust No One*
2009 Golden Heart ® finalist by Diana Layne

Excerpt:

"Who you working for, Keith?"

"No need for you to know," the man behind her said. He poked his revolver into her back. "You're gonna be dead."

She ignored him and focused on Keith. "How much money? Who's the target?"

"Stalling, MJ? Afraid to die?"

"I knew the risks going in. So did you. But what about the innocent people who'll die if you sell that information?"

"Sorry, baby, but I don't have time to debate philosophy." The sound of a distant engine made Keith pause and tilt his head to listen. "That would be the extraction team," he said.

MJ tightened every muscle, ready to spring. It well could be his team, but it could as easily be hers. Even if she wasn't in position for the original pick-up, she'd sewed a small tracking device in that backpack.

"No time for long good-byes." He raised the gun.

Now or never.

She dropped her left arm down, aiming the hoof knife for the man behind her. She caught the curved point in his crotch and jerked upward. The man's scream distracted the others long enough for her to snatch his falling .45 revolver. She aimed, squeezed the trigger, firing first at Keith, then the other man beside him. Boom. Boom. Two quick shots. Both men fell. The top of one man's head appeared to be blown off. Keith was lying on the ground. Blood quickly pooled beneath both men.

She vaguely registered a flash from Keith's gun before he hit the ground. She didn't have time to worry about it. There was still one bad guy to go.

She heard the man moving behind her. She dove to the ground, rolled to her back and popped off two shots into his head before he recovered enough to draw another weapon.

He fell.

Another hit.

Pain tore into her then, ripping through her gut. She grabbed her stomach. When she pulled her hand away, it was covered in blood. Keith's wild shot must have hit her as he fell. Gut shot and losing blood fast . . .
.

She heard the chopper but didn't know if it was the guys wearing the white hats or those dressed all in black. Injured and unable to escape, this could be her last breaths if it was the wrong side.

Trying to ramp down her heart rate, she took slow deep breaths, but with little effect. The warm blood flowed out making steam rise from her body in the frigid air. Good guys or bad guys coming, she was done for either way.

She saw two people rappelling from the chopper. When they dropped to the ground, a deep voice of authority snapped, "Check the men. Make sure they're dead."

Make sure they're dead? Did they know already that Keith had gone rogue? She wanted to ask, but no sound came out when she tried.

A man's face appeared before her. He had the most beautiful chocolate-colored almond-shaped eyes framed by thick, dark eyebrows. Great time to notice a man's eyes, MJ, she chastised herself. And yet, what better to notice if she was about to die?

"What about her?" the other man said. "She's as good as dead."

"No," the man with almond-shaped eyes answered. "We're getting her out of here." He pressed something against her stomach. She presumed to slow the blood.

"You and women," the second man said. "You can't save all of them." Though MJ couldn't see him, she heard the disgust in his tone and wondered what stick got shoved up his ass.

She blinked at her bizarre thoughts, tried to focus, tried to follow the conversation but her brain felt sluggish and inadequate. Blackness edged into her vision.

"Hang on, MJ," the man with the eyes told her. "Hang on."

***

www.ingramcontent.com/pod-product-compliance
Lightning Source LLC
Chambersburg PA
CBHW020322180626
46812CB00001B/9